PRAISE FOR JON LAND

"Land mixes his ingredients with a vigorous hand and cooks them at high heat, winding up with a zesty mind-snack."

—*Publishers Weekly*

"An adroitly told and fast-paced thriller."

—*Rocky Mountain News*

"A first-rate thriller."

—*Publishers Weekly* on *The Omicron Legion*

"Give me a crackling fireplace on a cold night, a damned good cognac and Jon Land's *Day of the Delphi* . . . then leave me the hell alone so I can enjoy myself."

—David Hagberg, author of *High Flight*

Other Books by Jon Land

JON LAND

THE FIRES OF
MIDNIGHT

FORGE

A TOM DOHERTY ASSOCIATES BOOK
NEW YORK

THE FIRES OF MIDNIGHT

Copyright © 1995 by Jon Land

Cover art by Thomas Snowdon-Romer

A Forge Book
Published by Tom Doherty Associates, Inc.
175 Fifth Avenue
New York, NY 10010

Forge® is a registered trademark of Tom Doherty Associates, Inc.

ISBN: 0-812-55252-0
Library of Congress Card Catalog Number: 95-35361

First edition: December 1995
First mass market edition: November 1996

Printed in the United States of America

0 9 8 7 6 5 4 3 2 1

For Toni

ACKNOWLEDGMENTS

All thanks must start with Toni Mendez, my agent, who's been there through all the beginnings of which this first hardcover is the most exciting. Of course, it never would have happened without the editorial brilliance of Ann Maurer and Tor's Natalia Aponte, who pushed for more with this one and got it. Tom, Linda, John, Yolanda and everyone else at the top of the Tor/Forge family never put product before people—the rest of our industry could learn something from them.

The challenge to make *The Fires of Midnight* technologically precise was one of the greatest I have ever faced and could never have been achieved without the genius and foresight of Dr. Alvan Fisher, Emery Pineo (who makes the impossible only a toll call away), and especially John Signore who explains blood work even more clearly than Hemo the Magnificent! Thanks also to John Rizzieri for the Brookhaven research, Michael Sherman for Cambridge locales, Dr. David Bihdelglass for Harvard, Walt Mattison for weapons assistance along with being my tutor in the field of Special Ops, Dr. Mort Korn for his typically clear critical eye, and Caroline Oyama of the New York Public Library.

I can promise you that the recipes that appear on pages 81–82, 111, 232–233, and 359 didn't come from my kitchen. For those tempted by them, these and thousands of others can be found in *The New York Times Cook Book**.

My final acknowledgment goes to Gordon Kinder, the actual author of the poem, "The Fires of Midnight." He penned it for me in exchange for two Pearl Jam tickets; I expect we'll be seeing his name in print again someday at a much fairer price!

*Craig Claiborne, Harper and Row, New York, 1990

FIREWATCH

CAMBRIDGE, MASSACHUSETTS,
SUNDAY, 3:00 P.M.

"Setting down now, Doctor."

Susan Lyle nodded at the pilot and leaned back in her seat as the helicopter descended toward Edwin H. Land Boulevard. The rotor wash kicked up dirt and debris on a normally bustling Cambridge thoroughfare that was deserted now save for the local and Massachusetts state policemen making a valiant effort to keep the milling crowds back. From farther up, those crowds had looked like a blanket draped over the adjacent streets, expanding continuously and rippling with motion as people poked and prodded their way forward to catch a glimpse.

She had determined the preliminary strategy based on a schema and map of the area faxed to her while in transit and relayed her instructions to authorities on the scene three hours before. In accordance with those instructions, the entire area around the Cambridgeside Galleria had been blocked off from the northern end of Charles Park to the entrance to the Monsignor O'Brien Highway to the south. The natural barrier of the Charles River cut off access from the west, and she could see police barricades all along First Street to the east. A ring of officers in riot gear guarded the primary mall entrance on the chance that anyone slipped through these apparently formidable lines.

The suspended traffic lights bounced as the chopper settled down in the center of Land Boulevard in front of the Royal Sonesta Hotel. Susan saw a man in a state police uniform approach with one hand raised to shield his eyes and the other clamped on his hat. She climbed out of the chopper and started forward, watching the officer lower the hand from his eyes, clearly surprised by her appearance. She wore brown slacks and a cream-colored blouse beneath a light summer-weight

jacket. Her blond hair bounced as she approached him, blown
carelessly by the rotor's slowing spin. Her skin was fair, her
eyes a shade hovering between blue and green. She appeared
to be of average height until she straightened her knees once
free of the blade's reach and looked the officer almost straight
in the eye.

"Dr. Susan Lyle," she said, right hand extended and voice
raised to carry over the chopper's whirring engine and the
persistent hum of murmurs from the curious crowds. "Firewatch Command."

"Captain Frank Sculley," he returned, taking the hand she
offered. "Got a command post set up in that park just across
the street."

"Have my orders been followed, Captain?" Susan asked as
they moved toward it.

"Best as we could manage."

"And the witnesses?"

"They're still together."

"On scene?"

Sculley gestured toward a trio of buses parked farther down
Land Boulevard and enclosed by police cruisers. "I comman-
deered those from a tour group. Figured that was as good a
place to hold them as any."

"What about the hotel guests?"

"Trouble there. We lost some of them."

"Some?"

"Dozens. Lots, actually. Guests from a wedding yesterday
checking out. Sorry, Doctor. By the time I got here—"

Susan stopped on the sidewalk directly before the officers
fronting the main entrance to the Cambridgeside Galleria.
"They've got to be tracked down and isolated, do you hear
me? There's another chopper en route with men inside who
can handle the details. I'll want you to coordinate things with
the hotel personnel."

Captain Sculley shrugged.

Dr. Susan Lyle's gaze drifted across Cambridgeside Place
to a restaurant called Rayz on the Galleria's ground floor, accessible via its own off-street entrance as well as from within
the mall. "I assume that was open."

"Until the local police closed it."

"And the patrons?"

Captain Sculley said nothing.

"My instructions were to secure the perimeter, Captain," Dr. Lyle snapped. "No one allowed out."

"Too late by the time all your instructions came through. In case you haven't noticed, things have been pretty crazy around here the last few hours." Sculley gestured with his eyes toward a second restaurant on the corner of Land Boulevard. "But as near as we can tell, no one in Papa Razzi was affected at all."

Susan remembered the schema. "No direct access to the mall, right?"

"No. What's that mean?"

Susan didn't respond. The less local authorities learned now, the better. Until just hours before, they had known nothing of Firewatch Command's existence, much less the helicopter on constant prep outside the Centers for Disease Control and Prevention in Atlanta. Whoever was standing watch could be anywhere in the country within six hours of an alarm being sounded, whisked there in a jet that was fueled and ready twenty-four hours a day at Hartsfield International. In the five years since Firewatch's formation, there had been only two such alarms before today: one false and the other easily passed off to a leak in a chemical storage tank a few miles from the afflicted area. If the initial reports were borne out, the Cambridgeside Galleria would mark the first incident potentially warranting full-scale-alert status. That decision would be Susan's to make.

"How many people have actually entered the mall?" she asked Sculley.

"I haven't counted. The Cambridge patrolman first on the scene, the ninety or so witnesses we've got in those buses. Just about all of them came out of the parking garage before we sealed it off."

"*About* all?"

"A few came out through the main doors."

Sculley's response scraped against Susan's spine. "Then the doors were open."

"Not for very long."

"Have any of those who came through them displayed any effects or symptoms?"

"They only stayed inside long enough to see—"

"Just answer my question, Captain."

Sculley's neck turned slightly red. "Not that we've been able to de-tect, no."

"And the equipment that was supposed to arrive from Mass General?"

"In that ambulance."

Sculley gestured behind them toward the command post set up inside Charles Park, composed of nothing more than four squad cars enclosing a rescue wagon and a small mobile home painted in blue and white police colors. A table had been set up outside it from which a pair of officers were frantically deploying reinforcements to those areas of the crowd line that seemed ready to give. The garbled sounds of status reports filtered through the air, mixing raspily with the voices squeezing out of the walkie-talkie clipped to Sculley's belt. Finally he switched it off.

"I'm going to assume, Doctor, that whatever's in that ambulance is something the hospital keeps just in case somebody like you from out of town needs it."

"That's correct, Captain," she said and started across the street.

Sculley stayed right alongside her. "Probably means lots of other hospitals are similarly supplied."

"In every major city."

"Like you were expecting this."

"Prepared for it, more accurately."

"You got your problems, I got mine. We got damn near a full-scale panic on our hands. I haven't got enough men on detail to hold all these people back from the perimeter. Plenty have pushed their way through. A few got close to the mall."

That got her attention. "But not inside."

"No," Sculley said, "not inside."

"What about the National Guard?"

"Governor's calling them up. It takes time."

"And the media?"

"News blackout, as per your orders. There've been some

leaks, rumors. You can't keep word of something like this quiet. If you ask me—''

"I didn't," Susan said. "We do nothing and say nothing until we determine the level of contamination."

Sculley turned his eyes toward one throng gathered at the back end of the park and another squeezed against the barriers across First Street as if they were waiting for a parade to start. "You wanna tell *them* that, Doc? Lots of folks in the crowd are next of kin to those inside. Parents mostly. Sunday at the mall, loaded with kids, you get my drift."

"Why don't we wait until we have something intelligent to tell them? Why don't we wait until I've had a chance to inspect the inside?"

The Racal II space suit was a poor fit, a generic medium when Susan could better have used a small. It was portable and contained a battery-powered air supply for use in the expected or likely presence of biohazards. The suit itself, apart from the helmet and air system, was also disposable—a necessity in events when rapid deployment usually meant the lack of elaborate decontamination procedures. The original Racal suits had been bright orange in color, but had been changed to white to attract less attention to the presence of emergency personnel in potential hot zones.

Susan had pulled it up over her pants and blouse inside the police mobile unit, then checked the miniature camera built into the helmet just over the faceplate. The camera's controls were located on a transistorized remote that could be affixed to either wrist with a strap. She fastened it over her left sleeve and made sure it was operational before exiting the trailer. Sculley was waiting when she climbed out and escorted her through the park to the security line set up before the Cambridgeside Galleria's main entrance.

"Anything I can do while you're inside?" he offered.

"I left a radio in the mobile unit for you to monitor my transmission. If something . . . happens, your good judgment will be put to the test."

"We're in this together, Doc."

Susan nodded and snapped her faceplate into place. The line of police fronting the entrance parted to provide passage across

Cambridgeside Place. She slid between a pair of sawhorses set behind them and approached the vacuum seal portal that had been installed in front of the glass doors beneath a huge, glitzy sign reading GALLERIA.

The thick, airtight plastic of the prefab unit wavered a bit in the wind. There were two additional off-street entrances to the Galleria and both had been similarly sealed and were also under heavy guard. The "door" to the vacuum seal was actually a zipper running up the plastic. Susan stopped inside and then resealed it before proceeding through one of the glass doors onto the first floor of the Cambridgeside Galleria.

She activated the camera's wrist control and made sure to rotate her helmet sideways as well as up so the tape would capture the entire scope of the mall. Later, computer enhancement and magnification would be able to lock on to and enlarge any specific point or area her rapid inspection might miss. The microphone built into her helmet sent a delayed, scrambled transmission to Firewatch Command, which would evaluate her analysis and take over the decision making should transmission break off suddenly.

The first bodies appeared almost instantly, stretched out on the floor as if clawing for the doors. Outside, Susan had managed to remain detached when Sculley broached the issue of the victims and their next of kin. At that point they were nothing more than theoretical concepts. But now those victims, or what was left of them, had become a reality. She felt her throat clog up and her breath quicken.

She imagined the mall as it normally was, bustling with patrons strolling about the floors, shopping bags in hand. Quiet music in the background maybe, clacking of heels against the tile floors. The shoppers were still here, all reportedly in the same condition as the grouping she hovered over now. The result was an eerie stillness that turned the air heavy, absent of sound save for a mechanical grinding she recognized as what, in bizarre counterpoint, could only be the mall's still-functioning escalators.

Susan forced herself to move on deeper into the Galleria's first floor, entering its atriumlike center formed by girders and glass. Three spiraling floors encompassing over one hundred stores. She noted their familiar names as she continued but didn't register them. A pair of kiosks had been toppled over by the last of those struggling to flee, spreading stuffed animals and glassblown creations all over the floor. The sun streamed down through the roof, reflecting off the glass and casting an eerie glow over the scene. To Susan it looked like an express elevator to the great beyond that had broken down from the overflow of passengers.

She was aware of each breath echoing in her helmet as she advanced. The rhythm of her heart came as deeper, quicker riffs in her head, seeming to expand the confines of her helmet with each throb. The worst came when she reached the back end of the first floor containing a food court. The litter of bodies turned it into an obstacle course she was reluctant to venture into. A clumsy misstep leading to a fall could result in her Racal II suit being torn, creating the very real risk of infection from whatever had caused all this. Her initial estimates, based on what she had seen by the time she was ready to move on, put the count of victims in the seventeen-hundred range conservatively.

"Condition of remains confirmed," she said into the microphone located just below her misting faceplate. "Confinement of exposure confirmed. Fatality rate from exposure on first floor . . . one hundred percent. Proceeding to second."

Susan backpedaled and retraced her steps around to the escalator. The down one, she noticed as she rode the up, had dropped a pile of bodies at the bottom, a thumping sound coming every time a moving stair pushed under a stubborn torso. Upon stepping off on the second floor, she leaned over the remains of another corpse to provide Atlanta a closer view.

"All evidence indicates presence of a Biosafety Level Four hot agent," she reported. "The agent has undergone extreme amplification of unprecedented scope."

She started down a concourse back in the direction of the main entrance, approaching a glass elevator with stilled limbs pressed up against its panels, hands that seemed to be reaching up for the sun pouring through the atrium-style Galleria roof.

"Full-alert status recommended," Susan continued. "All—" She cut herself off suddenly, stopping. A sound had caught her ear, something moving, rustling.

Something alive.

"Wait a minute," she continued. "I think I heard . . ." She aimed herself in the general direction from which the sound had come. When she heard it again, louder, she swung toward a store on the right, miniature camera swinging with her. "I think it came from inside that—"

A shape hurled itself toward her, rising for her faceplate. Susan threw a gloved hand up instinctively, but too late to prevent the impact that tumbled her backwards to the floor.

In Atlanta the broadcast picture scrambled, then died. A crack sounded just ahead of her garbled screaming that faded into oblivion as the transmission ceased abruptly.

PART ONE

MISSING PERSONS

CARDENAS, CUBA;
MONDAY, 1:00 P.M.

CHAPTER I

Blaine McCracken had a feeling something was wrong, even before he spotted the white-haired man sitting on the opposite side of the bar. His first thought was to back his way out before the situation deteriorated. It could be the white-haired man hadn't seen him, but McCracken knew better. The two men had crossed paths only once before, on an occasion when each had been given the task of killing the other.

But leaving the bar now could mean jeopardizing the mission he had come to Cardenas, Cuba, to complete. He had been contacted only the previous night by a former KGB Wet Affairs operative who claimed to have extensive information about the North Korean missile network. His instructions were to wait in the Buena Vista Hotel bar for a phone call advising him of the rendezvous point, and there was no contingency to fall back on if he deviated from the plan.

In the end that fact determined McCracken's decision. Nine-millimeter SIG-Sauer within easy reach beneath his white linen jacket, he glided around the long sweep of the bar, keeping his hands in plain view.

Years ago the Buena Vista had been one of the most fashionable establishments in the coastal resort community of Cardenas, before time and politics had stolen most of the region's luster. The shapes of other seaside hotels were marred by boarded-up windows and crumbling foundations, leaving the Buena Vista the lone reminder of Cuba's prosperous past, when people flocked to its casinos and nightclubs. Those casinos and nightclubs were gone, but more than just the polished mahogany of the Buena Vista's bar reaffirmed a stubborn attachment to the traditions of the past. The hotel's stucco exterior had been given a fresh coat of paint and the family of palm trees fronting it breathed green instead of the dying brown most of the country seemed to be afflicted with. The floor in the lobby was a checkerboard of Italian marble and the walls were paneled in glowing mahogany, the theme of polished wood picked up inside the bar.

When McCracken's path took him past the mirrored wall lined with shelves holding various bottles of liquor, he couldn't help comparing the glance he caught of himself with his glimpse of the white-haired man. Andre Marokov's shoulders were hunched and stiff, suggesting he could no longer make the lightning-fast moves required to survive in his chosen profession. His eyes were clouded and the hand clutching his drink was covered with liver spots.

The look McCracken had stolen of himself in the mirror, on the other hand, showed a man pretty much unchanged by the years. His black wavy hair had been shorter at the time of their first encounter and his coarse, close-trimmed beard had been all pepper and no salt. The emptiness in his eyes then had been replaced with maturity and cunning now. He was bigger in the chest and arms, smaller in the waist from daily three-hour workouts that had become ritual. And the scar that ran through his left eyebrow hadn't even existed until the day of his only previous meeting with Marokov.

The Russian sat at the bar twirling a straw through a drink that was largely ice, looking for the bartender who had vanished. Marokov had the entire far side of the bar to himself until McCracken straddled the stool two down from the Russian, ready to move if it came to that.

"Greetings, Comrade," Marokov said, sliding over to take the stool between them.

McCracken half expected him to have a gun in his hand, but all Marokov held was his dwindling drink. "I'd like to say it's been a long time, but . . ."

"Since we were never formally introduced, of course."

"We shared the same jungle and a burning village once. That's close enough."

Marokov smiled faintly and nodded. "A drink to old times, then, eh?"

He drew the glass upward and drained whatever liquid remained amidst the ice. The cubes collected against his lips, and only then did Blaine feel totally safe; no way would the

Russian have left himself in so vulnerable a position for that long if he had any hostile intentions. Marokov brought the glass back down and the ice cubes sloshed together, jangling.

"I'd offer you one, Comrade, but it is common knowledge the great McCracken does not drink."

"I did over there."

"We both did many things over there that I suppose are better left in the past. On that subject, congratulations are in order. After all, you won."

Marokov raised his glass in the manner of a toast but returned it to the hardwood bar without touching it to his lips. Once again he looked around for the bartender, seemed disgruntled when the man remained nowhere to be seen.

"I mean, Comrade, that's what our years in the jungle were all about: determining which way of life would prevail. There could be only one. There always can be only one."

Blaine studied him. He had not seen a file on Marokov in nearly five years and the Russian had aged even worse than his first glimpse had indicated. His eyes said it all, bloodshot and slow, bled of life and feeling, as if they had stopped seeing anything other than what lay directly before them.

"Not necessarily," McCracken corrected.

"Referring to the two of us, of course. You with your Operation Phoenix, me with my Spetsnatz squads. Opposite numbers, eh, Comrade?"

"Close enough."

"If your commanders only realized the hell your assassination teams caused us. Pity you hadn't started a few years earlier. Would have saved me the time I spent with those wretched savages."

"The savages were on both sides."

"And yet we fought with them."

"We were younger."

"And the times, Comrade . . ."

"Different."

"Simpler, clearer. Often I miss them. Especially now. I'm down here because I can't go home. Well, I could but there's nothing to go home to. Consider yourself lucky you still have a cause to fight for."

Marokov impatiently eyed the bartender, who had returned

to his post behind the bar, and pointed to his glass. The bartender poured fresh Scotch over the remnants of the ice cubes. Blaine waved the man off when he looked his way.

"To simpler times," Marokov said, raising his glass in the semblance of a toast again.

In point of fact, Blaine recalled, they hadn't been so simple at all. What the Russian had not admitted was that it had been McCracken's presence in Vietnam that had led to Marokov's assignment there. Operation Phoenix's assassination teams were causing so much disruption in the Vietcong's chain of command that the Cong's Soviet advisers had no choice but to send for equally proficient teams of Soviet Spetsnatz commandos. At the same time McCracken was being briefed on Marokov's presence, the Russian was being handed Blaine's intelligence file along with a termination order. Neither man knew of the other's sanction instructions and both set out, in typically expert fashion, to kill the other.

They weren't alone. Each was accompanied by a team, McCracken's in this case being composed of Vietnamese nationals who escorted him to the area off Highway 9 near Khe Sanh. Marokov's team members spoke perfect English and had been dressed and outfitted in the guise of American soldiers. Apparently the disguises worked too well, because the Soviets fell victim to an ambush by young Cong guerrillas operating outside the loop. Marokov and two other survivors found themselves seeking refuge in a small village Blaine's team happened to be approaching.

Of course no one knew McCracken was there; no one in command ever knew where he really was. So when the ambush of Marokov's team in American guise was reported to Eye Corps by friendlies nearby, an airstrike was ordered on the village off Highway 9 the hostiles had fled toward. Within seconds of McCracken's arrival, huge plumes of orange engulfed the bamboo huts and angular wooden structures. The deafening explosions roared one after the other, swallowing the oxygen and leaving pockmarks along the jungle earth.

McCracken had just managed to find cover when what looked like a trio of American soldiers, a pair dragging a wounded third between them, skirted the smoke before him. As Blaine emerged to help them, the second wave of bombers swooped in for another pass, more of the village perishing in gulfs of orange fissures. Blaine ducked back down and, before he could emerge again, heard the trio of "American" soldiers exchanging desperate words in Russian. He held his ground to let them draw closer, the smoke providing the camouflage he needed. The return of the first wave of bombers whistled overhead and then McCracken heard something else:

Children crying.

Blaine turned and saw them through a break in the smoke. A pair of kids, six or seven maybe, climbing out of a tunnel belching black, their faces darkened and bleeding. One dragging the other.

The wave dropped in fast.

McCracken didn't hesitate. Reshouldering his weapon, he bolted toward the tunnel and scooped up the kids in a single motion. The angle of the incoming rounds forced him into a dash that brought him to the outer rim of the jungle, just as the trio of Russians in American uniforms cleared the smoke line.

The Russians on either side of the wounded third had their M-16s raised and ready before McCracken could trade grasp of the kids for his rifle. But then the man in the center, moving with a savage fluidity that defied his condition, tore the weapon from one's hand and doubled the other over with a blow Blaine lost to smoke and speed. A single bullet emerged from the second man's rifle and stitched a savage line through McCracken's left eyebrow. That eye filled instantly with blood and the brief instant that followed gave him his only glimpse with his right eye of the man who had saved him: Andre Marokov. McCracken held the steel stare briefly, before lifting up the children and darting into the woods.

They had been the hardest eyes Blaine had ever known, but now, a generation later, they had lost all that, having traded purpose for Scotch. If eyes were truly the window to the soul, he figured the Russian had lost that, too. The country he had dedicated his life to had disintegrated, turning Marokov into the worst kind of rogue: one who has lost his past as well as his future.

"Something I always wanted to ask you," Blaine said. "Did you ever report sighting me?"

The Russian let the glass stay on the bar. "I was not inclined to."

"And the men on either side of you?"

"Regrettably they did not reach the rendezvous poin alive," Marokov said, and for just an instant the old life danced in his eyes. "I falsified the report. Made up some spectacular nonsense that had the brains behind everything fearing you more than ever."

"Told them you wanted to keep going after me."

"How did you know?"

"I did the same thing."

"Kept the game between ourselves, eh, Comrade?"

"We had plenty to do without the additional bother, Andre."

Marokov turned his stool toward McCracken at the latter's casual use of his first name. "A few minutes ago I was hoping you were going to ask me something else, Comrade."

"Like why you didn't kill me. I didn't ask that because I already knew the answer. If the situations had been reversed. I would have done the same thing."

"Because of honor?"

"And respect. The code makes us what we are. Others can' understand it and probably think we're crazy, but the thing is we're still alive. After twenty-five years of it we're still alive."

Marokov went back to the Scotch. "Some of us more than others."

"You weren't given the same chances, Andre."

The Russian kept his stool facing Blaine's way. "The truth is I've been doing some work for the Americans. One of your many layers, CIA, I think, but don't quote me. I'm here waiting for a phone call from them now."

McCracken bent a straw he'd been fiddling with in two. Thoughts flooded through his head, water from a broken dam.

"They have a job for me," Marokov was saying, pulling a folded picture from his pocket. "This man. Someone I believe you know."

Blaine gazed at the picture absently, registering it, but his mind was elsewhere. The two of them meeting in the same bar at the same time. Both in Cardenas. Both . . . *waiting.*

"Comrade?"

McCracken's gaze fell on the bartender, the man who had been missing from his post for several minutes after Blaine came in. He was now talking to a pair of men seated at the center of the bar, facing its mirror. New arrivals, their stools set back so there would be plenty of room to move; reinforcements undoubtedly summoned from the lobby when things had not gone at all as planned. They couldn't have known the truth about him and Marokov and now they would pay for it.

McCracken drew his SIG-Sauer in the same instant he jerked Marokov off his stool to the floor behind the bar's cover. He opened fire while the two men were still twisting and bringing their pistols around. Unable to properly aim, he was lucky for the shoulder hits that spun the gunmen away from the bar before they could start shooting. Blaine was just steadying the SIG on them again when he heard the familiar *click-clack* of a shotgun being cocked. He caught a glimpse of the bartender wielding a Mossberg sliced-handle pump in time to duck behind the bar's cover next to Marokov, who was fighting to steady an ancient Greysa pistol in a trembling hand. The first blast carved a huge fragment from the bar top and the second showered chunks of wood over both of them. Blaine bounced back up above the bar to find the original gunmen wheeling toward him, wounded, their pistols spitting orange. It took four more shots to drop them. But backing up to steady his aim had given the bartender a clear shot at him. The man had the Mossberg steadied dead on him when Marokov lurched up into its line of fire. A shotgun blast shattered the Russian's chest as he squeezed off a single round from his Greysa that snapped the bartender's head backward. Marokov's frame slammed back into McCracken, spilling both of them to the floor.

Blaine pulled himself from beneath the Russian and leaned over him. "Andre—"

Too late. The Russian's eyes had locked open in death, looking strangely at the end as they had in the jungle that day near Highway 9.

Blaine rose just as three men wielding Ingram submachine guns tore into the bar. McCracken drained the rest of his clip at them to cover his dart for the swinging kitchen door. He crashed through it and heard yelling in Spanish directed at

him, which ceased when the workers saw his gun. He bolted
past them and negotiated the clutter of stoves and counters
where chefs were busy preparing meals. That route took him
through a storage area lined with messily stacked shelves, the
bottoms of which held a number of propane tanks.

Blaine propped two of them against the other side of the
door, certain to be knocked over as soon as his pursuers came
crashing through. He backed down the hall, reloading, and
held his ground until the door rocketed open. In that instant,
McCracken fired twice, once for each of the tanks that had
clattered to the floor.

The explosions rocked the corridor and brought sections of
both walls and the ceiling tumbling inward. Blaine was close
enough to feel the heat of the blasts before he sped through
the exit that took him outside the Buena Vista.

Three jeeploads of Cuban militiamen had arrived, and the
last of the uniformed men were just racing toward the hotel.
He waited a moment until all of them had vanished inside
before lunging atop the lone jeep featuring a pedestal-mounted
machine gun. He turned his SIG on the remaining jeeps and
shot out two tires in each before speeding off.

The objective now was to get off the main avenue as quickly
as possible, use back roads to reach the extraction point at an
airfield a twenty-minute drive from here. Since this had been
a setup all along, though, chances were the airfield would be
covered by more Cuban militiamen before he reached it, and
no pilot in his right mind would chance a landing under such
conditions.

Blaine had no choice. The airfield was his only option.

He pushed the jeep on at top speed, the events at the Buena
Vista flashing through his mind. He and Marokov had been
set up, lured here by men certain that these two apparently
implacable enemies would not be able to resist the endgame
that had eluded them for so long. If only they had known the
truth . . .

The only truth that mattered at this point was that Mc-
Cracken had been lured to Cuba to do a job somebody wanted
done. Marokov had said he'd been working with some faction
of the CIA. Maybe he had outlived his usefulness to them and
this was their way of paying him back. Involving Blaine had

been a mistake they would be paying for now.

McCracken sped off the main drag and thumped down the back roads, hoping he could outrun the reinforcements certain to be summoned by the soldiers he had left stranded at the hotel. The ride passed uneventfully, and he had actually begun to relax by the time the thin, poorly paved road spilled out onto another primary route that would take him the last stretch to the airfield.

Then he froze, brakes jammed hard and jeep screeching to a sideways halt.

Directly before him, up a slight rise, an armored personnel carrier was parked sideways across the road. He glimpsed men scampering into better positions of cover behind it, weapons readied. Blaine swung the jeep around only to find a pair of troop-carrying trucks steaming toward him from a half-mile away.

He had resigned himself to fighting it out with the jeep's fifty-caliber machine gun when a distant whirring sound grabbed his ears. It was familiar and yet forgotten, as impossible as the sight that followed it out of the west.

An old Helio Courier, something he hadn't seen since the Nam days, banked free of the mountains and dropped for the road. It wasn't the craft Blaine had arranged for his extraction and this certainly wasn't the pilot. Helio Couriers had been used by Air America pilots to ferry Operation Phoenix personnel in and out of impossible situations. Utilized for their ability to fly low and to land with virtually no airfield, they had saved many a life, their pilots—like the famous Harry Lime—as crazy as the men they transported.

The Courier seemed to stop dead in the air and drop out of the sky, whining as it split the wind. Its wing-mounted machine guns began clacking, carving up chunks of the roadbed in the direct path of the troop carriers heading Blaine's way. The lead one swerved to avoid the fire and the trailing truck slammed into it. McCracken watched both spin onto the shoulder, while behind him soldiers hurried back into their armored personnel carrier to give chase.

But the Helio Courier was already into its rapid descent, kissing the road like an old friend and coming to a hunkering halt just two yards from Blaine's jeep. The cockpit hatch popped up, revealing a man dressed in a polyester Hawaiian shirt complete with lei.

It couldn't be!

But it was.

"At your service, Captain!" Harry Lime yelled down to McCracken, flashing a mock salute. "Better get yourself on board."

Blaine squeezed into the cockpit and took the copilot's seat as a spectator. The strands of Harry's lei bobbed a bit in the air. The wind caught his baggy Hawaiian shirt and ballooned it outward until Blaine sealed the hatch behind him. Then he watched Harry deftly maneuver the old plane back into takeoff mode, whizzing by the disabled trucks even as the closing armored personnel carrier's machine gun opened fire. If the bullets bothered Harry Lime, he didn't show it. He expertly skimmed the tree line low enough to leave branch scratches on the Helio Courier's underside and flew in zigzag fashion until he reached the Atlantic. Once there he gave the plane full throttle and let her hum over the water so low the ocean spray droppletted the windshield.

"You're better than ever, Harry."

Lime tried to smile, almost blushing, working an unlit cigarette from one side of his mouth to the other. "Good to see a guy like you still needs a guy like me, Captain."

"Castro'd be smoking me like one of Havana's best if you hadn't shown up when you did."

"Got my own reasons this time."

Only then did Blaine notice the quivery expression that had crossed Crazy Harry Lime's face. "Keep talking."

"You gotta help me. You're the only one who can. That's why I took this run. That's why I had to come get you. Leave you down there in Castro's shithouse and I'm fucked as bad as you."

"Hard to believe, Harry."

"It ain't, trust me. See, Captain, something happened. . . ."

CHAPTER 2

Susan Lyle had practiced laboratory work in full isolation gear many times. Nothing, though, could prepare her for the autopsies she opted to perform personally upon returning to Atlanta from Cambridge early Monday. Five bodies had been shipped in a refrigerated hold of the CDC jet that was now effectively hers. Normally a pathology specialist would handle this chore and Firewatch had a team that would take over after she had done the preliminary work. But something territorial had taken over Susan. She had trained so long and often in preparation for a crisis event that she was reluctant to delegate any responsibility, especially anything as sensitive as this. Beyond that, there was the danger factor to consider. Both of Firewatch's pathologists were family men, which in Susan's mind made the risk of exposure to the Cambridgeside corpses unacceptable for them.

This event had already made her no stranger to risk. The creature that had flown at her and smashed her faceplate back at the mall was a dog: frantic, terrified and somehow very much alive. The panic she'd felt when the potentially contaminated air rushed in through the shattered plastic had forced the breath to bottleneck in her throat.

It's happening. My God, it's happening to me!

The dog's tongue sweeping across her face told her she was okay. She recovered enough of her senses to quiet the animal down and remain inside the mall for another hour until a decontamination unit arrived from one of the CDC's six regional crisis management centers in Connecticut. She moved about, continuing her laborious trek with an almost maddening calm. Facing death had left her with the feeling she had gotten the upper hand on whatever Biosafety Level 4 hot agent had pen-

etrated the Galleria. It was hiding, *it* was afraid. The first round
had gone to her.

The autopsies formed the second. Accessing the isolation
wing where the bodies were waiting meant first passing
through several preparatory stages required to insure maximum protection. She was showered with both water and chemicals, air dried, wind blasted, powdered and dressed in several
layers of protective clothing that would all be burned at the
conclusion of her work.

Susan thought she'd be ready when the time came to enter
the wing, but the tension she felt made her heavy gloves bulkier and turned her space suit into an oven. Instead of being
outfitted with a portable air supply, this suit took its air from
a hose snaking from the wall to a slot custom-tailored for its
nozzle. The hose followed her like a chain wherever she went.
Every breath quickly became an effort and her faceplate kept
misting up until she calmed herself down.

The sights she recorded through that faceplate as she began
the first of the autopsies were clear enough, though. Her scalpel cut the flesh down the center of the torso like crinkled
cardboard. In years past, the use of scalpels or any sharp cutting instrument was strictly forbidden in the presence of a
suspected Level 4 agent, since slicing through a glove or
sleeve meant possible infection and even death. But the space
suits used by the Firewatch team had been outfitted with
gloves and sleeves reinforced with a thinner weave of the same
Kevlar material used for bulletproof vests.

As had been the case in the mall, Susan's helmet was outfitted with a microphone to record her observations. All she
had to do was speak.

"This body is a male thirty-one years of age. Weight according to recovered identification eighty-one kilograms.
Weight upon arrival at lab thirty-five kilograms. Height according to recovered identification one hundred sixty-two centimeters. Height upon arrival one hundred twenty-nine
centimeters."

She touched the rib cage and found the bones had taken on
a puttylike consistency. Parting the ribs was as simple as pulling them back with her hands and affixing a clamp on either
side, revealing the vital organs.

"Vital organs all intact but in the same dehydrated condition as the skin. Proceeding with inspection . . ."

Susan cut the heart out first. It fit easily in her gloved palm, reduced in scope and appearance to a baseball-sized prune, dry enough to resemble a balled-up piece of paper. She placed it in the digital scale eye level before her.

"Weight of heart one fifth of normal, confirming that loss of hemoglobin extended to muscle and vital organs as well as flesh. Condition of the skeletal system is similarly withered."

Susan grabbed a microscope slide from the ample supply resting on the table next to her and centered a fragment of bone upon it. Then she took it to the electron microscope and quickly located what she was looking for.

"Entire capillary system running through the sternum has collapsed. No living tissue present whatsoever in terms of stem cells or reproducing blood cells, leading to deterioration and decalcification of the skeletal structure."

Susan stopped here and returned to the body lying on the gurney. Strange how the absence of all but the isolation suit's antiseptic smell lent a dreamlike aura to the scene. She had come to associate the autopsy procedure with many things, scents foremost among them. Now the only thing she could cling to was the process itself, a process that had become almost routine by the time she completed the fifth body, realizing she was in danger of being late for the Firewatch Command meeting she had called. She had neglected to leave sufficient time for the repeat of the decontamination procedures and actually dashed the last stretch of the way to the communication center, after rushing through the process.

The communication center had no windows and the knobless door sealed after her entry. A computer keyboard and monitor rested atop a single narrow table in the small room's center, a chair tucked neatly behind it. The wall directly before the desk was made up of eight twenty-seven-inch television monitors. Each was connected to the computer's outputs so Susan could control the picture on each from her keyboard. Using the keyboard she could choose the picture she wanted the participants of the meeting to see, or divide their screens in up to four segments, even superimpose one broadcast picture over another.

The speaker boxes representing each of the participants enclosed her on both the left and the right, six to a wall placed atop innocuous-looking slate-black digital relay units, identifiable from the number glowing off a small LED screen atop each speaker. The voices that would emerge from those speakers belonged to members of the Firewatch Command control board, whose job it would be to evaluate her report and determine the appropriate response. She had never met a single one in person, although four or five of the voices were familiar to her, their identities placing her in awe of the position in which she had been placed. For the duration of the meeting that was about to take place, Susan effectively had the ear of the entire government.

Whatever she had been expecting the CDC to be like upon first signing on, this was nothing even close to it. She had come to the Centers for Disease Control and Prevention out of Duke Medical School, by way of three years' residency in internal medicine at Brown University in Rhode Island, rejoicing in an assignment most of her contemporaries viewed as sheer drudgery. When pressed on the subject, Susan claimed she found the research process both exciting and exhilarating. Didn't they stop to think that a doctor's ability to diagnose and treat was nothing if the proper treatments and cures were not available? Her work in the lab might someday allow her to save more lives in a week than her classmates might in a lifetime. The CDC people believed her. She was very convincing.

And it was all a lie, her true motivation too secret and painful to explain. She wanted no one to think she was on some obsessive crusade that might blur the clarity of her vision. But "crusade" was exactly the correct term for it.

Her expertise in the infectious disease field alone led to the CDC finding a position for her. But it was her ability to work with people as both leader and administrator which had accounted for her being chosen for the Firewatch program. Firewatch had grown out of the CDC's Special Pathogens Branch, which specialized in unknown viruses. But that branch lacked the capacity for quick response, something CDC officials deemed increasingly important with the rapid emergence of viruses and bacteria the world had seldom if ever seen before and was ill equipped to fight. Firewatch got the call when minutes mattered, while a crisis was still unfolding.

Accordingly, a Firewatch field leader *had* to be able to interact, had to be able to take charge on scene even as the inevitable number of agendas came into play. She had accepted the position primarily because it offered the most rapid advancement to the area where her true interest—obsession, actually—lay. And if she handled the Cambridge incident well, then perhaps that advancement would come sooner than she had anticipated.

Susan's eyes lifted to the camera suspended from the ceiling at the joint in the front and left side wall. The light beneath it changed from red to green, signaling the broadcast was now active.

"Let's begin."

"I can't help but notice your face, Doctor," came a male voice she couldn't put a name to out of box number five. "The written report you faxed to all of us yesterday was rather vague on the circumstances of your injury."

"Purposely so, sir. A dog jumped at me and landed on my helmet. Impact shattered the faceplate. It's not as bad as it looks."

"Did you say a dog?" asked the voice from box number two, which Susan recognized as belonging to the director of the FBI, Ben Samuelson.

"Never mind that," followed a voice from box number one. "My question is how could the dog have possibly been alive?"

"I'm not sure yet. It would be best for all of you—and me—to follow the events of yesterday in the order they occurred. I'll answer any of your questions, of course, but many of those answers may come in the natural progression of my report."

Standing, Susan worked the keyboard beneath her so that the screens of all the meeting's participants would be filled with the recording made by her built-in helmet cam the day before. "You are about to see on your monitors what I saw in my trek through the Cambridgeside Galleria yesterday afternoon."

Susan relived every step all over again, no less chilled this time than in any of her previous viewings. She had edited out her run-in with the dog and the result was a surreal walking tour through a graveyard gone mad.

"My God," said the voice out of speaker nine when Susan had leaned over to scan one of the victims in more detail.

"I'd like to see that again," from speaker six.

"In slow motion, please," requested a voice she recognized as belonging to Clara Benedict, deputy national security adviser to the president.

Susan hit four keys in rapid succession. Instantly the tape rewound and began playing again, in slow motion. She'd seen the shot a hundred times now and it still scared her. The body was not so much a body as a slab of dried, virtually petrified flesh. The slow-motion scene started at the head and worked downward, revealing a mouth that seemed to have been swallowed up by skin that had shriveled. The nose looked to have fallen into the skull, while the eyes bulged grotesquely outward since the lids, brows, and cheekbones had receded. The skin was a ghostly white, almost like chalk, with the texture of cracked leather.

The torso and neck had flattened into a shapeless mass before petrifying. The arms and legs were angular, molten piles of what used to be flesh and bone.

"We are to assume, then, Doctor, that all the bodies you found inside the mall were in this condition," proposed speaker four.

"That is correct."

"What is the count of fatalities?" asked the voice out of the sixth box.

"Approximately seventeen hundred."

"And how are we progressing in identifying them?" asked Clara Benedict.

"At this point, all we can do is use wallet contents to do the job. It's slow because of the safety precautions involved."

"Stop the tape, please," requested Clara Benedict. And, after Susan had done so, "Dr. Lyle, what exactly are we looking at? What *happened*?"

Susan cleared her throat. "They were drained of all hemoglobin. Blood," she added after a short pause.

"I hope we're not talking about vampires here," snickered

another voice she recognized, that of Daniel Starr, the chairman of the Joint Chiefs of Staff.

"No, because our examination of the bodies has yet to reveal a single wound in any of the victims through which the blood could have been removed. Add that to the fact that no blood whatsoever was found spilled at the site and we're talking about something else entirely."

"Like what?"

"Exposure to a foreign organism that ingested every drop present in the mall."

"Your initial reports called it a foreign 'agent,' " noted General Starr. "What changed?"

"No inorganic agent could possibly be this target-selective."

"Are you saying we're dealing with a virus or a bacteria here?"

"Very probably, but one that behaves like none ever previously charted."

"A bacteria or virus that goes after blood," General Starr picked up, "and doesn't stop until it's ingested every drop."

"Not *every* drop," Clara Benedict reminded. "There was that dog that broke out of the storeroom in the pet store and jumped on you. How do you account for such an anomaly, Dr. Lyle, considering all the other animals in the store were found dead?"

"I can't. Not yet, anyway."

"I'm more interested in your organism, Doctor," General Starr said. "Have you been able to identify it yet?"

"Only in terms of its baffling behavioral traits. No trace of it has been found in any of the bodies, meaning the organism likely dies when it is denied sustenance, in this case blood. A remarkably short and deadly life span, as borne out by the fact that the mall was actually clean, or safe, when I first entered."

"But you've maintained a limited quarantine anyway," from Clare Benedict.

"Standard procedure when dealing with any Biosafety Level Four hot agent. We don't know all the rules it plays by, and until we do we like to err on the side of caution."

"Then you can't rule out entry by hostile action," persisted General Starr.

"But I can't rule it in, either. At this point it's just one of the possibilities we're considering. Equally likely is the fact that we're facing a microbreak of unparalleled dimensions."

"Hostile action, microbreak, or whatever," Starr continued, "just how was this agent, organism, or whatever you want to call it introduced into the mall? And what stopped it from getting out?"

"Precisely what I've got to find out next, sir."

CHAPTER 3

"You're late," said Harry Lime, his face caught in the dull glow of the video game's screen. "I was running out of quarters."

McCracken checked his watch. Lime had asked to meet him at Captain Hornblower's on Front Street in Key West's Old Town section at nine P.M. Located a few blocks off Duval Street at the foot of Mallory Square, the bar was a bit shabby, not as trendy as its neighbors and therefore not as crowded. At this early hour, the outside tables were filled, but inside there was plenty of seating in the booths as well as stools set before the bar. A badly painted sign near the entrance advertised live jazz for the weekend just ended. The building's facade was painted white but much of it had peeled away to reveal the previous gray color.

Blaine had entered unobtrusively through the open front and found Harry focused on the bar's lone video game. Harry tilted the joystick hard to the right and Blaine saw his digital watch read nine-thirty, running thirty minutes fast, a holdover from his old flying days to make sure he was never late.

Air America had been set up back in the sixties to win the good graces of Laotian, Cambodian and Vietnamese warlords so they might aid in the war effort. Air America pilots flew drugs, guns, just about anything anywhere out of Ton Sun Nyut Airbase to keep the warlords happy. These pilots also doubled as ferrymen for the Phoenix teams' impossible missions. If men like McCracken were crazy enough to try, the saying went, then Air America was crazy enough to fly.

But none were as crazy as Harry Lime. Another pilot who'd been stateside long enough to know *Star Trek* christened him the man who went where no man had gone before. By Southeast Asian standards it was true, never more so than when he was working with the team led by Blaine McCracken and Johnny Wareagle, the giant mystical Indian who to this day remained only a phone call away for Blaine and sometimes even closer.

The game flashed GAME OVER and Lime whacked it in frustration.

"I got the record on this thing. Wanna see my initials?"

"Later maybe."

"You get to type them in when you set it. There, I think if we wait a few more seconds you'll see them. I got three of the top five scores ever." Harry seemed to finally register Blaine's answer. "Later, then."

He collected the rest of his neatly stacked quarters and led Blaine away to a table in the rear. As near as McCracken could tell, Harry was wearing the same Hawaiian shirt he'd had on that afternoon. Only the lei was missing.

"Careful when you sit down," he cautioned when they reached the table squeezed between the bar and a counter that opened into the kitchen. Blaine saw on the table an incredibly intricate one-story house Harry had fashioned by stacking cigarettes in symmetrical layers. He'd just started work on a surrounding fence when the video game had captured his attention. Five empty beer bottles littered the table as well.

"How long have you been here, Harry?"

"I don't know. Came straight here after we landed at Turnbull. Didn't want to be late."

That would make almost three hours, Blaine calculated. He slid into his chair, careful not to disturb Harry's house of Marlboros. The bar was old-fashioned, Key West-style enough to make Hemingway proud, featuring typical island fare such as Key lime pie, fish specialties and an assortment of tropical drinks, attractions that were lost on the other patrons who were in the bar when McCracken entered. He'd felt their eyes upon him, tightening either with recognition or concern as he approached Harry. He knew the kind of men they were from those eyes and stares, at least the kind of men they used to be.

"Recognize any of them?" Harry asked, realizing Blaine's gaze had strayed toward his friends again.

"Should I?"

"The Nam was a bigger country than people realize." Harry gestured at a Hemingway look-alike sitting at the bar next to a pitcher of Cuba Libre. "That's Papa. Can't tell you his real name. He was in White Star out of Cambodia." He turned his gaze on three men seated at a table waiting for their dinners to come, all their chairs cocked so they could watch McCracken. "Them there are Jim Beam, Captain Jack and Johnny Walker—we call him Red for short. Traded in their real names for what they drink."

Only then did Blaine notice that each had a bottle of his namesake waiting expectantly near the glasses they were cradling. He'd known lots of men who had drowned themselves in booze since the war, but these were swimming in it. He hoped they knew how far they could venture out before they went under.

"And that guy," Harry continued, eyeing a man in a bathrobe standing against one of the exposed beams as if he were part of the structure, "we call him the Sandman."

"Because of the bathrobe?"

"Because that's what he did in the Nam, Captain: put people to sleep. Something like you. Only he crashed a little harder. Six of us, the original Key West Irregulars. That's what the locals call us, anyway. We take care of each other, look out for one another. Sometimes that means making sure a man's got his booze." Harry's voice started to drift. "Sometimes it means a lot more. I told 'em you were coming. They thought I was making it up.

"And don't let the fancy menu worry you," Harry continued, noticing Blaine's eyes straying to the blackboard listing tonight's specials. "This place is all right. Serve good food, pour a good drink and leave you alone. So do the tourists, 'cept in the real busy season." Harry pushed his chair in a little closer to the table. "Thing is, any place worth drinking in's gotta cater a little to tourists or they can forget about making the rent."

"How have you been making the rent?"

"Got my commercial pilot's license—you believe that?"

McCracken tried not to let the shock show through on his features. The thought of Crazy Harry flying a plane full of people was enough to chill his blood.

"Don't worry, Captain." Harry smiled, reading his mind. "I don't carry no passengers. Zantop Airlines has an exclusive contract with me."

"Oh," Blaine said.

Zantop might have been duly registered as a commercial airline, but it had never carried a single passenger. Instead it functioned as the offspring of the old Air America, ferrying drugs and weapons from Florida's Patrick Airforce Base to various locations in Central and South America. Once again there were important people to be won over. Certain countries in that area were powder kegs waiting to burn and the right people in the United States wanted the right people on their side when the matches lit. The argument went, according to those of the old school, that these countries were a hell of a lot closer to home than Southeast Asia.

"Lucky for you I was laid over today. Got the word you were down there and hauled ass," Harry said, and plucked a Marlboro off the top of his cigarette house's roof. He stuck it in his mouth and began working it from side to side. "Was like old times today, wasn't it, Captain?"

"It was at that, Harry."

"You and me, we been there and back, ain't we? Wasn't for me hearing you needed a pickup, you'd still be wasting away in that shithole of a country."

"That's for sure."

Lime was playing with his house, not sure how to proceed. He fidgeted and twitched, turning about suddenly as if he'd forgotten where he was. Relaxed when he remembered and sat back.

"Hey, you want something to drink? I got a tab here."

"Let's talk first."

"Sure."

"On the plane you said something had happened."

Harry's face was blank. "I told you . . ."

"Yes."

"I shouldn't have. It's my problem."

"We're friends. That makes it mine, too."

"You mean that?"

"I mean it."

"What did I tell you?" Harry asked, with his head angled slightly to the side.

"Not much else. Just that something had happened. I got the idea you needed my help."

Lime shook his head and looked down, chin cradled on his chest. When he looked up again, his eyes were watery.

"It's a sad thing. And wrong. What they done."

"What'd they do? What was wrong?"

"My son," said Harry. "Josh."

Blaine looked up at that.

"He's gone. They took him."

Blaine just sat there, listening.

"Tough thing raising a kid by yourself. You remember when Maggie died. You came to the funeral."

"Funeral . . ."

"Yeah."

"Sad day."

"The worst. Kid needed me, so I came out of it. What the fuck you gonna do, right, Captain? You go on. You get over it, least past it, and you go on."

"That's all you can do."

A smile flirted with Harry's lips but tears continued to shadow his expression. "Everyone came to the funeral, all the old guard. It was like fucking goddamn Ton Sun Nyut all over again. A regular reunion. Coulda served Khe Sanh pie instead of Key lime. Was a better occasion, we woulda had a ass-kicking shithouse of a time."

"The kid," Blaine said.

"Smart bastard, lot smarter than his old dad, lemme tell ya." His eyes shook suddenly, mind veering. "I need another beer." A waitress saw Harry's upraised hand and came over. He ordered two Rolling Rocks. "I like the color of the bottle," he explained to McCracken. "Green. Drink the beer out of it and you can think it's green, too."

"Sure." Blaine uneasy now.

"I miss Maggie, Captain, but I was used to that. I'm not used to missing Josh."

"What happened?"

"They came and took him. Stole him. Happened a few months back, 'fore I came down here."

McCracken took a deep breath, steeling himself. "Look, Harry, I, I . . ." His voice trailed off.

"What is it, Captain?" asked Lime, looking hopeful.

Blaine sighed. "Who took him, the kid, I mean?"

"Don't know. He was just . . . gone. You should come to my house, see his room. I taught him video games. Then he kicks my ass 'til I start getting pissed off. Then he lets me win and I get more pissed off. You never got married?"

"No."

"You missed out." Harry's expression was changing every second now, like he couldn't decide how he wanted to feel. "Not too late. Gotta help me find Josh first, though. Gotta help me get him back."

Blaine nodded enough to reassure his old friend. "I'll make some calls, ask some questions."

"You will?"

"Just said I would."

"When?"

"Tonight. Soon as I can get to a phone."

The tears in Harry's eyes were happy ones now. He could barely contain his smile. "You're the man, Captain. You always were the man. You'll meet me tomorrow, first thing. Let me know what you find out."

"Sure."

"Did I give you my address? I don't remember if I did."

"Not yet."

"I'll write it down." Lime felt his pockets for a pen, his mind drifting. "Hey, be something if we got the old gang together to go after him, wouldn't it? You, me, your giant Indian friend . . . er . . ."

"Johnny Wareagle," Blaine completed for him.

"Right. Johnny." Lime looked agitated now. "I can get us a plane."

"Hopefully it won't come to that."

"Yeah, times is different."

Harry struck the table hard enough to collapse the walls of his Marlboro house. He spit the cigarette in his mouth onto the pile.

"You can have the shirt off my back and the balls from my sack, Captain. Harry Lime goes where no man has gone before and you're gonna go there one more time with me."

"That's a fact," Blaine said, hoping Harry didn't pick up the uneasy edge in his voice.

"What the fuck you want?"

"Nice greeting, Sal," Blaine said to Sal Belamo.

"That you, Boss?"

"Good to hear your voice, too."

"Hey, boss, it goes like this. Got four movie stations on my cable box now and access to those pay movies, too. You ask me, *that's* fucking progress. Trouble is I haven't been able to watch one all the way through yet, 'cause the fucking phone keeps ringing. I had more time to kill when I was inside the fucking loop. What am I paying—maybe fifty bucks a month for all this shit?—and I ain't seen a flick from beginning to end."

"Don't want to spoil your average tonight, now, do you?"

"Try me."

"Need you to run something down."

"What the fuck . . . shoot."

"Ever hear me talk about Harry Lime?"

"Sure. Old Air America pilot saved your ass more times than even I have."

"He just saved it again today. Get the file on him, much as you can and as recent as they got it."

"Anything specific in mind, boss?"

"Psychiatric reports and evaluations. Recommended treatments and therapy."

"What gives, boss?"

"I just left Crazy Harry in a bar down here in Key West. Told me somebody stole his kid, the one he had with his wife, Maggie. Said he hadn't seen me since the funeral."

"So?"

"So, Sal, there was no funeral. There couldn't have been a kidnapping. Harry Lime's never been married and he doesn't have any kids."

CHAPTER 4

"I think I got this nailed," Alan Killebrew reported Tuesday morning when Susan stepped into the trailer that had become Firewatch's on-scene command center, parked in Charles Park across from the Cambridgeside Galleria.

Killebrew was Susan's lead technician on the Firewatch team. He had arrived here just hours after her on Sunday and hadn't left since. Nor would he until their leads, clues and theories began to firm into fact.

Killebrew backed his wheelchair up and aimed it for the computer monitor; his mussed hair and tired voice indicated he had spent Monday night working behind it. "I'm talking about the way our organism made its way through the mall. I think I got it figured." He paused. "That and how it got in to begin with."

Before Susan could prod him further, Killebrew worked the keyboard and a computer-generated, animated graphic of the Galleria appeared in simulated 3-D. It was not unlike a video game; he controlled the flow of action by manipulating the computer's mouse.

"By analyzing the pictures from the mall's security cameras and studying the placement of the bodies on all three levels, we were able to determine that not all the victims were affected at once. Whatever killed them had to travel, the time difference minor but present and crucial. What you are about to see is a model of the progression."

The action began on the third level, the mall patrons denoted by flashing white dots. As the cursor swept past them, they stopped flashing and turned to red. The sequence was repeated on the second floor and then the first.

"Third to first floor, traveling downward, with a slight lag," Killebrew elaborated. "Then there's the dog. That storeroom he was locked in wasn't in the original plans for the mall. The temperature inside it was over a hundred and ten degrees, while the air temperature outside at the time of the event was ninety-four. Now, doors *must* have been open at some points after the organism's release. So it's virtually inconceivable that at least some of the contagion would not have slipped out, and yet all those afflicted were confined solely to the interior of the mall. Because something stopped it, literally, at the door."

"Temperature," Susan said, realizing. "My God . . ."

"The mall was a comfortable seventy-two degrees," Killebrew acknowledged, looking up at her from his chair, "thanks to the air-conditioning system. My computer-generated model of the invading organism's spread conforms perfectly with the flow of air through the Galleria's air ducts. Since the storeroom the dog escaped from wasn't built at the same time as the rest of the mall, it possessed no duct work for air-conditioning."

"Good work."

"There's more. The compressors which power the system are located in the mall's boiler room, which can be found here." Killebrew scrolled down his computerized schema of the Galleria until he came to the basement and a small square that was flashing red. "That's where the organism gained entry."

"Then let's go take a look at it."

McCracken had arranged to meet Harry Lime first thing Tuesday morning, which for Harry meant nine A.M. He lived in a first-floor apartment inside one of Southpark Condominium's six buildings. The buildings were similar to many others in the area, pseudo Spanish Colonial, and they had the advantage of being only three blocks from the ocean. Blaine figured Harry found the sounds and breezes calming.

When Harry's buzzer brought no response, McCracken hit two others and, as expected, was buzzed in without inquiry. He was carrying his SIG-Sauer under a baggy linen shirt worn out at the waist; not his preferred method of concealment, but a compromise to Key West's expected near-hundred-degree temperatures.

Once inside Blaine tried the doorbell and then knocked re-

peatedly with no response. He could picture Harry inside
Apartment 1A, passed out drunk or lost in the earphones of
some video game. Blaine sighed and went to work on the locks
with the picks he always carried with him. The dead bolt took
thirty seconds to work open, the knob lock barely half that.
Both Schlage—top of the line—though requiring a mere few
additional seconds' inconvenience for the professional.

"Harry," McCracken called, stepping in. "Harry?"

No response came and Blaine moved farther forward. The
living room was neat and well kept, a surprise considering
Harry's typically unkempt appearance. More surprising was
the stark nakedness of the walls. McCracken had expected
them to be cluttered with various posters, pictures and mem-
orabilia, just as Harry Lime's mind always seemed so cluttered.

The kitchen yielded no sign of Harry, and Blaine checked
the fax machine resting on the counter. Not surprisingly, it
was out of paper. He moved on to the apartment's two bed-
rooms. He came to Harry's first and gazed at the neatly made,
unslept-in bed. The room was plain and traditional, again not
what he had expected. The drawers were neatly packed and
arrayed, the twin closets leaving plenty of room after Harry's
meager supply of clothes—floral shirts and baggy trousers,
mostly—were hung.

McCracken checked the bathroom and then moved on to
the second bedroom. Save for a few stray pieces of miscella-
neous furniture, it was empty. If Harry really had a son, this
would have been his room. There would be posters plastering
the walls, a kid's bedroom set and workstation. Place for a
computer.

There was nothing. Just the excess furniture and boxes
Harry had never gotten around to unpacking. How long had
he been down here in the Keys flying for Air America's offspring? That question had not come up last night.

Blaine retraced his steps through the apartment, something
edgy scratching at his spine. He didn't like the feeling in the
rooms, found it too sterile. Even the carpets were neatly vac-
uumed, the lines against the grain still obvious.

To wipe out the telltale wash of footprints and signs of a
struggle, perhaps.

Why am I thinking that?

There was clearly no reason to; probably many nights when Crazy Harry Lime didn't quite make it home no matter where home was.

McCracken sat down on the white couch in the living room and pulled from his pocket the four-page psych report on Harry Sal Belamo had faxed to Blaine's hotel that morning. It said pretty much what he had assumed: Harry Lime was crazy as a loon, except when he was flying. His grasp on reality seldom extended beyond the cockpit, where he was still as good a pilot as there was.

Blaine read on but that was the nuts and bolts of it. They probably would have put Harry away if his flying hadn't been such a damnable asset. That made him the ideal patsy for the new Air America. Skillful and unfalteringly reliable when working. Easily denounceable and forgettable if caught.

Then again, McCracken also knew the door swung both ways. They weren't asking Harry to do anything he didn't want to. Flying was all he had, the only thing in his life that provided some measure of reality and balance.

That brought him to Harry's latest government file. Up until a decade before, 1985 say, the information jibed pretty much with what Blaine knew or expected. For the decade following, though, the information on the lines was strictly boilerplate, detailing Harry's reassignment to details and venues he couldn't have stomached for more than an hour. Humdrum stuff and transport missions. Some resupply to the Special Forces active behind enemy lines in the Gulf War. Advance missions to Panama and Grenada. Everything you'd expect.

And none of it in keeping with Harry's style. It wasn't that he wouldn't take on the more regular stuff; it was that the brass didn't trust him with it. He was too prone to turn creative on them, make things up as he went along. Just tell him where, when and what and he'd handle the rest. Anything that came down through official channels was jobbed to someone else.

Blaine grabbed a phone from a nearby end table and dialed Sal Belamo.

"Fax come through, okay, boss?"

"Better than Harry, Sal."

"Trouble?"

"He's gone and someone went through a lot of trouble to cover it up. Walls were wiped clean and everything but the wool got sucked out of the carpets."

"Keeping someone like you from seeing something, maybe. Christ, you think Harry really did have a kid who got snatched?"

"If he did, there'd be phone calls."

"Records easily obtained."

"I'll call you in an hour."

Even though all tests indicated that nothing was unsafe about the air inside the Galleria, procedure dictated that Susan and Killebrew don Recal II space suits before entering. For her the feeling brought on an eerie sense of déjà vu, even though the remains of the dead had been removed from the premises and transported to the CDC containment facility in the Ozark Mountains.

A service elevator brought them to the basement level and Killebrew wheeled himself along even with Susan down the corridor, sliding ahead of her when they reached the boiler room.

"Were any bodies found in here?" Susan asked him when they were both inside.

"No. We've managed to identify the three on-duty physical plant personnel among the remains in the mall and that's an anomaly in itself."

Each was able to hear the other thanks to the microphones built into the helmets' frames beneath their faceplates. Tuned properly they could talk to each other instead of to Firewatch, though precaution dictated that their conversation be recorded back at the mobile command center. The only thing technology could not manage was to make their voices sound less raspy and guttural when relayed through a miniature earpiece.

"Why?"

"Because according to procedure one of them was supposed to be inside at all times."

Killebrew pushed the door open and led the way in. The boiler room was a high-tech affair, hardly fitting its mundane title. There was no "boiler" per se visible, just the main heating elements, pump stations and air-conditioning compressors, which were shut off now, raising the mall temperature to just under one hundred degrees. None of this interested Susan so much as a wall that was composed from ceiling to desk level of built-in, twelve-inch-square black and white security monitors.

"Doesn't seem like these belong in a boiler room," she noted.

"This was originally supposed to have been the main security station. The developers decided to move it to the top floor after all but the finish work was complicated."

"Are these monitors functional?"

"I'm not sure."

"Assume they are," Susan proposed.

"Is that important?"

"I'm beginning to think it might be. What track has your investigation been proceeding on so far?"

"Microbreak of previously unidentified virus or bacteria."

"Accidental introduction?"

"Inadvertent, anyway."

"Assume hostile action."

Susan could see Killebrew's displeasure through his misting faceplate. "You're the government liaison here," he relented. "Not me."

"Play along. What do we know, what can we prove?"

"Whoever was supposed to be in here during the incident wasn't. Fact."

"Unless he himself was the perpetrator. Let's assume, though, that he was lured away by the actual perpetrator."

"Hypothesis," Killebrew said staunchly.

"So whoever that someone might be arranges to have this boiler room to him-or herself." Susan's gaze lifted toward the bank of monitors. "He, she, or they would then be able to watch the results of their handiwork live from a dozen different angles, assuring them of knowing when it was time to flee." Now she turned her eyes on the air-conditioning registers built into the ceiling. "You said the cooled air spread from the third floor down. That makes this the last place in the mall the organism would have reached. Proceeding with that scenario, how would the perpetrator have fled?"

"Continuing down the subbasement corridor we took to get

here brings you to an exit leading into the parking garage.''
Killebrew seemed to stiffen in his wheelchair. ''The same
place we found . . .''

"Found what?''

"I'd better show you.''

CHAPTER 5

McCracken took his time working his way back to Captain Hornblower's to follow up on Harry Lime's final moves the previous night. He strolled down Duval Street toward Mallory Square past an endless succession of bars, restaurants and clothiers featuring the trendiest of selections. There were any number of sidewalk pitchmen selling art, as well as numerous galleries, and there seemed to be a kiosk on every corner trying to lure tourists to sign up for the various water activities offered.

McCracken watched a collection of canopied cars roll by, dragged by a fake train engine and barely a third full of tourists busy with their cameras. An old-fashioned trolley followed close behind, also only about one-third full. The tourists inside looked bored and listless, as though trying to get all this over with before the day became too hot to stray far from the water.

Captain Hornblower's had just opened when Blaine got there. Inside, a bartender and a single waitress Blaine recognized from the night before were busy readying the place for whatever business might be coming in. Both remembered Harry leaving several hours after McCracken Monday night, having broken his own record on the video game at the expense of another handful of quarters and his usual number of Rolling Rocks.

McCracken was about to take his leave when he noticed the Key West Irregular Harry had called Sandman leaning up against the same support beam he had the night before. Could be he hadn't left, except Blaine was fairly certain this bathrobe was a different color.

"I know you," Sandman said, as McCracken approached.

"Don't think we've ever met."

"We haven't. I know you all the same."

"I'm looking for Harry."

"Come back later."

"I don't think he'll be here then, either."

"Harry moves around a lot."

"I think this time somebody made that decision for him."

What was left alive in Sandman's eyes flashed concern. "You talk to Papa?"

"Where can I find him?"

"Key West Harbor. Hustling charters."

Papa's boat was called the *Bell Tolls*. Seated there on the deck he looked even more like Hemingway than he had in Captain Hornblower's the night before. He seemed to have no interest at all in hawking his wares for prospective charter customers, preferring to spend his day pouring a pitcher of Cuba Libre into a plastic cup.

"Hello, Papa," Blaine said, stepping on board from the dock without waiting for an invitation.

The grizzled man turned and held back on his drink. "Do I know you?"

"You know Harry."

Recognition flashed through his bloodshot eyes. "You were in the bar last night."

"Harry needed me. Now he's gone."

"He does that sometimes, usually when there's something on his mind needs working out."

"Lately?"

Papa shrugged. "I suppose. He'll take a boat out late at night. Closest one he can climb into. Drunk, sober—matters not at all. Figures out how much gas he's got in the tank and goes out as far as he can before he has to turn around. Likes to push things, including his luck. Up till now, though, he always came back."

"Does he have a favorite boat?"

"Yeah: my dinghy."

"Can I see it?"

"Sure, if it were here. I showed up this morning and found it gone."

*   *   *

"We found this just outside the exit door on that subbasement level," Killebrew told Susan as he hovered over a table in the trailer with a number of items cluttered atop it.

The two of them smelled pungently of soap and powerful disinfectant, courtesy of the portable decontamination shower units contained in an adjacent trailer. Susan's hair was drying into gnarled, matted strands she paid no heed to whatsoever. Killebrew was seated in a different wheelchair since his regular one was still undergoing "cleaning" procedures. Susan watched as he leaned across the table and grasped a tattered and worn backpack made of blue nylon.

"I've catalogued the contents," Killebrew continued. "They're right there on the clipboard before you."

Susan ignored his suggestion and reached inside the backpack for herself. There were four books—tomes, in fact. Susan withdrew the one on top, a thick, tightly bound effort titled *Advanced Organic Chemistry*. The second, almost as thick, was called *Molecular Physics and Quantum Mechanics*. Three and four were both paperbacks masquerading in hardcover size, *Nuclear Physiology* and *Applied Chemical Engineering*. Susan actually recognized at least two of the books on sight, thanks to earlier editions she'd come across during her years preparing for medical school.

"Textbooks," she said to Killebrew, feeling about the now flattened backpack's innards. She fingered the rough blue fabric. "No name on any of the contents?"

"No. I checked."

She slid her hand inside the bag and it closed on a few stray pieces of paper which she pulled from the darkness.

"Receipts," she said, as she uncrumpled and spread them out. "Harvard Coop. Since the bag is on this table, I assume you haven't been able to match it up with any of the early witnesses on the scene we were able to identify."

Killebrew looked at her. "No match. And there's only one set of fingerprints present on it. We already ran them through the FBI and drew a blank."

Susan glanced at the slips she still held before her. "And these are cash receipts, so they'll be no help to us either. Well, they do have the time and date on them. We might get lucky there."

"Several weeks ago," Killebrew reminded, not sounding like he cared very much. "Doubtful we can expect anything. Harvard summer session, though, has a fairly limited enrollment, so following up on those students enrolled in classes requiring these texts shouldn't be too hard. Probably turn out to be some scared-shitless kid who slipped away instead of lingering like the others we've identified."

"Maybe," Susan said, turning her attention to a trio of identical eighteen-inch cylindrical shafts attached to rectangular high-tech meters next to the backpack on the table. The meters, both digital and curved, were built into the top of sealed boxlike frames with a number of tiny holes punched symmetrically across all sides. The objects were freestanding, thanks to tripods set at their bases.

"We found these late yesterday," Killebrew said. "Haven't been able to identify them yet."

"Don't bother," Susan told him. "I've seen them before— actually, not exactly like them, but close. They're air quality testers, left in confined spaces for extended periods of time to measure the levels of potentially toxic gases. Results of studies employing them have been primarily responsible for smoking bans in restaurants and malls to reduce the effects of second-hand smoke."

"Then we can assume their presence to be routine."

But Susan's mind was elsewhere. "Where is your sweep team?" she asked Killebrew, referring to the personnel responsible for collecting on-site data.

"Rechecking the mall for anything we may have missed yesterday."

"Tell them to get down to the boiler room. I want it swept again now."

"What exactly are they looking for?"

"Something I think they missed."

"Here's the way it plays, boss," Sal Belamo reported when Blaine reached him minutes after leaving Papa's charter boat. "Looks like your friend Harry liked to keep to himself. We got almost no calls going out, and only a few coming in."

"Any overlap?"

"Nope. But almost all the incomings originated from a single line in Cambridge. As in Massachusetts, boss, Harvard specifically.''

"Someone was calling Harry from *Harvard*?"

"A dorm room. Last call was made, let's see, Sunday afternoon about two. Big one, over twenty minutes in duration. Hey, I was just thinking. Harry have a fax machine?"

"No paper inside."

"From what you told me, it figures. Thing is, these records can't differentiate between a regular call and a fax transmission. Mighta meant something if there'd been paper.''

"Means I've got to catch the next flight to Boston," Blaine told him.

"As in Harvard? *Cambridge*?"

"The tone in your voice just changed, Sal. What gives?"

"Something went down there couple days ago you better know about, boss. . . .''

The man inspecting the original oil paintings stacked along the sidewalk waited until Blaine McCracken was well past him before slipping away and raising the cellular phone to his lips.

"McCracken's taken the bait," the man reported as soon as the party on the other end had answered.

Susan was reviewing the latest data when the soft beep sounded. She watched as Killebrew lifted a receiver from the communications board connecting him to the sweep team he'd dispatched minutes before to the boiler room. He listened to the report briefly, never taking his eyes off Susan.

"Your hunch was right," Killebrew said, voice sinking as his gaze fell on the backpack she had hastily repacked. "Fibers of blue nylon fabric were found in the boiler room.''

CHAPTER 6

"Doctor?"

The slumped form of Dr. Erich Haslanger remained motionless behind his desk.

"They're waiting for us at the test site. We'd be well advised to get started."

Erich Haslanger stirred in the high-back leather chair and with great effort lifted himself up and shuffled toward Colonel Fuchs, a creak in his bones for every step. He would be seventy-three soon, much too old for this kind of work but knowing no better or different. Without work Haslanger would have time on his hands and he feared time more than anything except sleep. Sleep terrified him most of all, so much so he had given it up altogether nearly two years before. He had good reason; sleep had almost killed him.

Haslanger drew even with Colonel Fuchs and found himself hating the man more than usual today. All prim and proper in his perfectly tailored uniform. Fuchs's skin was so tight it seemed ready to snap at any moment. Haslanger liked to imagine he sprayed the expression on in the morning and left it there all day. Usually by this time of the afternoon, his uniform would show some creases, his old-fashioned brush cut losing the battle to Long Island's humidity. But not today. Today the men from the Pentagon had come to visit Group Six and Colonel Lester Fuchs had made himself look early-morning fresh.

"Did you hear me, Doctor?"

"What? Excuse me?"

He and Fuchs were at the end of the corridor in front of the elevator. Haslanger couldn't remember making the walk, lost in one of the fugues he figured replaced his mind's need for slumber. The elevator door's polished steel showed him his face and he cringed at the sight.

Did he really look that bad?

A corpse, that's what he was becoming. His face was gaunt to the point of skeletal, pale puckered flesh making the cheekbones, jaw and chin more pronounced. His eyes were gray and lifeless and his white hair was a wild frizz. Besides all this his joints always ached and his neck was constantly stiff.

"I was asking you about the final staging you did yesterday for today's test," Fuchs continued.

"Yes. Everything checks out."

"You're sure?"

"Quite."

Fuchs's voice grew icy. "You were sure before the Reyvastat incident, as I recall."

"Hardly a comparable example," Haslanger returned without missing a beat. "Today's experiment is taking place in a controlled environment, not a war zone."

"Not yet, anyway," Fuchs followed grimly.

Haslanger ignored him, reviewing in his mind the litany Fuchs would soon be spouting off to his eager audience of Pentagon officials: the gospel of Group Six, starting with how the organization pursued its single-minded purpose isolated in the back end of the sprawling pine barren occupied by Brookhaven National Lab in the town of Upton on Long Island. Group Six had been so named because it was envisioned by the Pentagon as the "sixth" branch of the armed services. The Pentagon, specifically Chairman of the Joint Chiefs General Starr, had determined that the importance of technology meant its development should be centralized. The work of labs like Los Alamos, Lawrence Livermore, or Aragon often mirrored one another, untold man hours of research wasted toward identical ends. Group Six would change all that and in the process change something else as well.

This was the part Fuchs liked spouting off the most and Haslanger cringed just thinking about it.

The five groups currently charged with safeguarding the nation's interests were having a tougher and tougher time doing it. The Army, Navy, Marines, Air Force, even the newly formed Special Operations Command had found themselves in a post-Cold War world where the rules had changed more quickly than their collective ability to adapt to them. Fires kept springing up faster than they could put them out, and now a number of renegade countries held a match in one hand and a nuclear trigger in the other.

Although Group Six's original charge was to develop weapons of a nonlethal nature, the latest and more crucial mandate undertaken at the Brookhaven facility itself was to produce a weapon that would effectively neutralize the latest members of the nuclear family. The problem was that so far, under Colonel Fuchs's administrative leadership, it had failed miserably. Complicating matters further was the fact that Group Six's quasi-secret existence had recently been the subject of several media leaks. The president was furious. Congress was demanding a full investigation. Some of Group Six's primary supporters in Washington had started distancing themselves, wanting no connection to projects responsible for expending hundreds of millions of dollars with often disastrous results.

The most blatant example of this so far was also the most recent: an invisible, undetectable gas or liquid called GL-12 that, once released into the air or water, put anyone exposed to it asleep. Imagine the possibilities, Haslanger had boasted proudly. Imagine the ease with which a stubborn enemy could be defeated, casualties to U.S. troops reduced to zero. With the help of the army, Group Six arranged to test GL-12 in Bosnia, specifically the Muslim village of Reyvastat, which had come under brutal shelling by a Serb armed column entrenched in the surrounding hillsides.

According to plan, the GL-12 had been released in a secret airdrop directly over those hillsides. The problem was that Haslanger had failed to properly estimate the potential effects of the wind, which blew his sleeping gas instead over the besieged village. As a result, the residents were sent into an unplanned slumber from which hundreds never awoke when the Serb column attacked and massacred them as they slept.

Group Six, Erich Haslanger and Colonel Lester Fuchs, had become accessories to a mass murder. Although the nature of the mission kept the incident from ever reaching the attention of Washington circles, the very promising GL-12 was shelved altogether. Haslanger blamed GL-12 and the other failures on Colonel Fuchs's insistence that he follow through on any number of wide-ranging and mutually exclusive projects instead of patiently developing a select few. Fuchs blamed Haslanger for failing to live up to the expectations that had accompanied him to Group Six.

But Haslanger remained the best chance Fuchs had to earn his general's stripes and he knew it. All his hopes had fallen on the old man's well-documented, though controversial, genius. Haslanger had been achieving dramatic results for half a century, but his tenure at Group Six has thus far failed to produce the one superweapon that would affirm its efficacy and preserve its very existence. Today's test was another in a long chain of attempts and the first since the devastating failure in Reyvastat.

Haslanger longed for the simpler times following World War II after the Americans had sought him out. No one asked him any questions. He was given a job to do and no one cared how he did it. Failure was accepted as a natural precursor to ultimate success. Accountings were never required.

He was paying for that now, every time his eyes slipped closed and the shapes came to visit in the instant before he managed to shove sleep aside. Occasionally the products of his past almost reached him, just as they had two years before when he realized sleep and death were one and the same.

Haslanger held himself blameless for all he'd done prior to joining Group Six. He was ahead of his time, he told himself. In the early years, the proper technology simply hadn't existed to allow for the complete realization of his visions. That technology did exist today, but Haslanger could never have gone back even if the Pentagon wanted him to. Too many shadows and shapes had been left behind, horrifying night things that had doomed him to a life of wakefulness.

Sometimes Haslanger wondered what had become of his creations. Since he'd given up sleep and denied them their visits, however, he'd been getting better at forgetting them.

This afternoon's test site was a large open area between Group Six's headquarters and the Brookhaven perimeter fence line, layered with man-made hills and valleys to simulate battlefield conditions. A dozen soldiers and three jeeps were nestled comfortably between a pair of these hills. They were volunteers drawn from a nearby army base who liked the idea of participating in a top-secret government research project.

A quarter-mile away from the soldiers, five men in summer-weight uniforms stood near an M1A2 battle tank listening to the last of Fuchs's remarks as Haslanger cringed.

"Looks ordinary, doesn't it, gentlemen?" Fuchs said, turning his attention to the tank after completing his usual introductory ramblings.

The five men from the Pentagon followed the colonel's gaze to the M1A2.

"But a laser developed by Group Six personnel has been mounted on the underside of that M1A2," Fuchs continued. "It fires a series of bursts over either a narrow or wide area, depending on conditions. The desired effect, as you know, is temporary blindness of the enemy. This is in keeping with our desire to redefine the way war is fought today. Our goal is nothing less than one-hundred-percent survivability for American troops."

On cue a technician wearing a white lab coat who'd emerged from the tank's innards distributed a set of dark-lensed goggles to each man.

"If you'll join me over here now and don your protective goggles, please."

The Pentagon men slid away from the M1A2 and placed the goggles over their eyes. Haslanger eased past them and approached the tank, nodding at the two technicians perched outside its cab. They ducked back down and closed the hatch behind them. Haslanger heard a scratchy, whirring sound, indicating the laser's generator had been activated. He turned toward Fuchs.

"Fire when ready," the colonel said into a walkie-talkie connecting him to the men inside the tank.

Fuchs raised the binoculars to his goggles and watched the soldiers a quarter-mile away take their prearranged positions, the leader returning a walkie-talkie to his belt. Using live, unprotected volunteers for such an experiment would have been unheard of at Los Alamos or Lawrence Livermore, but not here at Group Six, especially not with what they were charged with creating.

Fuchs steadied his binoculars.

The laser's bursts of blinding light exploded in rapid succession as if from a massive strobe that fired lightning. For an

instant everything seemed perfect and Fuchs felt almost cele-
bratory. Then the sight through his binoculars made him gasp.

The clothes of the soldiers burst into flames. Even from this
distance he could hear their screams as they crumpled and
rolled in agony across the ground. It was Reyvastat all over
again, sure to draw even more negative attention since it had
happened here where containment and damage control would
prove difficult indeed. He felt his own frustration boiling over,
imagining what Congress might do with this. His gaze turned
on Haslanger, who seemed almost to be smiling.

"*What have you done?*" Fuchs screamed, grasping the old
man's arm.

Haslanger stood wide-eyed and awestruck, not able to take
his eyes from the flames as he responded.

"Not exactly the way we planned it, but equally effective,
I should think. With some slight refinements—"

"*Damn* you!" Fuchs rasped.

"Wonderful," Haslanger mouthed, scarcely believing the
accidental and wondrous discovery of this combustion ray.
"Positively wonderful."

CHAPTER 7

"You're from the government, I assume," the Harvard University registrar, Robert Mulgrew, greeted Susan Lyle when she entered his office on the second floor of University Hall.

Susan showed him her identification. "Centers for Disease Control and Prevention."

"Terrible what happened at the Galleria. We lost some students who were attending our summer session, I'm told. No confirmation. Still being sorted out. You'd be the person doing the sorting, I assume."

"One of them."

Mulgrew nodded as if he understood. "You'll want some addresses and backgrounds to go with names, then."

"Just one."

"Did you say 'one'?"

Susan nodded. "And I don't have a name," she said as she produced the list of books contained in the blue backpack. "These were found in the area of the mall."

Mulgrew took the list and raised his glasses. "I understand," he told her, fully believing he did.

"I want to know what courses call for these books and who might have been taking all of them."

Mulgrew glanced at it again. "That won't be a very long list." He reached for some folders lying on his desk and looked back at Susan before he opened them. "Do you know what it was yet, what killed them, I mean?"

"We're still investigating."

"I've heard the rumors, you see. Some kind of disease, people say, an epidemic. Victims in isolation wards. Victims who haven't been allowed to see their families."

"I can't respond to that."

"But, you see, people are scared. People are wondering if

they're safe. We've already lost two-thirds of our summer session enrollment to panic. It's difficult to reassure them."

"There is no epidemic. That much I can tell you."

"Well, that's a relief," Mulgrew said, sounding as though he meant it.

He located the course catalogue for the summer session and made a list of the most advanced science offerings, then cross-matched them with the book titles Susan had supplied. The course list compiled, he switched on his computer and ordered the machine to perform a search for all students enrolled in each of the courses.

"Here we are," Mulgrew said, with no trace of accomplishment in his voice.

A single name was centered on the screen: JOSHUA WOLFE.

"It's all so awful," Mulgrew said very softly.

"Can you print out his complete file, everything you have?"

"Yes, of course."

The file took several minutes to print. Mulgrew read it off the screen as it slid by.

"Isn't this terrible," he muttered barely above the printer's whir. "He's one of our regular-term students, as well, enrolled in the doctoral sciences program after completing his masters in a mere—"

Mulgrew stopped suddenly, got up and went to the printer. He lifted the stack up off the tray and inspected the top page.

"I thought I saw it wrong on the screen. I thought, I was hoping . . ."

"What is it?" Susan asked him.

Mulgrew's eyes had glazed over with shock. "Joshua Wolfe is only fifteen years old."

"I'll need to see his room," Susan said.

"Of course. I understand. I'll have security let you in."

Minutes later Mulgrew accompanied Susan and a uniformed security guard the brief distance across Harvard Yard to Weld 21, a room in a freshman dormitory used for summer-session students.

"If there's anything else I can do," Mulgrew offered, "I'll be in my office."

"Thank you," said Susan, and she closed the door behind her.

Weld 21 was actually a pair of rooms and would probably have been occupied by two or three students during the school year. But for the summer, clearly, only one had resided within it. The bedroom section contained a bed, a chair, a television and nothing else. There were no posters on the walls, no stereo with monster speakers, nothing that indicated occupancy by a teenager. The only things even remotely suggesting the presence of a youth were half-open dresser drawers and a collection of clothes that lay strewn about over the floor and bed, as if Joshua Wolfe had packed and left in a hurry. A glance into the closet revealed no suitcase. A number of wire hangers had dropped to the dull tile floor.

The second room was something else entirely.

It was dominated by computers. One of them she recognized as the Power Macintosh Series II 8100/80, the fastest, most powerful computer of its kind available. Two smaller computers were set against another wall, each boasting external hard-drive boosters. Bookshelves rested against every available wall, all of them packed solid.

Susan moved about the room slowly, taking it all in. She wasn't sure what she was looking for, and she picked up and discarded several items from desk or shelf until she spotted a thick, neatly bound report. She opened it and studied the title page:

IRREVERSIBLE EFFECTS OF POLLUTANTS ON THE ENVIRONMENT AND POTENTIAL SOLUTIONS
A Doctoral Thesis By
Joshua Wolfe
First Draft

The same shelf was stacked with notebooks. She lifted one up and skimmed its contents. Then another. And another.

All this boy's research notes and theoretical ponderings were centered around air pollution. One whole notebook was dedicated to global warming, another to the greenhouse effect.

The next three off the shelves had Susan retreating to a stiff-backed desk chair. They concerned the need for drastic and dramatic solutions to the pollution problem and detailed the devastating effects to mankind if that problem was not addressed in full very soon. Geniuses, she knew, were prone to be obsessive, and Joshua Wolfe's personal obsession was laid out in notebook after notebook.

Susan moved to the desk holding the Power Macintosh, dragging the single chair with her. She switched it on and accessed its menu list. Not surprisingly, all the hard drive's files had been erased. Disappointed, Susan started working her way through the desk's drawers in the hope of finding at least some semblance of a clue.

The second drawer down yielded much more than that in the form of a plastic storage case containing unlabeled floppy backup disks. Excited now, Susan popped the first one in and opened the single file it contained.

A poem appeared on the screen, the first in a long collection that made up the file. The poems were laid out in the chronological order in which they had been written. Susan hit HOME, returning to the first poem in the sequence. It read "*Josh, Age 3*" above the title:

"The Fires of Midnight." Eleven stanzas followed.

> *We all know how it feels to cry*
> *We've all sometimes had to lie*
>
> *But it's those of us whose spirits died*
> *Who life seems to have defied*
>
> *But here is a door*
> *And I will deny it no more*
>
> *The one thing the world couldn't ignore*
> *Soon I will be the one they all adore*
>
> *And with the midnight hour about to begin*
> *And the fires ready to burn within*
>
> *What you have but cannot see*
> *Is all I wish I could be*

If you've ever felt this way
You know it's no good to live for another day

So now you see you're not great
And the future holds a much worse fate

So walk a mile in these shoes
And my fires will teach you to lose

You can't escape
There's no one the fires don't rape

I cry for you
And I cry for the world
'Cause we all live together
And one day we'll be equal forever

Susan read the lines over, chilled by them, having to remind herself that a *three-year-old* had written "The Fires of Midnight." But hardly an ordinary three-year-old. A three-year-old already aware and frustrated by the fact that he was different. A three-year-old who must have been an outcast, who desperately wanted to fit in and knew he never could.

Heart hammering against her rib cage, Susan ejected the disk and slid a second into the slot. This one had a file menu and she began scanning through the contents. Joshua Wolfe's obsession with air pollution stretched far beyond its potentially catastrophic long-term effects and encompassed the development of drastic solutions. File after file was devoted to his experiments on various agents meant to attack it at the molecular level. Several of the technological references clearly indicated that the boy was playing around with some form of genetically engineered organism designed to suck pollutants right out of the—

Susan froze the screen, eyes fixed upon it. She had almost passed over this file, would have if a spark of recognition hadn't flickered in her mind.

Plans, blueprints . . .

She had seen them before, just hours earlier. Seen them in Firewatch's mobile command site.

They were the original plans for the Cambridgeside Galleria.

Susan tried to steady herself but her mind was racing too fast. She recalled the air-quality registers the sweep team had found in the mall, the connection to Joshua Wolfe's work unavoidable.

What do I know? What can I prove?

Start with a hypothesis. Assume Joshua Wolfe's presence in the boiler room, and the presence of those air-quality registers inside the mall, indicated he was conducting an experiment. Assume he had released an organism or enzyme of his own creation designed to destroy air pollution. Only it hadn't worked as planned and the result, the result had been . . .

> *And with the midnight hour about to begin,*
> *And the fires ready to burn within.*

The fires of midnight, Susan thought. Was that what Joshua Wolfe had inadvertently unleashed in the Cambridgeside Galleria two days before?

She found a semblance of the answer in the next file she accessed. Mathematical formulas and equations she could make little sense of dominated screen after screen until she locked on to a file devoted to what the boy apparently intended to release in the Galleria as part of his test: CLean AIR.

It was printed that way only as a title, replaced in later usages with the contraction "CLAIR." She scanned back a few files and realized Joshua Wolfe had named all of his experimental formulas after women. He was apparently as adept at turning a phrase as he was at turning a test tube, a poet indeed.

But it was his expertise with a test tube that interested Susan now. According to what she could decipher from Joshua Wolfe's equations, two vials of CLAIR would be required to cover the area of the Galleria. This was later amended to a single vial, at the last minute, actually, perhaps as late as Sunday morning.

That fact moved Susan's focus in another direction. What if, what if . . .

She reached for the phone, closed her eyes to remember the number Mulgrew had given her.

"I need something else," Susan told him. "The science labs

that Joshua Wolfe would routinely have access to—would he
be required to check out materials? Would there be a record?"

"I'm not sure," the registrar responded, pausing as if expecting her to explain further. "I can find out."

"And if such a list does exist, I'd like a copy."

"Of course."

"As soon as possible."

Susan hung up the phone. She settled back in the chair and
tried to settle her thinking, focusing on the moves immediately
before her. All of the materials in this room had to be im-
pounded and sent to Atlanta for more detailed analysis at Firewatch Command. Once there—

Susan felt a slight whiff of wind on her back and turned to
see the door to Joshua Wolfe's room opening. A broad,
bearded man entered and closed it behind him as she lurched
out of her chair.

"Who are you?"

"Sorry to interrupt," said Blaine McCracken.

CHAPTER 8

"I asked you who you were." Susan's voice was calm but her stance remained rigid as she half-eyed the phone.

McCracken turned his gaze about the room. "You've been busy. Accomplished quite a bit, by the look of things."

"What are you doing here?"

"Same thing you are, I suspect."

"Who sent you?" Susan asked him. "Washington? Atlanta?"

He was moving through the room, inspecting and cataloguing everything with his eyes.

"Well," he replied, "Atlanta sent you. I think we can call that a fair assumption." He locked his stare with hers. "You haven't found the boy, I assume."

Susan's eyes bulged and the red of her cheeks deepened. "*Who* are you? What are you doing here?"

"The name's McCracken, and maybe I always wanted to see how the CDC, specifically Firewatch Command, operates in a crisis."

Susan tried not to show her surprise. "You know an awful lot ordinary people aren't supposed to."

"I've never been accused of being ordinary, miss—excuse me, *Doctor*. I mean, it must be 'Doctor,' right?"

"You seem to know everything else."

"Friend of mine who told me what was going on up here didn't have time to dig that deep."

"What did he tell you?"

"Cambridgeside Galleria. That sufficient?"

"Plenty, but that doesn't explain what you're doing in this room."

"Like I said, the same thing you are: looking for the boy

who lives here.'' Those eyes sweeping again. ''Or used to, anyway.''

''His name. You didn't use the boy's name.''

''Josh. Happy?''

''Susan Lyle.''

''What?''

''*My* name. It's Susan Lyle.''

Turning his attention to the business at hand, McCracken began going through the desk drawers, barely ruffling the contents as he searched.

''You've been through these.''

''Not the bottom ones,'' she said, not sure why she was telling him.

Blaine went to work on those.

''If you do indeed know what I'm doing here,'' Susan went on, ''it seems only fair that you tell me what *you're* doing here.''

McCracken found what he was looking for and straightened up. ''This,'' he said, his eyes lingering on a snapshot that showed Harry Lime with his arm around the shoulder of a boy of about fourteen or fifteen. Both were smiling, Harry in a fresh tropical shirt that hung over his belt, the boy wearing his hair long and dark, the smile not looking right on him.

Blaine didn't want to let it go, as if doing so would mean letting go of Harry for the second time in twenty-four hours. He studied the boy's slightly blurred, smiling face. The long hair framed his face well. His eyes, even in the picture, were strangely intense and yet not quite mature. Harry's crazy, impossible tale suddenly made some kind of sense. Blaine made himself place the snapshot in Susan Lyle's outstretched hand.

''Joshua Wolfe,'' she said as she reached out to grasp it.

''You recognize him?''

''From a picture in the registrar's office.''

''Until a moment ago, I wasn't sure he existed.''

Susan looked up from the picture, confusion compounding her simmering suspicions. ''What are you talking about?''

''Man in that picture is what brought me up here.''

''Then we're not here for the same reason at all, are we?''

''I think we are; we just came from different directions.''

''You always make this little sense when you talk?''

"Until I trust the person I'm talking to, usually."

"I'm the one who's in the dark here. All I know is your name, while you seem to know just about everything."

"Not where I can find Joshua Wolfe."

Susan felt her features relaxing. "You know what happened at the Galleria. He could have been one of the victims."

"Possible, but not likely. Someone placed a phone call from this room on Sunday afternoon two hours after the disaster occurred."

"To your friend, the man in the picture?"

"That's where things get strange, Doctor, because when I talked to my friend he didn't say anything about a phone call. He was quite specific about the fact that he hadn't heard from the boy in quite some time. Thought he'd been kidnapped."

"And he wanted you to find him."

"That's right."

"And you'd be just the man who could."

"I owed him a favor, a big one."

"So you came here."

"I came here, Doctor, because my friend disappeared last night and this kid is the only clue I've got as to why. Only now it looks like Joshua Wolfe has disappeared, too."

Susan felt even more perplexed. "Why are you telling me all this, answering my questions?"

"Because I've got a few of my own and I figure both our interests would be better served by sharing information."

"My interests happen to be those of the United States government."

"Thanks to Firewatch Command. I know you've got jurisdiction and I know you're all doing your best to keep a lid on what happened. It's not working. It almost never does."

"Okay, so we're both trying to solve mysteries."

"And at the center of both is a missing teenage boy."

"He's fifteen," Susan elaborated. "Sixteen in September."

"Spending a summer at Harvard."

"More than just the summer; he's enrolled full-time."

That piqued Blaine's interest again. "For how long?"

"Since last fall."

"About the time the 'kidnapping' took place, according to Harry."

"And what is your friend's connection to him?"

"Harry thought he was the kid's father."

"No, his father's name is—"

"Don't believe everything you read."

"It was right there on the boy's transcript."

"Because that's the way they operate."

"The way *who* operates?"

"They buried Harry in Key West and then they made him disappear after the memory they provided got the better of him. Could be they went after the kid, too. Could be that's why he disappeared." It made perfect sense, until McCracken looked beneath the surface. "Of course, that wouldn't explain why you're here, Doctor, would it? Firewatch control officer leaves the primary site to spend an afternoon in a prodigy's dorm room in Harvard Yard—must have your reasons, I assume."

"Even if I were at liberty to tell you, what makes you think I would?"

"Because you're starting to realize I might be able to help you get to the bottom of things. But if you can't help me I've got no reason not to part company with you as soon as I've seen what this room's got to show."

"You *are* Washington."

"Used to be. Not anymore. Managed to maintain my security clearance, though." Blaine's eyes drifted to the phone. "Certain number you can call to check that, you want me to give it to you."

"I've got it."

"Use it."

"There's no need for that."

"Then tell me what you're doing here."

Susan Lyle hesitated, but only for a moment. "I think Joshua Wolfe caused what happened at the Cambridgeside Galleria," she said, "and I think it was an accident."

What happens now?" Susan asked, after explaining the conclusions she'd reached in this room. She had told the stranger named McCracken everything she'd pieced together, convinced there was nothing to hide any longer and that he could, in fact, help her. By the time she finished he no longer seemed like a stranger. Something about him invoked trust and deflected suspicion. Conviction rimmed his eyes and laced almost every word he spoke.

"You keep doing what you're doing," he told her, "while I keep doing what I'm doing."

"How do we stay in touch?"

"I can give you two very private phone numbers to reach me. One will be watched, the other not."

"What do you mean 'watched'?"

"Manned—by an ally. I don't suppose you're in a position to take similar precautions."

Susan thought briefly. "I can open a private voice-mail box. Would that do?"

"So long as you give only me the number."

"Is that really necessary?"

"It is if we want to keep whoever's behind Harry's disappearance from making the connection between us."

"Sounds a little paranoid to me."

"There's a fine line between paranoia and precaution, Doctor," McCracken told her. "I've been there before."

"I haven't."

"Until now."

CHAPTER 9

As was his custom, Hank Belgrade was waiting on the steps of the Lincoln Memorial when McCracken arrived. Belgrade was a big, beefy man who like a select few in Washington drew a salary without holding any official title. Technically, both the Departments of State and Defense showed his name on their roster, but in actuality he worked for neither. Instead, he liaised between the two and handled the dirty linen of both. He had access to files and information few in Washington had any idea existed.

Blaine had once saved his career back in the Cold War days by bringing a Soviet defector safely in after security had broken down, a leak detected. In return, Belgrade was always there for McCracken when he needed information. They met here on the steps of the Lincoln Memorial every time, Belgrade wearing his perpetual scowl, never looking happy to see him. Today Hank had a thick manila file folder wedged under one of his knees.

Belgrade was silent as he watched Blaine approach.

"I think I'll sit down, if you don't mind," McCracken said by way of greeting.

"Do whatever the fuck you want."

"Testy today, aren't we?"

"Not until you called. You got a real knack, MacNuts, you know that?"

"Thank you."

"Don't bother. I'm talking about shit and your unfucking-canny ability to step in it. Tell me something, how do you do it?"

"It just follows me around, Hank."

"Yeah, I wish you'd stop following me. When we gonna be even?"

"Whenever you say. Now, if you like. Leave. Take the folder with you."

"Fuck you."

"In such a historic location?"

"Last time, MacNuts! This is *it*!"

"Sure."

"Biggest shit yet this time. Least it ranks up there." Belgrade frowned and lowered his voice. "Your friend Harry Lime got about ten years washed out of his life. Him and maybe a dozen others who fit the same profile."

"Profile?"

"You know, crazy enough to control but not so crazy as to be unreliable. I haven't got hard numbers or even data. What I got's words, indications, and some cross-references make your skin crawl. And it all starts with something called The Factory. Ever heard of it?"

"No."

"We're talking capital *T*, capital *F*, and for good reason. The Factory was into shit, *doing* shit twenty years ago we can't even pull off today. And they didn't give a hoot about ramifications or morals. Cross a few species to see what you come up with? Why not? Radiate some mental patients? Who cares, if it gives us a better idea of the effects of fallout? Expose soldiers to a deadly toxin? Good idea, if it'll help us win a chemical and biological war. Cold War was going full tilt, and so were the boys at The Factory. Till the late seventies, anyway, when a single stroke of Jimmy Carter's pen effectively slashed it out of existence. Reagan managed to salvage it for a while but a year into his first term it was history. Too bad in many minds, I'd wager, 'cause the egg-heads there had just gotten into a new field big-time: genetics."

"Uh-oh."

"You got it, MacNuts. Files on what exactly they were able to pull off before the end have been wiped clean out of existence. But it's a safe bet they treated the DNA map like an Etch-a-Sketch game. Take the stuff we're just starting to figure out today and eliminate all the safeguards and precautions. Last recorded project they went operational with in '79 is what links Harry and the others in this folder together.

"Operation Offspring," Belgrade finished, after a pause long enough to slide the manila folder Blaine's way. "All I got's in here and it ain't much. Profiles of Harry Lime and the others. Reasons why they were judged the most able candidates."

"Candidates for *what*?"

"That's where I draw a blank, MacNuts. That's where I sign off."

Operation Offspring, Blaine reflected.

"We talking 1979 here, Hank?"

"Or '80. Thereabouts, anyway."

McCracken thought of the picture he'd found at Harvard of Harry Lime with his arms around the shoulder of a boy who was fifteen now.

Operation Offspring . . .

"You'll keep me in the loop with this one, okay, Mac-Nuts?"

"First time you ever asked me that, Hank."

"This one's got a real bad smell to it."

"It's like that every time innocent people get killed."

"Maybe Harry wasn't innocent. Maybe he volunteered."

"He and the others were *selected* to volunteer, Hank. I don't have to read the contents of your file to figure that much out."

"All the more reason to keep me in the loop. One thing I've learned about line items like The Factory. Slash 'em and they don't die; they just hibernate for a while until they get reborn with new call letters. This town's a fucking revolving door."

"Good thing for us it swings both ways," Blaine told Belgrade.

"I rolled the dice on Operation Offspring, boss," Sal Belamo explained over the phone several hours later, "and came up with snake-eyes. *Nada.* You get my drift. But those names fat Hank was kind enough to provide, they were something else again."

Belamo had been an efficient and trusted intelligence operative until he started working with McCracken. That eventually cost him any position remotely classified as formal. His past, though, had left him with a network of contacts who either owed him or wanted him to owe them. Consequently, there was little information the government possessed he could not obtain, much of it classified or red-flagged for restricted access. And when he couldn't find the answer himself, he found someone who could.

"A link?" Blaine asked him.

"Several. To begin with, none of them got active files anymore. You tell me Harry Lime's flying with the new Air America out of south Florida, but military data banks list him gone, no forwarding. Same thing goes for the other names. Their files just stop running, with no further updates."

"As of when?"

"1981."

"Around the time The Factory was dissolved."

"Which closed the front door. But you know me—the front door's closed, I go in through the back. Find that locked, too, and I try a window. This time I found a crack in the wall. Made myself real small and slith-ered in."

"To see what?"

"Damnedest thing. I ran the names fat Hank gave you in search of common denominators. Lo and behold there was only one: woman by the name of Gloria Wilkins-Tate. See, Harry Lime and the others were all military fringe players. The kind who can't go to the VA when they got a problem or expect to collect their pensions when they turn sixty-five. Trouble is, all the names on this list had psychological problems. Gloria Wilkins-Tate was their caseworker. Turns out she's about as qualified to help wackos as I am to teach kids manners. Ms. Wilkins-Tate is a spook herself. Goes all the way back to the OSS, when Langley was just a thought in the Company's forefathers' heads. The only woman among the original cadre. Rumor was she had an affair with Wild Bill Donovan himself. But her real specialty was salvaging and integrating Nazi scientists into our network. In fact, she helped create one mostly just for them."

"Don't tell me—The Factory."

"Gloria Rendine was one of its original founders."

"I thought you said her name was Wilkins-Tate."

"It used to be until she changed it upon retiring 'round fifteen years ago. Started herself a whole new career in the rare books department of the New York Public Library. I was you, I wouldn't call ahead."

CHAPTER 10

By Tuesday afternoon, Erich Haslanger's fascination with the results of that morning's test had become an obsession. The subjects' clothes had caught fire first, indicating that the focused light reacted with the material of their uniforms and explaining why that response had never turned up during animal testing. He was on to something tremendous here with unlimited potential.

Haslanger dimly registered the phone in his private lab ringing and felt for the receiver.

"Haslanger."

"It's been a long time, Doctor," came a familiar voice.

"What do you want, Larkin?"

"Want? Nothing. I'm calling to let you know someone's been making inquiries. The name Wilkins-Tate has come up several times."

"Ancient history," Haslanger said.

"Let's hope so for your sake. There can be no leaks, nothing that can lead back to you. If there are, it would be wise to eliminate them now."

"That's your job."

"I'm ancient history now, too, Doctor. A purveyor of information and nothing else. This crossed my desk. I thought you should know."

"Thank you."

"How is your new assignment going?"

"Well enough."

"I'd heard otherwise."

"A few setbacks, that's all."

"Glad to hear it, because we're both at the end of our lines now. Nowhere else to go. Make the best of what we've got."

"I always do."

"Let's hope I don't have to be in touch again."

Haslanger replaced the receiver and tried to refocus his thoughts on completing his analysis of the blindness weapon, but quickly grew distracted and decided to return to his office. He opened the door and froze. The lights inside were off, and he never, *never* even considered turning them off for darkness might bring on thoughts of sleep and such thoughts had to be avoided at all costs. He was fumbling for the switch when a powerful hand closed on his bony wrist at the same time a scratchy voice found his ear.

"Hello, Father."

"Dr. Lyle," General Starr, chairman of the Joint Chiefs of Staff, challenged, after Susan had finished the core of her explanation, "would you have us believe that the crisis we are confronting is nothing more than an *accident*, as you call it, at the hands of this *boy*?"

Starr's reaction had not surprised Susan and she was prepared for it. "I do, sir, because all indications point to that very conclusion. Joshua Wolfe was obsessed with the need to rid the world of air pollution and decided to do something about it."

"And what exactly did he do, Doctor?" asked Clara Benedict. "Or, should I say, where did he go wrong?"

"By far the largest portion of pollutants to the air—car exhaust, factory smoke, even the exhaust from lawn mowers—is composed primarily of sulfates and nitrates. These sulfates and nitrates possess a sequence in which the oxygen and nitrogen forming them share a specific and close proximity."

"In layman's terms, if you will, Doctor," someone requested.

"The sulfates and nitrates are indentifiable from the inclusion of OHN—oxygen, hydrogen and nitrogen—that form their molecules. Now, if you could teach a genetically produced organism to recognize and target those proximities specific to their chains, you would be able to effectively destroy them at the molecular level."

"You're saying that's what the boy did?"

"I'm saying that's what he *tried* do do. He made a mistake."

"Obviously."

"To him, it wasn't obvious at all. What Joshua Wolfe thought he had created was a living organism that, once released into the air, would attack and destroy the nitrogen-oxygen bond present in the air pollutants. The pollution would thus break down at the molecular level and cease to exist."

"Only that didn't happen," noted the voice from speaker number three.

"Yes, it did, but the organism didn't stop there." Susan settled her thoughts, continuing to speak without benefit of notes. "Normal protein structure is a twisting mass of strands in which space is shared by a variety of atoms forming molecules at various proximities. Unfortunately, human hemoglobin contains several complex amino acids, which results in additional twisting of the protein strands, thus bringing the nitrogen and oxygen molecules closer together. To a proximity, in fact, that almost duplicates the proximity the organism was programmed to recognize in the sulfates and nitrates of air pollution."

"In other words," started General Starr, "it kept on killing after its primary objective was achieved. Sounds to me like this organism liked its job a little too much."

"That's probably not far from the truth. The organism would need to ingest the nitrogen to produce more of itself. The desire for self-perpetuation defines its very role and existence. So when it identified something else determined to contain its target structure, it continued to attack—to, in essence, *feed*: on human blood. That accounts for the condition in which the bodies were found—the drying and general loss of cohesion."

"And Joshua Wolfe didn't anticipate this? As brilliant as you claim him to be, he didn't perform preliminary experiments on lab animals, exposing them to . . . what did you call it?"

"CLAIR," Susan replied. She had been ready for that question but her voice still lost a measure of its confidence as she continued. "And according to his files, he *did* and everything checked out. CLAIR tested perfectly safe. But in the Cambridgeside Galleria all the pet store animals, other than the dog that had been inside the storeroom, were found in the same condition as the human remains. I wish I could explain the anomaly, but I can't.'' Susan paused briefly. ''The boy planned everything out to the last detail. He had the air-quality registers perfectly placed. He somehow managed to lure phys-ical plant personnel out of the boiler room. He knew exactly how to use the air-conditioning system to spread his organism. He watched it all on the security monitors, and when it was obvious something had gone wrong, something horrible, he ran.'' She paused again. ''He must still be running.''

Silence again took over the cramped confines of the com-munication center as the audio participants struggled with what they had just learned.

''Have you been able to confirm what contained the spread of the organism to the mall?'' asked General Starr.

''According to the boy's notes, and confirmed by the sur-vival of the dog, he was working in the area of temperature sensitivity. His organism was programmed to survive within a very narrow temperature range, rendering it inactive above, say, seventy-eight degrees. The temperature at the mall was maintained at seventy-two degrees. The dog survived because it was in a room with a temperature considerably higher than seventy-eight.''

''We're talking about *air* temperature here, are we not?'' asked Clara Benedict.

''Yes, we are.''

''But the temperature of the human body is twenty degrees above your seventy-eight-degree window. How, then, could the organism have survived once it entered the victims?''

''I'm not sure. Something to do with the programming the boy wasn't expecting. Since the organism was airborne, my best guess would be a chemical reaction with the mucous membranes in the nose and mouth which caused a transfor-mation allowing heat tolerance.''

''Hold on,'' said the voice from speaker number one. ''If this transformation occurred as you have represented, why did the organism *still* stop at the mall doors?''

''Most likely the transformation only affected those cells that attacked the victims initially. When the cells divided, the original programming kicked back in. My associate Dr. Kil-lebrew is en route to our containment facility inside Mount

Jackson in the Ozarks to run further tests to determine the precise pathology of the organism.''

"Programming," repeated General Starr, clearly intrigued by her use of the word. "You talk as if this boy was working with a computer."

"Because, sir, through some advanced form of genetic engineering, that's exactly what he did. Joshua Wolfe created this organism to be task specific, only to find it performed its duties too well."

"Could he have purposely programmed it to kill people, Doctor?"

"If he desired, yes, but I don't think—"

"What steps are we taking to recover this boy?" General Starr interrupted sharply.

"As of this time, none. In fact, until moments ago I had shared the fact of his existence with no one."

"Good. I will supervise the search personally, then. I assume all other pertinent information has been forwarded to me."

"It has. Only . . ."

"Only what, Doctor?"

"I have reason to believe, General, that he will be heading to Key West."

"And what reason is that?"

"Materials found in the boy's dorm room at Harvard," Susan lied.

She had debated relaying McCracken's revelations and his insistence that the boy's Harvard file had been doctored. His admonitions to be leery of those with whom she shared information weighed heavily on her. But she didn't feel she had a choice. Shortly after McCracken had left Joshua Wolfe's room, the registrar, Mulgrew, had called with the inventory list she had requested from the labs at the Harvard Science Center. He read it to her over the phone. Joshua Wolfe had requisitioned *two* vials tailored to the specifications of the substance he called CLAIR. According to his original plans, that was how many he felt he required. But later analysis proved he only needed one, which was how many he had used in the Cambridgeside Galleria on Sunday.

That meant there was still another vial of CLAIR left. And the only way to get it back was to find Joshua Wolfe.

"I'm not your father," Haslanger managed, not wasting his time trying to pull from the iron grip.

"Close enough. Now, shut the door."

The words emerged as if the speaker had to force them through marbles held between his teeth. They were distorted yet easily understood, emerging from a terribly distended mouth that hovered at least a foot higher than the doctor's ears.

"A light first, please," Haslanger pleaded, as the shape slid away from him.

"Of course. That is where we're different, isn't it? You shy from the dark while I live within it, *live* for it."

Haslanger swallowed hard and shook his head. He wondered for a moment if he had actually nodded off and was dreaming now, one of his creations come back to get him. Yet he knew this creature was the product of reality, not nightmare. Haslanger felt his breathing turn shallow, as a coldness swept down his spine in the moments before his desk lamp was switched on. Angled down, its fluorescent bulb nonetheless produced enough light to quiet his nerves. A creak sounded as the huge frame of the visitor settled into his desk chair. Haslanger's eyes, starting to adjust to the semidarkness, made out the outline of his frame sitting there, the big chair lost to his bulk. He shut the door.

"You're early. I said eight o'clock."

"I knew you'd be returning before that. Anything that requires my services always keeps you from your work."

"This is a simple task, one I hoped wouldn't be necessary."

"Not yet . . . Father," the shape said, and Haslanger cringed again at the thought. "A man like me likes to savor such moments, since they provide the rationale for my being."

Haslanger swallowed hard.

"Of course, I'm not really a man at all, am I?"

Haslanger remained silent and watched the shape of something like a hand reach for the desk lamp.

"Answer me, Father, or I may choose to switch off the light."

"You are a man, and plenty more, *much* more."

"What is my name?"

"Your name . . ."

"Yes."

"Krill."

"Why?"

No response.

"Tell my why"—an elongated finger of bone scratched at the lamp switch—"or you lose your precious light."

"You couldn't say the word."

"What word?"

"Kill."

"Why couldn't I say it?"

"Your . . . mouth."

"Didn't form properly, did it? Had me putting the r's where they didn't belong, so 'kill' came out 'krill.' Not as you planned. Like my eyes. They have trouble with bright light. I see better in the darkness."

Krill's muffled, raspy breathing became the room's only sound. Eyes fully adjusted to the thin light now, Haslanger could see his contours clearly and most of his features. Krill's face was huge and elongated, supported by a massive neck banded by thick, overdeveloped strands of muscle. His skull was similarly too thick and large for the skin that coated it, leading to hollows, fissures and gaps in the cheeks, brow and both sides of the jaw. The mouth hung open, the teeth resisting all attempts to close it fully. His hair had never grown properly, covering his scalp in thin patches that looked like scabs.

Despite the horror of the rest of Krill's face, though, his eyes were the worst. They bulged out from sockets too small to contain them and lids that could barely close, looking like fat golf balls with black holes drilled in their center. Open as they were almost all the time, those golf-ball eyes focused incredible intensity forward. Peripherally they could extend vision to nearly 270 degrees, so they missed nothing, except when exposed to bright or sudden light.

The shape rose slowly from the chair and hovered over it. Haslanger had to tilt his head back to see the incredible girth of the chest and shoulders, a sight he viewed with his customary awe. The arms hung low enough for Krill to rest the whole of his Popeye-like forearms across the desk blotter.

"Now, what is it you have for me, Father?"

CHAPTER II

Colonel Lester Fuchs arrived at Group Six early Wednesday morning while the corridors were still vacant. He closed his office door behind him and moved to the closet. Inside, hidden in a garment bag, was a uniform jacket already complete with a general's stars. He traded it for the colonel's jacket he wore and sat down behind his desk.

Today was going to be a bad day, one of the worst. Today he would be called on the carpet for yesterday's debacle. Five of the volunteers had died. Three more would be scarred horribly for life. At the very least, he expected Group Six's scope to be dramatically reined in. At the very worst, his foes in Congress would get their way and he would be finished. The Washington forces who solidly backed Group Six's existence could de-vote only so much energy to damage control before someone had to take the fall. That someone would likely be him.

The phone on his desk rang, startling Fuchs. At so early an hour, who could possibly expect to find him in?

"Yes?" he greeted, receiver squeezed against his ear.

"Something's come up," General Starr's voice announced. "Something that may allow us to reverse the current trend we have found ourselves mired in."

Fuchs went rigid and slumped in his chair, as if afraid Starr might notice his bogus general's jacket.

"It's something Group Six needs to get involved in immediately," the general continued. "Tremendous possibilities. I'm faxing you the preliminary of what we have. It should be coming through now."

"One moment."

Fuchs rose from his chair and moved for the private message center that was built into the wall at his rear. There were three separate fax machines, in addition to a quartet of secure telephone lines. His hand was waiting when the first of the pages emerged from the machine reserved for Washington correspondence. The transmission ran only three pages. Waiting for the second and third gave Fuchs time to peruse the first. His hand was trembling when he returned the receiver to his ear.

"How confident is your information?"

"Very, by all accounts."

"We need this boy."

"My office has taken charge of retrieval. I believe I can arrange jurisdiction appropriately."

"And the woman, this Dr."—Fuchs had to look down again at page one—"Lyle. She could prove useful, given her now-expert knowledge. Can reassignment be arranged?"

"Why not?" General Starr returned. "After all, she works for the same employer we do."

Erich Haslanger found the door to Colonel Fuchs's office open when he arrived minutes later. The colonel's summons had reached him in one of Group Six's labs, a tone in his voice like none Haslanger had heard in recent weeks. Haslanger slipped through the door and found Fuchs seated at his desk, fingers interlaced beneath his chin, something that looked like a smile flirting across his lips. He'd never seen the man teetering so on the verge of emotion, his eyes alive with something other than desperation.

Fuchs held the fax out across his desk. "This just came in via Washington," he said, fighting to restrain his exuberance. "I want your opinion."

Haslanger took the pages and realized Fuchs was wearing a general's uniform. Fuchs followed his eyes to the stars and seemed not to care. Haslanger began reading. His eyes widened halfway down the first page when he came to the first mention of Joshua Wolfe. He knew the color had drained from his face and actually felt dizzy. He clutched the back of the chair set before Fuchs's desk.

"Well?" Fuchs prodded.

Haslanger heard his own words as if someone else was speaking them. "This substance is effectively a containable killing machine. Theoretically the target arena could be as small as a city block, as large as the city containing it."

"How?"

"If temperature sensitivity could be employed to control its spread, then so could finite cell division. It's a fairly simple formula, figuring out how many times the cells of the organism would have to divide in order to cover a predetermined area."

"Of *any* size?"

"With few exceptions, yes."

Fuchs leaned forward in his chair. "This could save us, Doctor. This is what we have been waiting for. Arrangements have been made for us to take charge of the boy's retrieval. . . ."

At that the colonel noticed the ghostly tint Haslanger's flesh had taken on. His skin seemed to cleave more tightly to the bone, turning his gaunt face into little more than a skull. He looked as if the breath had been knocked out of him.

"What's wrong, Doctor?"

"This boy . . ."

"Go on."

Haslanger slid into the chair before the desk, strategically arranged to assure that Fuchs was on a higher plane. "There's something you should know."

The fat man sitting on the bench leaned forward to better aim the bread crumbs he was tossing at the pigeons.

"You're not supposed to do this anymore, you know, Thurman," he said to the man sitting next to him. "Something about the birds being diseased. Makes me wonder."

Thurman fidgeted impatiently, trying to relax. He was tall and broad, too packed with muscle for suits to ever fit comfortably. The back of his neck was laced with knobby swirls that folded up every time his face changed expression. His head was square and angular, its size exaggerated by the stubbly, blond crew cut that adorned his scalp. But the feature that defined him most was an ugly scar that ran down the left side of his face from cheek to jaw.

"You see, Thurman," continued the fat man, thick wisps of hair bulging out from the sides of his head beneath a bald dome, "we experimented with pigeons; sparrows, too. Wondered if we had happened upon the perfect delivery system for isolated biological warfare. Imagine the possibilities! But the bastards proved unreliable. Decided to fly away and never come back." He tossed some more feed the way of the birds before him. "These could be their offspring."

"Trying to get on their good side, then."

"They're quite a delicacy, you know," the fat man said, settling back slightly with a contented sigh. "Not at this age, of course. No, they have a wondrous flavor only when they're squabs, too young to fly. They can be stuffed and roasted. Especially appetizing when cooked in a Madeira sauce with their livers. But don't forget to truss them. Can't trust butchers anymore to handle that chore. And the real key is to serve them on toast. Only the best chefs remember to do that. Soaks up all the juices. Then you have something simply delightful, young offspring gone to a good cause."

"Speaking of offspring . . ."

"Cambridge is being labeled an accident, just as we knew it would. We have nothing to fear on that end. Now, what of yours?"

"McCracken is still on the trail," Thurman reported.

"Are we keeping tabs?"

"If we wandered too close, he'd pick us out in an instant." He fingered his scar, remembering. "That risk is unacceptable."

"Yet one we tacitly accepted when we elected to utilize his services."

"A rushed decision. We didn't think it out long enough, the potential downside."

"If he fails, you mean?"

"No," Thurman told the fat man. "If he finds out what's really going on."

PART TWO

OPERATION OFFSPRING

PHILADELPHIA,
WEDNESDAY, 7:00 A.M.

CHAPTER 12

"Are you sure you don't want me to put that up top for you?"

The flight attendant's question jolted Joshua Wolfe from his daze and he twisted toward her nervously.

"Your bag," she continued, eyeing the black backpack that protruded slightly out from the seat in front of him. "You might be more comfortable."

"No," Josh said, clearing his throat. "It's okay."

The woman smiled and was gone. Josh lowered himself and squeezed the backpack farther beneath the seat. He had placed the test tube in the center, protected by notebooks and what few clothes they left room for. He couldn't feel its contours through the fabric, but he tried nonetheless.

He had spent Sunday night at a hotel in Boston before moving on to New York Monday. A train had brought him to Philadelphia and another hotel on Tuesday, the Airport Hilton in this case, to allow him to catch the first flight out for Miami this morning.

On the move, stay on the move . . .

Three hotels in three cities in three days with nothing to do but think, his eyes poised on the door, certain it would come crashing in at any moment. Sleep should have brought respite, but it didn't. It came instead in fits and starts, each brief slumber lasting only as long as it took for the pictures from the Cambridgeside Galleria to return to his mind. They came the same way he had seen the tragedy unfold on Sunday: lined up in rows, stacked atop each other.

It didn't make sense.

All his studies had checked out. Never in any of his laboratory experiments had any of the lab animals shown so much as an uneasy breath when exposed to CLAIR. Newspaper accounts, attributed to "unidentified sources," claimed the victims' bodies had been drained of blood. To Josh this meant CLAIR had somehow confused blood for its targeted molecules. It shouldn't have, of course. But the problem was that he must have made CLAIR too smart, too efficient. He had programmed it to reproduce itself by ingesting nitrogen in a specific chain. Surely it would have recognized the difference, however subtle, between human blood and sulfates/nitrates. Once the identification had been made, though, CLAIR could not turn away in the face of its own demise. It continued doing exactly what it was supposed to, straying only slightly beyond its prescribed parameters.

But why hadn't it behaved that way during his testing phase?

"Excuse me," said an overweight woman holding a boarding pass, her eyes on the window seat next to him. "I'm in there."

Josh rose and stepped into the aisle to let her pass. One of her sneakered feet brushed up against his backpack as she shuffled her way in. He felt his heart stumble a bit. When the fat woman had at last claimed her seat, he used the opportunity to lean over and remove a notebook from the pack's front zippered compartment.

The notebook was full of impressions and analyses he had begun writing out in search for the answer to what had gone wrong. But no amount of figuring could change the conclusion already obvious: getting CLAIR finished had become more important than getting it right. He was too sure of himself, too obstinate in his approach, too desperate to succeed. But nothing had ever gone wrong for him before. The leap from theoretical concept to finished product had always been a smooth and uncomplicated one so far as Joshua Wolfe was concerned. So why bother with the normal procedure of submitting a paper and requesting a sanctioned study? It would have taken years, if it had ever been granted at all. Bureaucracy moved like a train chugging uphill. Pollution would have overrun the entire planet before the top was even in sight.

All he wanted was to do something wonderful, to prove the worth of his meritorious discovery so no one could sweep it aside. Conduct his own study, obtain proof, and submit the results as part of an official paper, simultaneously released to the media.

Josh had gotten the idea years before, after performing an in-depth study on a designer enzyme created in the lab to eat the bonds which held oil together on the molecular level. The use of that enzyme had greatly advanced the fight against oil spills, saving countless wildlife in disasters in the North Sea as well as Alaska, and had him wondering why the same principle couldn't be applied to air pollution and water later as well.

Josh started with air.

Two years it had taken him to come up with his discovery, two years on top of all his other course work. He was obsessed, cared about nothing else, was never sure how he so easily breezed through advanced classes he paid virtually no attention to. The truth was, once he was finished, Josh couldn't make himself wait. He had to try it, had to *know*, had to . . . succeed.

He wanted to be a hero. And if things had gone differently at the Galleria, if only they had . . .

He had unlimited access to most of Harvard's most advanced research labs, located in the Science Center. And in the summer the wait for the most prized equipment was considerably shorter. Josh had been concentrating solely on the final round of testing and production of his organism since the end of the second semester. And when all his stages of lab testing on CLAIR checked out, he couldn't resist a larger-scale study of the organism's capabilities inside the Galleria.

Things had gone off without a hitch at first. He had lured the on-duty physical plant technician out of the boiler room, accessible via a set of stairs off the bottom floor of the Lechmere electonics store, by sending him a message on his digital readout beeper: NEED YOU ON THE THIRD FLOOR NOW!

The man had left immediately, the latch on the boiler room door not engaging all the way thanks to a piece of steel Josh had wedged between it and the jamb when the technician had last entered. His first step was to activate the security monitors on the wall. Then he placed his backpack on the desk and removed from it a vial that was a twin of the one he had with him now. He had learned from the Galleria's final construction plans the kind of air-conditioning compressors that would be down here and studied identical models for weeks. Eventually he rehearsed the process of gaining access through a six-inch-square hatch with his arm and pouring the vial's liquid contents into the start of the airway.

He had wedged the empty vial in his pocket and turned his attention to the screens. He pictured the freshly cooled air whisking his now-gaseous CLAIR up through the system, where it was free to multiply to the nth degree and spread through the Galleria. Forty seconds passed and then it began.

Josh shivered in his seat as the plane hurtled into the air at takeoff. The fat woman next to him cast a sidelong glance his way, then returned to her magazine. He tried to settle himself but the memories were too strong, chilling him.

The same chill had struck when he had watched the first of those on the mall's third floor stagger. They clutched for their throats before a series of horrible spasms racked their bodies, making them look like marionettes controlled by drunk puppeteers. It spread downward like a wave, Josh watching it all descending across the screens as it descended through the Galleria. A few of the patrons on the first and second floors had enough time to try for the exits before they were cut down in midstride, the floor yanked out from under them.

Josh's teeth had sliced his tongue. He felt his own breath fleeing and feared his own creation was about to claim him as well. He rushed from the boiler room into the corridor.

Josh had passed several people after crashing into the parking garage on Level C. He didn't warn them and wouldn't have been physically able to had he tried; terror had stolen his voice and his breath was coming in great gasps. He knew everyone was dying. He knew he was responsible. He was a murderer.

And no one would understand when he explained it to them; he had never been understood and now his desperate attempt to change that was going to accomplish quite the opposite by branding him an outcast. He was a block·from the mall when he realized he'd dropped his backpack somewhere in the parking garage. Knowing he couldn't retrieve it, he had returned to Weld 21 and started stuffing all he could squeeze into a second backpack, the one that now lay wedged beneath the seat in front of him. But he didn't want to be caught carrying the final formula for CLAIR in it, either hard copy or disk. Both represented evidence and both had to be destroyed. To lose the formula now, though, was to lose it forever, or at least for the foreseeable future. So he had faxed it to Harry Lime's paperless machine in Key West, knowing it would be stored in the machine's memory, waiting there for him to retrieve.

Since no one was looking for him, fleeing was not difficult. His concerns that the backpack he had abandoned at the Galleria might betray him melted away when he recalled that he had not written his name on a single item of its contents. They might track him to Harvard, but if nothing else he had bought himself some time.

His credit card had a three-hundred-dollar cash advance limit. Automatic teller machines, though, were easily fooled by someone who knew how to manipulate the electromagnetics that controlled them. Kindergarten stuff for Josh. He'd walked away from a Cambridge ATM with three thousand dollars in twenty-dollar bills instead.

The money had paid for the trains to New York and Philadelphia, a hotel room in each city, as well as today's plane ticket to Miami. The closest he came to leaving either of the hotel rooms was opening the door for the arrival of room service. When the food was gone and there was nothing else to look forward to, Josh found himself doodling with words in his notebook instead of pictures. His mind was spent. Nothing was coming and, for the first time in a long while, he began a poem. He'd used poetry to express his frustrations and inner rage as a child, when he first began to stand out as different from his peers. It was how he worked to resolve things, grew to understand them and himself. He had never discarded a single one and had eventually transferred the collection of works onto disk, where he could feel better about forgetting them.

Josh had remembered suddenly what it had been like to be three and four and five, and on. The poetry brought it back to him. The old rage was gone now, replaced by concession to who and what he was. The words stretched across the page, taking up space and little more. He couldn't make them work.

The plane settled into an even flight pattern and Josh felt

himself relax a bit. The fat woman next to him was doing a crossword puzzle, doing it badly. He gazed at the clues and the boxes and had the entire thing mentally solved in less than a minute. He ran a hand through his long brown hair and left it there, returning his eyes to his notebook. Perhaps the back-pack he'd lost had been discarded already, erroneously thought to have belonged to one of the victims or unclaimed by one of those first on the scene. Somehow, though, he didn't mind the fear for the attention it took from the guilt. He could live with fear; fear made him feel like a victim, the pursued, the hunted. Guilt reminded him that he had taken victims, hun-dreds of them, before becoming one himself. He deserved whatever happened to him because he was a . . .

Go ahead, say it! Think it!

. . . murderer. He could turn himself in, confess. What would they do to him? Josh was no expert in the law but he'd read about it as he'd read about everything. They had to prove intent, he thought. Without that there could be leniency, a suspended sentence. His punishment would be disgrace.

Could he make them understand the wonder of what he was trying to do, the importance of it? Could he convince them of the accuracy of his exhaustive studies on the state of the world a generation into the future if something wasn't done to im-prove air quality? Would they believe he had taken every pos-sible precaution before letting CLAIR loose in the mall?

"But why, Mr. Wolfe, would you take such a responsibility upon yourself?"

"Because, because . . ."

"Go on, Mr. Wolfe. The State eagerly awaits your answer."

"Because I want . . ."

"Want WHAT?"

"I want to be accepted."

Josh would try to tell them what it had been like all his life, feeling forever out of place. The stares children older by five or six years cast his way when he was seated in their class, always in the front so he wouldn't have to worry about seeing over their larger frames. The Galleria could have changed all that. He could have been a hero, his formula hailed as one of the greatest scientific discoveries of all time.

Now he would be hailed a murderer, by everyone except

Harry Lime, of course. Harry would understand. Harry would help him.

But Harry hadn't been answering the phone. Or maybe he was away from the apartment, the one in Key West where he had been placed after Josh had been taken away for the last time. Josh wasn't supposed to know what they'd done with Harry, but he'd gotten into the proper data banks months before and discovered where they'd moved him.

After the phone rang unanswered, he had sent the fax of the formula for CLAIR over the line. Now he was going down there in quest of the chip it was stored upon. Hopefully Harry would be home by then.

Josh felt himself nodding off and snapped alert suddenly, the indelible feeling of something terribly wrong plaguing him. He gazed to his right.

The fat woman was snoring next to him, one of her huge legs stretched out under his seat, foot pressed against his backpack. He saw the darkening splotch spreading across the fabric and realized the test tube inside must have broken just before the first of the plane's passengers began to gasp.

He leaped up to warn the rest, but his breath had been choked off, too. Nothing he could do but watch while their flesh paled and shriveled, eyeballs bulging outward as the skin around them receded. They just withered away, like the Wicked Witch of the West in *The Wizard of Oz*, their clothes suddenly robes over the shapeless masses puddling into the aisle as Josh watched it all . . .

"Excuse me . . ."

. . . wondering why he'd been spared. Wishing he hadn't . . .

"*Excuse* me."

He came awake with a start, to something like a persistent dog nuzzling his leg.

The fat woman loomed over him, trying to get by. Josh pulled his legs in tight.

"Thanks," she said, not smiling.

And Josh slumped back in his seat, shivering, the nightmare snatched from sleep not too far away at all.

CHAPTER 13

"Right through that door."

"Thank you," McCracken said to the escort who had guided him to the Bryant Park stack extension on a sublevel of the New York Public Library's main branch on Forty-second Street.

Gloria Rendine served as chief assistant to the curator for Rare Books and Manuscripts. She had been more than happy to schedule an appointment with him on the pretext of his donating a rather large collection of historical materials. Blaine wondered how she would respond upon learning he was here to dredge up her past instead.

McCracken entered and found Gloria Rendine in the midst of a page-by-page scrutiny of an elegantly bound, oversized volume.

"Excuse me."

"I'm sorry," the old woman replied, slightly startled. "I didn't hear you come in. You must be"—she consulted a pad on her right—"Mr. McCracken."

"That's right."

"Please, sit down."

Gloria Rendine rose and offered him a chair in front of her desk. She was wearing a light sweater over a simple print dress. Her silvery hair was tied up in a bun, but as he approached Blaine could see the stubborn vitality in her watchful eyes. Her skin looked to be unmarked by age or the environment. Different hair color and a fresh coiffure and she could easily have looked twenty years younger.

"I can't tell you how much we appreciate your generosity."

Blaine approached the desk but remained standing. "I'm afraid it comes with a price. You see, actually I'm here *in search* of something rare."

The old woman looked confused. "I don't see how I—"

"Specifically, a woman. On display for years before she removed herself from circulation. Catalogued under the name Gloria Wilkins-Tate."

Whatever response Blaine was expecting, he didn't get it. The librarian simply wet her lips and intensified her stare.

"What are you doing here?" she asked flatly.

"Research into a collection of a different sort made possible by Operation Offspring."

Gloria Rendine/Wilkins-Tate's taut expression wavered. She tried to look away, but McCracken's eyes bored into hers, riveting them to his face.

"I need to know what it is," Blaine told her, "what it involved."

The old woman gazed down at the book still open on her desk, as if to take refuge in it.

"I don't think we'll find anything about Operation Offspring in that. Or written down anywhere, for that matter."

"I could deny I ever heard of it."

"You could."

"And even if I had heard of it, Mr. McCracken, I'd need a very good reason to discuss it with anyone not in privilege."

"For reason, try Harry Lime, an old friend of mine."

The old woman fought against letting her expression trip her up, but it had been too long since she'd had to try. "And assuming I know this man?"

"Then you might be interested in hearing that he's disappeared, vanished. Someone very good made it look natural enough not to cause even a stir with the authorities."

"And you, I gather, don't exactly qualify there."

"Not in the traditional sense, ma'am. Some would say not in any. The point is that Harry Lime saved my life nine or ten times, most recently two days ago. I owe it to him to find out what happened."

The old woman sighed. "I'm afraid I can be of no service to you there."

McCracken used his words as a knife, digging them in. "Some Washington data bank has you listed as Harry's case-worker. Should we get back to my research, Ms. Wilkins-Tate? For instance, the history involving another dozen or so men and women that has you listed as their caseworker as well. That's the collection I'm talking about.''

The door to the office opened and a much younger woman entered, wheeling a cart of books before her. She smiled shyly at Blaine and then continued on for the desk on the other side of the room.

"There are some private collection rooms just down the hall,'' Gloria Wilkins-Tate said in almost a whisper. "I think we'd better continue our talk inside one of them.''

Krill never used the main entrance to a building, especially in daylight. He was more comfortable in the shadows; he *owned* the shadows. Service entrances squeezed into narrow passageways and alcoves were much more to his liking. The main branch of the New York Public Library didn't offer anything like that, but there was a series of doors accessible off the loading dock on Forty-first Street.

He chose one covered between a pair of trucks and took refuge along a dark corridor, glad to be able to remove the dark, wraparound sunglasses that protected his sensitive eyes.

Those sunglasses helped to minimize the problems his appearance caused him in public. He had learned to hold his arms crimped upward, keep his lips squeezed over his jagged rows of teeth, and hunch over to conceal his true height. People usually paid him little heed and, when they did, it was to regard him with pity or revulsion. As the freak their stares reminded him he was. Second looks were rare.

And today's assignment promised to minimize the chance of encountering even first ones. Libraries were always dark, filled with narrow, angular paths through the cavernous stacks of neatly rowed books. Even better, the woman he had come here for worked in the stack extension located in a basement level. That meant he wouldn't have to worry about windows, either.

Krill had memorized a map of the subterranean maze of corridors that led to the stacks beneath Bryant Park at the library's rear. He reached a door marked "Rare Books and Manuscripts'' and entered slowly. Inside a young woman was busy behind her desk cataloguing books.

"Excuse me,'' he said in his smoothest voice, stopping a

yard away and angling his eyes down, "I'm supposed to meet with Ms. Gloria Rendine."

The young librarian was afraid to break her concentration and scarcely looked up. "She should be back any moment."

Krill feigned checking his watch, hoped the young woman didn't notice the width of his forearm that would have made wearing one impossible. "I'm rather pressed for time," he sighed. "If you could just tell me where she's gone perhaps? This shouldn't take long."

The collection room smelled heavily of leather, darkened by the books lining the walls in the humidity-free and temperature-controlled environment.

"Tell me about the men like Harry Lime," Blaine demanded as Gloria Wilkins-Tate backed up against the farthest shelf. "Tell me about Operation Offspring."

"We have to start at the beginning," she insisted.

"Marked by your recruitment of Nazi scientists to serve in The Factory, no doubt. I suppose they made for your very first collection."

"Does that revolt you? For a man who seems to understand history, it shouldn't. They were advanced far beyond us. Under the circumstances, we would have been foolish not to take advantage of them, of their brilliance."

"And their gratefulness for not being jailed or executed."

"That's how we won their loyalty. We saved them."

"And in return you hoped they could save you."

"Not just us—the country." Gloria Wilkins-Tate moved to the room's single desk and rested her hands atop it for support. "Perspective, everything is perspective." She hesitated. "Let's talk about your history, your battles. Vietnam."

"It shows that much, does it?"

"It does to me. You believed in what you were doing over there. Otherwise it would have been impossible to perform the tasks required of you."

"Obviously."

"Well, *we* believed, too. Our enemy was different and so was the war. But we believed in the urgent need to defeat that enemy or at least keep him from defeating us. The fifties, McCarthyism, the Red Scare. The Communists weren't overflying in planes, they were moving in next door. The threat seemed real. Hysteria. Agreed?''

McCracken nodded.

''Then consider that desperate measures were called for, *any* measures that might help us destroy this menace. And if that meant using German scientists who offered substantial expertise in areas we had only begun to probe, then so be it.''

''And The Factory was built around them.''

''A misconception in most respects,'' the old woman told him, her voice hurried and cracking, sounding her years. ''There was no one 'factory.' Mainly the scientists worked independently, seldom aware of how deep our commitment to their collective use had become. Each thought he was special, not just a mere part but a whole in himself.''

''I imagine you also wanted to keep them away from each other. Collectively, they could make for a pretty formidable enemy.''

''That was a consideration as well. I was chief coordinator and as such I determined which projects were worthy of development and which were not.''

''Operation Offspring being one of them.''

''The last I approved, in fact. I never would have done it if the scientist who conceived it wasn't responsible for much of our most advanced work. The man had already displayed unlimited promise and potential:

''Dr. Erich Haslanger,'' Gloria Wilkins-Tate finished.

CHAPTER 14

"You should have told me this before, Doctor," said Colonel Fuchs, looking up from the stack of manila folders Haslanger had brought him.

"It wasn't your concern. It was . . . ancient history."

"Anything but, apparently, based on the most recent accomplishments of your prodigy." The edge in Fuchs's voice was tempered somewhat by the excitement he felt over the possibilities Operation Offspring raised. "Holding back is not a smart thing, Doctor."

"I haven't had anything to do with Joshua Wolfe or any of the others since they were mere toddlers."

Fuchs's thinking seemed to veer in another direction. "I find myself curious as to why you settled this boy and the others with guardians outside the laboratory."

"Geniuses can't be raised in a vacuum, Colonel. They must be exposed to the world to understand the effects of their discoveries. At the same time, though, we needed to control their upbringing. I approved of the individual guardians only after being assured by the parties responsible that their selection would allow for the control we sought."

Fuchs's lifeless eyes blazed across the desk. "Can I trust you anymore, Doctor? If you have any more . . . secrets you wish to share, this is the time."

"Only Krill."

"Hardly a secret. And his existence pales by comparison with that of Joshua Wolfe and the others."

"No, only Wolfe. The others did not pan out as hoped for."

"An expected ratio?"

"We did not know what to expect, Colonel. For us, this was all new ground."

"How did you do it?" Fuchs asked suddenly.

"Do what?"

"You created him during your tenure at The Factory, didn't you? I'm curious as to the procedure, the origins."

"Selective breeding," Haslanger responded in purposeful understatement.

"The residue of your work for a different regime, no doubt."

Haslanger didn't bother denying it. "The control of genius was known to be part of any future regime's hopes for hegemony. We wanted to create minds we could cultivate and control."

"Which 'we,' Doctor?"

Haslanger ignored him. "Oppenheimer, Teller—men like this would determine which way of life would thrive and prosper. Beyond the hydrogen bomb, beyond chemical warfare. Parties I was beholden to secured samples of sperm from some of this country's greatest minds. I never knew which, never cared. . . ."

"What about you?" Fuchs interrupted. "I mean, you would have considered yourself a genius, too, of course."

"Yes."

"Come, don't be shy, Doctor. You contributed a sample yourself, didn't you? Conceivably Joshua Wolfe could be your . . ."

"The odds would be dramatically against that," Haslanger said after Fuchs's voice had tailed off.

"But certainly he has lived up to your expectations."

"Exceeded them."

"How so?"

Haslanger nodded. "What he managed to create in the labs at Harvard following his entry into the sciences program indicates he has mastered concepts we at Group Six are at least a decade away from."

"Explain."

But Haslanger hesitated. Fuchs was no scientist and could seldom grasp anything beyond rudimentary principles, which meant he had to choose his words carefully.

"I'm waiting, Doctor."

Haslanger sighed. "Nanotechnology."

"What?"

"A new form of science the boy apparently has ventured into."

"Nanotechnology," Fuchs repeated, as if he understood it.

"In essence, the ability to build molecules atom by atom toward the accomplishment of a specific purpose or task. So far the only viable ongoing nanotechnological research has centered around repairing damaged human cells. Building what are essentially molecular machines designed to enter human cells and fix what is wrong with them, such as an enzyme deficiency or some form of DNA damage. In the future they could cure cancer, or birth defects within the fetus itself. The research the boy was apparently conducting indicates significant progress in this area."

"But that has nothing to do with what he caused in Cambridge."

"Yes, it does. Joshua Wolfe constructed a molecular machine, an *organic* machine, programmed to seek out and destroy air pollution by entering the molecules of nitrates and sulfates and breaking down the bonds in them between nitrogen and oxygen. What happened at the mall was a result of his machine breaking down the same bonds in human blood as well."

"Why?"

"A slight error in the formula for the molecular machine's creation, I suspect."

"An error that could be purposely recreated?"

"With the original formula in hand, yes."

Fuchs liked the sound of that, letting his voice drift slightly with his mind. "Imagine the wondrous things this boy's brain might yield given the proper environment, thanks, of course, to the superb preparation you provided him."

"That's the real problem: his background, according to the report that General Starr sent to you."

"What about it?"

"It followed my dictums to the letter, almost without variation. He graduated high school when he was eight years old and enrolled at Stanford, graduating three years later with a triple major in chemistry, biology and engineering. It was on to medical school after that, four years' curriculum completed in two."

"No plans for him to become a doctor, though, obviously."

"No. I wanted him to have a complete understanding of the functions of the human body."

"To make him more efficient in creating various means to destroy it, no doubt."

"Precisely. But who was following through on my original plan, Colonel? Who picked up where I left off?"

"It's too bad we can't ask this"—Fuchs gazed down at the pages spread on the desk before him—"Harry Lime."

"None of this seems to concern you."

"Because whoever they are, by all accounts they've lost their prodigy, leaving him out there for you to reclaim. You said the boy had exceeded even your expectations, Doctor. That means we may well be looking at development of the ultimate weapon, the savior of our very existence at Group Six."

"You're speaking of the organism from the mall."

"I am speaking, Doctor, of Joshua Wolfe himself, but we must have his organism, too." He lifted a folder and skimmed its brief contents. "Toward that end I have arranged for the services of the Firewatch team leader assigned to Cambridge. Her file is most interesting," Fuchs said, handing the folder across the desk.

Haslanger saw the name at the dossier's top. "A woman?"

"A very special woman, so far as our needs are concerned."

Haslanger scanned Susan Lyle's background. "I see."

"I thought you would."

CHAPTER 15

"Haslanger was a *wunderkind*," Gloria Wilkins-Tate continued.

"Best and the brightest of Hitler's Nazi youth . . ."

"Geniuses selected from screenings conducted of every child in the Reich, then spirited away to special schools and assignments. Haslanger was in his twenties during the prime years of the war, already a full doctor, and he was dispatched to the central Nazi research labs in Dusseldorf, the clearinghouse for all the advanced scientific research Hitler was obsessed with. Selective breeding, in-vitro fertilization, even species crossing—they were all tried behind those doors with varying degrees of success."

"Species crossing?"

"Since Watson and Krick didn't discover the existence of DNA until several years later, the work was very crude and the results by all accounts hideous. Suffice it to say that the Nazis in general and Haslanger in particular were well ahead of their time."

"And The Factory allowed him and the other scientists you recruited to stay ahead of it."

"With a far different end in mind, Mr. McCracken."

"Win at all costs, you mean?" Blaine challenged. "Not very different at all."

"*Survive* at all costs, more accurately. We could never foresee an end to the Cold War. We could see only a worsening leading ultimately to all-out war. We wanted to be ready for that war."

"So you let Haslanger and the others keep their blank checks."

"With certain limitations and parameters, that's exactly what we did. They were all brilliant men, but Haslanger had the sharpest mind and the ruthlessness to match. His early work showed great promise but virtually no tangible results." Her voice drifted and Gloria Wilkins-Tate tightened her sweater about herself. "Until the existence of DNA was confirmed. For Haslanger it was like opening a treasure chest. He began mixing and matching the strands of DNA from various species, searching for the proper match to create the ideal soldier, a perfect killing machine. But he didn't have the advantage of the identification and isolation practices and procedures available today. Everything was hit or miss and his end products were unspeakable, genetic nightmares. Most were killed within min-utes of birth."

"Humans included?"

"It was the experiments with humans that led to that part of his work losing its sanction. He began playing with the human genetic code long before he was ready. I don't know what he was mixing, or what exactly he expected to produce. I only know that the monsters he created . . ." The old woman stopped, trembling as she pictured once again the results of Haslanger's gene splicing. She settled herself with a series of deep breaths. "My history, Mr. McCracken. I let him go on much too long, until the seventies, when he began channeling all his energies into selective breeding."

"Bringing us to Operation Offspring."

"It was a much simpler, if less dramatic concept. We knew the wars of the future would be fought in the research lab, not on the battlefield. Toward that end, Erich Haslanger set out to create geniuses. If a mother and father both have genius IQs, imagine what their offspring would be like. Of course, the mother and father would never have to meet—that was the beauty of it. All Haslanger needed were the proper samples. He then paid female workers to bring the babies to term. Between 1979 and 1980, over eighty of Haslanger's children, a new generation of wunderkind, were delivered. They were raised en masse initially to allow for constant observation and quick identification of those with genius capabilities. Just short of their third birthdays, fourteen of these were selected for placement with individuals who were, for one reason or another, under our control."

"1981, then," McCracken calculated. "Maybe '82."

"Yes."

"And where does Harry Lime fit in?"

"Your friend was one of the guardians we selected."

"Even though he was crazy and all of you would have known it," McCracken followed accusingly.

Gloria Wilkins-Tate didn't bother with a denial. "Our choices were motivated by other factors as well."

"People who for the record, like Harry, could easily be made not to exist. People who had a close but tenuous association to the government. Harry would have fit all those qualifications perfectly. Who pulled the plug?"

"There were leaks, embarrassments. The Carter years were not good ones for us. The Factory was abolished, accounting for the file status of men like your friend and for my . . . retirement."

"What about the children?"

"Once Operation Offspring was abandoned, they were removed from their guardians and placed indiscriminately in adoptive homes."

"Not Joshua Wolfe."

"No," the old woman said, her voice hesitant and confused. "Apparently not." Her eyes sharpened, flashing fear. "Someone else must have continued to control and monitor him, picking up right where we left off."

"I don't suppose you have any idea who."

"It could have been anyone privy to our reports. That list was very small, but I don't have to tell you in Washington it doesn't necessarily stay that way."

"Could it have been Haslanger?"

"Not alone. He wouldn't have had the resources."

"I'm sure he could have found a benefactor." Blaine paused. "He'd done it before."

He reached into his pocket and produced the picture found in Joshua Wolfe's Harvard dorm room, handing it to Gloria Wilkins-Tate. She released her grip on her twisted sweater and accepted the photo, lifting her glasses on their chain to her eyes so as to see the shot of the smiling man with his arm draped over the shoulder of a long-haired teenager.

"Joshua Wolfe," was all Blaine said.

The old woman's stare was far away when she looked up.

"All the children we placed were given the names of animals for easy identification and coding. I didn't think I'd ever be seeing any of them again, even Wolfe." Her eyes caught life again. "Where did you say he is now?"

"I didn't, but it's Harvard. And he's not there anymore. Something happened."

"What are you talking about? You act like I should know."

"I'm sure you do. The whole country does. A shopping mall in Cambridge, Ms. Wilkins-Tate. Seventeen hundred people found—"

"*No!*"

"Joshua Wolfe was responsible, believe me. Prevailing theory right now is that it was a tragic accident, a botched experiment. But if Haslanger's involved, there's no telling. And if he gets to the kid first . . ."

"This can't be happening!" the old woman moaned.

"Rest assured it is. And I've got a bigger problem: Harry Lime's disappearance. Somebody arranged for it after he spilled his guts to me. You placed this kid with him, Ms. Wilkins-Tate. You gave Harry a dead wife to fill out the scenario and he started to believe she really existed, even thought I'd been to the funeral. Then one day last fall, whoever picked up where you left off came to take his kid away for good. They ship Harry down to Florida and the new Air America. Only once in the Keys, everything starts to break down. In Harry's mind the kid's been snatched, kidnapped. So whoever's running Operation Offspring now isn't just making geniuses, they're covering their tracks. Right up Haslanger's alley, isn't it? He's done that before, too, hasn't he?"

"You really think you can stop this?"

"I can find whoever killed Harry. That's a start. Where is Haslanger now, Ms. Wilkins-Tate? Where can I find him?"

"I don't know! You *must* believe that. If I did, I'd—"

She swallowed the rest of her words when the lighting in the collection room died, plunging them into darkness.

"Take my hand," McCracken said to Gloria Wilkins-Tate calmly. He could see no light whatsoever sneaking in beneath the door crack, indicating the power was out on the whole floor.

The old woman's rigid fingers flapped against his own. McCracken closed on them gently with one hand, while his other reached for the doorknob.

"This isn't unusual," she told him, "especially in the summer. Brownouts and the like, you see."

Blaine had worked the door soundlessly open. "The emergency lighting's out, too."

"Oh," Gloria Wilkins-Tate responded, understanding.

"We can't stay here. We've got to move."

He led her out of the collection room and to the right at the same time he steadied his SIG-Sauer. Inching their way through the blackness and using the wall for guidance, they reached the end of the short hall and rounded it. Blaine recalled the high-tech, movable stacks were to the right, while directly before them lay a huge expanse of traditionally shelved books.

A slight shuffling sound came from not far ahead of them, followed by a thump.

"Who's—"

McCracken laid a hand over the old woman's mouth too late to stop the single word from emerging. A shape shifted before him, whirling. Blaine felt it first, then caught a vague, soundless outline. He fired the SIG in the direction of the whirling shape, feeling again for Gloria Wilkins-Tate's hand in the process. But she had yanked it away at the ear-pounding burst from the SIG's barrel. McCracken was still flailing for a fresh grasp when the shape, a huge disturbance in the darkness, split between them. Blaine lunged aside, dipping free of an expected grab. He followed the shape with the SIG, afraid to shoot with the old woman's position before him unknown.

There was a gasp and a crack. Then the sound of something thudding to the floor. McCracken steadied the SIG and pumped off four rounds. The first three muzzle flashes gave him a view of a figure that stretched three-quarters the height of the stacks ducking in amidst the neatly shelved books.

Blaine crouched down and felt about the floor. His free hand closed on Gloria Wilkins-Tate's arm first and traced up it for her neck. There was no pulse. And something else, he realized, something all wrong.

The old woman's head was twisted all the way around, her neck snapped as easily as a twig.

Blaine reclaimed his feet, pausing briefly. The nearest exit was straight ahead and to the right, had he chosen to use it. But there were no answers to what was going on beyond the exit door; the answers lay here with whoever had just murdered Gloria Wilkins-Tate. So McCracken backpedaled down a row between two tightly packed shelvings of books, following in the killer's path.

Krill embraced the darkness, the advantage it provided him wondrous. His eyes, those hideous bulging spheres that so cursed him in the light, cut through the blackness and took in what lurked within it. His eyes worked much like an animal's under such conditions, recording motion more than shape.

And it was motion that told him the gunman was edging tentatively along the aisle he had dashed down himself after dispatching the old woman. Tall shelves cluttered with collections of first editions dating back centuries enclosed the aisle on both sides, creating a tunnel-like effect that would further obscure his new prey's vision.

Krill waited, thought about holding his position here until the man walked right into him, then discarded the notion in favor of a better one.

He saw the man edging along halfway down the aisle, a nine-millimeter pistol sweeping the air before him. He sidestepped to the right and started down the adjacent aisle, closing slowly.

Blaine edged his way through the darkness, hoping to find a hint of light to improve his vision. The dim glow of an exit sign at the rear of the first-edition stacks grabbed his attention when he was halfway down the aisle. It wasn't much, but at least it provided a destination.

The enemy had created the darkness to utilize it, obviously equipped with some sort of night-vision device, which provided an incredible advantage. Strange how he had gone for the woman first when he just as easily could have tried for McCracken, instead of alerting him.

Unless Gloria Wilkins-Tate had been his primary target, the

killing of Blaine just an afterthought. But who could possibly—

Books rained down around McCracken. He spun toward the origin of their fall, leading with the SIG. In the darkness a hand closed on the wrist holding the gun, the grip like nothing he'd ever felt before. A vise being turned quickly to maximum tightness. His hand wobbled, the pistol torn from his grasp and sent clanging to the floor.

A second hand joined the first through the litter of fallen books on a shelf even with the top of his head. It closed for his throat and McCracken just managed to deflect it with his free hand. He felt a powerful tug on the captured wrist and found himself slammed into the shelving, dislodging another shower of tumbling books. He flailed desperately to keep the fingers that seemed more like steel digits from finding his throat. With the shelving standing between him and his opponent, his legs were useless as weapons, leaving him only the single free hand he had dedicated to defense.

Go for the eyes, whatever he's wearing over them.

A strategy born of necessity, not choice, the risk lying in clear exposure of his throat to the enemy's inhumanly strong grip. McCracken waited until he felt another wrenching tug. When it came he shot his hand outward on an upward angle for where he judged the enemy's face to be.

The blow impacted on a face that might have been a skull, there was so little flesh covering it. The extra six inches to reach the eyes put the enemy in the seven-foot-height range, big as Johnny Wareagle. Blaine felt the huge head arching away as he jerked his hand upward and skirted across the enemy's brow.

He wasn't wearing any night-vision device at all. There were only . . . his eyes, and McCracken raked his fingers across one of them, trying to angle his thumb for a piercing jab. The enemy grunted in pain, and his grasp on Blaine's wrist slackened enough for McCracken to tear free. Momentum slammed him against the books on the other side of the aisle and several stacks of these went tumbling, too.

Blaine heard another loud, guttural grunt emitted just before the clanging noise of a metal-crunching collision. Still battling the darkness, he sensed more than saw a huge section of shelving caving in toward him, a shower of books spewing ahead of it. He darted sideways, just managing to avoid the initial spill and realizing the next section was starting to topple as well. The effect was not unlike dominoes and ultimately it caught up to him as he dashed down the aisle. McCracken felt himself pummeled by books and then his shoulder was racked by a huge section of shelving crashing down, pinning him beneath it.

CHAPTER 16

McCracken flailed at the books and debris covering him. He managed to extract himself from the bulk of it, only to have a stubborn section of shelving resist all his attempts to lift it. His angle was all wrong, no leverage possible.

Footsteps approached him, soft, barely grazing the tile floor and not striking a single fallen book in the process.

He can see me! Blaine realized. *Whatever this bastard is he can see me. . . .*

McCracken sent his hands raking frantically across the debris-strewn floor for his SIG, abandoning the effort when it was clear it would yield nothing. He could feel the eyes that were not eyes at all upon him, taking their time. Blaine returned his attention to the last of the shelving, felt it start to give. He could yank his legs out now and scamper away for the dull glow of the exit sign.

Toward what purpose?

A book slid across the floor as a foot kicked it from its path. McCracken held his position, pretended to be struggling desperately to extricate himself from the toppled shelving.

The shape stirred. Blaine felt it as a variance in the air, imagined its outline looming over him, and waited. Its breath touched him. An arm that was more like a tentacle clawed through the darkness.

McCracken propelled himself upward, pushing off on legs he had pretended were still trapped. His head caught the huge shape under the chin and snapped its cavernous skull backwards, gaining him the time he needed to lunge all the way to his feet. Something that felt like iron slammed into the side of Blaine's head and staggered him. The shape thrust itself his way, and McCracken ducked under the oustretched arms. He pounded the thing in the kidney with fists interlaced and tried to angle in for its throat or groin. But the figure turned fast and Blaine felt an impossibly long hand close on his throat, starting to lift him off his feet.

Find a weakness.... Gotta be a weakness....

McCracken thought of the monster's eyes that were so comfortable in the dark. Breath wedged deep inside him, he dropped a hand into his pocket, feeling for his key ring and the miniature mag light attached to it. His fingers closed on it and he brought it upward, working his fingers toward the button.

He found it just as his feet finally cleared the floor. Pressed it to angle the beam of light straight into the monster's line of vision.

The beam cut the darkness like a bullet slices air. The shape screamed and tossed him aside, flinging him hard enough into the shelving on the aisle's other side to buckle it. Blaine tried to regain his footing, grabbing his first clear look at the enemy. It was man-shaped, but everything else about it was all wrong, elongated limbs and a narrow, bony face beneath a patchy dome. But the eyes were the worst. They seemed to bulge outward, the sockets too small to contain them.

Half blinded, the monster flailed at him desperately, forcing Blaine to backpedal until he was up against yet another bookshelf. He resteadied his beam on the onrushing shape, its hand raised before its eyes to spare them further agony. McCracken seized the opportunity to duck under the monster's determined but unfocused surge. He joined its momentum and shoved it savagely forward into one of the uprights, mashing its face against the steel.

The monster bellowed and snapped both its arms backwards, forcing Blaine off. It twisted viciously, snarling, when McCracken's flashlight caught it again. Another guttural yell preceded a strike from the darkness Blaine never saw coming. The monster's hand caught him in the wrist, numbing it and sending his key chain and minimag light flying.

The beam glowed on as it rolled across the floor, giving Blaine sufficient light to dash off before the monster had totally steadied itself. But the spilled books slowed his pace enough to steal valuable seconds, and a powerful hand latched on to his shoulder from the rear just as he reached the head of the aisle.

The monster was done with subtleties this time. Blaine felt himself being hurled backwards, into the air, slamming into a wall not far from where Gloria Wilkins-Tate's body lay. Before he could recover his wind and his balance, the monster fastened both its clawlike hands on his lapels and jerked him backwards. McCracken felt his insides shake. His legs went wobbly. The monster threw a fist forward which Blaine just managed to duck under. Above him the wall cracked, showering him with plaster.

Everything was cloudy, growing dim. He blocked one strike, deflected another. But then the monster had him, fingers closing on his throat, the cartilage starting to contract under their power. Then, before he could even contemplate a response, the basement lights snapped back on.

The monster howled in agony, hands leaving McCracken to cover its eyes again. It backed up, staggering. Blaine gasped for air and saw the monster heading for the nearest exit door, disappearing through it before he could reclaim his feet.

The fat man answered the phone in a barely audible voice.

"Hello?" Thurman repeated.

"I'm here," came the reply, a bit clearer. "You caught me with my mouth full. I was just in the middle of lunch. Anguilles Quo Vadis. You know what that is, of course."

"No, I don't."

"We must give you some culture, Thurman, we truly must. Anguilles Quo Vadis are eels in a special green herb sauce I make myself from parsley, mint and chives. Of course you must have a special source to obtain eels at this hot time of year. Mine are frozen during the winter in their native Italy and shipped in special containers. Twenty-four hours and a phone call away."

"Speaking of phone calls . . ."

"Be quick with your report. The eels are best when eaten hot."

"I managed to keep McCracken alive," Thurman reported.

"He's not the sort of man who usually requires such assistance."

"He did this time: went up against one of Haslanger's creations in the main branch of the New York Public Library."

"Ah, then the good doctor is getting a bit nervous."

"He should be, with McCracken sniffing down his trail."

"As we expected he would."

"But there are more complications: Group Six is staking out Harry Lime's apartment."

The fat man's voice fell slightly. "We didn't expect that. How?"

"Cambridge was too much for them to resist. They made the connection faster than we expected."

Thurman could hear the fat man chewing again. "How unfortunate . . . I thought they'd be drained of manpower by now."

"Whatever they have left has been concentrated in Key West. We can't match it on such short notice, even if we wanted to."

"It would be ironic if our efforts end up helping Group Six achieve its goals. That is something we must avoid at all costs."

"There may be a way out of this," said Thurman.

"Go ahead."

"Let them think they've won. Let them have the boy."

"An inopportune suggestion."

"Not really. Because we have McCracken."

CHAPTER 17

Joshua Wolfe noticed the men watching Harry Lime's apartment as he biked down South Street in Key West. He was not surprised to see them, but there were more than he expected and they weren't making much of an effort to disguise their presence. There were three Ford Taurus sedans, a pair of men in each in addition to a construction crew, a mailman pretending to sort mail in his stalled truck and a trio of gardeners at work on the bushy landscaping that fronted Harry's building in the Southpark Condominium complex. Not to mention the one or two who would undoubtedly be inside.

Josh rode without breaking pace, disheartened. Until this point he had still clung to the hope that the tragedy in Cambridge would not be linked to him. But sending this many men to wait for his possible appearance could only mean that they knew where the blame for the Galleria lay. The damn backpack he'd dropped while fleeing must have led them to him, and the Handlers knew, ultimately, he'd come here.

The Handlers. . . . That was the name he had given the emotionless men who appeared from time to time in his life and were never far away even when they didn't. He knew none of them by name and in his younger years had viewed them as protectors. They always seemed to be there when he had a problem. He remembered walking home from high school one day when he was seven, remembered the beat-up Chevy that had pulled up, engine rattling. A creaky door thrown open on the passenger side. An ugly, unshaven man reaching over to grasp him. Josh had frozen, could smell the stink coming off the man as the soiled hand grazed his shirt.

A car had hurdled atop the sidewalk behind the Chevy. A pair of men wearing suits had lunged out and stormed forward. One yanked Josh free of the tightening grasp. The other dragged the unshaven man from his car and kicked his legs out from under him. The man's face broke his fall. That was all Josh saw before the other man brought him toward their car.

It was then that he realized the frequent moving he and Harry had done was the Handlers' doing. Their next move came almost immediately after the incident with the man in the Chevy. Josh heard the phrase "broken security" several times during the explanation.

The Handlers had appeared less frequently as he grew older, seeming ultimately to disappear when he was enrolled at Stanford. All the same, he knew they were there. Maybe the janitor in the apartment building, or the graduate student living in the unit down the hall. He wanted to believe it was still for his protection but in truth had figured out it had probably never been. Watching him was all about control. If he stepped out of line or tried to run, they'd be on him.

That lasted until medical school and then Harvard, when they'd tried to separate him from Harry Lime for good. No one had ever told Josh that Harry had been settled in Key West, and he never made any effort to disguise the fact that he had found out; in fact, he *wanted* them to know, and was sure they did soon enough. To flaunt it still more he had visited Harry over Christmas. But there'd been no contact since then, and Josh felt awful about that. He'd meant to call; he really had. But then his work constructing CLAIR started taking off and he couldn't tear himself from the lab.

He had done his utmost to keep CLAIR a secret from the Handlers, disguising the reason for his trips to both the Science Center and the Malinkrodt Laboratory. He doctored the logs to make it look as if he was working on something considerably more routine, and they had no reason to doubt him. If one had managed to follow him to the mall on Sunday, then that man would be dead now, the only one Josh didn't feel bad for.

What he needed to do at this point, though, was to get his life back together, and that started down here at Harry's. He had found the bike unchained in front of the youth hostel down the street and figured riding it would give the Handlers a tougher time spotting him. Besides, everyone rode bikes in

Key West, at least those who shied away from the pink or yellow mopeds that otherwise dominated the island. After passing Harry's building, Josh kept peddling down South Street toward the traffic light at the intersection with Simonton, planning his next move.

The presence of so many Handlers seemed to rule out any chance that Harry Lime was safe inside. They would have taken him away, so that Josh would have no ally nor any access to that ally's legion of friends. A lump rose in his throat as the irrational fear that he would never see Harry again struck him. It *was* possible, after all, and the possibility was enough to fill him with fresh resolve. He took strange comfort in the presence of the second vial of CLAIR in the backpack that had never left his sight on the flight to Miami or during the bus ride to Key West.

Of course, first he had to gain access to Harry's apartment, and that was a significant task in itself, but one he was prepared for. What the Handlers might not have known was that the four units in each of the Southpark complex's buildings had been built to be easily combined for the right buyer. A connecting door from the rear apartment on the first floor had been built into a closet, opening into a pantry just off the kitchen in Harry's.

He swung his bike down Alberta Street and then onto Washington, which paralleled South. As he'd hoped, he could see no men either posted on that street or watching the rear of Harry's building. He pedaled back to the Washington Street Inn and abandoned the bike on the sidewalk. Then he ducked down an alley that separated the inn from Harry's building. A fence formed the boundary and the pair of rotten slats were even looser than they'd been in December when Josh had visited. He slithered through and found himself on a six-foot grass strip between the fence and the apartment to the rear of Harry's.

One of the back windows was open, a screen in place. Josh thought he remembered that this particular apartment was rented on a seasonal basis. He could only hope the current tenants were absent as he worked the screen open and then hoisted himself up over the sill. Josh was no athlete but he was graceful enough to touch down lightly on the dhurrie rug covering a scuffed Spanish-tile floor. He caught his bearings and padded to the closet containing the door that led through to Harry's pantry.

The closet was open, and Josh pawed through a collection of coats and garment bags to reach the rear. Obviously no one had informed the current tenants what the summer weather was like in Key West. He squeezed behind the clutter and felt for the knob. Then he grasped the bolt holding the door into place. Sliding it free, he turned the knob and pulled gently. The door resisted at first, then gave with a scratchy rasp across the tile. He opened it enough to expose the rear side of the pantry and peered carefully forward to make sure no one was in the kitchen. Satisfied, he cleared the meager contents from the widest shelves and lowered his backpack through the resulting gap. Then he squeezed himself between the shelves and straightened up when he was fully inside the pantry.

Josh's heart was beating fast. His chest felt heavy. He was *home*, at least as close as he could come. Maybe it was the smell more than anything that confirmed Harry was gone, leftover pizza or day-old aftershave—all the things about Harry that Josh didn't want to let go of. His feet felt heavy as he started forward, afraid of what might await him or, rather, what wouldn't.

He had reached the doorway leading to the kitchen when a voice from the living room made him freeze.

"Anything?"

"Nothing on our end," came the raspy reply over what must have been a walkie-talkie.

"I don't think he's coming."

"You don't get paid to think. Just wait. You're due to be rotated in twenty minutes' time."

"I could use the sun."

Josh advanced through the kitchen, careful when he neared the wide breach that led to the apartment's living room section. There was a dining area as well, but Harry had seen no use for anything besides a small kitchen table. Josh slipped past the opening for the counter the fax machine rested upon. He caught no glimpse of a Handler and could only hope the man would not decide to suddenly enter the kitchen.

Josh reached the paperless fax and realized he had neglected to bring the screwdriver he needed to open it. No matter; Harry's junk drawer would undoubtedly yield a Phillips head. He pulled it open slowly, the clutter inside making that task a struggle. Working as quietly as he could, he riffled through the mess and found a Phillips just behind a can of pepper spray, one of several Harry had always left all over the house for Josh just in case. He must have forgotten Josh hadn't joined him on this move.

Josh focused his attention on the fax machine and turned it over, exposing its rear. Then he started working the Phillips on the first of the small screws. In December Josh had asked Harry why he never bothered to load the machine, and Harry's response had centered around making people who wanted to send him things feel better. Harry didn't care whether he saw the faxes or not; he never looked at the ones that came through anyway.

Josh left the screws in a pile and removed the machine's backing. Its innards were easily accessible and hardly cumbersome. Everything was solid state and identifiable for someone who'd had the back off before. Josh knew the purpose of each circuit, diode and chip, as well as their locations. He located the chip he was looking for and popped it out. He had a small Ziploc bag ready and sealed the chip inside.

He was busy reattaching the fax machine's back when the screwdriver slipped out of his hand. He tried to snatch it out of the air and nearly managed to pin it against the counter side. But it eluded him and hit the tile floor with a clang. A brief moment of total silence followed, panic rising as a lump in his throat. Then Josh heard the clatter of footsteps heading toward the kitchen. In a fraction of a second, he judged the distance to the pantry too great to manage in time. The first of a shadow had just scraped over the white kitchen tile when Josh returned his hand to the junk drawer and grasped the can of pepper spray, thumb finding the nozzle.

A man in a suit crossed into the kitchen in the same instant Josh lunged forward, compressing the pepper spray's nozzle. He'd never fired it before and had no idea what to expect. The first thing that occurred to him was the power and focus of the reddish stream. The stuff came out in a surprisingly thick jet that struck the man right in the face. His hands clawed instantly for his eyes as he pirouetted across the tile floor, screaming. The Handler tried to extract the walkie-talkie from his belt and came out with a thin wallet instead which went flying toward the sink. He slammed his shoulder into a storage closet and reeled against the stove as the closet's disturbed contents tumbled down.

The man was really wailing now, his face gone beet red. Josh watched him struggling to find the living room as he stopped to retrieve the man's wallet on his way back toward the pantry.

He grabbed his backpack and squeezed it ahead of him between the shelves into the closet connecting the two apartments. He checked his pocket for the Ziploc bag containing the fax machine chip just to be sure and then hurried back to the open window that had allowed him access. He went through it too fast and fell hard to the ground. He rose, feeling the wind knocked out of him, and had to lean against the building to get it back. When his chest started working again, Josh pushed the broken slats aside to clear a path through the fence and started down the alley behind the Washington Street Inn.

A green Ford Taurus screeched to a halt nearby. Josh spun and sped off in the other direction. A decaying steel fence blocked his route into the backyard of the nearest house and he hurled himself over it. He ran through that yard, then ducked under a hole in the fence on the other side. This yard had a six-foot wooden fence surrounding it on three sides. But the front gate was open a crack and Josh rushed through, finding himself on Washington Street.

He sped toward a run-down motel that featured Casa Key West Vacation Rentals in its parking lot. These rentals included mopeds, which were lined up across the sidewalk for tourists and locals alike. Hopping on one of them for escape seemed like the best option until he saw another green Taurus tear past and then abruptly halt, shift gears and shoot backwards.

Josh was running blindly now, his lungs on fire and the pounding in his head telling him to quit. But he thought of Harry, the Handlers coming to take him away, and found the rage he needed to keep going. He could hear at least one of the cars still roaring after him as he ran across a series of adjoining yards, through bushes and over fences. He emerged near a house that was little more than a shack; a pair of rusty jeeps resting on their rims were wedged in a driveway fronting Waddell Street. Perfectly green tennis courts lay directly ahead, enclosed by high iron fences denying him passage. If he had his bearings right, the beach was a mere block away, but the fence precluded a direct route to it even if he had wanted to head for the water.

Hearing the now familiar rev of one of the Taurus's engines, he ducked into the thick tangle of bushes and hedges that fronted the Coconut Beach Club. He felt as though he were in a jungle, in this case a jungle that ended at an underground parking garage he had no choice but to enter. He charged through the brightly lit concrete garage and emerged on the other side. Then the jungle was back and he gratefully accepted its cover as one Taurus zoomed by, followed almost immediately by another.

He stopped to catch his breath and parted the bushes enough to see what lay ahead. The street ended at the intersection with Vernon and a small bar or restaurant called Louie's Backyard. He couldn't make out all of the sign, because a red truck was parked in the way. A man in a blue uniform toted an overstuffed white bag down a set of steps and hurled it into the truck's rear, then retraced his steps inside.

Josh watched two Tauruses crisscross before him on Waddell Street. He noted there were fewer people inside the cars, indicating that the bulk of the Handlers had taken up the chase on foot. They knew the general area he was confined to, which made it only a matter of time before they circled in and trapped him.

He had to move now. But where?

The man in the blue uniform emerged from Louie's Backyard with another white bag which quickly joined the first in the rear of the truck. Overstuffed again, but with what? Josh's eyes widened.

Of course!

He found himself moving before he had time to hesitate. A quick dash, three seconds at most, was all it took to reach the truck and dive into its back atop the laundry bags full of what must have been soiled tablecloths, uniforms and maybe bed linens from the nearby inn. The driver returned with one more bag before sliding the door shut, plunging Josh into darkness.

The red laundry truck was already gone when the lead green Taurus made its next pass. Sinclair, the team leader riding inside, ordered a few more passes, but rapidly concluded that the boy had somehow slipped past them. Nonetheless, he had his team search for another half hour before calling Group Six.

"Get me Colonel Fuchs," he ordered. "Immediately."

CHAPTER 13

Killebrew slid his wheelchair over to the LED screen containing the readout from the electron microscope. Working in isolation gear made the effort extremely cumbersome but he was starting to get accustomed to it. And if he wasn't yet, he would be soon—this assignment promised to stretch over the course of several months, perhaps up to a year.

Working for prolonged periods with Level 4 hot agents took a special kind of person. Claustrophobia was only one of several factors that kept even the most ambitious technicians from doing it for very long. The main drawback was the lack of motion. Sitting for hours at a time without pause was required, since breaking the work up meant going through decontamination procedures over and over again.

Since he was wheelchair-bound anyway, sitting never bothered Killebrew. If anything, it was the only time the handicap he'd endured since being stricken with multiple sclerosis as a child seemed meaningless. He entered the world of viruses and bacteria and watched them swim about on the slides, immersing himself in the wild ride of motion he could no longer fathom for himself. The potential loss of the rest of his motor skills to another attack of MS made him cherish his work, made him appreciate the menial tasks everyone else took for granted as well as dismiss the risks of the dangerous ones everyone else feared.

Identifying the killer organism from the Cambridgeside Galleria clearly fell into the latter category. All of the remains had been transferred to the high-tech containment facility the Centers for Disease Control and Prevention maintained inside Mount Jackson in the Ozark chain. So many bodies greatly strained the facility's resources, especially considering the need to keep them in cold storage. They were at present stacked on specially constructed prefab gurneys five deep in the gymnasium-sized primary contain-ment center.

Killebrew's job was to gain a complete grasp of every facet of the organism's metastasis. Since this was medical science's first experience with a genetically engineered programmed organic machine, the potential seemed limitless. For one thing, Killebrew's work might yield breakthroughs in the area of cancer fighting and prevention. For another he might gain some insight into how to defend against the organism should humanity ever be faced with its release again.

He started work on three bodies which had already been positively identified. He rotated among them, studying tissue samples from matching parts of each to determine how the organism metastasized inside a host and then spread. His next task would be to identify any mitigating factors toward an understanding of precisely how the organism responded to certain stimuli. How, for example, did such random factors as age, gender, size, blood chemistry and a host of other variables affect the disease once it invaded the body?

Killebrew's first step, of course, had been to isolate and identify the organism itself. It had taken the whole of his first day at Mount Jackson to complete that task, and a single cell of it was presently displayed on the screen, caught in all its glory by the electron microscope.

"Particle of the organism," he said into the microphone built into his helmet, "seems to possess nine different proteins—nine different molecules—that I am unable to identity. It has the genetic structure of a bacteria, similar in shape and behavior to the anthrax bacteria. This refutes the preliminary hypothesis that the organism was a hot virus that bled out its victims on a scale akin to but well beyond something like the Ebola strain."

He paused and collected his thoughts.

"Its genetic structure is in keeping with the currently held assumption that it was a *created* rather than salvaged or discovered organism. Since none of the organism was trapped in an organic state, however, it is impossible to make confident judgments about how the strands of protein forming it interact to create metastasis upon encountering certain stimuli within the host."

Killebrew thought again of those "hosts," seventeen hundred of them, all killed within one minute of infection inside the Cambridgeside Galleria. There had been no further decay following that brief duration. Susan Lyle had found them exactly as they had been for the hours prior to her arrival.

"Speed of ingestion of blood enzymes within nitrogen-oxygen proximity contrary to everything previously thought possible. The organism was able to strike all points in its victims simultaneously, this based on the lack of any discernible spasm or locking in the remnants of the muscle. This refutes Dr. Lyle's preliminary assumption that the organism invaded its hosts using the lungs as a vehicle. More logical would be a transdermal means of entry since the extremities—hands and feet—that blood reaches last were affected with no significant delay. To further demonstrate this point . . ."

Here Killebrew wheeled himself away from the computer screen and back to one of the corpses laid out on a low table for him.

". . . I will take tissue samples from the extremities of a man identified as a seventy-five-year-old male Caucasian known to have been suffering symptoms of severe arteriosclerosis. If these samples show concentrations of the invading organism consistent with samples harvested from other areas, the theory of transdermal penetration will be supported."

Maintaining the corpses in cold storage had further complicated their already dried condition, rendering them so brittle that it became difficult to extract samples. As a result, Killebrew had traded his scalpel for an electric cutting device that looked like a soldering iron. Using that "hot scalpel," he removed four samples of tissue from each of the seventy-five-year-old man's hands and feet. He placed them in his lab tray, then sliced minuscule layers off with a traditional scalpel, made four slides and started back for the electron microscope.

The right wheel of Killebrew's chair stuck suddenly and his fresh samples tumbled from his lap to the floor.

"Damn," he muttered and returned to the table to slice off fresh ones.

Smoke was rising from the tray and Killebrew realized he had neglected to shut the hot scalpel off after putting it down. He quickly flipped the switch and was glad to see the flesh he had taken had been only heated up and not burned by the smoldering tip of the scalpel. He gathered new samples and brought them to the electron microscope, placing the slides in the proper slots for viewing. Then he returned to the screen and activated the initiating sequence.

The enlarged molecules of the invading organism appeared on the screen.

"Molecules harvested from extremities appear to be identical in all ways to those harvested from points in the body closer to heart and lungs. To affirm this fact I will superimpose them over those harvested earlier from the remains of the same patient."

Killebrew issued the proper commands and the screen split into two, a molecule on either side which the computer shifted toward each other until one had been placed over the other.

"Except for some slight deviations along the edges consistent with manageable decay, the molecules appear to be identical in all—"

Killebrew stopped, something on the screen having frozen his thoughts. A computer glitch, perhaps, or a trick played by his tired eyes.

He wiped those eyes, tried to relax, watched.

And it happened again. Or, more accurately, *continued* to happen.

"This can't be," he muttered to himself. "This can't—"

But then he turned back to his lab table, looking at the sample tray he had inadvertently rested the hot scalpel upon.

"Oh, my God . . ."

Hands trembling inside his Kevlar gloves now, he wheeled himself toward the main control console and lifted a phone receiver from it that linked him directly with CDC headquarters in Atlanta. He fitted the receiver into a slot that digitally enabled him to speak and hear through his helmet.

"Dr. Susan Lyle. Immediately."

As the seconds passed, Killebrew kept his eyes fixed on the computer screen showing the two molecules superimposed over each other.

"What do you mean you *can't* reach her? You've got to be able to reach her. She's—*what?* . . . What do you mean, *reas-*

signed? Where the hell is she? Never mind, I don't care. Just patch me through. Now . . . An emergency?" Killebrew's eyes fell on the screen again as he responded. "You could call it that."

CHAPTER 19

"Thank you for coming, Dr. Lyle," greeted Colonel Lester Fuchs when Susan was ushered through his office door. He tugged on the bottom of his uniform jacket to straighten the folds.

"I wasn't really given much of a choice, Mr. Fuchs."

"That's *Colonel* Fuchs, Doctor."

"My apologies."

"Leave us," Fuchs ordered the subordinate, who had escorted Susan from the main entrance of Brookhaven Labs. "And close the door behind you. Now, Doctor, if you'd like to take a seat, I'm sure I can clear up any questions you may have."

Susan had plenty. Her superiors had been atypically vague when informing her of her temporary reassignment. They congratulated her on a job well done in Cambridge and told her someone else would be able to pick up things from here. They provided nothing other than the Brookhaven Lab locale in the town of Upton on Long Island and her reason for going there.

"I was told I was being temporarily reassigned to Brookhaven," she started, "to oversee ongoing research into the cause of death at the Cambridgeside Galleria."

"That's correct, Doctor."

"No, it isn't, because where I am now, this really isn't part of Brookhaven, is it?"

"Very observant."

"Just obvious. Where am I, Colonel?"

"Group Six. We're government, one hundred percent, which explains how your transfer was successfully arranged and carried through on such short notice."

Susan fidgeted in her chair, confused. "What exactly does Group Six do, Colonel?"

"Oh, many things. In this case we take accidents and the products of research that didn't work quite as they should have and refine them to achieve our goals."

"And just what goals are those?"

"The same as yours in Atlanta, Doctor: to serve the country."

Susan leaned forward. "Colonel, what does this have to do with what happened in Cambridge?"

Fuchs fingered a folder on his desk. "I've read your report."

"That report is strictly preliminary. It wasn't meant to be circulated outside of Atlanta yet."

"A formality. You did brilliant work up there, Doctor. It was brought to my attention because of the possibility of continuing it here at Group Six."

"Toward what end?"

"Dr. Lyle—"

"Answer me, Colonel. Toward what end?"

"Why don't you tell me?"

Susan tried not to appear thrown. "I'm going to assume you're in the research business."

"Quite correct."

She studied his uniform. "And the fact that you're army suggests a certain slant to that research."

"I have been transferred here to serve my country in another capacity, just as you have, Doctor. Don't judge us or our work prematurely. Terribly important things are going on in this building that may have a profound effect on the future—"

"Weapons," Susan interrupted. "Group Six's research is about weapons."

"Specifically, Doctor," Fuchs continued, as if she hadn't said anything at all, "preserving the sanctity of that future." He pointed to the map of the world hanging behind his desk. "Those areas I have highlighted in red represent the world's hot spots, Dr. Lyle, simmering cauldrons of discontent releasing violence on an almost daily basis. Somalia, North Korea, Bosnia—I don't have to tell you about those. But look at all the other sites colored red and the additional trouble sites colored yellow that are currently under watch. The number stretches into the hundreds. The world is notoriously unstable, Doctor, and if the day ever comes when all these spots are colored red at the same time, that may be enough to tip it totally off kilter.''

''Then you're telling me Group Six is in the stability business.''

''*Preserving* stability, yes.''

''Through weapons research.''

''Through whatever it takes and, unfortunate as it may sound, weapons research plays an important role in maintaining stability.''

''That's military, not science, Colonel.''

''It's both, the latter serving the former.'' He looked at her harshly, no longer the gracious host with a tour guide's fake smile. ''You speak as though you've been offered a choice here, Doctor. You have been reassigned. Now, before you protest, you have my word that this transfer will end as soon as your report to us and follow-up on this matter is complete. That could be accomplished in a matter of days, a few weeks at most. I'm asking you to give us a chance. You may even find it mutually beneficial.''

Susan realized her mouth had gone bone dry. ''As you said, Colonel, I don't have a choice.''

Fuchs smiled and leaned toward the speaker on his phone. ''Could you come in please, Dr. Haslanger.''

The office door opened and Susan watched a frighteningly gaunt man who must have been in his seventies enter. His skin was a sickly shade of pale yellow, the sun and outdoors looking to be a long-forgotten memory. His face was cadaverous, the cheek and jawbones so pronounced they appeared almost to poke through his flesh.

''May I present the head of our special projects division, Dr. Erich Haslanger,'' said Fuchs.

Susan nodded at the old man as she replied. ''I would have thought all your projects were special.''

''Some more than others. Dr. Haslanger has some questions for you, Doctor.''

''I have read your reports on Cambridge,'' Haslanger started, ''along with your accompanying analysis. Not quite complete—''

"That's because they're preliminary."

"I am not speaking of the technical; everything there is quite complete and in order. No, I am speaking of the personal. I want to know why you think the boy went through with this, why he didn't wait until he was more sure his discovery would work as it was intended."

"First of all, according to his research, he had no reason to believe it wouldn't work as intended. Beyond that, I think he wanted to be a hero, to do something that would make him accepted," Susan said unhesitantly, as if she'd been waiting for someone to share her theories with. "He just wanted to fit in."

"All this merely to 'fit in'?"

"Yes, because that's what Joshua Wolfe craved more than anything else. He grew up isolated from children his own age, developing only the intellectual part of his life. I think he saw the Cambridgeside Galleria as his chance to change all that. If it had worked, if his organism had destroyed air pollution and nothing more, he would have been the hero he dreamed of becoming."

"And did it?" Fuchs raised. "Destroy air pollution, I mean."

"As a matter of fact, yes."

"But it didn't make him a hero."

"Not yet, anyway," Haslanger interjected.

Susan turned back toward him. "I don't think I understand."

"I think you do, Doctor," Haslanger continued. "According to you, in spite of all his wondrous abilities, all Joshua Wolfe ever wanted was to be normal. But he can never be that now, even if he could have before. Not after the Galleria. Not after being responsible for the deaths of over seventeen hundred people. Imagine how he must feel. The guilt, the worthlessness. How can he ever recover from what he caused on Sunday?" The old man looked at her long enough to be sure she wasn't going to answer before he did. "By being shown there was value in what he did, that something can be salvaged from it."

"Salvaged here, by you," Susan said, understanding.

"We want to see his talents suitably utilized," Fuchs picked up. "We alone can offer him a lifeline, Doctor. And we alone can insure that tragedy does not impair or even destroy his future. We can make all this go away for Joshua Wolfe. We can arrange for a wholly different explanation for what happened at the Cambridgeside Galleria to be released to the press."

The notion that Group Six possessed enough power to accomplish that sent a shiver of fear through Susan. "A lie, in other words."

"Quite."

"You'd need my cooperation, of course."

"And I suspect you'd give it willingly and without hesitation."

"For what possible reason would I do that?"

"Because your primary concern seems to rest with the fate of Joshua Wolfe now, just as ours does." The tour guide's fake smile was back on Fuchs's face, a mask of compassion that in no way fit him. "When we find this boy, I want you to help us."

"Why?"

"You seem to understand him. And I believe you could relate to him in so difficult a time far better than anyone else on my staff."

"Because I'm a woman?"

"You care for him. Yes or no?"

"I don't see what—"

"Answer. Please. Yes or no?"

"Yes."

Fuchs came closer to her. "You once experienced a great tragedy yourself, did you not?"

Susan winced as if suddenly in pain.

"There are no secrets from us, Dr. Lyle. We would never seek anyone's participation in our work without a full understanding of him or her. It was all in your file, information I suspect you did not even realize your CDC superiors were privy to. Tell me, Doctor, how were you able to recover from your catastrophic loss?"

Whatever answer Susan might have managed stayed stuck in her throat.

"I'll tell you what I think," Fuchs continued. "I think you

found purpose. I think that purpose got you through and made you the strong person that you are. I think Joshua Wolfe, above everything else, needs to find purpose in *his* life right now. You can't disagree with that.''

Susan remained silent.

''And if we were able to show him that something good can be made of this tragedy,'' Haslanger started, ''if we could convince him that those deaths were not senseless—that there was purpose to them—he could get past what he is feeling now, just as you did. Here and here alone, at Group Six, Joshua Wolfe would not be the social outcast he has always been. Here and here alone, he would *belong*.''

Fuchs tried to soften his rigid features yet again. ''You understand the implications of what he's discovered, yes?''

''I . . .''

''The principles and potential of nanotechnology, yes?''

Susan nodded.

''That would indicate your interest in Joshua Wolfe is not purely unselfish, either. Molecular machines capable of repairing individual damaged cells? Imagine the possibilities!'' Staring coldly at her once more. ''The diseases that could be wiped out. The lives that could be saved.''

''Are you offering me a deal, Colonel?''

''I'm merely pointing out that the good Joshua Wolfe does within the walls of Group Six does not have to be limited to weaponry, Doctor. I could arrange for you to supervise research conducted and applied into other areas. No need waiting for the National Institutes of Health or your own CDC to become aware of your true potential and interest. I can make it happen for you tomorrow.''

''And in return all I have to do is . . .''

''Help us make Joshua Wolfe feel comfortable here. Help us make him realize this is where he belongs and where he can thrive.''

Susan found herself speechless, saved from the effort of a response by the buzzing of a second phone on Colonel Fuchs's desk.

''What do you mean you 'lost him'!'' the colonel blared into the telephone receiver.

"He's still in the area, sir," Sinclair reported from Key West. "I estimate—"

"I don't give a shit about your estimates, Sinclair! You had the boy and you lost him."

"Our people are sweeping the area now, sir. I'd like to request reinforcements."

"You've got fifteen men down there now. I could never get more to you in time to do any good at all."

"I was talking about bringing in some locals."

"Locals?"

"The cover story should hold. I'm confident I can control them."

"You were confident you could bring in the boy, Sinclair. You told me that as soon as we realized where he was going."

"There's something else, sir."

"Go on."

"One of my operatives was assaulted by the boy and has reported his wallet is missing."

"Did you say 'assaulted'?"

"Yes, sir. It will all be in my report."

"I look forward to reading it. And the contents of that wallet?"

Sinclair listed them, one at a time.

"Is it the habit of your men to walk around with such items?"

"This team was assembled posthaste. Many of the members were channeled directly from transit. I don't think we have to worry. This man was top flight. The contents of his wallet won't lead anywhere."

"Just find that boy, Sinclair. Find him before he has a chance to prove you wrong."

Susan Lyle sat in the Group Six office Colonel Fuchs had provided for her, contemplating her next move. What she really wanted to do was walk out. Get up right now and head through as many doors as it took to get away from here, even at the expense of her career. But she couldn't, because of Joshua Wolfe. She didn't dare leave him alone for Fuchs and Haslanger to do with as they pleased, once they captured him. It was abundantly clear to her already that Group Six didn't play by the same rules everyone else working under government charter did. In pursuit of its mandate, this organization was capable of anything, and that did not bode well for one fifteen-year-old boy who had accidentally discovered something Fuchs and Haslanger wanted very badly.

But that wasn't all. Susan wished it were.

"You once experienced a great tragedy yourself, did you not?"

Actually, absurdity might be a better way to describe it. Her parents had died of liver cancer within six months of each other while she was a junior in high school. Doctors told her the odds against such an occurrence were fifty million to one. But when her brother was diagnosed with leukemia two years later, they rated the odds of her becoming afflicted with that or some other deadly cancer in her lifetime as better than seventy-five percent.

"Tell me, Doctor, how were you able to recover from such a catastrophic loss?"

Susan hadn't been able to respond to Fuchs and doubted he much cared. He simply wanted her to know he knew, that he was capable of knowing *anything*. The truth was she was able to recover and forge on by fighting, a battle waged in labs with test tubes and microscopes, as she became intimately acquainted with virulent diseases both infectious and noninfectious.

Eventually that study had brought her to Atlanta and the CDC, where she came to regard the infectious disease department and later Firewatch as springboards that could propel her into a position of real power there or somewhere else. Chief of genetic research, perhaps, at a major biotech firm. The cure for cancer lay somewhere in that realm and Susan desperately wanted to be a part of the process, as much as anything because its deadly specter was almost certain to lurk in her future as well.

"That would indicate your interest in Joshua Wolfe is not purely unselfish, either. . . ."

Fuchs was right and Susan hated thinking it made her no better than he. So she had to prove to herself that she was better by helping the boy. She knew what it was like to live with a single obsession. If Joshua Wolfe let the tragedy of the

Cambridgeside Galleria dominate the remainder of his life, he would fall victim to it just as Susan had to cancer, without yet being stricken by the disease. He would spend his life in an emotional vacuum in which every potential relationship became a reminder of hurt and loss, instead of a possibility of hope.

And yet she could not help thinking that Joshua Wolfe had become *her* hope. For that she wanted him as much as Fuchs did. Perhaps the colonel's offer was worth considering. Perhaps the boy's best chance did lie with—

No! *No!*

Fuchs and Haslanger would destroy the boy to get what they wanted or, worse, let him destroy himself. They were too self-absorbed to realize that would be the emotional upshot of what they would be asking him to do. Design new and more precise ways to kill. Make him relive Cambridge over and over again. Get as much out of him as they could before he cracked.

She couldn't allow it. Saving the boy from Group Six meant saving at least a small part of herself. She had to get him out of here before Fuchs's claws sank in too deep to pry off.

But how?

Krill was waiting in his chair when Haslanger returned to his office, lit only by the fluorescent glow of his desk lamp.

"I trust things went well," the doctor greeted.

"The woman wasn't alone," Krill reported, handing something out to him.

In the thin wash of light, it took Haslanger a moment to realize it was a black and white picture attached to a manila folder.

"This man was with her," Krill offered for explanation. "I identified him from one of Washington's data bases—a number of them, actually. His name is Blaine McCracken."

Haslanger looked at the grainy picture and then flipped open the folder. "You knew where to search?"

"It wasn't hard. You might say he's one of a kind. McCrackenballs."

"What?"

"Page three. Skip ahead. McCrackenballs—that's what some call him. Care to hear why?"

Haslanger didn't bother turning to page three.

"Because some years ago he shot out the balls of Winston Churchill's statue in London after the British upset him. I dare say he does not like to be upset." Krill paused. "He's upset now."

"You left him *alive*?"

"Someone else at the library intervened."

"An ally of McCracken's?"

"Perhaps. It doesn't matter."

Haslanger sighed, the file a lead weight in his hand. "It does if it means Group Six has been compromised. It does if we're facing a threat from more than a single man."

At that, Haslanger could have sworn he saw the trace of a smile flicker across Krill's fleshy lips.

"Keep reading."

"You're a real pain in the ass," Hank Belgrade said, from his usual position on the steps of the Lincoln Memorial. "From now on, you call, talk to my voice mail."

McCracken sat down edgily next to him. "Erich Haslanger, Hank."

Belgrade flashed his open palms. "Notice I came empty-handed. There's a reason for that. Haslanger's file reads deceased as of 1983."

"But you and I know better."

"I don't know how you step in the shit you do, MacNuts, but the piles just keep getting bigger." His stare tightened. "Group Six. Heard of it?"

"Bits and pieces."

"Use your imagination."

"Haslanger?"

"Gainful new employment for the son of a bitch. I don't know how you dug up all you did on him, but lemme tell you, the info could embarrass plenty of people who like to stay out of the news."

"What are my chances of getting in to have a talk with him?"

Belgrade frowned. "You'd have a better chance of getting an audience with God. Nobody gets into Group Six through the front door without the kind of clearance you ruled yourself out of being granted a long time ago.''

"Even if somebody on their staff is responsible for the larg-est mass murder in U.S. history?''

"What?"

"I was in Cambridge yesterday.''

Belgrade's oversized jowls seemed to quiver. "Oh, shit . . .''

"I know who engineered the massacre at the Cambridgeside Galleria. I was in his dorm room at Harvard. Child prodigy, born about 1980. Sound familiar?''

"Operation Offspring . . .''

"It's still active, Hank, and my guess is that Haslanger never stopped running it. For Group Six now.''

"This kid was behind the whole thing?''

"That's right, and Harry Lime served as his guardian up until the kid started work in the doctoral sciences program at Harvard last fall. Rest is still sketchy but it leads to Group Six because that's where Haslanger can be found.''

"And the kid?''

"Gone. Disappeared.''

"You saying Group Six was behind what happened?''

"If I did, would it help me get granted access?''

Belgrade shook his head. "MacNuts, aren't you hearing me? Group Six is protected to the highest level. Their fuck-ups are handled strictly in-house. So you wanna go around playing crusader, all you're gonna do is let them know you're coming.''

"Could be it's just Haslanger who's responsible. Would that make a difference?''

"Sure, maybe for the worse. Pentagon's gone through a lot of trouble to keep Haslanger's participation secret. You go stirring things up in the typical MacNuts fashion and they'll batten down the hatches.''

"I guess I'll just have to find a way in on my own, Hank.''

"Was me, I'd walk away from this one.''

Blaine's eyebrows flickered. "I'm not you.''

"Sure, and you can never walk away, either. Run into trou-ble, though, and no one in these parts will know you. Mem-ories in the good ole D. of C. are fickle. Calling in debts won't save you and friends won't be worth shit, you take these peo-ple on.''

"I'll try not to step on any toes.''

CHAPTER 20

Joshua Wolfe waited until the maid was just finishing the room on the tenth floor of the Hyatt Grand Cypress in Orlando before he slid through the open door.

"Perfect timing," he greeted, pulling his backpack from his shoulders as if he belonged.

The woman smiled at him and was gone.

He had escaped the men at Harry's apartment barely five hours before, beating them to Key West Airport and sneaking his way on board a forty-two-passenger U.S. Air commuter plane bound for Orlando. He hid in the single lavatory for twenty minutes before the plane started to board and then claimed a seat while the flight attendant was busy ushering passengers on. He chose one in the very first row, figuring it would be easier to work his way backward in search of another if the real occupant appeared. Fortunately no such passenger arrived and the flight attendant seemed none the wiser.

Upon arriving in Orlando, he simply joined the flow of human traffic to the main terminal via a futuristic tram that was packed solid with eager and weary travelers, mostly families with children. He followed the bulging crowd to the baggage claim area, his eyes sweeping the various carry-on bags the newly arrived visitors shouldered or hauled. He was looking for the kind that held a laptop computer inside, an advanced model featuring a built-in modem. When he found the type of case he was looking for, Josh fell in behind the man holding it and melted back into the crowd. A woman walked alongside the man, two boys and a girl trailing slightly behind. A family of five, then, and that meant lots of luggage, which would serve Josh well.

The family reached the carousel where their bags would be arriving. As hoped, the father unshouldered the computer

carrying case and rested it on the floor near the rest of their
carry-ons. Then he slid forward to claim a spot in front of the
carousel before the tread began to move. The two boys were
playing a video game, the girl holding her mother's hand as
she stood between her brothers and the father. A loud whine
sounded and the motorized tread started to churn, the first bags
winding their way toward their owners. Judging by the number
of people squeezed tightly together, the flight must have been
packed. Everyone seemed to push forward en masse, except
the two boys busy with their video game.

Josh cut a direct path for the computer case, crouched to
mock tying his shoe, and started into motion again with the
case in his hand and backpack still slung over his shoulder.
He followed the signs for ground transportation and never
looked back. He made straight for the taxi stand and gave
Disney World as his destination to the dispatcher. The cab slid
away from the curb, Josh gazing behind him only then to make
sure no one had given chase.

When the cab deposited him in the sprawling Magic Kingdom parking lot a half hour later, the laptop was squeezed into
his backpack in place of a discarded sweatshirt. He bought his
admission ticket and rode the monorail to the actual park entrance. Once there, the expanse of the place both amazed and
intimidated him. But the presence of so many other teenagers
proved a comfort: even if the Handlers had already traced him
this far, they would never be able to pick him out amidst such
a crowd. He would be inside the Magic Kingdom for only as
long as it took to hide the second vial of CLAIR. Carrying it
around just added more complications to his plight, and the
lighter he traveled the better. The vial might have added only
a few ounces but its presence was starting to weigh heavily
on his mind.

He was in the park for barely an hour before he located the
perfect hiding place and then reached the Hyatt via its private
shuttle bus. Staying in one of the Disney hotels would have
been simpler logistically, but that would be where the Handlers would begin their search once they traced him to Orlando.

The maid had barely closed the door to the room in the
Hyatt behind her when Josh set up shop on the room's double

bed, spreading the contents of the Handler's wallet atop it in a semicircle around the laptop. There were nine separate pieces of identification encompassing six different names. The process ahead could prove long and arduous—challenging, Josh preferred to think, and he loved a challenge. The business about men like the Handlers being untraceable was bullshit mostly. *Everyone* left a trail, especially in the case where an operative from one agency was loaned out to another, a scenario that Josh suspected had been the case yesterday.

He plugged the computer into a wall socket and ran a cord from the telephone jack to the built-in modem.

"The boy's in Orlando," Sinclair reported.

"Orlando?" returned Fuchs.

"He was seen approaching a commuter plane bound for there in Key West. We arrived too late to meet it, but got to the baggage claim area in time to hear a man insist a boy meeting Josh Wolfe's description stole his computer."

"He stole a computer?"

"We're not sure where he went from the airport, but we're questioning all bus and cab drivers to find out."

"And rental car companies, Sinclair."

"But the boy's only—"

"With a computer and modem, he could make himself any age he wants. Make a rental reservation, have a car ready and waiting. Billed to the President's credit card, or yours or mine, if he knew who we were."

"I'll check, sir."

"Keep me informed."

Josh knew the passwords to get in the front door of virtually any of the nation's prime data banks. His plan was to scan the personnel records of various agencies in search of a match for the six different names the Handler went by, according to his wallet. If successful, ultimately Josh would learn who had dispatched him to Key West and thus who was behind Harry Lime's disappearance.

The process was both harder and easier than Josh had expected. Easier because of the simplicity of accessing the information he wanted. Harder because of the depth of it. The files for active agents working for any of the various Washington agencies were immense. Josh tried searching for a match with any of the names the Handler's wallet contained. After an hour, he found one through the FBI.

Under the alias of Cole Chaney he had been retained as a surveillance specialist in a case involving a major international drug bust. Chaney was not carried on the regular Bureau rolls, but his assignment had been duly authorized and logged.

Josh stayed with that name, running searches through all the data banks he could access. As it turned out, Chaney had worked for just about every three-letter group at some time or another, and a more in-depth search revealed that his other identities were all logged in the CIA in a file grouping labeled "Cousins." Cousins must have been the spy agency's version of temps, as opposed to full-time "brothers" or "sisters," called in when specific tasks required men the agency lacked the funds to keep on permanent staff.

The next phase was chronology, determining *who* exactly had retained Chaney for his assignment today in Key West. "WORKING" appeared on the laptop's monitor and lingered there for the long minutes he waited impatiently for a response. This was a difficult search even for the most sophisticated computers to perform. Beyond that, there was the very real possibility that Chaney's participation hadn't been entered yet and never would be.

Josh's fear subsided, replaced by excitement when fresh information began to roll across the screen. There wasn't much, just a few lines, but it piqued his curiosity.

CHANEY, COLE   ASSIGNED GROUP SIX 6/30/96
ACCESS ZO–9XR–57, ROUTING OUT OF DALLAS,
NO CLOSE OUT

He had it! Josh had no idea what "NO CLOSE OUT" meant but it was the other mysterious phrase that commanded his attention:

Group Six.

He had never heard of such an organization, had no idea what it was. But its connection to himself, the Handlers, and thus Harry's disappearance through Chaney was almost certain.

Intrigued, Josh typed in the access code provided. Nothing. Just more of Chaney. He needed to get in, if not through the front door, then the back. He had no password for Group Six, no way to reach the guts of the system. Josh tried the access code again, keeping the same ZO prefix but changing the configuration of the letters and numbers that followed. When this failed to get him anywhere, he repeated the process with 57 as the key instead, again with no results. As a last shot he typed in the 9XR center code. His heart leaped when a single word on the screen prompted him further: SPECIFY.

He was in! Well, almost. He keyed in 9XR again, followed by 1XA, chosen at random. It took a few moments for the Group Six database to respond: WAITING.

He had done it! The primary data banks of Group Six, whatever it was, were open to him.

Josh curled himself into a tighter ball and began typing.

"Yes," Fuchs said into his intercom.

"This is Larsen in the com center, Colonel. Sorry to bother you, sir, but we have a bit of an emergency here."

Fuchs looked at Haslanger and put the call on speaker. "Go on, Larsen."

"I have just been alerted to an intrusion into our computer network from the outside. Someone's gained access to our system. I'd like your permission to shut down and reboot."

Fuchs felt a chill slither through him. "Can you trace the origin of intrusion?"

"Yes, but it will take several minutes. Whoever's broken in could do untold damage by then."

"Run the trace," Fuchs ordered.

"But, sir—"

"Run the trace."

For Joshua Wolfe, the work had been reduced to the information flying across the laptop's monitor. There was no room around him, no bed beneath him. There was only the screen and his fingers working the keyboard to make it live.

He had dug his way deep into Group Six's data banks and

was utterly fascinated. If this wasn't the most sophisticated, advanced and well-equipped research facility he had ever encountered, it was close. Harvard's top labs were nothing compared to those of the mysterious organization he had never heard of until just minutes ago. With their equipment, he could for starters fix what had gone wrong with CLAIR in Cambridge, identify the specific part of the formula where the error was and correct it.

Josh's enthusiasm dampened somewhat as reality interfered with the information rolling across the screen. If Group Six had retained Chaney, it was Group Six that must have been after him and, by connection, must have been responsible for taking Harry away. Why? What exactly did Group Six do?

Josh turned his attention back to the machine and began to read again.

Group Six's command and communications center was located on the third floor. Larsen had just isolated the source of the intrusion into the computer network when Fuchs stormed in, followed closely by Haslanger.

"We've got it, sir: Orlando, Florida. Hyatt Hotel." Larsen's eyes came off the screen. "Permission to shut down system now, sir, *please*. He's in deep, into classified reports."

"No," said Haslanger. "Not until we've got him."

"*Time*, sir. A few more minutes and he'll be inside any part of our system he wants to. He could *wipe out our data banks!*"

Fuchs was already holding a phone to his ear. "Patch me through to Sinclair in the field in Orlando. He's on cellular."

Josh was staring at the screen. Over the past several minutes, he'd slowed his scan significantly, amazed by the depth of what Group Six had accomplished but frightened by the scope of it.

Weapons. They made weapons. The best equipment, the best technology, the best hardware and software in existence, and they used it to make weapons.

What did they want with him? What was Group Six's connection to the Handlers? Lacking answers, Josh felt his mind pull back in another direction.

The best equipment . . .

Their inventory and laboratory development was unprecedented, made what he'd had to work with at Harvard look like a grammar school chemistry set.

Josh began scanning again. Strange how he could access all of Group Six's most intimate secrets, but nowhere in any of the data banks could he locate its address.

Maybe, he thought, *I don't have to.*

"We're moving into position now, sir," Sinclair reported.

"We've got him, Doctor," Fuchs said to Haslanger.

"Something's wrong," the old man responded. "The boy would know we could trace him."

The colonel looked back at Larsen. "Is he still scanning?"

Larsen checked his screen, hit a few keys. "Yes, sir."

"Can you bring up what he's seeing?" Haslanger asked.

"I think so. Let me just run a loop and bypass here. . . . Yes, he's spent the last several minutes going over our experiments involving molecular technology."

Haslanger and Fuchs looked at each other.

"What's he looking for, Doctor?"

Haslanger couldn't take his eyes off the screen. "I don't know."

Sinclair's team still consisted of fifteen men, not enough to blanket the spacious grounds of the Hyatt Grand Cypress, but easily enough to take the boy, who, according to reports, was in room 1063. The room overlooked the spacious pool complex consisting of three separate but inter-connected pools sprawled across a rocky mountain motif of waterfalls, tunnels and water slides. A single man with binoculars posted on the man-made beach confirmed Joshua Wolfe's presence in the room before Sinclair moved. He spaced the remainder of his team strategically across the tenth floor. He left three lined up shoulder to shoulder a yard back from the door to room 1063, while a fourth affixed a sophisticated listening device attached to a set of earphones to the door. He listened briefly and then turned back to Sinclair.

"He's not working the computer," the man with the earphones reported. He yanked the device free as a large man replaced him before the door. "But his position seems to be unchanged."

Sinclair stepped back and used his walkie-talkie to contact the man down on the beach. "Can you still see him?"

"Negative."

Sinclair felt his nerves tug at him and decided to waste no more time.

"Do it," he ordered the large man who had taken up position directly in front of the door.

One swift kick from his steel-toed boot crashed the door inward. It banged up against the wall and might have bounced closed again if the three men with tranquilizer guns drawn hadn't rushed in just ahead of Sinclair. They froze in matched firing positions, their crouches allowing Sinclair to gaze past them at a solitary figure seated on the bed, a laptop computer resting unplugged on one side of him and a black backpack on the other. The figure stood up and grabbed his backpack casually, working a wad of gum through his mouth.

"What kept you?" asked Joshua Wolfe.

PART THREE

CLAIR

WASHINGTON,
WEDNESDAY, 10:00 P.M.

CHAPTER 21

"It ain't good, boss," Sal Belamo announced grimly as he stepped through the door of the room in Washington's Watergate Hotel. He was holding rolls of blueprint plans under one arm and an attaché case in the other. "Got everything you asked for and more," he said to McCracken. "Satellite overviews, original schemas, final retouched blueprints, confidential budget summaries, development file, personnel. Yup, I got it all and what I got I don't like."

McCracken stood there looking as Belamo dropped the blueprints onto the double bed and laid the briefcase down next to them. Besides the slightly scarred ears and bumpy nose that angled sharply to the right, Sal Belamo was generally nondescript. The nose had come courtesy of Carlos Monzon, who had broken it both times Sal had made the mistake of getting in the ring with him. Belamo had learned life on the streets, boxing and killing at about the same time. Like Blaine, he never seemed to change. Certainly the bald spot on the crown of his combed-back short hair was a little more prominent, and the lines under his liquidy eyes might have deepened into furrows. But the important things, like the cocky way he held those eyes and his perpetual sneer, were worn, Blaine guessed, even in his sleep.

"How much you know about Group Six, boss?"

"Beyond their name and function, not much. I also know that quite a stink's been raised since their existence became public knowledge."

"Their existence is about the only thing that's gone public. Group Six's function varies depending on who you ask in Washington. Everyone on the in knows they're out there but the specific knowledge depends on the person's role. Different stories to suit different needs, you get my drift."

"Sounds like standard government politicking."

"Politicking, yes. Standard, no. We're talking a major bullshitting job here. Next best thing to keeping Group Six's existence secret altogether is to keep it confused. Ask ten different people what they're about and you get at least five different answers and five repeats of the runarounds the respondents have been given."

McCracken nodded. "Not the first time."

"No, the same runaround was given about Los Alamos and the Manhattan Project way back when. Group Six enjoys the biggest scientific commitment the government has ever made since then and, depending how you balance the books, that includes NASA. Hell, Group Six could get funding for a Mars trip if there was a chance the voyagers might come back with new weapons for the twenty-first century."

"Nice to see our future's in good hands."

"Yeah, well, Group Six has got so many layers that most of 'em probably don't even know about the existence of the others."

"The Manhattan Project again."

"And again the layers fit together without the kind of seams that usually rip." Belamo pointed at the briefcase. "Their personnel roster is somewhere in there, but don't bother yourself with it. The big boys aren't listed, including your Nazi Haslanger. Group Six's director is an army colonel named Lester Fuchs who's been on the outskirts of the big time his whole career. Any medals he's got on his chest come from surviving administrative battles. Son of a bitch never saw war, and here he is trying to redefine how it's fought. Thing is he's in deep shit himself. Seems like the real powers behind Group Six in Washington are starting to lose patience with the lack of return on their investment. All they got is a string of zeroes to show for all the zeroes on the checks they've made out. Most recent major fuck-up was yesterday."

"Yesterday?"

"Dozen soldiers got themselves microwaved by some ray that didn't work according to Hoyle."

McCracken raised his eyebrows, then gazed down at the stack of blueprints. "Where is this place?"

"The grounds of Brookhaven National Labs in Upton, Long Island."

"And to think I almost bought a summer place around there once."

"Not on the grounds of Brookhaven you didn't, boss. Take a look at these."

Belamo unrolled the first of his blueprints and fished through the briefcase for the proper eight-by-ten photographs, courtesy of pilfered satellite reconnaissance, to plop down over it. "To start with, Brookhaven's got its own private community on the order of fifteen square miles, all of it fenced in and guarded on what used to be the property of Camp Upton 'round World War II. See the heavy tree cover that hides the facility from passersby on the William Floyd Parkway? Whole place is built into a scrubby pine barren atop a watershed area. EPA probably wouldn't let you build it today, but this is Brookhaven we're talking about. Got their own post office, minimart, and direct freight line running off the Long Island Railroad lines. No passenger traffic, 'fore you get your hopes up."

McCracken's eyes finished scanning the photographs Sal had laid out. "Lots of buildings. Which one's Group Six?"

"None of these. Some of 'em are old, most new. Each has its own designation and purpose. Got a weather station in one, particle accelerator in another, and a nuclear breeder reactor in this big tower here, just for starters. Rest are divided between genetics, advanced molecular shit and assorted other biotech specialties I can't even pronounce." Sal lowered his finger to a spot in the center of the overview blueprint. "And here we have your ordinary, run-of-the-mill, toxic waste dump. Locals just gotta love that. Complaints of ground water contamination have gone up tenfold in the past five years."

"Don't tell me—since Group Six opened."

Sal smiled and nodded. His finger plunged downward again, popping against a crease near the right-hand corner of the map. "Got itself headquartered right here in Brookhaven's northeast corner. Can't even see its private security fence from the rest of the installation, 'cept maybe for this farmland over here they're growing God knows what on. Thick pine growth handles the natural camouflage. Rear of the base has plenty of terrain for full-scale weapons testing.''

McCracken's eyes fell on the blueprints. "So how do I get in?"

"You don't," Sal said flatly. "What Group Six has got protecting it inside their fence gives a whole new meaning to the term 'three-zone security.' ''

Belamo unrolled three of the blueprints and scattered another series of enlarged satellite photos from inside his briefcase randomly atop them upon the bed.

"Group Six may be contained on Brookhaven property," he continued, "but every connection between the two of them ends there. What we got is a facility within a facility. In fact, the only reason Group Six's base is on those grounds at all is because Brookhaven had this shell of a new addition built before the powers that be determined they had run out of money and need. Group Six came in with plenty of both. Finished the facility in record time and was laying in the security even as the first filing cabinets started to arrive. Security like nothing we've seen before.''

"And me thinking we'd seen it all . . ."

"Big day for firsts, boss. See, the way it is most times, high-security installations aren't prepared to fend off one intruder. They're set up to defend against a full-scale armed assault or terrorist action. But Group Six is different. Group Six's primary concern is sabotage or espionage, which one or two men can work more efficiently than a group, and all their security is set up with that in mind. Wait till you get a look at these, see what I'm talking about.''

Sal leaned over to visually highlight the objects of his discussion. His knees cracked and he had to hunch his back to bend.

"Like I said, what you got is your basic three-zone-security model, except there's nothing basic about it. The electrified fence around the complex doesn't even count, so the first zone runs along this grid.'' Belamo traced his hands across a blue strip that circled the entire building on the overview plans. "Motion detectors laid with underground, interconnected wire and rigged to changes in ground mass above. You take a step, you disturb the dirt and bam!—they know you're there.'' Sal's finger moved to a red strip that encircled the complex inside the blue strip. "Here we have your basic ultraviolet spools of light that register intrusion when broken. Thing is they don't just run in straight symmetrical lines or squares; they criss-cross on an ever-changing computer-altered basis. Prevents anyone on the inside from selling the schema to ambitious sorts like us. In other words, we're fucked."

"And you've only mentioned two of the three zones."

"You don't want to hear about the last one, boss, believe me."

McCracken looked down at the unrolled plans and realized there was no third color grid to complement the blue and red. "So where is it?"

"Everywhere."

"What do you mean?"

"I brought you a picture so you could see for yourself." Sal riffled through his briefcase and extracted a single eight-by-ten photograph that was clipped to the top of a formal memo. "Here, have a look."

Blaine took the packet and examined the photo. The picture showed what looked like a huge steel mushroom, a foot-long shaft attached to an umbrellalike top.

"Looks like an underground sprinkler."

"And it works on pretty much the same principle, boss. Fact, I think it says somewhere that's where the idea came up for it, 'cept it fires death instead of water. They got maybe five hundred of them rigged belowground and wired to the motion detectors and infrareds."

"Wired to do what?"

Sal removed still more enhanced satellite reconnaissance photos from his case. "First I want you to take a look at these shots. Tell me what you don't see."

"What I *don't* see?"

"Yeah. Won't take you long."

McCracken scanned the shots that caught various angles of a large dark slab of a building sitting in a clearing. Belamo was right: it didn't take him long to see what was missing.

"No perimeter guards," Blaine pronounced. "Nobody in evidence patrolling."

"A thing of the past, boss, at Group Six. Rendered super-fluous, you might say."

"Because of those mushrooms?"

"*Laser*-firing mushrooms. Motion detector and/or the ultra-violet rigging picks up an intruder and tracks him at the same time it sends a message instantly to mushroom control. Mushroom things rise out of the ground and home in on the intruder's signal, firing automatically once he enters one of their grids. Nothing left to chance that way."

Blaine turned his attention to the overview schema, then lifted it aside to check a more complete blueprint of Group Six's headquarters. "What about an airdrop onto the roof here, Sal? Say off a glider or a quiet-running chopper?"

Belamo shook his head. "Forget it, boss. It doesn't show up clearly in the plans, but the roof surface is electrified."

McCracken nodded slowly, still checking the plans. "Where does Group Six's power supply come from?"

"Doesn't matter. They got backup generators capable of running the entire security system at eighty-percent efficiency. Not to mention that in the event of a power failure, all exit doors are automatically sealed with cobalt bars. More to keep people in than out in this case, figuring a power failure would create the ideal diversion for an infiltrator to escape."

Blaine was looking at the plans like the page of a book he'd been over a dozen times. "Diversion might be just what we need."

"Better be an awful big one, you ask me."

"When exactly does this security system stand down?"

"According to some boys at the Pentagon who've seen it firsthand, never—not even when someone authorized's coming or going."

"Down this road . . . here." McCracken traced a route that wound its way through the Brookhaven complex starting at the main security gate.

"Yup."

"Deliveries?"

Sal Belamo shook his head. "No truck even gets close. Everything is off-loaded on Brookhaven grounds and picked up by Group Six personnel."

"Security is made to be broken, Sal. There's always a flaw. The trick is finding it." McCracken checked the plans again. "According to these, Group Six's building has three complete underground levels, along with these high-confidence storage holds here, here and here." He traced his hand farther outward well beyond the scope of the building. "And there are these underground passageways that run from Brookhaven outward. Unfinished, it looks like, when Brookhaven abandoned the building Group Six ended up occupying. I think you can get maybe halfway into the security zone before you run into a wall."

"Not far enough, you ask me."

"Wait a minute," McCracken said suddenly, his eyes drawn back to something on a blueprint enlarged to contain the area encompassing the toxic waste dumping facility to the start of Group Six's security zones. He tapped his finger against a spot on the original plans marked in red. "Take a look at this."

"Holy shit," Sal muttered, gazing over Blaine's shoulder. "I never . . ."

"Think it's big enough for a man?"

"What's the difference? You can see from the plans it don't go far enough."

"Just tell me if it's big enough."

"You got something figured, boss?"

McCracken was comparing the blueprint sketches to some of the photos Sal had scattered atop them. His eyes kept coming back to one area.

"I might," he said. "Now what about my question?"

Belamo started leafing through a thick book of bound computer printouts. "I don't know. It wasn't on the original specs list for Brookhaven and Group Six never had a need for it, so . . ."

"Can you get me into Brookhaven, Sal?"

Belamo shrugged. "I can throw some shit, see if it sticks on the right walls. Thing is, you gotta have a way out, too."

"A two-man job, then."

"For sure, boss."

"Johnny's already on his way."

Belamo chuckled at the prospects of that. "Need one big fucking wall now, but what the hell? Be nice if you told me what you're looking at 'fore I start throwing."

McCracken smiled. "Glad you asked. . . ."

CHAPTER 22

"They're just passing through Brookhaven's main security gate, sir," Larsen reported, when Colonel Lester Fuchs reached Group Six's communications and security center.

One of the two dozen monitor screens built into a huge console on the floor's center showed a convoy of three cars snailing past the individual research buildings lining the front of Brookhaven en route to Group Six. Another trio of monitors, equipped with substantially more sophisticated pictures and imaging, picked up the convoy as it continued on a journey that would take seven minutes.

"I'm heading down," Fuchs announced, tightening a miniature earpiece in place so he could keep in touch with the communications center.

En route to the garage, Fuchs again considered the best strategy for dealing with Joshua Wolfe. Four hours earlier he had met with Haslanger after the doctor had completed his inspection of a fax machine re-covered from Harry Lime's Key West apartment and flown straight to Group Six.

"Brilliant," Haslanger had muttered in his private lab, leaning over a table littered with tools. Centered on the table was the fax machine with its back removed. "Positively brilliant, and just as I expected." He turned his gaze on Fuchs. "It's gone."

"What is?"

"The chip. Understand, Colonel, that a fax machine operates on the same principles as a computer. The machine doing the sending digitizes the material and transfers it over line where it is reassembled and printed by the receiving machine. In this case Joshua Wolfe has removed the chip responsible for that reassembly."

"Why?"

"What did I tell you as soon as I removed this machine's back?"

"That it was out of paper."

"Precisely. And since the received information could not therefore be printed, it remained stored on the chip inside the machine. When the boy removed it, he was effectively removing all fax communications that had come in since the paper ran out. So if he faxed the entire formula for CLAIR to himself, he would have had to venture to Key West to retrieve it."

"Quite a risk."

"Well worth it, I would suspect."

But thorough searches by Sinclair had not turned up the fax chip either among the boy's possessions or in the hotel room he had appropriated for himself in Orlando. Fuchs wasn't worried, fully expecting Joshua Wolfe would be ready to tell him where the chip could be found shortly after arriving at Group Six.

"Standing down security, sir," Fuchs heard Larsen's voice report through his earpiece as the elevator slid down to the third sublevel. "Opening gate now."

A pause.

"Lighting approach route."

The standing down of security applied only to the narrow, two-lane stretch from Group Six's security fence to the entrance to the ramp that permitted access to the underground garage. For the rest of the grounds, all normal procedures and safeguards remained in effect. Understandably, then, the approaching convoy would be careful to stay between the lights and not stray from the road.

"Tell Dr. Haslanger that it's time," Fuchs ordered as the elevator doors slid open on the garage level.

Haslanger had been watching the convoy approach on the single monitor in his office and rose from his chair at almost the same time Fuchs started for the garage. He had reached for the remote control to turn the monitor off when a voice from the rear of his office stopped him.

"I'd like to watch, if you don't mind."

Krill . . . In the quiet of the room and the excitement Haslanger was feeling, he'd actually forgotten Krill was with him.

"No," he said, uneasily. "Of course not."

"A first, I should think."

Haslanger looked back at the Krill's massive, misshapen silhouette, illuminated by the meager light shed by the monitor screen. "What do you mean?"

"Two of your creations so close together at the same time. I should have thought it was obvious."

Haslanger wished he'd been closer to the door. Krill was his creation as well, yes, but a poor comparison to Joshua Wolfe. After all, the boy could function in everyday society. Krill's appearance, of course, made this impossible. Haslanger had nearly terminated him as he had the vast majority of the others shortly after delivery from the womb. Only on second glance did he see enough reasonable features to provide hope. Krill wasn't the first to avoid swift termination, just the first whose life was not claimed by a myriad of physical problems during infancy. He held on stubbornly, showing a persistent will to live from that first day.

What surprised Haslanger most, though, was his brain capacity. He showed tremendous aptitude for reading and gained an appreciation for music at a very early age. Standard education was never meant to be part of his training, but Krill educated himself during the long hours of isolation that had come to define his existence. He was the product of an experiment that doomed him to life in a lab even after the research was over. Haslanger had set up quarters for him here at Group Six where he read in the dark and usually emerged only when the doctor called for him.

"And interesting, too," Krill continued. "After all, the boy and I represent the sum total of your life's work. I should like to meet him, discuss all we have in common. But that is not why you have taken me from my books."

Haslanger opened the door that blocked most of the light from the hall with his frame. "I've been looking into the man you identified from your visit to the New York Public Library, this McCracken."

"So have I."

"He's dangerous."

"I know."

"But we have no way of being certain his meeting with Gloria Wilkins-Tate concerned me."

"If it did, he will find you."

"I don't exist anymore."

"Neither did Gloria Wilkins-Tate."

"You think he'll trace me to Group Six, then."

"I think he'll be coming. Inevitably."

Haslanger could feel Krill's eyes bearing down on him.

"This is the first time I've ever failed in my work, Father. So I intend to be here when he does."

Dr. Susan Lyle was escorted to the garage level by one of Fuchs's plainclothes security men.

"Ah, thank you for joining us, Doctor," the colonel greeted ebulliently, relaxed in his full-dress uniform. "I hope you didn't mind me sending someone with you, but I wasn't sure if you knew the way."

"I appreciate the thoughtfulness."

Haslanger arrived just after her and Susan tried to avoid looking at him.

"I will introduce both of you to the boy straightaway," the colonel continued, and then looked at Susan alone. "It would be most helpful if you at least made an effort to seem a part of us. Further confusion can only upset this boy's already unsettled mental state. He needs to see structure, order, so he may choose to embrace what we can offer him."

"He won't hear otherwise from me," Susan said, trying hard to disguise the edge in her voice.

A door that was actually a huge segment of the front wall rose suddenly, allowing the headlights of the lead car in the convoy to burn into the primary receiving area. It pulled in far enough to allow easy access for the two that followed it down the ramp into the garage that was located three levels below ground. None of the occupants of the middle car exited until the ones on either side of it climbed out and took up rigid stances, as if at post. Then its back doors opened, allowing another of the security men to emerge, followed by Joshua Wolfe.

The jeans and shirt he wore would have made him fit in anywhere with kids his own age. Add the fashionably long hair and the white bead necklace worn loose around his neck, and he could have been any fifteen-year-old boy.

But the eyes were not those of a teenager. That, Susan figured, was where everything changed. Those deep blue eyes were almost menacing in their intensity, missing nothing in their sweep. Susan wanted to say that the stare was cocky or even arrogant, but she knew it merely held one of the means by which this boy with an IQ in excess of two hundred processed input to his wondrous brain. Swallowed everything he could see, especially when confronted by new surroundings. In familiarity could be found comfort, and that was what Joshua Wolfe sought now.

"Good evening, Mr. Sinclair," Fuchs greeted the man who had preceded the boy out the backseat. "I trust your trip went well."

"Uneventful," Sinclair returned, reluctant to take his eyes off Joshua Wolfe.

The boy had stopped between the colonel and the car, seeming to register Fuchs as he took in the rest of these new surroundings. Fuchs moved to the boy and extended his hand.

"Colonel Lester Fuchs. Director of Group Six."

Joshua Wolfe accepted the hand in a weak grip, eyes still absorbed in processing what lay around him. The boy looked the colonel up and down, obviously not impressed.

"I remember your name from the personnel files I accessed."

"I trust you found that and the others interesting, Josh. May I call you Josh?"

"Sure. I couldn't access some of the most interesting stuff, though . . ." Josh waited the length of a breath. ". . . Lester."

Fuchs cleared his throat uneasily. "We can change that if you like, provide access to any file, system or laboratory you wish." He turned back toward Susan and Dr. Haslanger. "On that subject, there are two other people here I'd like you to meet." The boy's eyes veered their way and narrowed. "This is Dr. Erich Haslanger, and this is Dr. Susan Lyle."

Haslanger nodded, fascinated at meeting this creature of his own devising, and yet wary. Susan forced a smile, remembering the picture Blaine McCracken had found in the boy's dorm room. Though it had been taken only a year or so before,

Joshua Wolfe looked considerably older standing before her now. It must be the eyes again, she thought. Whatever innocence had been present in that picture was long gone, far more than a year's worth lost. Susan remembered the smiling man standing next to the boy in the picture, the one whose disappearance accounted for McCracken's involvement. She wondered how Fuchs would handle that if Joshua Wolfe brought it up.

"Dr. Haslanger is in charge of research and development," Joshua Wolfe announced matter-of-factly. "I could find nothing in his file that predates his assignment to Group Six." The boy looked at Susan a little curiously. "And your name wasn't listed at all."

"I was just transferred," Susan said, quite comfortably. She could almost feel Colonel Fuchs seething.

"From?"

"The Centers for Disease Control and Prevention."

"Oh," the boy said, and his head dropped a little. His face came back up enough to shyly meet her eyes. "I know why you're here. The file wasn't in the system yet, but you must have thought what happened, what . . . I did, was a disease at first."

"It was the first option we had to rule out," Susan affirmed.

"You were the one who figured out it was me, weren't you?"

"Yes."

"How? It must have been the backpack. If I hadn't dropped it, I wouldn't be here now, would I?"

Susan looked at Lester Fuchs, who had gone red from the collar to the roots of his hair. "Neither of us would be."

"But you tracked me down from it. I should have gone back after I dropped it. I thought about it but, well, I didn't." Those intense, almost omniscient eyes softened and looked like a child's for the first time. "Then again, it was a big day for mistakes."

Fuchs edged forward to join Susan. "We know what you were trying to do, Josh," he said, and she noticed how the hollow confines of the garage gave his words a twanging echo. "Admirable, commendable."

The boy's eyes flashed back to their normal liquidy brilliance. "But it's not what you do here at Group Six, is it, Lester?"

"As you know full well, it is not."

"So what was commendable about Cambridge? What I tried to do, or what I ended up doing?"

"I would never purport to rejoice in the deaths of innocent persons, but neither would I advocate letting those deaths go for nothing." Fuchs tightened his stare. "Especially, young man, when those deaths could actually prevent thousands and thousands more."

"Is that the business you're in?"

"You read our files. You should know."

"That's why I figured I'd better ask."

Fuchs remained stoic. "Yes, that's the business we are in."

"So what do you want with me? What is it you think I can do?"

"Isn't it obvious?"

"No."

"For starters, we want CLAIR in its original form, the one released in the Cambridgeside Galleria."

"Doesn't seem to do much for your mandate."

"That depends on one's perspective," Fuchs responded, "especially considering our mandate is the development of weapons for use in limited arenas."

"To kill."

"Only if necessary."

"Isn't it always?"

Fuchs took a step forward. "Not necessarily, which is why I want you to give us a chance to show you some of the discoveries we've developed here."

"Give you a chance? You mean I have a choice?"

"You're not a prisoner, Josh. Say the word, and I'll have Mr. Sinclair arrange for you to return to Cambridge." Fuchs frowned. "Of course, by now I would expect we aren't the only ones interested in finding you, but we may be the most understanding."

"What if I didn't want to go back to Harvard? What if I wanted to go to wherever you took Harry Lime?"

"I'm not sure I know what you're talking about."

"You know my file, Lester, just like I know yours."

Susan waited for Fuchs's answer as expectantly as Josh.

"Oh, I know about Harry Lime's role in your upbringing," he replied. "But I'm afraid I know nothing of his current absence. Inquiries are being made. He could be off on an assignment. With no formal records, such work is difficult to access, even for us."

"Those were your men in his apartment today." ·

"Yes."

"They never saw him?"

"No."

"It would mean a lot to me if you could find him, Lester."

"As I said, we're trying."

"I'd like it if you could bring him here, so we could be together."

"A good idea. Definitely something to consider. In the meantime, why don't we let Dr. Haslanger show you around? Any problem with that, Doctor?"

The old man shook his head nervously. "No."

Joshua Wolfe's eyes shifted to Susan. "What about Dr. Lyle?"

"She'll catch up to you, young man. After we've spoken."

"Your assessment, Doctor," Fuchs requested, after a nervous Haslanger had led the boy off.

"Assessment?" Susan asked.

"Of the boy."

"We've been through this before, Colonel. I'm an infectious disease specialist, not a psychologist."

"What about your assessment of him as a person?" Fuchs asked her. "And a woman."

Susan raised her eyebrows at his final query. "You're not used to working with women, are you, Colonel?"

Fuchs shrugged. "When you've been in the military as long as I have . . ."

"I suppose you're even less used to being around children."

"Then you see Joshua Wolfe as a child."

"Albeit an exceptional one. But emotionally he's prone to suffer the same maladies and upheavals all children do."

"Do you see that as a problem?"

"I'm not sure I know what you mean."

Fuchs's eyes scolded her. "Dr. Lyle, I wanted to speak with you alone to reiterate the primary issues here. Joshua Wolfe has something that we at Group Six want. We have chosen not to interrogate him or force him to do anything against his will. We want him to cooperate of his own volition, and we are relying on you to help convince him that course is in his best interest."

"And how do you expect me to go about that, exactly?"

Fuchs smiled. His voice lowered and became almost amicable. "Dr. Lyle, I understand the reasons for your ambition, your pursuits, as well as the desperation that drives them. But how far away are you from the kind of appropriate leadership research position you seek? Group Six has rather powerful friends in Washington. Should you assist us in this matter, we would certainly be moved to intervene on your behalf in any capacity you desire."

"I never said I was unhappy where I was."

"You didn't have to. It's clear to me the CDC was just a stepping stone for you, as was Firewatch Command. Both worthy endeavors but hardly meeting your goals or skills. Why not regard your visit here as yet another stepping stone, and an extremely fortuitous one at that?" He drew uncomfortably close to her, making Susan want to shrink away. "I understand your ambition. You and I are not that much different in terms of what drives us. Our motivations are distinct, true enough. But we both seek positions from which we can better our efficacy. Joshua Wolfe can help both of us in that regard, Doctor, and we can help Joshua Wolfe."

"Is that what I'm supposed to convince him of?"

"The power of an organization like ours can offer many things, but one of the most valuable is insulation. Insulation from mistakes, retribution and traditional punitive punishments. At the entrance to Group Six, a person leaves behind what he was before. From that time he, or she, is defined only by the extent of the contributions they are able to make." Fuchs paused briefly. "We can insulate Joshua Wolfe from what happened in Cambridge. We can wipe his complicity in the deaths of more than seventeen hundred persons off the books and, more, we can provide justification for it in his mind. Something good must be shown to come out of it, and with your help, Doctor, I think we are quite capable of demonstrating that to him.''

In that instant Susan Lyle looked into the revealing stare in Colonel Lester Fuchs's eyes and knew; perhaps she had known from nearly the beginning, but only admitted it now: no matter how this worked out, Joshua Wolfe belonged to Group Six. The rest of his life would be charted accordingly. What he offered was too valuable to let go and too dangerous to set free. Everything else, her presence included, was pretense.

In offering her access to the boy, though, Fuchs did not realize that, thanks to Blaine McCracken, she knew the truth about Harry Lime's fate and thus grasped to what means the colonel would stoop to achieve his ends. That truth galvanized her resolve to help the boy, to convince him that anything was better than accepting the offer to remain at Group Six.

''I'll see what I can do,'' Susan told Fuchs.

At the Centers for Disease Control and Prevention containment facility inside Mount Jackson in the Ozarks, work had come to a standstill since Killebrew had made his startling discovery the previous day. He had suspended all research and experimentation on the remains of the Cambridgeside Galleria victims until he could reach Susan Lyle.

Killebrew felt as scared as he did frustrated. All his efforts to locate Susan had been stymied and he was finally told that she had been temporarily replaced as project head by a CDC director he knew only from promotional videos. Killebrew wasn't about to share his shocking discovery with a total stranger, wasn't about to tell anyone other than Susan what he had learned the day before:

The CLAIR organism wasn't dead at all.

CHAPTER 23

"Doctor?" Josh Wolfe asked again.

"Excuse me?"

"You were saying . . ."

Haslanger didn't know what he'd been saying and back-tracked in his mind. For twenty minutes now, he'd been taking Joshua Wolfe on the rounds of Group Six's laboratory facilities. There was little need for narration; the boy recognized and understood everything he was seeing at first glance, often supplying the narration himself and looking to Haslanger only for confirmation. He seemed to possess total recall of everything his relatively brief perusal of Group Six's data banks had imparted. For Haslanger it was merely a matter of filling in the blanks or helping the boy connect a project he remembered to its principal point of research.

That's where they had left off, Haslanger recalled, catching up. He'd been praising the virtues of Group Six, indoctrinating Joshua Wolfe slowly, with an eye toward bringing him around to accepting the importance of the work that went on here.

"I was saying," Haslanger continued, "that in spite of what much of the information you accessed indicated, a large portion of our work has been devoted to the development of non-lethal weapons of war."

The boy turned quizzical at that. "A contradiction in terms, it sounds like."

"Only because Group Six's purpose lies in redefining how wars are fought. Actually, I suppose, the redefinition has already taken place and we are merely responding to it. Let me show you what I mean."

They moved farther into the spacious and open lab they had entered. Haslanger stopped at a long, black table and handed Joshua Wolfe a piece of shiny material.

"What does this feel like to you?"

The boy ran it through his hands. "I don't know. Aluminum foil, I guess. Only it doesn't crinkle."

"You're not far off," Haslanger complimented. "The material you're holding makes up a shroud designed to engulf an enemy vehicle, even a tank. The shroud molds to its target's shape and locks in place, rendering the vehicle instantly inoperative."

When Haslanger finished speaking, Josh snatched a large clip from a stack of papers and wrapped the foillike material around it. True to Haslanger's claims, it adhered easily and there seemed to be no prying it off afterwards.

"The shroud can be fired any number of ways," the old man indicated. "The speed it picks up after being expelled from a barrel provides the force that both spreads the shroud outward and allows it to encase its target. An offshoot of this same material has also been used to create a new form of net that can be fired into large groups of angry, rioting masses. They are trapped just where they are standing and are held there while virtually no damage is done to them."

Haslanger knew he had the boy's attention now and loved every second of it. More than Joshua Wolfe's approval, he wanted the boy to accept him, to consider him an equal.

"The point," he went on, "is that the United States must not be forced to resort to total war every time we take up the cause against some rogue or insurrectional government. Terrains are too hostile, deterrent weaponry too sophisticated and prevalent. The rules must be rewritten. The projects we have in various stages of development number, literally, in the hundreds. Some deal with dramatic changes in sensory inputs, such as light, smell or sound. Others are more chemical or organic in nature—for instance, microbes we are developing which eat engine hoses, belts and electrical insulation."

"Not all successes," Joshua Wolfe said suddenly. "The files I accessed were rather detailed. Some of your experiments did not turn out as planned. GL-12, for instance."

The sleeping gas disaster, Haslanger recalled with a chill.

"An entire town was massacred as a result, I believe. Can you get me a sample?"

Haslanger nodded uneasily.

"I think I can improve its stability for you. That's where its problem lies, from what I was able to tell. And earlier this week, only yesterday, I think, the data was cryptic but it was clear your weapon that causes temporary blindness still needs some work."

Haslanger wondered if Joshua Wolfe was mocking him. The data banks, after all, included nothing about the disastrous results of his most recent test, which meant the boy had figured something had gone wrong simply by analyzing the material provided, just as he had with GL-12. Haslanger tried not to let his expression give his thoughts or feelings away. He didn't bother denying either of Joshua Wolfe's assertions. Growing defensive, he settled on a different track instead.

"In science, young man, the process of discovery is often painful, achieved at a cost we as scientists must be willing to pay. We test and we analyze but reality holds the only true proving ground. Failure does not rule out success; it merely tempers it. We must accept failure, and the sometimes difficult price it exacts, as a normal part of the discovery process."

"But all this, what you do here, isn't about science; it's about war."

"I prefer to believe that it's about survival. Do you believe in the concept of deterrence, young man?"

"It kept the world out of World War III."

"Why?"

"Because the superpowers each feared total annihilation from the other's vast arsenal of atomic weapons."

Haslanger nodded. "Well, those vast arsenals have been rendered impotent by their capacity for overkill. A stockpile of a thousand warheads is useless against a country, a terrorist group or a madman with a single weapon. By the turn of the century, my guess is scores of countries will possess atomic devices, either for their own use or to be brokered on the open market."

"I don't think lasers, sleeping gas or tin foil can do much to hold those kinds of people in check."

"My point exactly. We need something else, something . . . more."

The boy's expression wavered slightly, losing its sureness. "CLAIR was meant to save people, not kill them."

"And what happened in its only application?" Haslanger
followed quickly, seizing the advantage.

"You know as well as I do."

"For nothing? Is it to be for *nothing*? Can you accept that?"

"Could you accept all the people in that Bosnian town dying?"

"I was trying to save them, young man." A pause. "Just
as you were trying to save the people in that mall."

Haslanger stopped there, not wanting to go any further. The
truth was that the boy's mastery of the principles of nanotechnology, his development of the first truly functional organic machine, had far greater ramifications than CLAIR. A
whole new generation of weapons and the means for assuring
worldwide dominance and control lay on the horizon. The potential was limitless. CLAIR was first generation, created by
accident. What Joshua Wolfe could do in the succeeding years
in the labs of Group Six . . .

"But I didn't," the boy said suddenly. "I killed them."

Haslanger made his voice its sternest yet. "I believe in intentions and I believe in the final products that result from
those intentions. Everything else can be dismissed as the superfluous meanderings and banter that the average mind
spends it lifetime dwelling on. The exceptional, those bent on
accomplishment, dismiss all but what they seek and what they
ultimately achieve. Otherwise," he said, knowing he was
about to reveal too much of himself, "you run the risk of
sharing your life with ghosts."

Josh remembered the dream he'd had on the flight from
Philadelphia to Miami, CLAIR eating up all the passengers
while he stood there and watched.

"Who are your ghosts?" he asked Haslanger.

"Tell me what you think."

"Your accent is German, and you're probably in your seventies, which means you may have served with the Nazis."

"Very good, but little to do with my ghosts, young man.
The ghosts came later, because no one was able to help me
the way I want to help you. The pressure was tremendous,
intelligence and applied theory exceeding the limits of available technology." Haslanger let the boy see him gaze fondly

about the lab. "If I'd had this place from the beginning, there would be no ghosts."

"The beginning's already passed for me, too." Josh shrugged.

"Still salvageable, young man. The ghosts can be controlled. Let us, let *me* help you."

"I know what went wrong with CLAIR," Josh said, interrupting Haslanger's line of thought. "I know how to make it identify the nitrogen-oxygen proximities in molecules more precisely so it will be able to discriminate between sulfates and nitrates and human blood. If you want to help me, that's what you'll let me do. Here, in these labs."

"I'll have to take that up with Colonel Fuchs."

"Make sure he knows I won't help you otherwise. That includes providing the original formula. I'll just walk out of here and face the con-sequences and the ghosts."

"I'm sure he'll agree. He wants you to stay as much as I do." Haslanger watched the boy stiffen, maybe fighting back tears, and resisted the urge to reach out and touch him. Instead he simply lowered his voice. "We both understand how you have been punished your entire life for your wondrous skills and abilities. You have been made an outcast, as many who are deemed superior are. But at Group Six you will face no such problems. Here you will belong. You can be free to be who you are as you help us preserve the future of this country and this planet."

Haslanger thought he saw the boy's features starting to soften when the woman entered the lab.

"I hope I'm not interrupting."

"No," said Haslanger, trying to hide his agitation.

"Colonel Fuchs asked me to escort our guest to his quarters as soon as you were finished."

"I believe we've covered enough for now, anyway."

"I want to start working tomorrow, Doctor," Joshua Wolfe insisted sternly. "First thing."

"I'll see the colonel about that right away."

Haslanger escorted the two of them into the hall and then headed off in the opposite direction.

"Working on what?" Susan asked when he was gone.

"CLAIR," Josh said.

Susan elected to drop that subject. "It will take five minutes for us to reach your quarters. That's all the time we have to talk; all the living quarters in this place are sure to have been bugged."

They started off slowly.

"I've got to tell you something and I'm not really sure how. It's about your friend. It's about Harry."

The boy's eyes blazed into hers.

"I met someone, a friend of his. The trail he was following led to you, to your room at Harvard the same time I was there."

"What trail?"

"Harry's. He thought something had happened to you and he asked this friend to help."

"That would be just like Harry," Josh said with a faint smile.

"Then he disappeared and this friend was trying to find him. He didn't think he was going to. He was after the people responsible."

"Fuchs and Haslanger . . ."

"That's what your presence here would seem to indicate. No matter what they promise you, no matter what they say, you can't trust them. They're not going to let you out of here under any circumstances."

Josh considered that. "And you're the one who gave me to them."

"I didn't even know Group Six existed when I issued my report back in Atlanta. They had me brought here, same as you."

"Then we're both prisoners."

"We might be. I know too much." Susan paused. "Even more than I told them."

They reached the elevator and Josh looked at her.

"I know there's a second vial of CLAIR you must have hidden somewhere."

The elevator doors slid open to reveal an empty compartment. Susan stepped in and Josh followed reluctantly. The doors hissed back closed. Susan leaned forward and pressed 5. The elevator began its climb.

"I don't want them getting their hands on it," she continued very softly. "I don't work here, I don't work for them and I know what all this is about. Right now CLAIR is the only thing that can save Group Six from the scandal brewing in Washington. They need something to prove themselves to their supporters and you've got it. Beyond that, everything else you can accomplish here can elevate Group Six to a level on par with the CIA. That's why they can't let you leave. You're too valuable. They don't want to share you and they're not about to let anyone know you even exist. That means you're not going anywhere. You're Fuchs's express ticket to his general's stripes and Haslanger's ticket to the ultimate weapon he's always sought. The bastard is still trying to win World War II. Only the sides have changed."

The elevator stopped on the fifth floor and the doors slid open. No one was waiting or in sight nearby. Neither Susan nor Joshua Wolfe made any move toward stepping out.

"Why should I trust *you*?"

"Because I'm going to help you get out of here."

"I read some of your poems," Susan offered as they started down the fifth-floor hallway. As Josh's features narrowed and tensed, she added, "I liked them. They made me feel like I knew you, at least knew who you are."

Josh nodded. "That's why I stopped writing. It made me think about that too much. It made everything hurt. It was easier not to think." He stopped, but then looked over at her again. "Which was your favorite?"

"The first," Susan replied without hesitation. " 'The Fires of Midnight.' "

"I remember when I wrote it, how mad I was, how unhappy. Maybe it was the first time I realized how different I really was. I hated everything and everybody. The fires were my rage. I wanted to let it out, to let them burn." He stopped again. "And they've been burning ever since. CLAIR was supposed to put them out and the only thing it did was make them so high and hot that maybe I'll *never* be able to put them out. That was Haslanger's argument, sort of. He's got a point."

"The burning will never stop if you stay at Group Six. They'll make sure of that."

They reached the door to Josh's quarters on the fifth floor, just around the corner from Susan's.

"Can you do it? Can you get me out of here?"

"I don't know. I think so. I think I've got a way. But you'll have to help."

"How soon?"

She put the coded plastic slab Fuchs had given her into the proper slot in the door. It whisked open. "The sooner the better. Tomorrow night."

"That would give me one day in the lab."

"Yes."

"I need that."

"Why?"

"Insurance," Josh told her.

Alan Killebrew continued to keep himself busy by rechecking his data, running repeat tests to be sure of his original findings and new ones to expand his understanding of the CLAIR organism.

From the point the Cambridgeside Galleria had tested clean, the assumption had been that, like any parasite, CLAIR died when its host did. But all indications pointed to the fact that it had been lying dormant instead. Denied sustenance, it had gone into a state of indefinite hibernation Killebrew had inadvertently ended.

He returned to his computer console and reran the original program. He had been superimposing molecules of the organism over each other to see if they maintained the same genetic shape when harvested from different areas of the body. His own words filled his ears.

"Except for some slight deviations along the edges consistent with manageable decay, the molecules appear to be identical in all—"

He had stopped when on the screen one of the molecules had begun dividing, expanding well beyond the borders of the one superimposed over it. He had split the computer screen back into two at that point. The molecule on the right, the one he had just harvested from the arteriosclerotic subject's extremities, continued to grow before his eyes, part of a tissue sample he had sliced off with an electrically heated scalpel, left to smolder beneath it when he had neglected to return the scalpel to its tray.

His next step was to take the temperature of what was left of the sample. It measured 97 degrees by that point, having dropped considerably. The other samples he had been working on were all considerably under that temperature after a much briefer exposure to the heated scalpel. At 97 degrees the sample showed no signs of reanimation. Killebrew increased the temperature in tenth-of-a-degree increments. There was no re-activated growth until he reached 98.7, a mere tenth of a degree above human body temperature. At that point CLAIR came back to life and began to grow at an alarming rate, continuing to do so once reanimated even after the temperature dropped below the confirmed threshold.

Body temperature—that was the key!

In transforming itself to be able to survive within the human body, CLAIR had also managed to find a way to survive once its host had expired. The temperature of the body drops almost instantly upon death. To avoid being starved, CLAIR had taught itself to recognize this and use that drop in temperature to move into a state of dormancy, waiting for the temperature to rise again so it could feed. The organism could not know under normal circumstances that could never have happened. It was merely behaving in a logical manner, devoid of creative thought.

Just like the machine it was, Killebrew reflected.

He spoke as he watched the cells dividing yet again on the screen before him.

"I have now confirmed that accidental exposure to the heat scalpel and the according rise in tissue temperature returned CLAIR to its active state. It's probable that the organism becomes dormant after its host metabolism expires. I would further theorize, contrary to Dr. Lyle's original assertions, that CLAIR's violation of its original programming to expire at temperatures exceeding seventy-eight degrees did not result from exposure to some amino acid found in the mucous membrane linings of the nose and mouth. Instead it was most likely a result of exposure to a protein found in the upper layers of skin the organism encountered as it ingested the bodily fluids of its victims from the outside in."

Killebrew stopped again and considered the ramifications of his own words.

"Further, because of the transformation brought on by exposure to this protein, the temperatures that would have destroyed CLAIR in its original form become the very means to bring it back to life. I have isolated and contained the organism in a vacuum seal. But if not contained and subjected to extreme heat, the mutated strain would be free to multiply exponentially with no presently known mechanism to impede it. I will continue subjecting the reactivated samples to decreasing temperatures to find out at what temperature growth stops and the organism returns to an inactive state. However, if in this mutated state the organism is no longer subject to the controls of temperature sensitivity—"

Killebrew stopped suddenly, realizing the import of his words, realizing that within Mount Jackson lay the power to destroy mankind.

CHAPTER 24

"I don't have you on any of my lists," the single guard at the front gate of Brookhaven National Labs told Blaine McCracken Thursday afternoon.

"You're not supposed to. That's why they call it a surprise inspection." Blaine made himself pause, hoping it would help make his point. "Just check our credentials again."

The guard did just that, leaving Blaine to turn to the figure in the seat next to him. Johnny Wareagle had scrunched his legs under the dashboard so that his knees rubbed against the glove compartment. But his head still touched the car's ceiling; no car had been made with his seven-foot, three-hundred-pound proportions in mind. In the confines of the sedan, Johnny looked stiff and lumbering, a condition that would disappear as soon as he was free to move about outside. Blaine had never met a man who could move faster than Wareagle or accomplish more when he got where he was going.

Sal Belamo had arranged one of the few covers guaranteed to gain them rapid access to Brookhaven. They had the credentials of Environmental Protection Agency inspectors who were responding to increased complaints from neighbors about toxic chemicals found in their ground water. And, assuming someone at Brookhaven did call the EPA to check up on them, they would find that two agents had indeed been dispatched toward that precise end. Sal Belamo was nothing if not thorough.

The guard leaned out the sliding window of his small gatehouse, phone still at his ear. "Someone's coming down to escort you in. Sorry for the inconvenience."

Blaine nodded at the guard. He and Johnny didn't have to wait long. A tan car bearing the same insignia the security guard was wearing on his shirt pulled up on the other side of the open gate. The passenger door opened and a man in a white lab coat climbed out.

"I'm Dr. Childress, chief administrator of Brookhaven," he said as he approached McCracken's open window. "I was in a meeting when you first arrived. Otherwise you would have never been kept waiting so long."

"We'd really like to get started, Doctor," Blaine said, impatience ringing in his voice. "We've got a long afternoon ahead of us."

"Well, I'm quite happy to say that you'll be wasting your time. The last inspection team found no suspected release of toxic substances, and neither did the one before that."

"Tell that to the people who can't drink their tap water anymore. We're being thorough for their sakes."

Childress nodded concedingly. "If you don't mind leaving your car in the visitor's lot, we can drive up to the main building together."

"We've got a lot of gear," Blaine told him.

"Then just follow me" Childress replied and walked back to the tan security vehicle.

Colonel Fuchs had greeted Joshua Wolfe with the news personally Thursday afternoon, having made him wait through the morning in the hopes the boy might let his guard down in his enthusiasm to get working.

"I've reserved labs one and two for you for the rest of the day. I'm sorry it took so long to free them up."

The boy eyed him emotionlessly. "I've got plenty of time."

"To make your refinements on CLAIR, of course, as per your request relayed to me by Dr. Haslanger."

Josh accepted the news stoically. "Alone. No one else but me."

"Dr. Haslanger has asked that he be allowed to—"

"Alone," the boy repeated.

"On the chance that you require something—"

"Dr. Lyle can get it for me."

"As you wish."

"It was never completed," Childress insisted, when McCracken laid out his intentions to inspect the huge discharge pipe running out from Brookhaven's toxic waste dumping plant he'd spotted on Sal Belamo's plans. Childress's words were aimed at Blaine, but he was having trouble taking his eyes off Johnny Wareagle. "Couldn't get EPA approval for another feed line, as a matter of fact."

"Not completed by you, anyway," Blaine returned.

He held McCracken's stare. "You mean . . ."

"Look, Mr. Childress—"

"Doctor."

"Dr. Childress, I can't get access to Group Six. You know it and I know it. And you and I both know that the ground-water contamination is somehow coming from them. Now, I've got a theory here I want you to work with me on. I think they secretly completed your discharge system at the same time they were finishing off construction on your abandoned addition. If I can prove that's the source of the contamination, I'll do everything I can to shut Group Six down, including going public, unless they're willing to cooperate."

The sincerity in Blaine's voice seemed to win Childress over. "You'd do that?"

"Somebody's got to."

"Why?"

"Because they've got to be stopped."

Winning the cooperation of Brookhaven's chief administrator had been an unexpected bonus for McCracken. His plan hadn't depended on it, although reports made out by Childress obtained by Sal Belamo were scathing when it came to Group Six. The fact that the Pentagon had based them here had set plenty of Brookhaven personnel on edge, a situation exacerbated by repeated reports of leaking toxins Brookhaven was getting blamed for. Further, the unconfirmed reports of human guinea pigs and hideous experiments being performed on animals had increased speculation as to what might be going on within the blacked-out windows of Group Six's building.

"I've never been inside there," the chief administrator explained. "No one here at Brookhaven has. Our only association with them is passing their . . . guests onto the premises."

"I understand."

Johnny and Blaine carried their heavy equipment duffels

down a long hall on the second sublevel of Brookhaven's waste treatment facility, which led to the access point for the unfinished discharge system for toxic waste. They had spent a good part of Wednesday night and part of today acquiring the equipment and learning how to use it. Of course, it was conceivable all of these efforts would go for naught, that they would find nothing at the end of the discharge pipe Blaine felt certain Group Six was using. If his suspicions were justified, though, he and Johnny would have free passage beneath the complex's impenetrable grounds and access to what lay within Group Six.

And that was where Blaine expected to find Erich Haslanger. Everything about Harry Lime's disappearance indicated Haslanger was responsible and implied Group Six was complicit. It made sense. When The Factory was shut down, Haslanger had maintained Operation Offspring with the help of General Daniel Starr, currently chairman of the Joint Chiefs of Staff and the same man who had secured his assignment to Group Six years later. If this indeed lay at the root of what had cost Harry his life, it was going to cost Group Six and Haslanger more.

"None of your predecessors asked to see this part of the complex before," Childress explained, continuing to lead Johnny and Blaine down a little-used, poorly lit hallway.

"They were going through the motions. I'm not."

They stopped at a heavy steel door. Childress plugged a code into the keypad and the door slid open. The room beyond smelled moldy with disuse. Nonfunctioning machines and equipment lay stacked on the floor, some of them still in their original crates. Tables and other, specially proportioned bases stood empty.

"This was to have led to a second and more secure dumping point until the EPA shot us down," Childress explained, leading them inside. "Primary access into the ground would have been right over here, through this hatchway."

He led them to a hatch slightly more than a yard in diameter. It made Blaine think of the variety found on submarines and just the thought of passing into it made him feel claustrophobic. Childress turned the wheel and pulled open the hatch. Only darkness lay ahead.

"It goes two hundred yards down on a forty-degree angle."

"Taking it under Group Six's section of the property."

"Just barely."

"We'll see," McCracken told him.

"He trusts you, Dr. Lyle," Colonel Fuchs told Susan when they were alone. "We must make that work for us."

"Whose side do you think I'm on, Colonel?"

"Your own, just like me. I know better than to believe you're on the boy's side. You want him for what he can provide you. You want an answer, a cure, before your insides begin to rot away as your parents' did. It hurts, doesn't it, having the potential solution to all your problems so close and yet not available? Working with me and Joshua Wolfe can help us both."

Susan shook her head. "You should really stop and listen to yourself."

"I'm nothing more than a realist, just like you. The molecular technology this boy has mastered holds the potential for individual cell repair—the cure for cancer, Doctor. A worthy endeavor and one I am fully prepared to let the boy undertake once he has produced what we here at Group Six want."

"You want to save yourself."

"Something else we hold in common that the boy can achieve for us. But let us dispense with this bickering and face the fact that he must give us what we want. We both know that. This can be simple or it can be difficult, and if it is difficult for us then it will be doubly difficult for your young friend." Fuchs stopped and eased himself closer to her. "Make him talk, Dr. Lyle. Convince him to give us his original formula for CLAIR."

"And if I do?"

"You remain as his guardian and overseer, while I secure you a top position in cancer research at the National Institutes of Health. Once you are in place there, I will allow Joshua Wolfe to focus a portion of his energies on developing a cure you will take credit for."

"What about him?"

"His contribution must remain secret."

"That's not what I was asking."

"He stays here."

"Indefinitely?"

"As long as I desire, working for both of us, of course. I'm trying to be fair."

"I'm sure you are and I want to be as well. That's why I want you to understand something, Colonel: once I'm out of here, if you take any steps, any steps at all, to further complicate this boy's plight, I won't stop talking until the entire country knows the *whole* truth about what goes on in this place."

Fuchs looked at her for what seemed like a long time before he spoke. "You have become involved with the highest levels of power, Doctor. You would be wise to keep that in mind."

"Thanks for the advice."

Johnny and Blaine changed into contaminant-proof space suits complete with sophisticated air filtration devices built into the helmet and a fifteen-minute emergency supply of oxygen in the event that wasn't enough. They parted company with Childress and entered the sloping shaft dragging one of the duffels between them. The shaft was too narrow to allow shouldering it, so Johnny pushed it forward from his position just behind Blaine.

The going wasn't hard. The steel was shiny and cold and easily covered when moving downhill. A pair of powerful flashlights provided their only illumination, Blaine measuring off their progress in his mind.

The discharge shaft ended, Childress had explained, at a second, automated hatchway that provided access to the primary waste pipe extending a half mile down into the earth. If Blaine got there and found a dead end heading toward Group Six, his theory would be disproven and he and Johnny would have no choice but to retrace their steps.

"End of this shaft's coming up, Indian," he called behind him to Wareagle. "I think I see the hatch."

McCracken shined his flashlight farther ahead. The hatch Childress had described leading deeper into the ground was there all right. But that was all. A hard-packed earthen wall lay where he hoped the continuation of the shaft originating at Group Six would have been.

"Looks like the end of the road, Indian."

"Maybe not, Blainey. Something's missing."

McCracken shined the flashlight about them again, focusing on what it wasn't showing him. "Dust," he realized.

He slid around the automated hatch and pressed up against the earthen wall. "Hand me a—"

He turned back to Wareagle to find him already holding a hammer. Blaine took it and tapped lightly against the jagged wall, then harder. No pieces coughed dust or broke away. He struck it a few more times as hard as he could. Again there was no dust.

"Gotta give Group Six credit, Indian," Blaine said, satisfied. "They do damn good work."

Wareagle edged up alongside and felt the earthen wall with his hand. "Some sort of steel layered with epoxy." He kept feeling and probing. "No means to activate its controls from this side of the shaft, Blainey."

"If it's steel, we can melt it, Indian," McCracken told him. "Let's get those torches out and go to work."

Through the course of the afternoon, Joshua Wolfe might have been alone in the labs, but he did nothing without being watched. Cameras followed his every move, virtually all of which took place within a pair of Group Six's most advanced laboratories dedicated to genetic and molecular research. Group Six's research staff could do nothing but look on in awe, scarcely understanding what they were witnessing.

For much of the afternoon, the boy had focused his attention on information pouring out of one of Group Six's Cray supercomputers. Erich Haslanger monitored his every move, his screen carrying the very same data Joshua Wolfe's did. But it changed too fast for him to keep up with or comprehend what the boy was working on. After a few hours Joshua Wolfe had moved into the labs, spending the bulk of his time guided by an electron microscope as he worked robot arms in a vacuum-sealed room, the mechanical hands and fingers capable of adjustments and manipulations a thousand times more delicate than the human variety.

"What's he doing now?" Fuchs asked Haslanger as they

watched the scene unfold via closed-circuit television monitors.

"I believe he's completing another stage in a compound he intends to mix with CLAIR in its present form," Haslanger replied.

"Toward what end?"

"He wants to correct the flaw that accounted for his original formula mistaking human blood for sulfates and nitrates. That compound he's creating must contain genetic markers meant to enhance the organism's specificity."

Fuchs's frustration was obvious. "I was under the impression that accomplishing that required that he reveal the original formula. *You* gave me that impression."

"I was mistaken. The data I've reviewed so far indicate he has revealed only those parts of the formula directly affected by the compound he's creating today."

"Your suggestion last night, I believe, Doctor, was to provide the boy access to our labs in the expectation he would have to expose the entire CLAIR formula in the process of his work."

"I said hope, Colonel, not expectation."

Fuchs's attention returned to the screen, where Joshua Wolfe continued to work on what was now a vial full of clear liquid. "I find myself growing distressed with your attitude in this matter."

"I'm afraid I don't understand."

"Come now, Doctor. Your 'creation' of this boy does not give you the right to play the doting father. If there is any pride to be taken in his work, it must come at his revelation of the original CLAIR formula. General Starr was quite clear on the ramifications of Tuesday's failed test. We have precious little time left to preserve our very existence. Certainly no time to waste coddling and appeasing this boy."

"My concerns are long-term, Colonel." Haslanger spoke with his eyes glued to the screen, watching Joshua Wolfe's each and every move with reverence. "If coddling and appeasing him will eventually make the boy more comfortable in our midst, what he will eventually produce for us is limitless."

Fuchs's expression shifted between a sneer and a smile. "Oh, he'll produce it all right, and soon. You see, I've prepared a different strategy. . . ."

CHAPTER 25

"You wanted to see me," Susan said, from the other side of the isolation lab where Joshua Wolfe was working.

He looked at her through the thick glass. "There are some items I need from ordnance." His voice was picked up by an unseen microphone, just as hers was.

As they had planned before, Susan had made sure to sit behind a computer Josh had already keyed into the one he was using, forming their own private network. Knowing Fuchs and Haslanger could hear and see everything they did, Susan rested her hands innocently and unobtrusively on the terminal keys. The angle the computer was set at prevented the video camera from getting a clear view.

Josh was well aware that everything which flashed across his screen was relayed to Fuchs and Haslanger, so he had arranged some camouflage. He had already keyed in a program that would broadcast random repetition of his work in place of what he was actually typing. All he had to do was give the proper command and Group Six's electronic eavesdropping on him would cease temporarily.

"How are you coming with the addition to the formula?" Susan asked.

Josh's response was to continue typing in apparent disinterest. He looked up and nodded ever so slightly.

"It's ready now," he said, the intent of his words clear.

And she typed a message that appeared instantly on his screen:

WHEN WILL YOU BE READY?

THIRTY MINUTES, Josh typed.

Eight o'clock sharp, Susan calculated, fingers ready on her keys again, as the next part of Josh's message appeared on her screen:

YOU HAVE TO GET WHAT WE NEED.

I'M NOT CONVINCED THEY'LL GIVE THEM TO ME.

DON'T WORRY. THEY WILL. THEY'LL GIVE YOU
ANYTHING I TELL THEM TO GIVE YOU.

Susan continued to speak in meaningless rehearsed banter
while she waited for more of Josh's words to slither across
her screen. When none came, she typed:

HOW MUCH TIME WILL WE HAVE?

His answer was immediate. ELEVEN MINUTES.

She waited for him to print out his list of requirements and
then moved for the door.

The hatch caved inward under the force of McCracken's
shoulder, revealing the expected presence of a second tunnel-
like pipeline meeting the first to form a sharply slanted *V*.
McCracken ran a chemical sensor across the walls and
checked the readouts on the miniature LED screen.

"Clean, Indian," he said to Wareagle. "Been a while since
they dumped anything. Makes this our lucky day. We've got
our road in."

A difficult road, as it turned out, since going uphill along
the cold, smooth surface was much harder than going down.
With only the tube's siding to use for handholds, Blaine found
his progress coming painfully slow. It took over thirty minutes
to reach the first break in the piping Group Six had secretly
installed to link up with Brookhaven's abandoned secondary
toxic waste dumping system. Straight before them lay a hatchway, while the line itself banked sharply to the left.

Blaine ran his hands along the hatch. "What do you say we
have a look behind this?"

Johnny had already broken out a fresh torch and was moving forward to take the first shift. He fired up the torch and
started it along the top of the hatchway's perimeter. Another
thirty minutes passed with Blaine and Johnny trading places
as they worked. McCracken was holding the torch when the
blue-hot flame at last finished outlining the hatch's perimeter
at the weld points. This time no shoulder was required; the
hatch simply dropped inward. Blaine shone his flashlight inside and saw what could only be described as a temporary
holding chamber. A number of weapons already into produc-

tion sat stockpiled against all four walls. McCracken quickly
realized the ease with which they could be disposed of, thanks
to the hold's proximity to the dump hatch. That, of course,
was the idea. In the event of attack or attempted takeover, the
contents of this hold could simply be flushed away with the
rest of the discharge originating elsewhere in the Group Six
facility.

"This wasn't on the plans, Indian."

"We are beneath the complex's final sublevel, Blainey. This
chamber must link up with a tunnel that runs most of the
length of Group Six." Johnny swept his flashlight about.
"Through there."

McCracken's eyes followed the beam. "Doesn't look
good."

The room's only door resembled that of a bank vault, much
too thick to break through with either the torch or the explosives they had brought along.

Blaine moved closer to the door and ran the flashlight's
beam down its length slowly. "Electronic seal alterable only
from the outside, unless we can figure out a way to short-
circuit it from in here."

"The control panel must be inside one of these walls."

"Let's see if we can find it, Indian."

Susan moved down the hallway, keenly aware of the closed-
circuit cameras that no doubt followed her every move. She
hurried to the ordnance control area with the memo Josh had
given her on the pretext of needing certain items to complete
his work. The clerk read the list, raised his eyebrows and read
it again. There was a desperate, breath-stealing moment when
he dialed up a superior for authorization. His expression was
unchanged as he hung up the phone.

"This will take some time."

"I'm not in any rush," Susan told him.

The case he handed her several minutes later was light
enough for Susan to carry easily down the hall to the lab where
Joshua Wolfe was closeted. She walked with the fear that
Fuchs or Haslanger could appear at any moment and ask to
inspect the case's contents. Or perhaps they had been testing

her all along and would be waiting to intercept her outside the lab.

But she reached the lab without incident and waited for Josh to buzz her in. Inside she closed the door behind her and rested the case on the closest table.

"Get ready," he said softly.

His fingers flew across the keyboard of one of the computers, while she used hers to open the case. She had just removed two sets of night vision goggles, rendered less cumbersome and bulky than ordinary ones courtesy of Group Six, when Josh hit the execute key.

McCracken was working futilely with the wires revealed behind a plate in the wall next to the vault door when the overhead light he had managed to find died. A metallic click sounded at the same time he located his flashlight and switched it on.

"Power failure, Blainey," said Wareagle, turning his on as well.

"Means that click was the backup security system being activated to keep intruders from getting in here."

"But not keeping us out."

"My thoughts exactly," Blaine said, and returned to his work.

Not more than a minute later, he succeeded in crossing the proper two wires. A second click sounded as the backup system disengaged and the door's electronic seal parted. Wareagle eased it forward effortlessly. It opened onto a narrow corridor that, as expected, wound tunnel-like beneath the installation.

"I don't know where this leads, Indian, but it's got to be better than where we are now."

Blaine noticed the duffel they had dragged with them was now overstuffed with equipment Wareagle had selected from among the stockpile the chamber contained.

"For when we get there, Blainey," Johnny said, hoisting it effortlessly over his shoulder.

Every bit of power inside the Group Six complex had died. Josh's earlier preparation behind the keyboard and most recent commands had also cut off the emergency backup system from the grid. The generators had been automatically activated, yes, but the juice they spewed outward never reached the feed lines.

The plunge into utter darkness stunned Susan, even though she had prepared herself for it. Joshua Wolfe was only a yard from her but she had totally lost her bearings and felt panic rearing to overtake her.

"Here," the boy's voice called. "I'm here."

She pushed her panic down and reached over to Josh. He took one of the goggles from her hand and fit it over his eyes, then helped her do the same. With only the outside light sneaking in through the mirrored windows to use, the updated goggles were of minimal aid. Enough, though, to see a number of yards forward and anything that lay directly ahead of them.

"Come on!" Josh shouted, taking Susan's hand and heading for the door.

She had made sure not to let it seal all the way so they wouldn't be trapped as most everyone else in Group Six must have been. The electronic keying necessary to leave or enter virtually any facility could effectively turn the complex into a prison if the proper circumstances were introduced. That was what had made Josh so confident about this plan. His eleven-minute estimate was based on the amount of time it would take Group Six control room personnel to run a bypass and override his command to the physical plant of the system.

Josh and Susan had the hall to themselves and they ran hand-in-hand down it, following the path she had memorized to the garage area. They could enter it by stairs through doors not fitted with keypads or slots. Josh had already ordered the computer to switch various bay doors in the garage on the third sublevel to manual operation. At that point any of the parked cars would do nicely as an escape vehicle, gunning up the steep ramp and then toward the fence with no fear of the motion or infrared detectors setting off the immobilized lasers.

Susan estimated they reached the stairs just past the two-minute mark and would reach the garage with still more than eight to go. Allotting three to find a vehicle and then open a main bay still left five to flee the grounds.

Plenty of time, she thought, and kept running.

*   *   *

Johnny and Blaine followed the circuitous length of the darkened tunnel in single file, searching for hatchways that might provide entry to the primary installation. McCracken figured this passageway had been constructed to allow for the transport of hazardous material from one section of the installation to the other without the risk of contaminating the entire facility. If he was right, there would be access points at regular intervals.

"Blainey," Johnny Wareagle signaled, when they came to the first one: a hatchway a foot above them, accessible by a ladder built into the wall.

McCracken took the rungs and balanced himself awkwardly. He spun the wheel attached to the hatch until he heard a click. He felt it release and then lowered it slowly. A familiar smell flooded his nostrils.

"Think I know where we—"

A gush of light streaming through the hatch from above forced McCracken to cut his words off. He dropped off the ladder and clung to the wall opposite Johnny, pistol ready when he heard the voice.

Joshua Wolfe and Susan Lyle dashed down the steps. The night vision goggles, hardly bulkier than a sophisticated swimming set, gave the darkened stairwell a dull orange hue. Three floors down Susan pushed through the door that opened onto a corridor leading to the garage. Josh was at her side when they reached the door at its end. Susan threw her shoulder into it. The sea of vehicles swam in the orange-tinted darkness.

Then an incredibly intense burst of light, like an ultrapowerful flashbulb, burned her eyes. Her hands flailed for her goggles and she stumbled as she tore them off to see the garage aglow with its normal lighting. Her eyes watered, ravaged by pain, clearing to reveal Lester Fuchs and Erich Haslanger standing before her, flanked by two broad-shouldered men in sports jackets. Behind them, clinging to the shadows nearer the wall, loomed the massive shape of a man who didn't look like a man at all.

"I gave you a test," greeted the colonel. "You failed."

CHAPTER 26

"You have to pay for that," Blaine heard the voice continue after a pause long enough for the sound of footsteps to clack across the floor. "You and the boy both, Dr. Lyle."

Susan Lyle . . . the Firewatch team leader he'd encountered in Joshua Wolfe's room. Now their paths had crossed again, and this time the boy was with her.

McCracken gazed at Wareagle, whose eyes were riveted on the open hatchway, expecting an assault through it any moment. None came; the attention of those in the garage above was focused too intently elsewhere to notice the anomaly.

"I think we can dispense with the pleasantries," the voice continued, sounding farther away from the hatch. Fuchs's probably, or maybe Haslanger's. "Krill," he said, "bring her."

Blaine stiffened when a number of barely discernible footsteps clip-clopped across the asphalt. He recognized the sound from the assault on him in the New York Public Library by some hideous mutant, a *living* creation of Haslanger's, most likely.

McCracken waited until the sounds of voice and footsteps had vanished before he reached for the ladder again, his eyes seeking out Johnny's. "Find us something to travel in, Indian, and get ready for a rough ride."

"What am I to do with you?" Colonel Fuchs accused Susan and Joshua Wolfe, shaking his head as he closed the door to the test chamber behind him. "I don't want to be unreasonable, in spite of your abuse of my trust. Let's just talk for a moment."

The chamber where his guards had escorted Susan and Josh consisted of a small viewing gallery looking straight through a glass wall into an inner room that was currently dark.

"Sit, please," Fuchs ordered.

Susan and Josh took chairs at the observation room's single table. The broad-shouldered security men stood rigid at either end. Dr. Haslanger lingered behind Fuchs, but it was the man-shape who had accompanied them up from the garage Josh found both repulsive and fascinating at the same time.

"I see Krill has secured your interest, young man," Fuchs continued.

"He makes me sick."

"He shouldn't: you're very much the same, he and you."

The boy's face knotted up in puzzlement.

"You belong here, my boy, just as he does," Fuchs continued. "You are as much a part of this place as any of the other experiments we have conducted. You are nothing more than the residue of one lost in the past before our tenure began."

"Why don't you tell him the truth, Colonel?" Susan shot out suddenly. "Why don't you tell him the only thing he's here for is to save your ass? Washington's ready to toss you out and shut this place down." She stole a quick glance at Josh before proceeding. "Don't bother to unpack your bags."

Fuchs's eyes blazed her way. "I'm most impressed, Doctor. It would seem your expertise at research does not stop with test tubes."

"You looked into my background. I looked into yours."

"And it all comes down to backgrounds, doesn't it? Yours, mine . . ." His stare swept back on Josh. "His."

Josh returned the stare wordlessly.

"Come now, young man, can it be that you have not come to suspect the truth even in the aftermath of your conversation with Dr. Haslanger last night? Think of his past."

Josh's eyes flew from Fuchs to Haslanger and then back to Fuchs. He looked dumbfounded. His lips trembled.

"The connection should have been obvious to someone of your intelligence. Dr. Haslanger *created* you. You are the product of one of his early experiments before he joined Group Six. It was called Operation Offspring. And its purpose was the *creation* of genius, to be used in any way its creators desired."

"My God," Susan muttered.

Fuchs let his eyes wander to the man-monster, ignoring her. "Now, Krill was created for an entirely different purpose altogether. The desired genetic elements of other species identified and blended to form . . . well, you can see what they form. Not all the products of the good doctor's work turned out as they were supposed to, but Krill is as close as he ever came."

"You're the real monster here, Colonel," Susan said sharply.

But Fuchs didn't so much as gaze her way. "You, my boy, on the other hand, are exactly what he envisioned you would be. But circumstances forced him to abandon your development, the careful grooming that would have assured you achieving an even higher level of your capabilities. Regrettable but necessary."

"Bullshit," said Joshua Wolfe. "You've been steering my life for as long as I can remember."

"Not us, I'm afraid. We would have handled the situation with considerably more tact and responsibility than Dr. Haslanger's replacement. Beyond that we would have provided you with the resources that would have much more fully allowed you to realize your potential. As proof I offer this."

Fuchs placed a small vial that had been found in Joshua Wolfe's pocket on the table before the boy. "A most productive day on your part," he said, "thanks to the wondrous facilities we are blessed with."

The boy remained silent.

"I am assuming the contents of this vial represent your attempt to 'fix' CLAIR."

The boy nodded.

"Of course, there is nothing wrong with CLAIR. From our perspective it worked just fine in Cambridge and we would like to acquire it in precisely that form. I would ask that you now provide us with the formula."

"So you can kill more selectively than you've done so far," Susan broke in. "Not the kind of track record that inspires any faith. Where would you test CLAIR out first, Colonel? Where would you botch things next time?"

Fuchs finally looked at her. "I would suggest you are no

one to speak. A woman who took her maternal instincts too far. You interfered, Dr. Lyle. I trusted you and you abused my trust.''

"You set me up from the beginning.''

"A safety net, nothing more.''

"You knew I'd help the boy escape. You knew I couldn't let you have him.''

In that instant Josh realized all eyes in the room were on Susan. Before any stares turned back on him, he reached forward and snatched the vial of clear liquid, bringing it into his lap before stuffing it into his pocket.

"Because you are unfalteringly predictable. Of course, the methodology of your and the boy's plan was obvious. All we had to do was wait for you to commit yourselves.''

"I was right to try. This proves it.''

"And tell me what it's gained you. Do you feel better, more motherly, for the effort? Do you think you have somehow beaten back the dreaded cancer that is probably just beginning to show itself as microscopic cellular abnormalities no one can detect in your system? You can't save yourself, Doctor, and you cannot save Joshua Wolfe. There are bigger things than both of you.''

"You, for instance.''

"Me? No. Group Six, yes. To pursue what this country needs to survive, there is no rule that can't be broken, no step I will not take.'' Fuchs nodded to himself and turned back to Joshua Wolfe. "The formula for CLAIR. Now, please.''

Josh shook his head in stiff defiance. "I won't give it to you. I won't give you anything.''

"Please reconsider.''

He shook his head again.

Fuchs sighed in genuine regret and nodded to the two broad-shouldered security men. As Josh watched, they grabbed Susan, hoisted her from her chair and dragged her to another chair set away from the table. One plunked her down into it while the other tied her arms behind her.

"What are you doing?'' Josh demanded. "Let her go!''

"I will, young man,'' Fuchs assured him. "All you have to do is cooperate.''

"Let her go!"

Krill stepped forward and pulled an odd-looking object, like a single-barreled gun with a button instead of a trigger, from his pocket. A foot long maybe, its exterior shining in the room's dull light.

"You know what that is, of course," Fuchs prodded.

"No," said Josh, "I don't."

"Dr. Haslanger, if you don't mind . . ."

The old man moved slightly forward. "You are familiar with the Taser electric shocking device, I assume. This is a variation we have developed here, equipped with variable voltage settings instead of a single one. The barrel shoots out a pair of prods at a distance we have raised to thirty feet, capable of delivering shock ranging from incapacitating to fatal."

"Ten settings," Fuchs picked up. "We'll start at five."

Krill switched the shock gun to the proper level.

"There is no need to feign bravery at this point, Dr. Lyle," Fuchs told her. "You are among friends."

Krill stood ten feet in front of Susan, optimum distance.

"Now, Dr. Lyle, I suggest you advise your young friend to give us what we want. I suggest you advise him to tell us where the fax machine chip containing the formula for CLAIR can be found."

"Go to hell," she said, trying hard not to look at Krill.

"Young man," followed Fuchs, turning his attention to Josh, "I suggest you show some maturity where Dr. Lyle is clearly not prepared to. Your brother Krill is even less patient than I am. Please give us what we want."

Trembling, Josh looked at Susan for guidance. Her rigid expression told him what he had to do.

"I'm not giving you anything." He swept a hand through his hair and found it was shaking badly.

"Krill," Fuchs signaled.

The giant steadied the shock gun.

"Wait!" Josh shouted, leaning forward without leaving his chair.

"Have you changed your mind, young man?"

"I, I . . ."

"Fire."

Krill pressed the button.

*   *   *

McCracken pinned his shoulders at the break in the corridor leading to the room Susan Lyle and Joshua Wolfe had been ushered into and studied the guards posted on either side of the door twenty feet from him. Twenty feet was too much to cover in a single dash. Blaine was considering his options when he heard the scream. A woman's scream, a high-pitched wail elevated by awful pain.

Susan Lyle . . .

The realization reduced his options to one.

McCracken hurled himself into the hall, both his gun and his eyes aimed away from the guards, pretending to be one of them, approaching as if panicked.

"Is the colonel inside?" he yelled, not quite turning.

The two men gazed at each other, hands near their guns, clearly unsure of how to react.

"Is the colonel—"

That was all McCracken needed to add to bring him close enough to dispose of them. He slammed the barrel of his pistol into the jaw of the closest and then lurched toward the second man, who had just drawn his gun. Blaine rammed his tightly curled knuckles straight into his windpipe, shattering it and sending the man's hands clawing for his throat as he slumped, eyes bulging. The first man managed to turn on him, face a mess of torn flesh and dripping blood, and McCracken slashed his SIG butt-first into the bridge of his nose. Blaine felt the bone crack and recede. The man crumpled.

McCracken turned instantly and pulled from his pocket a prewired pack of C-4 plastic explosives. He peeled the protective coating off the detonator and wedged it against the door near the frame. Then he popped the detonator outward. Its trigger had a twenty-second delay, which gave him plenty of time to poise himself against the wall a safe distance away, pistol ready and ears plugged.

The shock gun hadn't so much as moved in the giant's hand. He activated the retracting mechanism and the barrel swallowed up the miniature electric prods once more. Susan was writhing in the chair now, spasms racking her body. A trickle of blood slid from her mouth where the convulsions had forced her teeth into her tongue. Finally she slumped as low as her bonds would allow.

Fifteen feet away, Josh's eyes tried to find life in her cloudy gaze.

"Stop," he mouthed, then said out loud, "Stop it."

"We want the formula, young man," Fuchs told him. "Give it to us."

Josh looked at Susan, back at Fuchs.

"Krill," the colonel said, "turn the setting up to seven." Eyes back on Josh. "I'd speak now if I were you, young man."

Josh watched the giant steadying the shock gun on Susan once more. "It's here," he said, words racing ahead of his thoughts.

Fuchs looked at Haslanger briefly. "What do you mean it's *here*?"

"The fax chip. It's in my room. I brought it here from Florida."

"You were searched thoroughly in the hotel. Sinclair assured me of that."

"Not thoroughly enough. I stuck the chip in the center of a piece of gum and stuck the gum inside my mouth. I took it out in the bathroom on the plane."

"Where in your room, young man?"

Josh swallowed hard. "She needs a doctor. I want you to get her a doctor first."

Fuchs turned toward the giant. "Krill."

Josh sprung from his chair. "Candy jar. One of the pieces near the top. Inside the wrapper."

Fuchs smiled. "That's better."

"Now get her a doctor!"

Fuchs's smile disappeared, a vile and toothless sneer taking its place. "No need. You must be taught a lesson. You must learn what happens from this point on if you disobey me."

"*No!*"

"Raise the setting to ten," Fuchs ordered Krill. "Then kill her."

Josh stood there, suspended between thoughts, ready to give it all up. "There's another vial! Of CLAIR!"

"Did you say . . ."

Josh watched Krill steadying the shock gun, huge elongated finger going for the fire button, and threw himself into motion forward, intending to crash into Susan and take her from the deadly path of the prods.

He had just reached her when he heard a soft popping sound at the same time the Taser's prods lodged against him. It was like grazing up against something hot and not being able to pull away. Everything seemed to lock up and stiffen as he was caught between breaths. Even his eyes locked open, watching the door when it exploded inward.

The force of the blast tumbled Susan's chair over and took Josh with it. McCracken vaguely recorded that sight as he followed the remnants of the door into the room. The fall had separated Susan Lyle from the chair. He stripped the rope from her wrists and yanked her to her feet at the same time he recognized the still form of Joshua Wolfe lying spread across the tile floor. He shoved Susan behind him, covering her with his body as he opened fire on the pair of big men the explosion had hurled against a glass wall.

They had managed to free their guns when his bullets found them, slamming them back into the glass with enough force to crack it. Meanwhile, he turned his focus on a pair of figures forced to the floor by the exploding door and scampering for cover.

"Watch out!"

Susan Lyle's scream alerted him to motion to his right just as he was angling to steady his gun on who could only be Fuchs and Haslanger. The monster he recognized all too well from the New York Public Library was steadying something with a barrel on him. He dove as the monster fired and felt a pair of sizzling electrodes shoot over his head. He opened fire on the monster with the rest of the SIG's clip while still in his dive, his bullets off the mark but close enough to force the monster to lunge behind a toppled table. Blaine used the opportunity to jam a fresh clip into his pistol and open fire on the thick table to keep the monster pinned behind it, giving him time to hoist the limp form of Joshua Wolfe up in one arm.

"Go! *Now!*" Blaine ordered Susan, who, though unsteady on her feet, managed to stumble into the hallway.

Once he joined her, McCracken shifted Josh to his left shoulder, leaving his right hand totally free to use the SIG, just as a half-dozen security guards rushed forward with pistols drawn.

"Down!" Blaine screamed at Susan and drained the rest of his second clip.

The men dropped in eerie precision before him and Mc-Cracken hardly had to break stride to speed by their bodies, the boy he recognized from Harry's picture bouncing upon his shoulder.

"Take a left here!" Blaine told Susan. "Second stairwell on the right. Then straight back to the garage."

He sensed her stiffen at the mention of their destination and didn't bother explaining his reasons for the instruction. They had just reached the stairwell in question when the emergency alarm began to wail throughout Group Six.

Johnny Wareagle was waiting for them in the garage next to a six-wheel RV-type vehicle made of solid black steel. The top hatch was open, the engine warming, and the nose angled straight for an open garage bay.

"Best I could find, Blainey," Wareagle said, taking Joshua Wolfe from him.

"Get the boy inside! Her too!"

"You drive, Blainey."

"We'll have to get through those lasers, Indian."

"That is why you must drive."

"Hurry!" Susan pleaded desperately. "I don't think he's breathing!"

Blaine noticed Joshua Wolfe's lips were turning blue as Johnny lowered him into the RV. Spittle was running from the corners of his mouth and he seemed to be convulsing.

Susan had climbed into the armored RV cabin first and helped Johnny ease the boy across one of the seats. His body was utterly still now.

"No," she moaned. "No . . ."

"Go, Blainey!" Johnny urged when McCracken was barely settled behind the wheel.

The RV's huge tires spun and screamed as McCracken shoved it into gear. Wareagle ducked down and reached for a riflelike weapon with what appeared to be a shower head at the end of its barrel. He also shouldered a pair of packs containing what looked at first glance to be field radios but were something else altogether. Blaine recalled they were among the items Wareagle had recovered from the storage chamber and packed away. Clearly, he had figured out their purpose and operation.

Susan's pumping adrenaline enabled her to shake off the tingly, numbing effects of her own shock and she began compressing Joshua Wolfe's chest in the familiar motions of CPR. Then she tilted his head back and forced breath down his throat.

"Come on! Come on! *Don't quit on me!*" Heaving for breath herself as she went back to chest compressions, pushing the blood through his body.

McCracken drove through the bay and up the steep ramp that led back to ground level.

"Uh-oh," he muttered as the climb neared its end at a twin door Johnny had obviously not manage to get open. "Hold on!"

Blaine drove the RV straight into the door, accelerating all the while. It didn't break or shatter but snapped off its hinges and flew to the side as McCracken tore off across the grassy field.

Susan held Josh steady through it but his body still bobbed limply, limbs spraying in all directions like a puppet with its strings cut. In the rearview mirror Blaine watched her alternate again between chest compressions and forced breaths, while Johnny prepared for the next stage of their escape.

"They're out!" Sinclair reported from the garage.

An out-of-breath Colonel Lester Fuchs had just reached the command center, handkerchief pressed against his head to stanch the flow of blood from a wound suffered from flying glass.

"Do not pursue!" he heaved. "Repeat, do not pursue! We'll let the lasers disable them."

"Security systems all functional," Larsen reported from his station. "All lights are green."

"Confirm automated mode."

"Automated mode confirmed, sir."

Fuchs steadied himself against the back of a chair and turned back to the security monitors before him as the first of the perimeter's cameras picked up the RV speeding forward.

Johnny Wareagle had popped opened the RV's top-mounted hatch and squeezed himself halfway through, his face and torso braced in the warm night air.

"Lasers, Indian," Blaine called back to him. "Coming up!"

Wareagle flipped a switch on the first of his unidentified packs and hurled it outward, ahead of them to the left. He did the same with the second and tossed it far away and to the right. He ducked back down quickly into the RV and closed the hatch behind him.

No explosions followed, just a brief ear-rattling whine that chilled the spine like fingernails down a chalkboard. Blaine felt the RV buckle, waver, and nearly stall. The instruments on the dashboard were going crazy. The clock went out altogether.

"I'll be damned," he said as they surged farther into the night.

The monitor screens containing shots of Group Six's front perimeter all died at once; at the same time the complex's lights blinked once and then came back on, slightly dimmer.

"What happened?" Fuchs demanded of Larsen. "What's wrong?"

"They must have used the NEPPs," said Haslanger, who had just appeared in the command center. He leaned against the wall, his face a mass of small cuts and lacerations.

"The *what*?"

"Nonnuclear electromagnetic pulse packs. Setting them off has effectively shut down the motion and infrared sensors in the field, as well as our monitoring systems."

"What about the lasers?"

"They're powered from here," Larsen answered. "Should still be functional."

"Then use them!" he ordered, forgetting about the gash in his skull and letting the blood trickle down his collar to the back of his uniform. "Switch to manual!"

"We'll be firing blind, sir."

"I don't care! Just *fire*! Fire at anything, fire at *everything*! Now! Do you hear me? *Now*! . . ."

CHAPTER 27

Susan had stopped her CPR long enough to lower an ear to Joshua Wolfe's chest.

"He's breathing! He's breathing!"

Suddenly the boy began to convulse again, body twitching and writhing as if trying to tear from her determined grasp. Susan pulled Josh against her own body and held him tight as his damaged nerve endings tried to shake the life from him again.

In front of them Johnny Wareagle, his head and shoulders again squeezed through the RV's ceiling hatch, brought the strange-looking rifle up to his shoulder like any normal gun. It was equipped with an infrared zoom sight that functioned like the close-up lens of a camera. Group Six personnel would be firing the lasers on manual now without benefit of their sophisticated sensors. That evened the odds enough so that, along with the power and strength of the RV's hull, this weapon of Johnny's would hopefully safeguard their escape from the Group Six complex.

It delivered a powerful stream of aerosol through its showerheadlike muzzle, an aerosol that turned metal brittle on contact, rendering it useless. The laser firing devices that looked like underground sprinklers were made of metal.

The aerosol contents were held under pressure in a thick, canlike magazine just in front of the trigger guard. Johnny had wedged three additional clips in his belt for easy access. He swept the area with his naked eye, aerosol gun ready, when a series of lasers to the RV's right began firing wildly in all directions. A pair of beams sliced across the RV's fender and rear quarter panel, leaving blackened metal in their wake. Johnny swung the gun toward the position of the mushrooms, sighted and fired.

A narrow stream of the instantly corrosive aerosol shot outward. It took only a short burst to render the lasers inoperative and Johnny quickly settled into a rhythm. Since the gun had no kick whatsoever, aiming it along the sight and then firing was really all he had to do. The stream went where he was looking.

"On the right, Indian!" Blaine called to him. "Lasers coming up!"

Wareagle swung that way, adjusting the firing nozzle in the process. As expected, he was able to widen the stream to cover more of the lasers with a single burst, at the sacrifice of distance. An unexpected bonus came when a glance through the sight showed him its field had widened to the same extent as the aerosol stream. He fired and the burst knocked out a whole nest of lasers that had barely missed the RV. As that unit of blue beams of deadly light ceased abruptly, Johnny turned his weapon on another grouping that had just popped up.

A single blind-fired laser managed to pierce a wheel well and tire. The RV bucked and rattled but kept going. Wareagle used the rest of the first can to disable the grouping that laser was a part of and quickly inserted a fresh canister.

"Front, Indian!" Blaine signaled. "Both sides!"

Lasers had begun firing in erratic, crisscrossing beams fifteen yards from them on both the left and right. McCracken braked hard to stop from crossing their path and give Wareagle more time. Johnny fired to the left first and gray smoke from the suddenly corroding, brittle metal replaced the flashes of blue light on that side. He swung the other way just as a trio of beams hit the RV dead on in the front. Another tire blew out and the engine sputtered.

"Come on!" Blaine urged. "Come on!"

The RV responded, but it was badly hampered now. A lesser vehicle with normally thin steel and rubber would never have made it this far. But the RV's reinforced armor sheeting had kept the engine intact. The fence was in sight, and Blaine drove the RV on straight for one of the sections of steel link.

Another series of lasers opened fire directly before him and McCracken ducked an instant before a pair of slashing beams cut a neat slice right through the windshield. Fuses must have blown, because the RV's cab went totally dark. But Johnny

was up to the task yet again, calmly capturing the required
grid through his sight and spraying the aerosol with calculated
aim. Once again, the mushroomlike devices smoked, hissed
and gave up.

McCracken pushed the RV on, picking up as much speed
as possible en route to the fence. The remaining lasers were
still firing, out of Johnny's range now. Blaine could only hope
they wouldn't pierce anything vital, such as the gas tank, and
cause an instant explosion. Instead the beams that found them
only damaged the rear of the vehicle, blowing out the back
window and showering Josh and Susan with glass. Susan tried
to shield him as best she could with her own body, and felt
the shards pricking and digging into her back and arms.

"We're out of their range, Blainey."

"Then get yourself back inside, Indian, and hold on."

The nonnuclear electromagnetic pulse packs Johnny had
used had not affected the cameras mounted atop the fence. In
the Group Six command and communications center, the three
working screens showed their own updated RV bearing down
on one of the sections of fence. Fuchs watched helplessly as
the fence simply caved in and vanished under the RV's charge.

"Sinclair!" Fuchs called through the intercom system.

"Here, sir."

"They're out. All security systems disabled. Take up pursuit."

"Yes, sir."

With that, the four chase vehicles Sinclair had loaded with
men hurtled toward the open garage bays. Suddenly their
surges slowed to bucking skips. Then the engines died.

"What the fuck . . . Colonel Fuchs!" Sinclair called into his
communicator.

"We can't see you. Where are you?"

"We're stalled, sir. They must have done something to the
engines, sabotaged them. We're not going anywhere in these."

"Damn!" Fuchs blared, realizing McCracken's cohort,
whoever he was, must have also found and utilized the com-
pounds Group Six had developed that turned diesel fuel and
gasoline into jelly. But he was certain there weren't enough
samples stockpiled to cover all the vehicles in the motor pool.

"Listen to me, Sinclair. Check all the cars. Some of them will still be functional."

"Tires on the others are cut, sir."

"Take eight men around to the rear visitors' bay. There are two cars inside they couldn't have gotten to. I'll send down reinforcements to change those tires."

"Acknowledged, sir."

"Move!"

Fuchs punched up a fresh line on the phone next to him. "Brookhaven Security, come in."

"Brookhaven Security."

"This is Colonel Fuchs at Group Six. One of our vehicles has been stolen by intruders and is heading your way. Seal off the gate, but do not approach. Repeat, *do not approach!*"

The RV thumped and hunkered its way toward the gate at Brookhaven's main entrance.

"Here we go. Hang on!" Blaine called back to his passengers.

The RV slammed into the gate and shattered it, sending it swinging wildly sideways. McCracken managed to right the RV, even though it had taken on a leftward list. He bypassed the more heavily traveled William Floyd Parkway for a residential thoroughfare called Longwood Road.

"Two vehicles following, Blainey," Johnny Wareagle called from the rear of the RV.

"No way we can outrun them. This thing's gonna die on us any second." He stole a quick glance behind him at Susan, who was still working on the inert form of Joshua Wolfe. "Doesn't look like getting away on foot is an option, either."

The RV had begun to waver from side to side and he was powerless to keep it steady.

"That means we must make a stand, Blainey."

"Tough odds to beat without—" McCracken stopped when he saw the sign on the side of the road. "What do you think, Indian?"

"We could hope for no more, under the circumstances."

McCracken managed to swing the RV to the right toward a long, rectangular building, shiny letters rising into the night

from the front of its roof: LONGWOOD CENTRAL MIDDLE
SCHOOL.

Fuchs stared at the image of a bearded man caught by the
security cameras and then digitized for clarity by one of Group
Six's computers.

"His name is Blaine McCracken," Haslanger said from behind him. "Krill had a run-in with him yesterday. I think
you'll find his file most interesting."

It took a few seconds to bring up and Fuchs had just started
reading when the call came from Sinclair.

"They did *what*?" he demanded.

"They've pulled around behind the school building out of
sight," Sinclair reported.

"The vehicle?"

"Disabled. I'm certain."

Fuchs would have felt triumphant if not for the contents of
the file running down the screen before him. "Sinclair, I'm
ordering the bulk of our security force into the field to join
you, to make sure there are no surprises this time. Forty men."

"I hardly think I'll need that many, sir."

Fuchs was still reading. "You will. Believe me."

CHAPTER 28

Johnny Wareagle laid Joshua Wolfe across a lab table in one of the classrooms in the vacant school's science wing. They had passed the nurse's office, locked up for the night, on the way. Blaine had shot his way through the door and emerged with a first-aid kit in hand.

"Here," he said, offering it to Susan.

She didn't so much as look up from Josh's inert body. "Unless there's a portable defibrillating machine in there, don't bother."

She was compressing the boy's chest again as Blaine positioned himself to take over the breathing portion of the CPR.

"This is no good," she said, her breathing growing labored. "We're going to lose him."

"No defibrillator. Sorry."

"Not yet," Susan said, looking around the room before fixing her stare on Johnny Wareagle. "Take over for me. Please."

Johnny slid into place without missing a beat, his motions surprisingly gentle considering the power he was capable of exerting.

Susan disappeared briefly into an adjacent storage room located between this and another science lab. She reemerged holding what looked like a long, thin black box. Blaine recognized it as a simple voltage capacitor, a staple in every school science lab for use in any experiment dealing with electricity. He watched as she stripped the wires free of its back, revealing two pairs identical in all ways but color. She left the capacitor on another table near the closest electrical outlet and then strung the red and blue wires toward Josh. Johnny Wareagle suspended his rhythmic pumping long enough to allow her to strip open the boy's shirt and place the ends of the wires on either side of his pale chest.

Blaine couldn't believe his eyes. "You're not going to . . ."

"He'll die if I don't try."

Johnny went back to pumping, Blaine to breathing. Susan returned to the capacitor and lowered the white and black wires toward the electrical outlet.

"Stand clear on my signal. Ready . . . *now*!"

A brief sizzling sound followed and the lights dimmed momentarily as Josh's body lurched upward. Blaine started administering CPR again while Johnny felt the boy's heart. He looked at Susan and shook his head.

"Get ready to stand clear again. Ready . . . *now*!"

And again she jabbed the black and white wires into the wall socket, pulling them out after a single count.

Josh's body jumped again, back arching as the current jolted his body. Johnny Wareagle gave a great sigh and nodded.

"He's breathing!" Blaine proclaimed as Susan rushed back to the boy.

"Normal cardiac rhythm," she announced happily, raising the ear she had lowered to his chest.

Watching her making use of whatever she could find to save the boy's life was eerily familiar to McCracken. In Vietnam he had seen plenty of medics at work in the field, poorly equipped and under intolerable conditions, men who could save kids who'd lost a chunk of their stomachs or skulls with no more than what they could carry in their backpacks. Holding them tight, soothing them with words while they waited for the drugs to take effect. Miracle workers in every sense of the word. It was easy to rip flesh apart. The real heroes were the ones who put it back together.

Watching Susan now, that was what he thought of. She moved with the same refined urgency the Nam medics did; she had the same *eyes*. Professional and unyielding. They could look into the gristle of a grunt's shrapnel or bullet-scorched wound and tie the ruptured arteries off with a shoelace, if that's what it took.

"He's not out of the woods yet," she reported. "Far from it."

"It won't matter unless the Indian and I can work *our* kind of magic," McCracken told her.

"In here, Blainey," Johnny said from the entrance to the storage room.

McCracken joined him inside and saw the chemicals lined up in jars and containers filling shelves from floor to ceiling.

"Charcoal . . . sulphur . . . and . . . saltpeter," he said as he pulled each from the shelves. "Everything we need, Indian."

"Just about, Blainey."

McCracken was nodding, his thoughts mirroring Wareagle's. "Some one-inch PVC pipes—foot-long connectors, preferably—and seals to go atop them."

"Heavy-duty twine, too, for fuses," Johnny added.

"All likely to be available in the wood or metal shop," McCracken suggested.

Johnny hurried off, leaving Blaine to his part of the work. He had no idea how long they had before the school would come under siege by Group Six troops. It would take a certain amount of time to gather and equip Fuchs's men as well as transport them to the school. Say half an hour maybe, twenty minutes at the very least.

He cleared off a table in the center of the storage room and placed on it the three jars he had pulled from the shelves.

"Gunpowder," Susan said, reading their labels from the doorway.

"How's the kid?"

"His vital signs are normal. He's stable for now."

"Good, because I need you. There are some candles there on the right." And, after Susan quickly located them, "Break them into small pieces while I start mixing these powders up. Then melt them. You'll find the Bunsen burners over—"

"I see them."

He half watched her pile the resulting fragments of wax into a dish over a Bunsen burner he had found on another shelf. The hiss of its blue flame splashed heat upward and the wax began to melt almost instantly.

Satisfied, he turned his attention to emptying the proper amounts of sulphur, saltpeter and charcoal into a plastic bowl and swirled them together. That done, he located a tray containing a dozen large test tubes and rested it on the table next to the bowl half filled with what was now gunpowder. The tubes jangled together in their slots. He stuck a funnel in the

first and held it in place while Susan filled it. They repeated
the process with the other tubes, enough gunpowder to fill ten
in all.

When they were finished, Blaine searched the shelves until
he found a glass jar containing potassium nitrate.

"What's that for?" Susan asked him.

"Turning our twine into fuses once the Indian gets back
with it."

He had just poured the potassium nitrate into a steel bowl
when Johnny Wareagle returned and set a box down on the
counter adjacent to the table Susan and Blaine been working
on.

"Eight pieces of PVC piping," he said to both of them,
displaying one of the sections. It was a foot long by an inch
and a half in diameter. McCracken laid the pipes out in a neat
row before him while Wareagle began the process of sealing
their bottoms with hard rubber stoppers. Susan, meanwhile,
got ready to pour in the contents of the test tubes they had
filled.

"Not yet," Blaine told her, his eyes sweeping about the
shelves again. "One more thing we've got to add . . ."

By the time Wareagle finished sealing the bottom ends of
the PVC pipes, McCracken had found what he was looking
for: a jar of phosphorus. He took the first finished pipe and
filled it almost to the one-quarter point with the shiny gray
powder. He repeated that process with the remaining seven
while Wareagle poured a bit of water atop the evened-off powder and Susan funneled the melted wax into a narrow beaker.
Then she poured a small measure atop the water in each of
the eight plastic pipes.

While Susan poured the wax, Blaine turned his attention to
the twine Johnny had brought with him from the shop. Working in tandem, they cut off eight foot-long strands and laid
them in the bowl of potassium nitrate to soak, turning them
flammable.

Turning them into fuses.

By that time the wax had hardened, trapping the water and
phosphorus inside the pipes and assuring separation from the
gunpowder they poured in through funnels. Susan managed to
locate eight hard rubber test tube stoppers of the proper di-

ameter to fit the top of the pipes, each equipped with a hole which would save them the trouble of drilling one to accommodate the makeshift fuses. Blaine twisted the stoppers into the open tops of the pipes and squeezed them in as far as they would go.

Johnny had already removed the foot-long strips of twine from the bowl of potassium nitrate and laid them across some paper towels on the table.

"Five minutes to dry, Indian."

"Leaving us time for other projects."

"*Other* projects?"

"The spirits were kind to us tonight, Blainey. I found something else in the shop area we can use."

"Not bad, Indian," Blaine said when he saw what Johnny had waiting for him in the lobby.

The logistics of the school's sprawling layout made enacting an elaborate defense difficult at best. The two-story main wing of the building, which contained the science labs and lobby, ran north and south, while a pair of parallel one-story wings connected to it here and next to the nurse's office ran east and west. The main wing was closer to the woods lying on the outer rim of the playing fields which extended the length of the parallel corridors, all the way to the street beyond where the enemy was undoubtedly amassing. Primary points of access, then, were three: the main entrance, and the two hallways accessible via a second school entrance too far away—and close to the street—to be defensible. Clearly they could not stop the enemy from entering; their strategy turning toward cutting off their approach to the main wing. And the twin tanks Johnny Wareagle had hauled up from the school's shop would certainly prove beneficial here.

"Acetylene," Blaine said, gazing at them.

Johnny had placed the tanks at the head of the hallway on the school's right side where it joined with the lobby. They would be visible from atop the stairwell leading to the second floor directly behind them but, more importantly, not from the main entry doors on the right past the main office.

Blaine watched Wareagle produce a hammer from his back pocket and carefully begin tapping the valves on each of the twin tanks. Too soft would have too slow an effect. Too hard might pop them off prematurely. Johnny fell into an easy rhythm, the *chink-chink* sound no louder than a clock's ticking.

"One more hard knock will do it, Blainey," he said when McCracken returned from the nearby school library with a pair of huge dictionaries.

Blaine gazed down the hall that led to the library and the other wing of the building. A pair of double doors stood at the foot of a slight decline sixty feet away. Anyone entering from the opposite end of the building and taking this corridor would have to pass through those doors to get to the main wing.

Johnny followed his eyes and his thoughts. "They open to the outside, Blainey."

"Meaning someone coming toward us from the other end of the building would have to *pull* them. . . ."

They looked at each other, no need for further discussion. Together they centered the tanks directly in front of those doors at the very start of the hall's decline. While Johnny held the tanks in place, Blaine positioned the books so the loosened valves would strike them if toppled. Then he fastened one end of the heavy twine they had used to make fuses for the pipe bombs to the top of the acetylene tanks at the same time Wareagle ran the remainder out all the way to the closed double doors. He looped the twine through both handles and pulled until it stretched taut while McCracken held fast to the tanks so they would do no more than wobble from the strain.

"That's one route of access to us covered, Blainey."

"And I've got an—"

"Hey," Susan Lyle called from near the stairwell that spiraled up to the school's second floor. She was holding a large glass jug in either hand. The strain of lugging them had turned her face beet red. "I thought you might be able to use these."

Blaine gazed briefly at Johnny before speaking. "What are they?"

"This," she said, looking to her right, "is ammonium hydroxide. Doesn't like oxygen. Mixing the two makes lots of problems for whoever's around." Susan looked to her left now. "And this is sulfuric acid. Doesn't like water. Soon as they mix . . ."

"We get the idea," McCracken told her. "Kid still holding his own?"

"For now, but until he regains consciousness we won't know how deep the damage goes. Serious electric shock is known to, well . . ." Her voice faded out at the end, almost breaking.

"What is it?"

"It should have . . . been me. The charge . . . He dove in front of it."

"You saved his life. Makes you even."

"Not if he doesn't recover."

"Blame Fuchs."

"That won't help if he dies."

"You've got to *make* it help, Doctor. It's how you get through."

"We were talking about me, not you."

"Lessons of experience. Figured I'd share them."

Wareagle's eyes shifted to the wall-length window that ran along part of the hallway, attracted to it like a dog to a sudden scent.

"They're here, Blainey," was all he said.

"Is there anything else I can do?" Susan asked both of them.

Blaine looked at Johnny before responding. "As a matter of fact, there is."

As promised, forty men had joined Sinclair across the street and out of sight from the Longwood Central Middle School. It had been twenty minutes since he had made his call to Fuchs, but according to the men he had posted at discreet distances around the building, no one had exited. That meant McCracken and the others were still inside, either seeking refuge or preparing for the inevitable battle.

Sinclair had planned for the latter. Each of the men dispatched from Group Six was wearing a flak jacket. Almost all carried M-16s, some of which were equipped with sniper scopes. A few carried the M-79 version, which combined the M-16 with slide-loaded grenade launcher mounted beneath its barrel. Others wore fragmentary and percussion grenades hanging from their belts or vest straps. Since this encounter was going to be fought on the move in restricted and limited confines, there was no reason for any weapons packing more firepower than these.

Colonel Fuchs had drawn Group Six's security personnel from the top government pools of former soldiers who were battle-hardened. Many had seen duty in covert operations co-ordinated by the CIA. Others had done stints as mercenaries in whatever country could pay them the most. The men arrived geared up and already divided into groups in response to Sinclair's specifications. He gathered the individual commanders at his car because it contained a direct link to Colonel Fuchs back at Group Six.

"Colonel?"

"Here, Sinclair."

"Sir, I am about to order the commanders to move their units into position. Gentlemen," he continued, holding the mike so Fuchs could hear, "move to your strike points and report in over C band on your walkie-talkies when you are in ready position." C band was a private, scrambled channel McCracken could not listen in on, assuming he had a com-municating device with him. "No one goes farther until you hear so from me. Is that clear?"

Five nods told him it was.

"Under no circumstances is there to be deviation from the parameters of the plan as I have expressed them. I know who we're dealing with here. You do not. My orders are in the best interests of this mission."

The nods came again. Sinclair was glad there hadn't been adequate time to brief the men assigned to him in more detail on Blaine McCracken and his Indian friend.

"Move out," he ordered, and the commanders scattered back to take their units.

They were back in the science lab, Susan Lyle again hovering over Joshua Wolfe while McCracken and Wareagle completed the task of assembling the pipe bombs by wedging the dried, flammable twine down into the gunpowder. Before leaving the storage room, they each wedged four into their belts

and checked the cigarette lighters Blaine had also found, ironically, in the nurse's office not far from the first-aid kit Susan
had quickly discarded.

They joined Susan as she was checking Joshua Wolfe's
pulse.

"Wait until you hear the first blasts, Doctor," Blaine reminded when she was finished.

"Don't worry about me. Just make sure you get back."

"Count on it." Blaine moved toward Johnny. "Let's go to
work, Indian."

CHAPTER 29

"Unit One, report," Sinclair said into his walkie-talkie.

"Unit One in position. Building front."

"Unit Two, report."

"Unit Two in position. Right rear flank."

"Unit Three, report."

"Unit Three in position. Left rear flank."

"Unit Four, report."

"Unit Four in position. Holding at east perimeter."

"Unit Five, report."

"Unit Five, in position. Holding at west perimeter."

"Snipers, report."

"Red in position."

"Blue in position."

"Green in position."

"White in position."

Sinclair nodded to himself, pleased at the execution. "Units Two and Three, begin your approach."

At the back end of the school building closest to the street, sixteen black shapes darted forward into the night, eight on each side. The style was classic military advance, groups of two seizing ground and providing cover for the next pairs to rush ahead. The process continued until all members of both groups were in rushing distance of their selected access point.

"Unit Two prepared for entry."

"Unit Three prepared for entry."

All timing now, Sinclair reflected as he steadied the walkie-talkie against his lips. "Move when ready."

A pause followed.

"Unit Two in."

"Unit Three in."

"No resistance."

"No resistance."

Sinclair breathed easier. "Close on building front," he ordered. "Unit One, begin your approach."

The seven members of Unit One scrambled forward, ultimately seizing positions on either side of the main entry doors leading directly into the building's lobby.

"Unit One prepared for entry."

"Move when ready," said Sinclair.

Unit One's commander hand-signaled a soldier holding an M-40 grenade launcher. The soldier lunged out directly in line with the glass doors and pumped out two rounds in rapid succession. The first was a standard charge that blew out the doors, frames and all, and sent glass cascading through the lobby. The second poured coarse gray smoke in after it that would totally obscure Unit One's charge into the building.

"Unit One going in," reported its commander softly and then whipped a finger through the air, signaling his troops on.

McCracken waited at the top of the stairwell, holding his breath against the noxious smoke rising upward and trying not to cough. He knew the soldiers had expected bullets to meet them, the coarse smoke meant to camouflage their entry.

It did its job. Blaine felt more than saw their shapes sliding through the lobby, but he had no intention of using bullets on them. Instead he raised the glass jar of ammonium hydroxide Susan Lyle had provided overhead and hurled it over the railing into the center of the lobby. The glass shattered on impact and, as the freed contents mixed with air, the effects were immediate. Blaine still could see almost nothing, but the sounds were enough to tell the story. A cacophony of gagging, coughing and choking echoed as the toxic vapors entered the enemy's throats and noses. By the time Blaine grabbed a pair of the pipe bombs from his belt, his own eyes and throat had started to burn. He lit the makeshift fuses and counted the seconds. Beneath him, shapes were struggling up from their knees, gloved fingers groping for their faces. Some were trying to stagger blindly from the building.

Blaine tossed the first pipe bomb between that group and the door, the second into the congestion of smoke where the heaviest concentration of men was still centered. The explosions were dizzyingly bright, thanks to the phosphorus, and the screams told him the rest of the contents had done their job as well. Blaine backed off, covering his eyes and trying to swallow the pain that had started to rack his throat.

"Ground Leader, come in!"

"Unit One, what hap—"

"They hit us! They hit us hard! Grenades! Bio shit!"

Sinclair felt a vise grasp his innards. "They don't have any—"

"I got men down! I got casualties here! It's a fucking mess!"

"Units Two and Three, building front is your target. Confirmed presence in building front," Sinclair reported, playing it by the numbers when something inside told him retreat would have made for a better option.

"Sinclair!" Fuchs's voice barked. "What's going on? Sinclair, can you hear me?"

Before he could acknowledge, a wash of bright orange flames blew out a section of the school's long, single-level wing in a horrific blast that swallowed the screams behind it.

Unit Two had followed the left-hand corridor from the back of the school building toward its front, two-level wing. As the troops approached the double doors leading onto the last stretch of hallway sloping to the lobby, the unit leader signaled two men ahead to take the lead. The rest hung back until this pair had yanked the double doors open, at which point they were to pour through in a single file with random spacing to negate the effects of an ambush.

The resulting pull on the heavy twine attached to the handles on the double doors toppled the acetylene tanks waiting at the head of the corridor. They smacked into the heavy books stacked beneath them, knocking off the valves Johnny Wareagle had all but removed. The vast contained pressure vented with a *whooooooooosh* and the tanks shot forward like a missile, their volatile contents freed to mix together. When some of the first troops through reacted instinctively by firing their M-16s, the heat and muzzle fire created the spark needed for combustion.

The blast shook the entire school building and carved a huge chasm out of the corridor, with flames reaching out from it. The ceiling came crashing down onto the blue-hot flames that quickly turned to orange. The walls along the immediate stretch of hall to the main lobby buckled and cracked, the screams of the victims all but lost in the lingering rumble. A backwash blast of hot wind reached McCracken on the second floor and nearly toppled him as he continued to struggle for breath. He steadied himself briefly against a wall and then moved off.

"Unit Two! Unit Two, come in!" Sinclair barked into his walkie-talkie. "Unit Two, are you there?"

The sight of flames engulfing the midway portion of the school's long corridor gave him his answer. Whatever McCracken had hit them with had knocked the whole unit out.

"Ground Leader! Come in, Ground Leader."

Sinclair pulled the walkie-talkie back to his lips. "This is Ground Leader, Unit Three."

"What the fuck's happening? Something big just hit this building."

"Where are you, Unit Three?"

"Approaching main wing, almost to the library."

"Exercise extreme caution, Unit Three. Repeat, ex—"

"*What the hell is . . .*"

"Unit Three!"

"Jesus . . . Open fire! *Open fire!*"

"Unit Three, what's going on in there?"

Sinclair heard the screams, and the walkie-talkie shook in his hand.

Safety goggles fastened tightly in place, Johnny Wareagle continued to spray the contents of the fire extinguisher atop the sulphuric acid he had spread evenly across the hallway. He had waited until the approaching troops' feet were all sliding through it before pinching the handle and letting the stream go.

The effects surprised him with their suddenness. White clouds of what looked like steam rose, carrying the noxious vapors with it. Johnny heard the hissing above the enemy's footsteps and ducked back into a doorway leading into the library for cover.

The approaching troops began to stagger, clutching at their eyes, digging into them in horrible agony. Their screams were high-pitched at first but turned raspy fast as the acid compound burned away all their mucous membrane layers. From within the library, Johnny watched some claw at their faces as if to scratch their ravaged flesh away.

A few from the rear recovered enough of their bearings to fire wild sprays through the library windows, trying for a bead on Johnny. He lit one of his pipe bombs and hurled it at a trio lunging for the doorway. It struck the floor, rolled, and ignited in a white-hot flash that blew two of the men backwards. Books and shelving toppled. One of the men was still screaming when the third twisted through the doorway, firing a constant stream from his rifle. Johnny hit the ground and rolled away from the spray, at the same time firing his Desert Eagle pistol until the clip clicked empty. The third attacker keeled over, blood staining the glass of the door behind him.

Wareagle jumped back to his feet and rushed for the library exit door on the other side.

"Unit Three! . . . Unit Three!"
When it was obvious there wasn't going to be a reply, Sinclair knew he had no choice but to play his last cards.

"Units Four and Five, come in."

"Unit Four here."

"Unit Five here. Do you mind telling us what—"

"Back wing of building has been compromised. Concentrate all efforts on main wing, first and second floors. Move in now!"

Sinclair was glad he had prudently held back two units of six men each. If these final two units could only manage to flush the opposition outside, McCracken and the others would make easy targets for his four snipers.

"Sinclair!" blared Colonel Fuchs's voice through the microphone he'd returned to his stand. "Talk to me, Sinclair!"

"Sir, we've encountered heavier than expected resistance."

"Don't lose them, Sinclair. Don't let them fucking out of there!"

"We've still got them, sir," said Sinclair, not as surely as he had intended.

The advantage, he told himself, still clearly belonged to his forces. He had positioned his snipers in the cover of the woods which surrounded the school on three sides, watching for the expected flight of his targets. They weren't going anywhere fast, which meant they weren't going anywhere at all.

Upstairs McCracken had just opened the stairwell door when he heard the quiet shuffling of men who knew how to move in near silence. Several of the footsteps had started up the stairs in his direction.

Blaine let the door close slowly, SIG-Sauer in hand. He had this clip and one more to go, along with two remaining pipe bombs. He backtracked quickly down the hall, reached the junction with the adjacent corridor and swung onto it.

Johnny Wareagle was waiting there, back pinned tight against the tile in the near blackness. The only illumination came through classroom windows in the form of stray beams from outside security lights. Johnny leaned against a spot on the hall the slivers could not reach.

"Twelve men, Blainey," he reported. "Armed as the others were."

"Trying to trap us?"

"Or flush us outside."

"Snipers?"

"It's what we would have done if the situation were reversed."

The first of the figures emerged from the stairwell onto the second floor at the far end of the hall.

"Looks like we've got to alter the strategy, Indian. Can you handle the snipers?"

"Given time."

"How much?"

"Depends on their spacing. Ten minutes, if the spirits are kind."

"Get going. And stay clear of the building."

"Blainey?"

"It's time to do some flushing of our own."

*   *   *

Johnny gave Blaine two of his remaining three pipe bombs and disappeared into the nearest classroom to make his exit through a window. He might draw some sniper fire upon himself, but McCracken knew Johnny would melt away into the night before the shooters could home in; he'd witnessed similar demonstrations time and time again.

Pressed in the recessed frame of a classroom door, Blaine heard a second group of the enemy approaching from the head of this hall as well. They were converging on him from both corridors, then, which left only the stairwell behind him at the junction of the two halls for escape. McCracken waited as long as he dared before flicking a flame out on his lighter and touching it to both fuses of Johnny's pipe bombs simultaneously.

Then he darted out and rolled them toward both concentrations of the enemy.

"There!" Blaine heard a voice scream out as he slammed through a door onto the stairwell. A barrage of automatic fire traced him as he lunged down the first set of steps, the gunmen giving chase.

The pipe bombs exploded simultaneously before he had covered half the flight, earlier than expected. There were a few screams, but not enough. A few men downed, the rest still able to fight.

He reached the bottom of the stairwell and twisted toward the front wing's back hall, ready to head for the science wing where Susan Lyle would be preparing his final surprise.

CHAPTER 30

Susan had gone to work following McCracken's instructions as soon as the second series of screams had drifted up to the science wing. She had already lowered Josh into a chair with wheels on its bottom to facilitate moving him when the time came. She left him in the storage room and eased back into the lab. This lab, along with the other five on the hall, contained piped-in gas to allow for the proper completion of experiments. The spigots controlling the flow were located in the front of each room near the teacher's high-top demonstration table. She reached the first one quickly and twisted it fast and hard. The hissing sound of escaping gas started immediately.

Then she headed for the door leading into the corridor. Another lab room with its neatly arrayed black slate tables lay directly across the hall from her, and she darted into it. The lights beyond the windows did a decent job of guiding her to the spigot and she activated its flow of gas as well.

She repeated the same process in three more of the labs and then returned to Josh to prepare him for their coming escape.

"Josh?" She shook him gently. "Josh . . ."

He moaned, but didn't stir.

Holding him at the shoulders, she began wheeling the chair forward, out of the storage room and into the lab. The wheels squeaked slightly and she slowed to less than a crawl to silence them when she passed through the doorway into the hall. There was an exit to the right at the school's rear where McCracken said he would meet her. She started to wheel the chair down the dimly lit corridor for it as quietly as she could.

"Susan . . ."

The sound of McCracken softly calling her made Susan turn toward the other end of the hall near the nurse's office. A smile lit her face in the instant before she felt an arm grip her tightly around the neck and a pistol press against her temple.

By the time Blaine saw the man he was too close to Susan Lyle to chance a shot. He froze in his tracks, holding his SIG in one hand and one of his final two pipe bombs in the other.

"Drop it!" the man grasping Susan commanded, and Blaine could see the fear building on her face. She had managed to get Joshua Wolfe into a desk chair that rested just behind her. "I'll kill her!"

The desk chair seemed to be . . . moving. No, Blaine realized, it was Joshua Wolfe reaching out with a hand, reaching out for the man holding Susan.

Blaine let a finger dangle through the SIG's trigger guard and crouched slowly so the man could see him place it on the floor. He had actually touched it down against the tile when Josh's fingers closed on a strap on the man's flak jacket and pulled.

In the same instant, Blaine snatched the SIG back up from the floor and steadied it on the figure of the man struggling to regain his grasp on Susan Lyle.

Susan ducked.

Blaine fired.

The bullet snapped the captor's head back and spilled him atop Joshua Wolfe, toppling both of them to the floor.

"Josh!" Susan screamed.

McCracken lurched to his feet at the same time another phalanx of Group Six men appeared at the other end of the first-floor hall near the ruined lobby. He lit the fuse on the pipe bomb and hurled it toward them.

Under cover of the resulting explosion, Blaine ran toward Josh and Susan, covering the last stretch in a sideways burst of motion that allowed him to keep the head of the science wing hallway covered with the SIG. He caught the faint, sickly stench of gas seeping into the air, his plan carried out just as he had instructed. His eyes had barely met Susan Lyle's when a sound from the head of the hall led him to twist back that way. A gunman spared by his most recent pipe bomb had risen into firing position behind the wall's cover and opened up.

Blaine snapped off four shots from the SIG to hold him and any others behind him at bay.

"In there *now*!" he ordered, gesturing toward the nearest lab on the side of the school bordered by woods.

McCracken fired five shots more to cover Susan's short dash and then drained the rest of the clip while dragging the once-more unconscious Josh after him. Blaine slammed the door shut and pushed in the lock. He snapped home his last clip in the SIG and accepted Susan's help in getting Josh across the room to the window overlooking the school's playing fields. He hurled a chair through the window just as a barrage of fire cut through the door behind him.

"Get outside!" he ordered Susan, returning the fire with a quick series of shots to hold Group Six's men at bay. "I'll hand him to you!"

Susan climbed hurriedly through the jagged glass, tempting the shards. Her feet had barely touched the ground when McCracken hoisted Josh out and lowered his frame toward her.

"Sniper Red to Ground Leader. I have three targets in scope. Two clear. I don't have McCracken."

"Sniper Blue to Ground Leader. I have three targets in scope. Also two clear. No McCracken yet."

Sinclair could scarcely believe his ears. Out of this disaster, hope for a successful finish had blossomed.

"When all three are clear, you have a go. Make sure you have McCracken locked on. *Make sure*!"

"Roger that," from Sniper Red.

"Acknowledged," from Sniper Blue.

"Get him away from here!"

Susan started dragging Josh across the first in a series of fields separating the school from the woods. Satisfied she was safely away, Blaine swung from the window and watched the lab door burst open.

He emptied the remainder of his SIG's clip, scattering the gunmen back into the hall, then heaved himself through the hole in the window glass. As he hit the ground, he flicked on a lighter and touched the flame to the fuse of his final pipe bomb. McCracken had to rise to hurl it for the shattered window and never saw the red line trace his way from a concealed position in the woods beyond.

"Sniper Blue to Ground Leader. I have McCracken in the grid."

"Roger that, Blue," Sinclair responded. "Red, do you still have the woman and the boy?"

"Affirma—"

"Sniper Red, please say again. . . . Ground Leader to Sniper Red, please say again. Do you have the woman and the boy in your grid?"

No response.

"Sniper Blue, this is Ground Leader."

"Waiting, Ground Leader."

"Take him out."

Sniper Blue had positioned himself in a tree providing clear view of the windows overlooking the field side of the school. He watched McCracken fly out of the window through his Zeupold night scope. McCracken stopped to hurl something back through the glass, then turned and fled.

Sniper Blue tightened his finger on the trigger and waited for the red laser beam to steady on his target before pulling. It locked on McCracken's chest and he started to pull, intending to fire at the end point of his exhale.

The piercing bolt of pain between his shoulder blades forced the rifle barrel upward and sent the red light spinning into the overcast night. A single crack rang out before he lost his grip on the rifle and flailed for the pain in his back. His hands locked and spasmed halfway there and he dropped from the tree branch, death overtaking him before he struck the ground.

Johnny Wareagle met him there seconds later and yanked his knife from the man's back. This was the fourth and final sniper Johnny had found and dispatched since exiting the school building. The first two had been poised on the ground, safely hidden, they thought, amidst thickets of bushes and shrubs. Eliminating the men had been as simple as finding them. The elevated positions of the third and fourth had allowed them each seventy-degree-angle sweeps of potential exit points from the front of the school building. Right where Johnny expected them to be as well.

"Sniper Blue, report," a walkie-talkie on the final sniper's belt whined. "Sniper Blue, come in. Sniper Blue, do you read me?"

Johnny had just turned to look for McCracken when a horrific explosion reverberated in the stillness of the night.

A hundred yards from the school building, Blaine felt the ear-shattering blast scorch the air, the freed gas ignited by his final pipe bomb. The pressure caught him in its grasp and hurled him forward. The ground cushioned his fall and he braced himself to withstand the blanket of heat that surged outward.

Another hundred feet away, it seemed to Susan Lyle as though someone had torn her feet out from under her. The explosion had swallowed the entire main wing of the building in a blazing orange fireball that belched black smoke in all directions. Debris leaped into the air and rained down in shards and hunks that left blackened etchings on the summer-thick grass. Secondary fires caught one after the other, forming a dull afterglow that made for insane contrast with the orange waves still lapping at the remnants of the building.

Susan felt herself to make sure she was whole. She was hot and singed, but there seemed to be no damage, just a ringing pain in her ears and the aftermath of the bright flash behind her eyeballs. The light of the flames showed Josh lying motionless on his stomach nearby.

Susan was crawling toward him when a figure emerged from the flames' shadows, silhouetted by the smoke, appearing more as specter than substance. The figure stopped briefly to let a larger shape draw even with it. Susan watched both shadows become solid as Wareagle and McCracken approached her. In the distance a chorus of sirens wailed, drawing closer to the school.

"You get her, Indian," Susan heard McCracken say. "I'll get the boy."

She felt herself hoisted effortlessly to her feet and supported there by Johnny Wareagle. Seconds later Blaine stopped next to her, Joshua Wolfe cradled in his arms and his eyes gesturing toward the woods dead ahead.

"Come on, Doc. We're getting out of here."

PART FOUR

THE VALLEY
OF THE DEAD

GROUP SIX,
FRIDAY, 1:00 A.M.

CHAPTER 31

"Tell me this night wasn't a total loss, Doctor," Fuchs said, disturbing Haslanger's work at the computer. "Tell me the information on that chip we found inside the candy dish in the boy's room was what we were hoping for."

"Our computers are analyzing the formula now," Haslanger told him, angling his chair the colonel's way.

"But it *is* the original formula for CLAIR. You've confirmed that much, anyway."

"Everything points to that fact, yes."

Fuchs felt himself to relax. His eyes wandered to Haslanger's monitor screen. "I assume that is what you're analyzing now."

"No, it's not," Haslanger said, and turned the screen so Fuchs could have a look. "This is what Joshua Wolfe was working on during his lengthy stay in our labs this afternoon. He thought he erased the data but our computers were too smart for him."

"I should think, Doctor, that you would be better advised to concern yourself with the CLAIR formula."

"This is all a part of it. He wanted to fix what went wrong with CLAIR in Cambridge."

"We found the vial he produced when we captured him in the garage," Fuchs recalled. "It was on the table during his interrogation."

"But we searched the room following his escape and failed to find it. That means it left here when he did."

"I fail to see—"

"I'll tell you what I see," Haslanger interrupted, pointing at the monitor. "What I see in these theorems and equations has absolutely *nothing* to do with reworking the CLAIR formula to assure there are no more tragedies." Haslanger paused and the computer continued to whir softly. "In other words, Joshua Wolfe lied. I don't know what was in that vial he took out of here, Colonel, but it doesn't do what he told us it did."

After a twenty-minute walk through the woods, McCracken and the others found themselves in a tangle of residential streets in Middle Island. Johnny Wareagle had taken Joshua Wolfe from Blaine and carried him the whole way, not even breathing hard for the effort when he at last lowered him in the shadow of a backyard fence. At that time of night, any vehicle left outdoors was ripe for the taking. Given the circumstances, Blaine selected a minivan for the ample room it provided for the boy. He also pried three additional sets of license plates off other cars to change at regular intervals along the way.

"How's he doing?" Blaine asked Susan Lyle.

"His vitals are still stable. Beyond that, I can't tell." She looked up. "We need to get him to a hospital."

Blaine shook his head. "Sorry, Doc. Our friend Colonel Fuchs will have alerted every hospital within five hundred of miles of here by now, expecting us to do exactly that."

"You talk like Fuchs is in charge of an army."

"It's the country's army and he's got access to it. Oh, not the country you know; it's the country the Indian and I have learned to survive in. More like the underbelly where it's always so dark nobody can tell what's really going on."

"You can."

"I know the territory."

Susan looked down at Josh. "We've still got to get him to a hospital."

This time Blaine nodded. "I'm gonna make a phone call soon, see if I can set a few things straight. Then when we get to a hospital, the same army will be on *our* side."

Susan accepted the proposal with a shrug.

The first leg of the journey lasted forty minutes and brought them to a pay phone outside a closed convenience store that advertised it was open twenty-four hours a day.

"Morning, Sal," Blaine said to Belamo.

"How'd it go at Group Six?"

"Different than expected. No Haslanger to show for my

efforts. Two others in his place."

"Par for the course."

"Not this time. One of them's Harry Lime's nonexistent son in the flesh."

"Wow!"

"That's not all. Lots more to tell, but no sense wasting time you could better spend getting me safe haven in Washington. It's time to pull the plug on Group Six, end this here and now."

"You start the process already?"

"Their facility's looked better and they lost some people tonight."

"A shame."

"*Lots* of people. Combat freelance types."

"Certain to cause some complications."

"Just wanted you to know."

"Call me back in an hour. I'll have your reservations by then."

"Reservations canceled," Belamo greeted an hour later.

"You're a lousy travel agent, Sal," Blaine replied.

"And you're a lousy storyteller, 'cording to certain parties in the D. of C. Seems they got you pinned for wasting a whole mess of dudes and doing several million dollars of damage to Group Six. Makes you persona non grata in the worst way. People down here figure you're on one of your crusades."

"In other words, no help from the inside."

"Shit, boss, right now the only ticket I could book is to your own hanging. They got you pegged bad this time. Lots of people are out looking already. Wouldn't be surprised to see you on a wanted poster at this rate."

"Or a milk carton, Sal, the way these men operate."

"Was me, I'd drop the whole thing."

"No, you wouldn't."

"You're right," Sal followed quickly, his smile easy to picture. "Just thought I'd try it out."

Blaine thought of Joshua Wolfe. "What about hospitals, Sal? We still need one."

"Big problem there. Case you didn't catch my drift before, you're a wanted man. They got a description of your lady friend and the kid—sketches, too—distributed to every hospital and clinic with a published address. You walk into any one of them with a red flag around your neck, and you might as well hoist yourself up the pole.''

"Doesn't leave me a lot of choices.''

"Let me work on it, boss. Meanwhile, you keep yourself moving and call in when you get somewhere.''

Susan didn't take the news well, especially that going to a hospital was out of the question.

"I can't do anything more for him without the proper diagnostic equipment.''

"You'd be able to do even less if Group Six gets their hands on him again, Doc. I've got a bad reputation in some quarters, and Fuchs and those above him are using that to their full advantage. They've got half the people that matter thinking I'm on a crusade against Group Six and the other half figuring someone hired the Indian and me to trash the place. That means no safe haven until things get sorted out. That means we keep playing by my rules.''

"I have a suggestion, Blainey,'' said Johnny Wareagle.

The fat man was already on his usual bench when Thurman arrived at the park. It was too early in the morning for the pigeons, only a few strays gathering at the promise of food dangling from the fat man's lap. As Thurman approached, he could see the fat man was eating picnic-style out of a wicker basket, an ample napkin tucked neatly across the front of his jacket.

"I knew you'd be late,'' the fat man greeted. "Thought I'd make myself some sandwiches to while away the time.'' At that he slid a neatly wrapped package out toward Thurman. "May I tempt you?''

"No, thanks.''

"A shame. I have quite a selection. Not sandwiches exactly, but *smorrebrod*: just a bottom slice of bread, no top, but well garnished, I assure you. Originated in Denmark. There is much we can learn from those beyond the borders of this country we are so determined to preserve.'' He probed his hand through the basket. "Let's see, I still have a roast chicken, a

Danish cheese; here's lumpfish caviar." The fat man looked up at Thurman almost sadly. "I suppose a ham and egg might have been more to your liking."

"You've heard the news."

"Word of Group Six's mishap is all over Washington," the fat man said happily, raising a fresh *smorrebrod* toward his mouth. "That's why I'm celebrating. Perhaps McCracken deserves a bonus for his efforts."

"Fuchs isn't giving up. I just got a call myself," Thurman told him, "looking for specialists to take up the chase. That's why I'm late."

"What did you tell them?"

"That I was already employed."

The fat man chomped off a hefty bite, chewed quickly and swallowed. "A pity I can't interest you in the fringe benefits."

"McCracken's isolated. We couldn't have asked for more."

"Not quite." The fat man dabbed the corners of his mouth with his napkin. "The trick now is to find him."

CHAPTER 32

To implement Johnny Wareagle's plan, they drove virtually nonstop across the country, the landscape and the level of heat the only thing that varied. Everything else was a blur through the regular changing of vehicles and occasional calls to Sal Belamo to update him on their progress. They lived off food from rest-stop snack bars and restaurants. Thirty minutes was the longest stretch they went without driving.

Joshua Wolfe continued to hold his own but showed no signs of any real improvement, prompting Susan Lyle to fear he had suffered some degree of brain damage. In spite of herself, she dropped off to sleep from time to time, hours of vigil lost to the exhaustion that overcame her.

"What's on your mind, Indian?" Blaine asked Johnny after watching Susan nod off. They'd been rotating shifts behind the wheel and Wareagle's latest one was nearing its close.

"Realities, specifically whether this course of action is the best one."

"Am I missing something here?"

"I think you are, Blainey. This pursuit, though it seems familiar, is vastly different from our others."

"Elaborate."

"A question: what has most of our work this past decade centered around?"

"Stopping madmen who figured they alone knew what was best for the world or the country."

"And their means?"

"New technology mostly—weapons, or discoveries that could be turned into weapons."

"We destroy them."

"We have to."

"And this time?"

"No one madman and no weapon, either."

Johnny looked from the road to McCracken. "Right on the former. Wrong on the latter."

"You're talking about Josh's discovery of CLAIR?"

"I'm talking about the boy himself. *He* is a weapon, Blainey, because of what he is capable of producing."

McCracken grasped where Wareagle was headed. "But he's innocent, and we also specialize in saving innocent lives."

"Is he?"

"You're talking about his mind, Indian."

"We cannot even begin to conceive of its reaches, Blainey."

"That's not his fault. He didn't ask for it, any more than the others we've fought to save didn't ask for their lots. Any more than . . ." Blaine stopped himself, not ready to articulate his thoughts and glad when Johnny saved him the trouble.

"But if he developed a formula Group Six so desperately wanted by accident, what might he be capable of developing on purpose?"

"If he fell into the wrong hands, you mean, and it's our job to keep that from happening."

"And what if we fail, Blainey? How far will he go with the knowledge he possesses if he is hurt again? His soul has been scarred now. Harry Lime is dead. He was nearly killed himself. He is becoming as we are, but with a different potential for response. His mind may be adult, but his emotions are still immature. And we cannot forget the manner by which he came into this world."

"Meaning . . ."

Wareagle took a deep breath. "We grew into our purpose, Blainey. The boy was born for his."

McCracken didn't like considering those prospects. He searched for an argument to refute Johnny's, but as always the Indian had thought things out in a maddeningly logical manner.

"He killed all those people in that mall," Wareagle continued, "in the name of trying to do good. Next time it will be in the name of something else. There are many names, many opportunities, many rationales."

"This is a tough one, Indian."

"The toughest, Blainey."

Alan Killebrew had never been more nervous. All his attempts to reach Susan Lyle had failed and his superiors at the
Centers for Disease Control and Prevention were beginning to
get impatient with his failure to issue any reports on his findings.

*"Share whatever you discover with no one else but me. We
don't know how deep this goes or who can be trusted."*

Killebrew was taking Susan's last instructions to him very
seriously. The most deadly force mankind had ever known lay
frozen inside Mount Jackson, temperatures exceeding 98.6 degrees all it required to become active again. He was not about
to release that information until after consulting Susan.

But how to stall? How to keep any additional personnel out
of the Level 4 isolation lab and the entire wing that accessed
it?

Killebrew could think of only one course of action to buy
the time he needed. He wheeled his chair over to the wall and
reached up for a red button, one of six wired throughout Level
4. He felt it compress and then yanked his hand backwards as
if the button had been hot.

Suddenly an electronic alarm began to wail. Red lights built
into the ceiling started flashing as a dull mechanical voice
issued a warning throughout Mount Jackson:

*"Code Red. Level four has been contaminated. Emergency
procedures are in effect. Code Red. Level four has been . . ."*

Right now magnetic seals would be sliding into place over
all doors accessing the entire wing, cutting Killebrew off from
the outside world.

"We're here, Blainey," Johnny Wareagle said late Friday
night from the driver's seat of the Jeep Cherokee that had
taken them the bulk of the journey west into Oklahoma.

McCracken noted Johnny's voice had the slightest of edges
to it. Returning home after so long, apparently, was no easier
for him than anyone else.

The Sioux had taken a huge stretch of acreage in the rolling
hills and plains here and turned it into a self-sufficient com-

munity. They suffered none of the painful stereotypes that plagued other reservations because they had stubbornly clung to the old pride and the old ways. The only compromise the tribe had made with modern times, Blaine saw, was in the construction of their cabinlike homes. Sturdily built structures dotted the landscape along the road that led through the reservation's center, visible through the night's darkness. There were no stores or shops; the government-sponsored one was a boarded-up relic.

Ceremonial tepees frequently rested near the more modern homes. There were lean-tos as well and a number of outdoor cooking stoves that were little more than grates propped up over a wood fire. McCracken figured the reservation could support a village of five hundred or so, people attracted by the prospect of living the old ways.

Johnny eased the Jeep to a halt not far from the largest tepee Blaine had seen. An old man who looked nearly as scorched as the earth itself was standing outside in front of the flap, arms by his side, smiling slightly. The layer of dust on his clothes indicated he'd been standing there for some time.

Wareagle dropped out of the Jeep, gazing back at Blaine. McCracken nodded and joined him on the ground, but didn't follow as Johnny approached the old man.

"I expected you sooner, Wanblee-Isnala," greeted Johnny's spiritual father, Chief Silver Cloud. "I hope you have brought rain with you."

"We saw some early today back east," Johnny responded. "Not since."

"Even if it had followed you, it would have skipped right over us. The spring was too wet, the summer too dry. Our spirits are close to broken. I'm glad you are here."

"I had no choice."

"Home is not a place you need to choose to come."

"You do not understand."

"I think I do."

"There is great trouble."

"That was as clear to me as your coming, Wanblee-Isnala. And there will be more following in your path; I saw them, too. Their souls were sallow. I have known them before; not these, but others like them."

Wareagle gazed briefly back at McCracken, standing by the Jeep. "Warriors?" he asked.

"The vision was not sharp enough to be sure, but some assumptions are safer to make than others."

"I am sorry to bring this upon you."

"Bring *what* upon us? What we have so often brought upon *you*? I am glad you have come, Wanblee-Isnala. You have fought many battles for us. Now we may have a chance to stand with you and . . ." He stopped abruptly, ancient eyes turning to McCracken. "This is the white face you have so often spoke of?"

"It is."

Silver Cloud smiled. "I feel we have met before. He is welcome here."

"There are two others, a woman and a boy."

"The spirits told me of their coming, too." He set his stare back on Johnny, suddenly somber. "That boy troubles me, Wanblee-Isnala."

"He troubles me as well."

"His aura is very mixed and difficult to read. The light and the dark are jumbled as one, instead of battling for control. You know what this means."

Johnny nodded. "He is capable of evil without meaning to cause it."

"There is something more. A chasm in his soul the essence of his aura has retreated to. The chasm is wide, Wanblee-Isnala. It is nearly open enough for the rest of his essence to fall in. You understand?"

"Loss of hope."

"A bad thing for someone of so mixed an aura. His essence sits on the edge. Should it ever slip over, there will be no retrieving it."

"Can he be pulled back?"

The old chief seemed to have no response, but suddenly a distant knowing glint showed in his eyes. "In the vision of your coming, I saw the boy as a black sparrow. You know of this symbol?"

"In some of our myths, the transporter of a man's soul to its final resting place."

"And the omen of the sparrow's nesting?"

"Foreboding, a warning of bad tidings it brings with it. The transformation of order to chaos, and perhaps death."

"Where has this boy made his nest, Wanblee-Isnala?" When Johnny made no reply, Chief Silver Cloud turned toward the tepee just to his side. "Will Darkfeather, our medicine man, is waiting inside. I told him you'd be coming."

"What are you saying, Doctor?" Fuchs demanded, rising out of his chair.

Haslanger looked up at him in front of the desk. "That the formula on the chip from the fax machine is not the CLAIR organism that the boy released in Cambridge."

"Meaning he tricked us yet *again*?"

"I don't think so. He faxed it to Harry Lime's apartment for his own benefit, not ours. Why would he hold something out? And if it was incomplete, why not just hand it over earlier?"

"What does that leave us with?"

"I'm not sure."

"But you are saying there is no way we can recreate CLAIR now."

"That's not what I'm saying at all. You see, there are two equally important stages in the creation of this form of organism. The first is its construction. The second is devising an agent, an enzyme of some sort usually, which induces it to divide or replicate. Remember, after all the construction atom by atom, you're still only left with a single cell. But identify the activating agent and that cell becomes two, and two becomes four, and four becomes eight. The formula he gave us *does* identify this activating agent."

"I fail to see what—"

"The last words the boy said before McCracken's untimely appearance was that he had another sample of CLAIR, obviously hidden somewhere. If we were able to obtain that sample, inducing replication through a polymerase chain reaction would produce a potentially inexhaustible supply for us."

"Joshua Wolfe was searched in Orlando. The hotel room was searched. No vial, test tube or anything of the sort was found."

"But the investigation was suspended after we learned he

was at the Hyatt. Where else might he have been? Find out and we find the missing vial.''

Fuchs hit the intercom button on his phone. ''Please send Mr. Sinclair in.''

CHAPTER 33

Almost to the tepee, Wareagle took Josh from Blaine's arms and parted the opening.

"I'm going in, too," Susan insisted, and placed herself in Johnny's shadow.

Johnny glanced at Chief Silver Cloud, who hesitated, then nodded stiffly. Wareagle let Susan follow him inside.

"Wanblee-Isnala has told me much about you, Blaine McCracken. I feel you are one of us."

The old chief's words caught Blaine by surprise. He hadn't been aware of Silver Cloud moving up next to him. "If Johnny told you the truth, you wouldn't want me to be one of you."

"Not according to him. He says your spirit is worthy of our people. He says you have the soul of a warrior." The old man smiled. "But, most important, he says you are starting to grasp what he teaches you."

"I'm a slow study."

Silver Cloud gazed at the tepee. "Wanblee-Isnala is troubled."

"I know."

"The boy troubles him."

"I know that, too."

"Does the boy trouble you?"

"I'm not sure."

The old chief nodded knowingly. "You must understand that my spiritual son was raised under the old ways and lives by their code today. That means he still recalls the tale from long ago of the warrior from another tribe who learned to use fire as a weapon. Enemy tribes feared him, hatched plots to kill him at all costs. They never had to. Do you know why?"

"Because his own people killed him first."

"Very good. Why?"

"He turned the fire against them."

"By accident? Maliciously? Out of desire for power?"

"It doesn't matter," Blaine told him. "They felt they had no choice."

Will Darkfeather helped Johnny ease Joshua Wolfe atop a blanket he had spread across the hard ground inside the tepee. A pleasant-smelling fire was burning in its center, sending reddish flames climbing for the vent at its top. He reached behind him for a black medical bag and seemed to notice Susan Lyle for the first time.

"I don't remember inviting her," Darkfeather said to Johnny. Compared to Wareagle, he was a small man who barely resembled a full-blood Sioux. His hair was cut short and neatly combed. His shade of skin looked more vacation-tanned than naturally bronzed. His eyes bounced about furiously, intensely.

"I invited myself," Susan told him.

"Did you?"

"I'm a doctor."

"So am I."

"I mean a trained physician."

"So am I. Now, make yourself useful and tell me this one's name."

"Joshua Wolfe."

"Wolf?" Darkfeather gazed at Josh's figure. "He's no wolf. He's barely a cub. I think I'll call him Cub." He pulled a stethoscope and blood pressure gauge from his bag. "Yes, that's a good name for him."

"His vitals are stable. I just checked them. Pulse a little low, though. Pupils reactive. I think there may be some brain damage. He hasn't had any seizures but—"

Darkfeather pulled up Josh's left eyelid and lowered a small penlight toward it. "No brain damage."

"How can you be so sure?"

"I'm a medicine man, remember? Kind of thing they can't teach you in medical school."

"This boy needs more than a medicine man," Susan snapped, sliding closer and ready to take over.

"Chief Silver Cloud believed our tribe needed more than

one, too.'' Darkfeather finished the left eye and moved to the right. Then he lowered his stethoscope over Josh's heart. "So he sent me to Johns Hopkins Medical School. The government paid. I finished third in my class."

Susan stopped and held her ground.

"And you know what I learned at Johns Hopkins, Doctor? I learned that sometimes the old ways of our people are more effective than modern medicine can ever conceive of. I learned that what I was born with and what was handed down to me combined for more than I could ever be taught."

He opened Josh's shirt and found a pair of twin black and blue marks where the shock prods had wedged against his torso.

"Any idea how many volts?"

"No. Enough to kill, though. Based on his response to—"

"I'll take over from here, if you don't mind." Darkfeather was fingering the skin around the prod marks. "Here's the thing, Doctor. Goes back to modern medicine versus the old ways. Now, I know what the book says about how to treat severe trauma resulting from electric shock, and I've got everything we need to follow through with it at my clinic. Trouble is I think the cub here's gonna go comatose on us while we wait for it all to work."

"You have an alternative to propose?"

"I don't propose, Doctor, I cure. Good thing for the cub we've got the old ways working for us as well."

Johnny smiled from the entrance to the tepee, then turned and went out as Darkfeather reached behind him for a medical bag of a different sort in the form of a rucksack of cleverly woven wool held tight at the top by thin rope laced through the stitching. He undid the rope and flattened the sack out to reveal its contents.

Susan Lyle recognized none of them. All were contained in plastic Ziploc bags of varying sizes, one of Darkfeather's concessions to modern times. There were powders, one the color and texture of wood ash, another an equally fine brown. There was a bag of a chalky substance the shade of charcoal. But Darkfeather reached for the Ziploc containing a reddish substance that looked like ground-up dirt.

"This is a rare bark from the echinacea family," he explained to Susan. "Grows only in the Pacific Northwest. I harvested this batch myself."

"What does it do?"

"Makes people better."

"Who've suffered severe electric shock?"

"Who've been disconnected from themselves, sometimes *as a result* of electric shock. Sometimes epilepsy or another seizure disorder. Apparent symptoms may be different but inside what's going on is the same. This bark works inside."

Susan looked at him disparagingly. "Oral administration?"

"Not quite. Watch."

Darkfeather poured a hefty portion of the reddish ground bark into a small black frying pan and added a half ounce of water. He stirred the contents briefly, softening the gritty texture of the bark, and then added the rest of the ounce. After more mixing, he fastened the pan into the wire holders placed low over the sweet-smelling fire inside the tepee.

"Takes a few minutes."

"Then what?"

"You'll see."

Susan leaned over to inspect the pan's contents more closely. Its texture had already changed from moisture-starved bark to a pastelike compound that looked like wet clay. Darkfeather placed another, much smaller amount of the bark in a plate and added enough water to turn it sticky. Then he rolled a wooden spoon about in the reddish muck until the curved end came away with a thick coating.

"Know why I'm doing this, Doctor?"

"You want to stir the contents heating up in the pan, but you don't want any wood fibers from the spoon to disturb the chemistry."

"Very good," the Indian said honestly. "There's hope for you yet."

Darkfeather moved his coated spoon into the pan suspended over the fire and began to stir gently, careful never to bring the spoon all the way out of the mixture. The paste took on the texture of watery oatmeal. It bubbled in places, coagulated in others. Darkfeather tried to keep the mix as consistent as possible. As he did so, Susan noticed the smell for the first time. The first thought that came to mind was dried leaves being burned on an autumn day, until an almost sickeningly sweet smell began to permeate the tepee seconds later.

"Aroma's part of the therapy, Doctor," Darkfeather explained. "Don't ask me why, but breathing the vapors seems to work together with topical application in effecting healing."

When the contents were thoroughly bubbling, he lifted the pan from the wire slats and placed it alongside Joshua Wolfe's midsection.

"Okay," Darkfeather continued, "here we go. . . ."

He grasped what looked like a paintbrush from his open rucksack and dipped it into the bubbling bark-turned-paste. Then he brought the bristles down upon Joshua Wolfe's exposed torso and brushed it first over the marks the prods had left. The boy cringed involuntarily when the paste met his flesh, whether from the compound's heat or the effects of its contents, Susan wasn't sure. Darkfeather kept smearing it on, looking like an artist at work on a human canvas, until the whole of the boy's stomach and chest up to his neck were covered. Then he covered the boy's face with it, massaging an extra amount in across his temples and squeezing it through his hair to his scalp.

"I guess I shouldn't ask how this works," Susan said.

"You can but I couldn't answer you because I don't know. And, like traditional medicine, it doesn't always." He leaned back and inspected his finished product. "We'll know by dawn. Either way."

Thurman reached the fat man shortly after midnight, caught him munching on something and was glad when the fat man chose not to bring whatever it was into the conversation.

"We've found McCracken," Thurman reported.

"Splendid. How?"

"Calls made to a contact who's en route to him now."

"I would have expected anyone working with McCracken to utilize more secure equipment."

"It's the most secure available anywhere: he obtained it from us. It pays to hold on to the necessary ciphers."

"What about the boy?"

"With McCracken, if he's still alive."

"Either way, this must be finished. You'll handle it personally?"

"Of course."

"I have already arranged for the personnel required to eliminate the remaining traces at Mount Jackson. There must be no links back to us. No evidence any of this *ever* occurred. Understood?"

"Clearly."

The fat man took a relaxed, easy breath. "You know, Thurman, I'm beginning to think we may salvage some measure of success, after all."

"We need to talk, Blainey."

Wareagle had found McCracken within sight of the tepee looking out over the vast fields of the reservation.

"How are things going in there, Indian?"

"Will Darkfeather is treating the boy with the old ways."

"Doctors know best. . . ."

"That is not what we must speak of, Blainey."

Blaine caught the note of urgency in Johnny's voice. "Go on."

"Chief Silver Cloud was expecting us."

McCracken shrugged. "Yeah, I got that impression."

"He expects others as well."

"Group Six?"

"He is not sure."

"You think he's right?"

Wareagle's gaze was noncommittal. "He was right about us."

A hot night wind blew past them. McCracken stiffened against it.

"They show up, you got a plan?"

"I do," came the leathery voice of Chief Silver Cloud from behind them.

Alan Killebrew came awake with a start and reached for his cup of bitter-tasting, overly strong coffee. Before him, through the glass of the observation room, the Level 4 isolation lab was deserted. Killebrew rolled his chair closer to the glass and ran his hands over his face. How long had he been sleeping?

Long enough for someone else to have entered the lab to confirm the contamination he had reported? No. When they realized no such contamination had taken place, they would have confronted him for all the undue stress he had caused.

Beyond that, he doubted anyone at the Mount Jackson facility would risk entering a contaminated area. He clung to the hope that his cover story would hold until Susan Lyle finally returned his desperate calls. She had told him to trust no one but her, hinted there was something more going on here she wasn't ready to discuss yet. He had left a number of messages just as she had instructed him to, but none of them had been returned. Perhaps the CDC was responsible for her disappearance. Perhaps they would be coming for him next.

Killebrew returned the coffee to the sill in front of the glass. The high-octane caffeine and the secret he was harboring had combined to turn him into a jittery paranoid. He realized that if there was any way other personnel could have watched him they would, just as a sanitation team would have stormed the lab if Level 4 hadn't been sealed off from the rest of the complex.

But that wouldn't hold Dr. Furlong Gage, director of the CDC, back much longer.

"Dr. Killebrew."

Gage alone had the codes that could open the magnetic locks currently keeping Level 4 inaccessible. So far Killebrew had given him no reason for activating them.

"Dr. Killebrew."

Hours had passed, though, since their last conversation and Killebrew found himself out of both answers and explanations.

"Killebrew!"

Killebrew realized he'd been dozing again and snapped alert, jarred by Gage's voice over the speaker.

"Here, sir."

"You will vacate Level Four immediately."

"Sir, my readings—"

"—do not jibe at all with the off-site analyses. If Dr. Lyle put you up to this, I want to know now."

Killebrew stiffened in his wheelchair.

"If you are a party to what she is involved in, I suggest you own up while there is still time."

"I don't know what you're—"

"Dr. Lyle is currently a fugitive from the law, Dr. Kille-brew. I am asking you to cooperate in helping us uncover what damage she has done. I am told she purposefully contaminated the hot zone in Cambridge because she was involved in an unauthorized experiment."

Killebrew's mouth dropped.

"It went wrong and she got caught," Gage continued. "I am offering you a chance to save yourself, Dr. Killebrew. The proper authorities are standing by. The—"

Killebrew slammed the disconnect button and steadied his hands on the wheels of his chair. This was worse than he or Susan possibly could have imagined. His gaze turned back toward the isolation lab beyond the glass.

They want the organism. That's what all this must be about. . . .

There was nothing he could do about the bodies stored in another section of the complex. But he could destroy his own records and conclusions. Make them start from scratch and pray to God that Susan got the truth out before they caught up with her, too.

First the doors. Short out the magnetic seals. Make them cut through steel to reach him. Buy himself a few extra minutes, anyway.

All he needed.

Chief Silver Cloud gazed into the west, toward the hills and past what the moon could claim from the night. "The Valley of the Dead," was all he said.

"An ancient burial ground, Blainey," Wareagle explained, "built on the site of a legendary battle. Sacred and tremen-dously powerful."

"It has been a last line of defense for our people for cen-turies," the old chief picked up. "It has advantages too great for any opponent to overcome. We are prepared for this. Since times long forgotten, we have been prepared."

"If battle does come, the landscape of the valley will give us what we need," added Johnny. Some of the confidence drained from his face. "But there's one catch, Blainey, and you're not going to like it. . . ."

CHAPTER 34

"You want the duty?" Darkfeather asked Susan.

"My pleasure," Susan replied, hoping it meant he would leave her to start treating Josh on her own.

"Okay, here's how it goes. In two hours, you need to apply a fresh coating of the bark over the initial one." He placed the black pan containing the hardened paste between the two of them. "Reheat this until it softens and begins to bubble again. Clear?"

Susan nodded.

"You don't need to put on as much this time and you don't have to wipe the original layer off. It'll look different smeared atop that layer instead of on flesh, but don't worry. It's strong enough to permeate right through. Clear?"

She made herself nod again.

"Check his vitals every twenty minutes and come get me if you think there's a problem."

Darkfeather rebundled the contents of his makeshift rucksack, rose and slid through the break in the tepee. Susan had her hand on the medical bag he had left behind when the sound of his voice made her stop short of reaching inside.

"It isn't medicine or even the bark that will help him now, Doctor," Darkfeather said, only his face visible inside the tepee. "Your spirit is close with the cub's. Alone the two will join and he will feed off your strength. That's why I'm leaving you alone with him. You have plenty of strength to spare."

Susan moved her hand away from his medical bag.

"Sacred land," Chief Silver Cloud elaborated for Johnny, "must not be defiled."

"You're telling me we can't kill any of them, right?" Blaine asked, even though the answer was clear.

"Not if we expect the spirits who call the land home to aid us, Blainey," said Wareagle. "Nor can we use any weapons not available to the tribe who fought the original battle."

"Bad guys won't be up on the rule changes."

"Our advantage."

"They're going to bring plenty of firepower."

"That is all the better," broke in Chief Silver Cloud. "In the battle of legend, ten braves held off five hundred of the enemy long enough for the rest of the tribe to flee."

"That how many we're going to have with us?"

"We will have eight, Blainey. The two of us makes ten."

"All you will need, just as it was all that was needed in times before," added Silver Cloud.

"What about the rest of the village?" Blaine asked the old chief.

"They are my responsibility. It will be now as it was then."

"You're prepared."

"Part of surviving the present is reliving the past."

"Be nice if there was a future for us, too, after today."

Joshua Wolfe came around slowly. The first thing he remembered was trying to open his eyes. In that instant all of his other motor skills seemed to shut down. He could not feel his hands or feet, much less make them move. It felt like all his limbs were asleep at once. He tried to speak but his lips wouldn't budge either, and his tongue felt bloated and swollen, his mouth like someone had taken sandpaper to its inside.

"Josh? . . . Come on, Josh. Wake up. You can do it, I know you can."

A familiar voice, soothing and warm. He felt pressure on one of his hands, recognized it was someone squeezing. He made himself squeeze back, trying to summon the effort. When at last he managed to open his eyes he could make out the shape of Susan Lyle hovering over him, taking his other hand in hers now.

"Can you hear me? Do you know who I am?"

He muttered her name and watched the tears brimming in her eyes as the life drained back into him like water filling a glass.

"Where am I?" he managed, turning his head to look about.

"An Indian reservation."

"What?"

"Long story."

"Doesn't feel like I'm going anywhere anytime soon."

He felt Susan's arms slide around him and draw him close. Josh feebly returned her embrace, not wanting to let go.

"You saved my life," she said when they finally parted. "You saved my life."

"Least I could do," he managed in a scratchy voice. "You're the only one who's tried to help me since Harry Lime."

"There's someone else now."

"Harry Lime's friend," Susan said after Josh had managed to sit up, crossing his legs gingerly before him. "He saved both of us back there at Group Six."

"Where is he?"

"Outside. I can get him."

"No, not yet. I wanna just . . . sit here for a while." Josh slid closer to the fire, seeming to notice the paste painted onto his exposed chest for the first time. "I've read about stuff like this. What is it, do you know?"

"Some kind of bark."

Josh sniffed at a portion on his arm. "Strong."

"So long as it worked."

"Just like CLAIR," Josh said.

He stared at the fire for what seemed like a long time before speaking again. "I did a lot of thinking while I was inside Group Six. It's what I do best, you know—think. I don't know where it all comes from. I don't know how I do it. At least I didn't used to. Now I know about Operation Offspring. I know my parents were a pair of test tubes Dr. Haslanger put together. He could even *be* my father. I do take after him. We both have . . . ghosts. And we're both murderers."

"That's not tr—"

"Yes, it is. And we both do what we do in the name of science and progress. Motivations don't really matter, only results." Josh wrapped his arms around himself, shivering slightly. "I wanted to make things better. I wanted to make a

difference. I wanted people to . . . like me. Harry did and he's
dead. I know that now; I guess I did all along. You did and
you were almost killed. McCracken might but if he couldn't
save Harry, why should I think he can save me?''

"Because it's what he does and he's good at it."

"Just like I'm good at what I do. That's why I let them
catch me and bring me to Group Six. I needed a way to take
care of myself, to keep them off me for good, hold them back.
I would have told you about it as soon as we were out, but
then . . .'' He took a deep breath. "Nobody can save me, except me, and that's just what I'm going to do."

"Sentence yourself to a life alone with only your obsession
for company? It'll follow you everywhere, determine everything. Believe me, I know."

"How?"

"I've been there. I *am* there."

"Not where I am, not even close. If you've got a home to
go back to, you've got a choice. I don't have either anymore.
Before Cambridge I still had a chance, but afterwards—no
way. I can't own up to what I did because it would just set
more Group Six types after me. So what do I do? Go back to
Fuchs and hide at Group Six, help him and Haslanger kill
more people? I think you get my point. See, you were right
about the existence of that second vial of CLAIR. I hid it in
the Magic Kingdom where nobody will ever be able to find it
except me."

Josh felt suddenly for the pocket of his jeans and relaxed
when he found the vial of clear liquid he'd produced at Group
Six bulging out from the fabric. "Thing is, it all comes back
to that first poem I wrote that you liked so much."

"'The Fires of Midnight.' "

"I finally understand what the fires are and what they're
for. And you know what else?"

"No."

"Midnight's coming anytime I want."

McCracken turned when he heard the footsteps emerging
from the tepee, expecting to see Susan Lyle instead of the
figure of Joshua Wolfe stumbling almost drunkenly toward
him.

"I guess I should thank you," he said, stopping a cold five feet away.

"Don't bother."

"I know who you are. Harry showed me pictures all the time. He said you were the best friend he ever had. That's why you came to Group Six, wasn't it? You were looking for the ones who killed him."

"Yes."

Tears started running down Josh's cheeks and he brushed them aside. "Why'd they do it? Harry of all people . . . He'd never hurt anyone."

"They thought he could hurt them, I guess. Harry . . . couldn't handle being alone. When he was with people he was okay. Like when he was part of the team during the war, or when he was with you. But after you left he lost touch a little. Ended up thinking you'd been stolen from him. He came to me for help. Wanted me to find you. Told me you were his son and that you'd been kidnapped."

"When did he come to you?"

"Monday. In Cuba."

"Cuba?"

"I was working down there. Harry pulled me out like he did maybe a hundred times before, lots of years ago."

"In Vietnam."

"Right."

"He talked about it a lot. Used to tell me how much he missed it. Said it was the only time he was really happy."

"I don't know, I think he was pretty happy when you were around."

If that made Josh feel better, he didn't show it. "Because he was able to pretend it was real."

"Wasn't it?"

"It . . . wasn't supposed to be."

"*Wasn't* it?"

"Yeah, I guess so. He took me fishing. We did things." Josh paused. "Harry used to talk about you a lot, too. Told me stories. He said you were the toughest guy he ever knew."

"Second toughest; he knew Johnny, too. He tell you I ask a lot of questions?"

"No."

"Here's one for you: had you ever heard of our friend Dr. Haslanger before you ended up at Group Six?"

"Not by name. I knew somebody was in charge of what was going on, but I never really cared who."

"In charge of what?"

"Me, I guess. The way they moved me around, placed me in special schools and kept changing so nobody would take special notice." The boy's expression changed. "Funny thing is, at Group Six they denied anything to do with it."

"Haslanger denied it?"

Josh nodded. "But if it wasn't him, then who . . . I mean, somebody had to be behind the Handlers."

"Handlers?"

"That's what I called the men who were always around, watching, checking up. Making arrangements. I never asked their names and their faces changed all the time. I didn't really care. Harry and I ever needed anything, they took care of it." The boy smiled thinly. "But we always had fun sneaking away from them."

"Like when you went fishing."

"I never got a damn thing."

"Did Harry?"

"Nope. It was still fun." Almost a laugh. "Once we stopped at a fish market on the way home. A couple carloads of Handlers were waiting for us, and Harry plopped the fish straight in the lead one's lap." Josh sighed. "You were Harry's best friend."

"That means a lot to me."

"It would mean a lot to him that you're doing this, that you came after the people who . . ." Josh lost the words and let them go, choosing new ones. "Revenge, right? That's why you were going after Haslanger."

"Sometimes, kid, it's the only thing we have left."

"Does it make you feel better?"

"Good question. I'm not sure 'better' is the right word. Maybe 'worthy' is more like it. You've got to stand up for the people who have stood up for you. Without Harry, I would've been dead a dozen times over. I owed him, and when you come right down to it, sometimes that's what the closest relationships are based on—debt."

"Would you have killed Haslanger? *Will* you?"

"I honestly don't know."

"But you found him. You found him through me. Is it true what Colonel Fuchs said? Is it true Haslanger created me just like he created the *thing* that tried to kill Susan?"

"You saved her life."

"You're avoiding my question."

"Not my style. I just wanted you to know what you did counts for something."

"Then answer my question."

"Yes."

Josh seemed surprised by Blaine's honesty. "Most people would have qualified their answer."

"Not my style, either."

"He doesn't sleep, you know."

"Who?"

"Haslanger. He doesn't sleep, hasn't for a couple of years now ever since it almost killed him. He told me he couldn't handle the ghosts anymore. He doesn't sleep because he knows the next time he does that's when they'll get him and he'll never wake up. I think I'm getting to be the same way. The whole time I was out after the shock hit me, I didn't dream. But I know the nightmares will start again anytime I nod off now."

"Everybody's scared of something."

"Even you?"

Blaine nodded. "Lots of things. You can't avoid fear; you just want to make it work for you."

"How?"

"By channeling it. By turning it into something you can use. You understand?"

Through his jeans Josh fingered the vial he'd produced inside Group Six.

"Yes," he said, "I think I do."

Sal Belamo arrived at the reservation an hour after dawn, looking as ragged and dust-covered as the beat-up rental car he was driving.

"Hell of a trip, boss," he said, stepping out and moving for the trunk when McCracken and Wareagle approached.

Blaine's last call to him before arriving at the reservation had
included a well-planned shopping list just in case. "Got everything you asked for. Wasn't easy getting it here. You ask me,
next time call Federal Express."

"We won't be needing it," Blaine said with an eye on
Johnny.

Belamo had fitted the key in the trunk lock but didn't turn
it. "I hear that right?"

"Rules have changed. So has your role."

"Maybe you better hear what I got to say 'fore you make
any changes, boss. Two serious-looking dudes were at the airport waiting for another flight to come in when I got there.
One of 'em looked familiar. Vietnamese midget used to be
called Colonel Ling. Presently associated with a man you
made a candidate for plastic surgery, old friend named Thurman."

"He deserved it."

"Should have just killed him."

"I couldn't; he was too valuable to the network. This was
the next best thing."

"Blainey?"

"One I never told you about, Indian. Thurman was part of
White Star, run out of Cambodia. Had a nice thing going on
the side with the local drug lords. All well and good until he
started using Special Forces detachments to terrorize villages
where the stuff was harvested. Some Vietnamese allies of ours
asked if I could do something. Thurman took offense to my
interference, sent some of his people to pay me a visit. I paid
him a visit after I finished with them. Turned out to be pretty
good with a knife. Pretty good."

Belamo took it all in. "I didn't hang around long enough
to see Pretty Boy himself, but while I was there, a third guy
shows up in a truck." Sal looked at Johnny. "An Indian."

"A tracker, Blainey."

"Silver Cloud's vision . . ."

"Coming true."

"Time out, boys," Belamo interrupted. "Somebody mind
telling me what the fuck is going on?"

*   *   *

"Good to see you up and around, Cub," Will Darkfeather said after thoroughly examining Josh.

"That paste was yours, wasn't it?"

"Belongs to the spirits, Cub. They let me borrow it for a while. Good thing. A few more days you'll be good as new."

"That's good," McCracken said from the entrance to the tepee, "because he's leaving."

Josh shot a cold stare his way. "They're coming again, aren't they?"

"Somebody is and I don't want you or Susan around when they get here."

"You can't stop them. You can slow them up, but they'll keep coming."

"Look, kid—"

"Don't call me that. You call me kid and"—Josh gestured toward Darkfeather—"he calls me Cub. I've got a name."

"Sorry, Josh," Blaine relented. "Now, if you'll let me finish. I can't afford to look beyond today. You may be right. Maybe we can never stop them from coming. But don't forget: I've been here before and I know the game. Just play along."

"It's my battle, too, in case you forgot."

"And maybe you're forgetting what it's all about: Harry," Blaine finished when Josh shot him a withering glance. "I found you because of him, and I'm doing what I know he'd want me to do."

That quieted the boy. His voice lowered when he spoke again. "I wish this could be the end of it."

"Agreed."

"But it won't be. It's never going to be over."

"We'll see about that," Blaine said, as convincingly as he could manage.

"Indian's right on this one, boss," Belamo said as Susan and Josh moved together for his car.

"I didn't know we were voting."

"You know what I mean. Look, I know where you're coming from." Belamo's callused face softened a little, but his eyes remained resolved and sure. "But there are things I can do you maybe can't."

"What do you mean, Sal?"

"You know what I mean, boss, and you know it's the only sure way out of this."

McCracken gazed at the boy again. "I can't accept that."

"Not like you."

"Like *me*? That's the problem. *You're* like me." Blaine turned briefly to Johnny. "The Indian's like me. We live for what we do and when it's over all I can think of is the next time the call comes. If it stops, I stop, because what I am is what I do. That's all I've got to hold on to and there's nothing behind me to exchange it for. I look at Joshua Wolfe and that's what I see. He doesn't fit in any better than me or you or Johnny. He didn't ask for that, but he's got to live with it all the same."

"He is desperate, Blainey, desperate to be understood and accepted," Wareagle said, drawing up even with McCracken and Belamo. "He acts toward these ends just as we act toward ours. But his are doomed never to be achieved. His desperation will continue to grow, and desperation is an emotion that has never empowered our actions."

McCracken gazed at the boy's silhouette through the rental car's rear window. "He didn't kill anyone."

"Not on purpose, maybe," reminded Belamo.

"He's not a killer," Blaine said, leaving it at that. "And I can't give up on him. Giving up on him means giving up period. I've never done that. I don't know what it's like."

"He is like us, you and me, Blainey?"

"Yes."

"As we are or as we were?"

"What's the difference, Indian?"

"Plenty. I was lost once in the woods, before you found me and brought me back. You were lost once in exile, before you drew yourself back in. What we might have been capable of then, we are not capable of now. The wrath we were hiding then has been vanquished. The boy's is a long way from that."

Blaine was still looking at the car. "I'm telling you he's not a killer, Indian. Something in my gut tells me he's not."

"We are accepting a great responsibility, Blainey."

"So what else is new?"

*   *   *

Killebrew again faced the image of Dr. Furlong Gage, director of the Centers for Disease Control and Prevention, over the video monitor in the Mount Jackson communication center. A pair of security guards flanked him on either side. Back in the isolation lab, one had actually readied a pair of handcuffs before seeming to realize Killebrew's handicap made them superfluous. But that had been hours ago and so far his interrogation had consisted of the same questions being repeated over and over again.

"I am at a loss to understand your persistent silence, Dr. Killebrew," Gage started once more, his voice tired and strained. "All I'd like to know is whether you have some way of explaining your behavior?"

Killebrew remained silent.

"Were you conspiring with Dr. Lyle? Can you tell us where she is?"

Killebrew swallowed hard.

"You destroyed your data, Dr. Killebrew," Gage continued. "I would like you to reconstruct it for me. It is vital that you share everything you have so we—"

At CDC headquarters in Atlanta, Gage stopped when a blinding flash of light swallowed Killebrew's image. He passed it off briefly to transmission problems, until the sounds of a horrific explosion rumbled through his monitor's speaker.

"Killebrew, can you hear me?"

But the transmission died altogether as the CDC's containment facility vanished into oblivion, its remnants blasted out through the side of Mount Jackson in a huge gush of fiery heat.

CHAPTER 35

The day had turned hot and dry early. Dust whipped in funnels and sprayed the air. The four cars carved their way through it slowly and warily. Virtually all of the passengers had drawn their pistols or readied their submachine guns at the first signs of the reservation.

"Stop," said the Indian tracker named Birdsong from the backseat of the lead car.

The driver slowed the Crown Victoria to a halt. Birdsong climbed out before the car had come all the way to a stop, followed closely by Thurman. His boots crunched against the gravel as he walked about the neat collection of small, rustic cabins dotting the center of the reservation.

"What is it?" Thurman asked, drawing next to him.

Birdsong crouched down and sifted some gravel through his hand. A cowboy-style hat hid so many of his features that it was impossible to tell his expression or age. His entire face was bathed in shadows. But his voice, when he finally spoke, belonged to a man past the midpoint of his life.

"They're gone," Birdsong reported.

"They're *what*?"

Birdsong indicated an indented line in the gravel and Thurman followed his gesture.

"Where did they go?"

Birdsong turned back and glanced at him from beneath his wide-brimmed hat. "Two directions." He pointed to the right. "One large group headed north, that way into the fields. Another, much smaller group headed west toward—"

"That's the one!" Thurman beamed. "That's the one we want. Now, where did they go?"

Birdsong aimed his eyes straight ahead, where in the distance shimmering hills rose out of the plains. It might have been an illusion, or a picture waiting to become a postcard. "To the west: the Valley of the Dead."

"Is that supposed to mean something to me?" Thurman asked.

"Only if we have to enter it."

Birdsong stopped the convoy again when the road began to arch upward, bending toward the hills they had glimpsed from afar minutes ago. They looked far less foreboding now, and yet somehow still distant. He checked the ground in several areas.

"It is as I feared," he told Thurman. "They have entered the Valley of the Dead."

"How many?" Thurman demanded.

"Ten, I think."

"Is the boy among them?"

"He seems to be."

Thurman advanced slightly ahead of the Indian. "What is this Valley of the Dead?"

"Sacred Sioux burial ground," Birdsong told him. "Site of a legendary battle where a small group of Sioux braves defeated an army of Pawnee."

"You're not Sioux."

"No," acknowledged Birdsong. "I'm Pawnee."

Thurman swung back to the cars. His men had climbed out and were stretching their legs impatiently. They were freelancers the fat man had retained to help his group achieve the varied purposes it pursued, under the command today of Thurman. To avoid questions and possible recriminations, the primary members of the team were all foreigners. The largest, Goza the Bosnian, reached his massive arms for the sky. The tiny Vietnamese Ling stood next to him, dwarfed in his shadow. The Arabs Aswabi and El-Salab stood alongside each other, inseparable as always in their silence, taking in the surroundings like a pair of eager predators. Standing further back next to a South American named Guillermo Rijas were three Russians who had come over from the Wet Affairs division of the KGB. This group had been joined by seven battle-tested American mercenaries hired at the last minute. The fat man made sure they had the arsenal they required: plenty of high-powered stuff, including grenade launchers and heavy-caliber machine guns.

"What are we waiting for?" Thurman asked Birdsong, swinging back his way.

"We are outsiders, not permitted to enter, especially . . ." Birdsong's voice tailed off. His eyes drifted over Thurman's silent, milling troops.

"Especially *what*?" the big man demanded.

"Those who do enter the Valley of the Dead may not bring the tools of the present with them. Machines and weapons threaten the land with desecration. Those who enter must bring with them only the past."

"Bullshit," said Thurman. "Back in the car, tracker. Lead us on."

Birdsong gazed up past the sun into his eyes. "You are making a mistake."

"I'm making a decision."

The road up the hill was no more than a trail, not meant for tires. As a result, the convoy thumped and bumped up the rocky way, clawing for every yard behind revving engines. They traveled in single file, the windshields of all but the lead car paying a heavy price for being in the path of stones being kicked backwards by spinning, grinding tires. Chips of glass were lost to the dust, scarring the windshields by the time the cars reached the crest of the hill.

"Looks like nothing special to me," Thurman commented as the lead car started down.

Birdsong shrugged and tightened his hat atop eyes that tried to see in all directions at once. Whatever marked graves or warning totems there might have been were long lost to the years. The Valley of the Dead was a stretch of rolling, sloping land that lay enclosed on the east and west sides by hills that steepened as they rose. The north held only a narrow passageway permitting access, helping to explain how such a small number of Sioux had managed to defeat an army of Pawnee all those years ago. The ground flora was surprisingly rich in bramble, vine and tumbleweed, thin trees dotting the landscape like skeletons thrust out of the ground.

The hills standing on the western side of the valley were

pockmarked with caverns and craters. Birdsong knew these had been the defensive positions taken by the Sioux braves during a portion of the legendary battle. But he had left that part out in his earlier narration to Thurman. Even now he could not see how access could be gained to them, what footholds the Sioux braves had used to sequester themselves inside a hundred and fifty years before.

The lead car crested over the hill and began its descent, brake pads squeezed and tortured. The dust thickened once more, caking its windshield. The driver sprayed washer solvent and the glass cleared under the force of the wipers, only to brown quickly again. The process became constant and unavailing, Thurman ultimately rolling down his window to better his own view.

The road leveled off. The convoy started across the valley. There was no longer even the semblance of a trail to aid them and the cars bucked accordingly. Shocks strained to their utmost, the cars continued on, passengers jostled, shoved up against the roof and then snapped back down. In one of the trailing cars, the massive Goza held his hands to the roof to cushion his skull.

The lead car's driver hit a patch of soft earth and felt his tires sink. He revved his engine, rocked the car from forward to reverse and back again until he felt the tires regain their hold and push forward. The convoy settled onto a straightaway, an unimpaired stretch of the valley lying ahead in the blowing dust.

Twenty yards later, the lead car simply sank into the yielding ground, all four wheels dropping at once.

"What the . . ."

Thurman's voice was lost as the ground gave way, the whole car swallowed by the earth, lost to the hood line.

"Doors won't open!"

"Windows, then! The windows!"

The engine sputtered, barely enough power salvaged to drive the windows down. Slowly they descended and finally jammed against the supporting rubber.

Thurman was the first to pull himself out and back to the surface.

"Shit!" he bellowed.

Upon seeing the lead car eaten by the dust, the car immediately behind it had screeched to a halt too fast for the third
car to avoid it. A metal-jarring crunch jolted the occupants of
both vehicles, who poured out to inspect the damage. The
radiator of the third car was hissing gray smoke. The back end
of the second was bent inward and lost to a deep bank in the
valley floor, nose tipped upward as if to gasp for breath. The
fourth car had tried to avoid it all by swerving and had ended
up buried in a sinkhole half as deep as the one in which the
lead car was mired.

"Get the weapons!" Thurman shouted at the troops scur-
rying from the vehicles. "Get the weapons!"

Trunks were snapped or pried open, heavy guns yanked out
behind the determined pull of powerful arms, while the two
Arabs and Rijas swept the ancient grounds with their rifles and
eyes, wary of an ambush. The rest of the group rushed to gear
up behind the cover of the cars' ruined carcasses and natural
depressions in the earth.

"Birdsong!" Thurman screamed, looking for the tracker
through the gathering dust. "*Birdsong!*" He shielded his eyes
and continued to search, to no avail.

"He's gone," Ling reported, pistol in hand.

"Son of a bitch!" Thurman scowled.

He heard a whizzing through the air, a biting sound like the
wind cutting itself. He dropped instinctively into a narrow fur-
row within the pit where the lead car was wedged and readied
his M-16. He cautiously raised his head and swept his rifle
from side to side.

The first series of screams came from the right. Thurman
followed the sound to the men who'd been unloading gear
from the trunks. An arrow lay imbedded in Goza's shoulder
and another in the leg of a Russian named Perochin.

A third man tried to duck away, squeezing a load of ammo
in his arms. An arrow took him in the hamstring. He crumpled
and the ammo went flying, including a grenade separated from
its pin.

"Down!" Thurman bellowed.

The explosion blew apart the car with the ruined front end.
It became a flaming carcass that spewed chunks of glass and

metal into the air when the gas tank ignited. More screams sounded.

Thurman lunged out from the depression that had swallowed the lead car and joined Ling and Rijas behind a pair of boulders.

"Those caverns," he said, pointing to the pockmarked hillside facing them from the west. "That's where the arrows came from. Ling."

The tiny Vietnamese was already zigzagging back toward the heaviest concentration of the team. Thurman watched him disappear into the dust. Seconds later fifty-caliber machine-gun fire split the air, echoing through the valley as it sought a bead on the mysterious openings in the hillside. With fifty-caliber fire covering them, the two Arabs burst up and fired five forty-millimeter rounds each upward. Four of the shots were dead on target with the caverns and four others close enough. Huge plumes of dirt and debris were blown out of the hillside, showering down in avalanche fashion. When the shower cleared, some of the black openings had disappeared altogether while others had become even wider, jagged tears in the hillside's structure.

Thurman crept off to check on his casualties. The wind sounds mocked him and kept Birdsong's warnings about defiling the land alive. Thurman stilled his massive frame briefly in a depression and focused his thoughts on the rational. Birdsong had placed at ten the number of opponents who had entered the valley ahead of them. The archers among these who'd been in the caverns had surely been taken by the strafing barrage. So Thurman calculated the opposition had been reduced to seven at most.

His count put his own mobile force at ten now, including Goza, who had somehow pried the arrow from his shoulder. The grenade blast had taken two lives and added another wounded to the other two who'd been shot by arrows. Fortunately their entire arsenal remained intact. The element of surprise that had worked for McCracken was expended. The tables were about to turn.

Staying close to the ground, Thurman bolted out and helped drag one of the Russians to safety, keeping an eye peeled toward the hills at all times. In actuality, McCracken's forces had hampered them only minimally; Thurman would have posted men at the rear of his group's advance anyway. Now it would be the wounded who were given that task. He made sure the three men who qualified were well armed and properly placed as Ling readied the remainder of the force to move.

"Cover our rear," Thurman ordered, before rushing up to join the others.

Chief Silver Cloud was smoking a long wooden pipe in his tepee when the flap parted and Birdsong stepped through.

"Sit, my friend," the chief beckoned.

The tracker moved toward him and removed his hat, revealing a shock of graying hair. "I did as you instructed."

"They went along?"

"Couldn't get into the valley fast enough."

"Of course, and their weapons must be many."

"Indeed."

"That is a pity." The old man smiled between puffs.

"I told them I was Pawnee."

"They believed you?"

"I guess to them," Birdsong said, "we all look the same."

CHAPTER 36

The Valley of the Dead's confines worked like a wind tunnel, twisting the desert-dry dust about in all directions. The long drought had scorched the land, and it shed its anger by coughing itself into the air.

At the head of the procession, Thurman simply gritted his teeth and pressed on. His team could see ahead, but not very far. Their arsenal of weapons should more than compensate for this. McCracken's Indians might have held a logistical advantage, but as soon as they showed themselves in any number his commandos would be free to slice them down at will.

Thurman's experience with guerrilla-type fighting was nothing compared to that of Colonel Ling, who'd mastered the art of it in Vietnam. For this reason he had sent Ling on slightly ahead to serve as scout. Ling had been on the other side of this form of battle often enough to sense from where the enemy's next strike would be coming. Thurman could barely see him out there ahead in the dust swirl. He strained his eyes to catch sight of the small man and almost jumped when Ling appeared right in front of him.

"Trouble," the Vietnamese said through the whipping dust.

The old depressions in the ground had been easily camouflaged. Wareagle had taken three braves with him for this particular task, and in laying the groundwork he had the odd sensation that he was repeating part of the very strategy the original defenders of this valley had employed.

The wind made it tough to hear the men passing atop them, but Johnny could feel them and knew the braves could as well. There had been no set signal to rise, just an apportioned amount of time to wait after the last set of boots had passed overhead. Wareagle lurched out from his hiding place beneath the ground mere seconds ahead of the three other warriors. Spread well apart, they vanished into the wind for the next stage of the plan.

Ling pointed out the Indian figures hidden in the brush up a slight rise that gave way to the last of the valley. Thurman continued on briefly before dropping into a crouch, opening up with his M-16. The rest of his men joined in instantly and the gunshots echoed in a continuous rattle through the hills.

"Cease fire!" Thurman signaled finally, the echoes lingering after his men had obeyed. "Hold positions. You two, with me."

Thurman led Goza and Rijas forward into the cloud of gun smoke that sifted through the dust. The stink of gunfire hovered over them every step of the way as they neared the brush.

"Fuck," Thurman muttered.

What was left of the targets they'd been firing at hung from the trees. Other remnants lay tied to bushes. Pieces of straw and fabric were still fluttering through the air, caught by the whims of the breeze.

"Fuck," Thurman said again.

Dummies, scarecrows . . .

"Four more men missing!" a voice bellowed from the rear of the pack.

Taken while we were firing, Thurman realized, gnashing his teeth.

"No more games," he said to Ling. "And no more hiding places. Let's finish them."

And Thurman led the way south over the rise into the last of the valley atop a dry riverbed. He was careful of his footing once the parched remains of what had once been the bottom began crackling underfoot, testing the land for more potential traps. The remainder of his men followed him onto the plain confidently, Goza bringing up the rear, the Arabs and Ling in the middle with Rijas.

Suddenly Thurman heard the now familiar whizzing noise through the air and dove for the ground.

"Arrows!" he screamed. "Down!"

Thurman had been right about the arrows, but wrong about their intended targets. They surged through the air, tips aflame, coming up strangely short of his troops. Thurman rejoiced at first until he realized the purpose of the fiery arrows.

"No!" he bellowed and lunged back to his feet.

Too late. Just as similar ones had done in the legendary battle over a century before, the flaming arrows ignited the kerosene freshly soaked into the ground around the plain. The hard-packed brush and weeds, bone-dry from the drought, quickly became an inferno and effectively sealed Thurman and the remainder of his team in a ring of fire.

They spun around, weapons firing furiously at nothing.

"Stop! Stop!" Thurman ordered.

The enemy wanted them to panic, giving in tantamount to giving up. The front wall of the flames was the weakest, showing several breaks.

"There!" Thurman pointed. "Through there! Out that way before they come! Take them as they charge in to finish us. Go!" he instructed, urging his men on when they were reluctant to leave him. "Go on!"

Weapons poised, Thurman brought up the rear to provide cover. When the last man hurled himself forward through slight cracks in the front wall of flames, he backed up to allow for the same running start his troops had utilized. He peered through the wall of fire for something to leap for.

And realized his men were gone. Thurman slid close enough to the flames to feel them licking at his flesh. Eyes starting to water, he squinted and saw a dark ditch rimming the front of the fiery plane, the ditch his men had plunged into when they lunged to safety.

A crack snapped through the air and the leather of a bull-whip closed on Thurman's throat and yanked backwards. His weapons dropped from his grasp as he flailed upward to tear the whip's death wrap off. Backpedaling, he felt his legs go out from under him and his head hit the parched ground hard. Then the whip was torn free, taking some of his flesh with it.

"Get up," a voice commanded.

Thurman rolled onto his side and saw Blaine McCracken standing there with him inside the ring of fire. He had discarded the whip but something else was gripped in his hand—tied to his wrist, it looked like.

"Get up, Thurman."

Thurman propped himself up slowly, feigning weakness in order to prepare himself for a lunge toward his lost weapons. He sneaked a glance at them.

They were gone.

"It's been a long time," Blaine continued.

Thurman rose to his feet. McCracken tossed him the other end of what was tied to his wrist, a thick leather strap.

"Tie the thin edge around your left wrist, just like this," Blaine ordered, and held his up for Thurman to see.

Thurman held the strap, but that was all.

"No more games," he said staunchly, jutting his jaw forward.

"This is the way it has to end, Thurman, just like it did over a century ago."

Thurman stiffened and tied the edge of the leather strap around his wrist. Blaine tossed a shiny, hand-molded knife his way. It thumped down on the hard-packed ground beneath him.

"Second chances," McCracken told him. "Take your best shot."

Thurman leaned over to pick the blade up. The flames licked at the air in the circle of flames around them; so even and symmetrical they looked as though an artist might have painted fire onto the landscape. The wind blew the heat inward, drenching both men in waves of sizzling gusts.

"We're improvising here, Thurman, but I think it's good enough to satisfy the spirits." Blaine made sure Thurman could see the knife's twin grasped in his own hand.

"You're a fool," Thurman said, handling the knife nimbly and sticking out his massive chest.

"Tell me who you're working for and maybe I'll let you survive this."

"You really are a fool. Who do you think saved your life in that library by turning on the lights?"

"Why'd you bother?"

"Because we needed you," Thurman said, and whirled in at McCracken with knife leading.

McCracken anticipated the move perfectly and tugged on the strap connecting them just as the big man committed to his thrust. The move dragged Thurman off balance and sent his swipe terribly off target. Blaine sliced at him as he surged by and the blade caught his side, Thurman just managing to arch from its path. He swung and tried to fool McCracken by yanking. But Blaine countered by entering into the move and kicking Thurman under the chin.

He followed the strike with a thrust of his knife. Thurman, learning fast, used the leather strap to expertly deflect the blade and then wrapped it around Blaine's wrist. A quick tug provided the opportunity for an equally quick lunge. McCracken used his left strap arm to block it and took a nasty gash on his forearm for the effort.

Thurman backed off, grinning. "I've learned a little over the years."

Blaine grimaced in pain, trying to judge how much he could rely on his strap arm now. Sensing weakness, Thurman could either go for the kill now or prolong things by waiting until an opening was more evident. Probably the latter.

"What do you mean you needed me?"

"To find the boy for us, after he disappeared."

And then Blaine realized. "You were the ones who took over Operation Offspring. . . ."

Thurman jabbed again with his knife. McCracken backed out of its way and kept backing up, avoiding swipe after swipe until the highest flames licked at his back.

"Where's the boy, McCracken? Hand him over and you can walk away from this."

Thurman was trying to reel him in like a fish, wrapping the leather strap around his wrist to draw him closer, daring Blaine to strike at him with his own knife.

McCracken finally took the bait and lashed outward. Thurman used the strap to capture the blade in a tight loop and yank. Stripped from Blaine's hand, it skidded across the hard-packed earth and stopped near another section of the flames enclosing them.

"I'll find him anyway," Thurman sneered.

And then he lunged. Blaine moved when the tip of the Thurman's blade had nearly found his stomach. Thurman felt only air where his target had been and went surging by. Instead of stopping him, McCracken used the now tightly wound strap to hurl the big man around toward the wall of fire he had been ignoring in his desire for the kill.

McCracken heard Thurman's agonizing screams as he entered the flames, his knife totally forgotten as the fiery pain stretched mere moments to seeming hours. He was still screaming, covering his eyes, when McCracken yanked him out at the same time he snatched his own blade up off the ground. Thurman was still in motion when Blaine slashed the knife across the right side of his face, the slice almost identical to the one scarring the left.

"Now they match," Blaine taunted.

Thurman's mouth dropped in shock, about to scream when McCracken kicked his legs out and held the knife poised over his throat.

"Son of a bitch," Thurman rasped, the blood running out of the gash.

McCracken brought the blade down closer.

"Live or die, your choice. Who are you working for? Who's kept Operation Offspring up all these years?"

"Go to hell."

McCracken jammed the blade down, buried it in the fleshy part of Thurman's upper arm, just a flap on the outside of his tricep but enough to hold him just where he was. The big man screamed.

"*Who?*" Blaine demanded.

"Fuck you! You should have died in Cuba. I told him I could handle this myself."

McCracken felt something shift deep in his gut. "What do you know about Cuba?"

Thurman would have smiled if it wasn't for the pain. "Give me some credit."

"*Jesus Christ!* You set everything up to get me down there, so Harry could come to my rescue. You set me up to kill Marokov. He was working for *you!*"

"And you fucked it up, fucked *everything* up."

Then Blaine remembered the picture Marokov had shown him just before the shooting had begun in the Buena Vista bar.

"They have a job for me. This man. Someone I believe you know."

"Looks like you must have fucked up somewhere, too, Thurman," McCracken told him. "Marokov was in Cardenas waiting for a job: your execution.''

"Go to hell!''

"He showed me your picture. Looks like someone figured you'd outlived your usefulness. I'd say you're on borrowed time even as we speak.''

Rage filled Thurman's features, squeezing out through the pain in scarlet fury. "That *son of a bitch!*''

"Who?''

"The fat man.''

"*Livingstone Crum*? That's who you're working for? That's who's behind this?''

Thurman didn't bother nodding.

"I guess the Company didn't phase out his private little group, after all,'' Blaine continued. "All the bad press on those radiation tests conducted on the mentally retarded must not have been enough for them. Where'd you fuck up, Thurman? How'd you get on the fat man's bad side?''

"Joshua Wolfe,'' Thurman said with sudden calm. "The operation was mine all the way. I was the only link back to him.''

"What operation?''

"It wasn't the boy who killed seventeen hundred people at the Cambridgeside Galleria. . . . It was us.''

CHAPTER 37

"We had monitored his every move," Thurman continued, wanting Blaine to know, proud of it. "Studied all his research. It was our scientists who realized how easy it would be to turn CLAIR into a killing machine. Just a slight modification in the formula, I'm told. Barely even noticeable."

"You and the fat man really do belong at the same table."

"Look, we didn't know the kid was going to test it in that mall."

The flames continued to encircle them, moving ever closer, shrinking the central patch. If either noticed, he didn't show it.

"But you didn't stop him, either," Blaine said accusingly.

"Our people lost him inside. They were still inside when . . ."

"So there was no one to follow him when he ran, but you needed him back to reproduce the formula for you."

"And who better to find him for us than Blaine Mc-Cracken?"

"Through Harry Lime. I'd never suspect anything that way, even though I should have." Blaine paused, everything falling together. "I guess you can count yourself fortunate Joshua Wolfe escaped in the first place. Otherwise Marokov's kill order would have stood. You'd outlived your usefulness to the fat man, until the kid disappeared and he turned to you again."

"The bastard told me about you and Marokov. He had me set the whole thing up."

"He played you for the fool you've always been, that's all."

Thurman bared his teeth in a grimace of pain. "I think I'll surprise him."

"You're not up to it, Thurman. He'd eat you for lunch—literally maybe. Leave him to me."

Friday night had run into Saturday morning by the time Erich Haslanger had finished running computer diagnostic tests on the compound Joshua Wolfe had created in the Group Six labs. He confirmed early in his work that the compound in and of itself was as innocuous as it was generally unidentifiable. That indicated it was some sort of activator the boy planned to mix with his original CLAIR formula. If not toward repairing it, though, then what?

Even for supercomputers capable of performing a million commands a second, the diagnostics took time. After all, there was no hard data for them to work from, no actual analytical samples. There were only two formulas, neither of which was totally complete. Haslanger tried to be patient. He knew what it was like to wait for the night to end just so morning would come and keep him from a slumber he knew he would never awake from.

Because the ghosts would come for him.

It had been worse in the dreams than it had been in reality, for in the dreams his discarded subjects were shown all grown up. Not just heaps of freshly delivered, misshapen, stillborn flesh or shapeless things that had somehow managed to survive long enough for him to mercifully end their brief lives. In the dreams he saw them matured: the extra or missing limbs, the disfigurements and mutations, the scale of development all horribly wrong.

Reaching for him, trying to hold him in their dark dream world. The ghosts had come close the last few times he had chanced sleep years before. The next time he would remain their prisoner. Waking would never come.

Last night he had come dangerously close to nodding off. Feeling himself start to drift, the glow of the computer monitor the room's only light, the pills not working. Once he jolted himself awake from a slide into darkness, convinced scratch marks would be left on his body where the ghosts had tried to drag him down with them. Terrified, he had barely been able to catch his breath or still the hammering of his heart.

Now, late on Saturday morning, Haslanger heard a series of

beeps as the computer signaled completion of its program. His eyes locked on the monitor and read the final results. A pang of fear, even worse than the one his near-sleep had wrought, slid through him. He backtracked through the program, hoping for an error.

There was none. Haslanger double-checked, and checked again.

He rose so quickly from his chair that it toppled over backwards. He burst out of his office. The hallway beyond burned with light, hurting his eyes. He looked at his watch, realizing he'd gotten through another night, seeing that it was nearly noon. But the emptiness of the first hallway made him fear he was actually sleeping and this was his eternal prison, the ghosts sure to step out from the doorways at any instant.

Just around the corner, though, he heard voices and footsteps. A few workers greeted him, but Haslanger hurried past them, picking up speed, out of breath by the time he reached Colonel Fuchs's office.

"The spirits smiled upon us, Blainey," Wareagle said, as they made their way through the Valley of the Dead under the careful watch and cover of the remaining Sioux warriors.

"Your people lost some good men today, Indian," he told Johnny by way of apology.

"The chief saw this in his vision, Blainey. He will be saddened as we are, but not surprised."

Entering the village, they expected to see Silver Cloud waiting, the knowing half-smile etched over his lips. The old chief was there, all right, but he wasn't smiling and he wasn't alone.

Sal Belamo was standing next to him, the dust-coated rental car parked nearby off the road.

"We got problems, boss."

"An hour down the road," Belamo was explaining, his eyes glassy and distant, "we stop at a diner and I go in to get some food. Kept my eye on the car the whole time. Kid was inside that car right until the time I turned to the counter to pick up my order. I get back to the car, open the door, and next thing I know I'm waking up almost two hours later."

"GL-12."

"Huh?"

"A sleeping gas developed by Group Six. The kid must have smuggled some of it out. That's what he used on you, Sal. Released it into the car and made his getaway just before you returned."

"Shit. But what the fuck for, boss? I mean, we're on his side, right? What the fuck is he doing?"

"I don't know, Sal."

"I do," said Dr. Susan Lyle as she gingerly emerged from the car.

"What are you saying?" Fuchs demanded.

Haslanger was pacing rapidly up and down the office, his face beet red. "Heat. It all comes down to heat."

"What does?"

"Joshua Wolfe's original formula for CLAIR. He programmed it to be heat sensitive, so it wouldn't be able to survive above a certain relatively low temperature."

"You said that already."

Haslanger stopped in his tracks. "He can take it out."

"Take *what* out?"

"Heat sensitivity, the defense mechanism. That's what the compound he created in our labs does. We thought he was solving the problems surrounding the organism's recognition of oxygen-nitrogen proximity, becoming more specific with its programming so it would attack only the molecules present in air pollution and bypass those forming human blood."

"But he wasn't."

"No. According to its programming, CLAIR should have died when it entered the human body. The boy theorized that exposure to certain amino acids present in the outer layers of the skin neutralized the temperature-sensitive defense mechanism he'd given his compound, and he was right. The substance he created in our labs is meant to *synthesize* those amino acids on an extremely concentrated level. Once mixed with the original CLAIR formula, it will permanently remove the defense mechanism that prevented the organism from spreading beyond the Cambridgeside Galleria."

"Are you saying that—"

"If he combines the new compound with CLAIR and releases the resulting product, there will be nothing to impede CLAIR's spread, nothing to stop it.''

Fuchs stood up very slowly. ''In which case . . .''

''Joshua Wolfe could destroy the world,'' Haslanger completed.

''*All* human and animal life?'' McCracken asked, not believing what Susan Lyle had just explained.

She nodded. ''He told me as much last night but I didn't realize he'd actually do it, actually release them.''

''Release what?''

'' 'The Fires of Midnight,' the title of the first poem Josh ever wrote. It describes his frustrations over being so different, over not fitting in. He had tremendous rage even then, and now it's boiling over. He's fed up. He wants a way to make sure everyone will just leave him alone.''

''By threatening to destroy the world if they don't . . .''

''He believes that's the only way to keep the Group Sixes of the world off his back. He can live with anything, I guess, except being forced to perpetrate more Cambridgeside Gallerias.''

''He didn't do it.''

''*What?*''

''A CIA splinter group that's been monitoring him all along tampered with his formula. They're the real murderers.''

''But he doesn't know that.''

''Not until we tell him. If what you say is true he's got to have a sample of the original CLAIR formula stashed somewhere, right?''

Susan nodded slowly.

''Disney World, Doctor.''

''What?'' Haslanger had trouble rising out of the torpor he had sunk into upon returning to his darkened office. He had left the lights off, almost daring sleep to take him, preferring that to facing what Joshua Wolfe was prepared to unleash upon the world. He felt beaten, duped. All the time he and Fuchs had been trying to fool the boy, he had been fooling them. And Haslanger had fallen for it, blinded by the pride he felt for what he had created. He knew he was finished here, just as he knew there was nowhere else for him to go.

"The people Sinclair dispatched to Orlando have confirmed that Joshua Wolfe was inside Disney World's Magic Kingdom shortly before he broke into our network from the hotel," Fuchs elaborated.

"His second portion of CLAIR . . ."

"Interesting hiding place, don't you think? Provides hope for us in spite of everything."

"Hope?"

"Your revelation about what the boy has the potential to do changes nothing so far as the preservation of Group Six is concerned. Our survival still depends on locating the remainder of CLAIR. I'll alert General Starr toward that end. I'm sure he'll give us however many men we require to accomplish the task."

"You'll never find it," Haslanger insisted.

Fuchs glared at him quizzically through the dark. "I wasn't talking about finding it. I was talking about finding *the boy* and letting him lead us to it. I mean, thanks to you, Doctor, we now know exactly where he must be headed. All we must do is wait."

"McCracken will be accompanying him, or following close behind."

"Then we have to make sure to take enough men to deal with him once and for all as well, don't we?"

"Why didn't you tell me all this before?" Blaine demanded.

"Because I was afraid it would confirm everything you feared about Josh already, everything your Indian friend already believed."

"He didn't do anything. We know that now."

"You didn't then. If I'd told you he had another vial of CLAIR hidden, if I'd told you what he was planning to do with it . . ."

"What?"

"I was afraid you'd kill him."

"What kind of man do you think I am?"

"Someone who does what he thinks is the right thing."

"Killing innocent people is never the right thing."

"Until this morning you didn't know Joshua Wolfe was innocent. But everyone's been after him because of the terrible things they thought he could be capable of: you from one side, Group Six from the other. But what about the miraculous things he's capable of?"

"In your hands, instead of Group Six's?"

"Among others."

"And after you get what you want, somebody else gets their turn, right? Point is, sooner or later we're right back where we started—with Group Six or somebody else just as bad ending up using Joshua Wolfe."

"We all want something," she managed. "Even you."

"All I want right now is to keep this kid from mixing his two test tubes together. Let him know that he didn't kill anybody, after all."

"And just how do you plan to go about that?"

McCracken shrugged. "For starters, Dr. Lyle, it looks like I'm going to Disney World."

"Regrettable, Mr. Thurman, most regrettable," Livingstone Crum lamented when Thurman reached him by cellular phone from the Valley of the Dead.

"Pack it in. This one's finished."

"Thanks in no small part to you."

"We can divvy out the blame later. For now shut everything down. That includes Mount Jackson. Suspend the operation. Recall the team."

"I'm afraid it's already too late for that."

PART FIVE

MIDNIGHT

DISNEY WORLD,
SATURDAY, 6:00 P.M.

CHAPTER 38

"For he's a jolly good fellow, for he's a jolly good fellow.
For he's a jolly good fellow, that nobody can deny. . . ."

The song continued to ring in Turk Wills's ears as the cake was brought out. Took two people to carry it. Hell of a lot bigger than the one they'd had for his retirement as captain in the Florida Highway Patrol twelve years back at the age of forty-two. Since he was the first black to reach that rank in the patrol's proud history, it hadn't been easy to force him out. But Wills had gone against his superiors' express orders by continuing an investigation into the misuse of federally owned lands. When the evidence came up short of indictments, someone had to take the fall and it was he.

One thing was for certain: this cake had to feed lots more people than the one they'd given him for his last retirement. As head of security for Disney World's Magic Kingdom, Wills had upwards of five hundred people working under him.

"Speech, speech, speech!" the vast assembled crowd squeezed into the command center was chanting. Turk Wills stepped toward the cake to blow out the candles.

Funny thing about retiring when you work in Florida; where do you retire to? Wills wanted to spend more time with his family like everyone else, but the grandkids had all cried when he told them he was leaving Disney World. No more special treatment, they thought, no more backstage passes and tunnel tours. They were too young for Wills to explain it to them. How credit card theft and counterfeiting were by far the biggest problems facing Disney World today and how others were better suited to handle those kinds of problems. He had a street cop's mentality, and snaring criminals with wads of plastic jammed into their Jockey shorts just didn't cut it anymore. Fifty-four years old—it was time, anyway.

Turk blew out the candles and caught his smiling reflection in the glass partition. Still firm and well muscled for a man his age, he packed at least a portion of the build that might have made him an all-American offensive lineman if he hadn't blown out his knee halfway through junior year at Clemson. He worked out as often as he could, proud that from a distance he looked ten, maybe fifteen years younger. Lately he'd even been thinking of letting his hair grow back, a rather extreme change since he'd been shaving himself bald every day since high school.

Turk had enjoyed a good run down here at Disney, but he was glad to be getting out now, before Park Number Four officially opened. That was what everyone had been calling it for the three years of construction on the Osceola side of Disney's forty-three-square-mile property. Even the workmen had no idea what they were building and every blueprint Turk had seen told him less than the one before. He had learned the truth only four months before in a high-level meeting that at Disney meant representatives from sidewalk sweepers on up. Park Number Four's theme was safari and would feature the world's largest and best-stocked zoo. An enclosed tram would wind through and over versions of the plains of Africa, the jungles of the Congo and Amazon, and other regions brilliantly reproduced to create natural habitats for Disney's ambitious stock of animals.

Patrons would be able to watch these animals sans bars, walls or fences from a tram car. There would also be a dozen petting zoos, chimps conversing with paying customers in sign language through interpreters, along with the world's largest aviary and reptile collection. Safariland areawise would be Disney's largest theme park, as big as Epcot and MGM combined. It had been scheduled to open in the summer and Disney attractions always open as scheduled.

But this would prove the exception.

Never before had live animals entered into the Disney mix, and their care, upkeep and the unexpected logistical problems all partially shared responsibility for an indefinite postponement of the opening. Partially because the final and arguably most stunning attraction in Safariland had turned into a nightmare:

Dinoworld.

It was meant to be a real Jurassic Park populated by robotic dinosaurs every bit as real as the ones from the hit movie. The problem was software. The programs written to control the dinosaurs' movements were the most complicated in history and initially required a pair of supercomputers to handle. Even then the programs kept developing bugs, and mechanical breakdowns came with every change in the wind.

Since Safariland and Dinoworld weren't going to be ready as planned, a compromise had been reached so that summertime patrons who'd made their plans long in advance wouldn't be disappointed. The working robots of two favorites, Tyrannosaurus rex and Stegosaurus, would be on display and performing starting on the Fourth of July. Wills asked the Disney brass if they knew what that would do to crowd control. They told him that was his problem, the last he would face before officially stepping down. So, added to the hundred thousand people, parades and fireworks on the Fourth of July, Wills was going to have to deal with dinosaurs being proudly unveiled.

He got to the last candle on his cake and stopped. The single ornament in the center of the icing was a T. rex. Wills scowled. Everyone else laughed.

"Let's see," he started dramatically, "today being July third makes tomorrow my last day on the job. Then I'll leave you assholes to all the new problems caused by—"

"Turk," his assistant called from the doorway leading to the inner office.

"You're interrupting my speech, son."

"Sorry. Phone call."

"Headquarters?"

"No, sir," the young man replied, a dumbfounded expression on his face. "Washington."

"You?" Haslanger raised incredulously.

Fuchs's neck stiffened. "Can you think of anyone else capable of supervising this mission? Certainly not you, Doctor."

"No, not me."

"Of course not. To oversee recovery you would have to leave the confines of Group Six. Not very likely, is it?"

Haslanger said nothing.

"You would be well advised to keep that in mind while I am gone. Your performance as of late has been most disappointing, I'm afraid. The failures with GL-12 and then your blindness ray, followed by your bungling of CLAIR."

"*My* bungling?"

"The boy was your creation. As such you should have been able to control him. Instead, by your own admission, he was calling every shot, captured only because he wanted to be, because we possessed the technology he required. It would be a terrible thing if he escaped Disney World with the only remaining portion of CLAIR, a terrible thing for both of us."

"A terrible thing for the entire world, you mean."

"Then you'd better hope my efforts are successful. And another thing, Doctor. If I am removed from Group Six, consider your own fate. You may find my successor to be far less sympathetic to your idiosyncrasies than I have been. But we should not stray from the matter at hand. Luckily, General Starr has supplied me with the manpower I need to accomplish what I must." A slight smile stretched Fuchs's lips. "I must tell you, I'm looking forward to the opportunity."

Haslanger's eyes urged caution, tentatively. "What of McCracken? He'll be there, of course, certain to know everything we know."

"No argument there, and for just that reason I would ask that you summon Krill. I think it best he accompany me south."

"Disney World?" the man on the other end of the line asked incredulously through the staticky connection.

"General Starr has assembled an army to meet Fuchs there," Thurman told him. Ordinarily use of a standard phone line in such a situation would have been avoided at all costs. In this case, though, he had no choice.

"But not you."

"I've decided to take some time off."

"Why call me?"

"I thought you should know. McCracken's going to need help."

"You think there's anything *I* can do?"

"I knew you'd want to try."

"You available?"

"Like I said, I'm taking some time off."

"Doesn't leave me with much."

"More than McCracken's got now."

Haslanger faced Krill from across the desk in his darkened office.

"The colonel wishes you to join him in Disney World. He knows he will need you to finish this affair to everyone's satisfaction."

The dim light caught Krill's catlike eyes, the room's shadows further elongating his already out-of-proportion features.

"I need you there, too, for both our sakes," Haslanger continued. "The colonel has made it his business to learn too much about me. I would venture he is the only man who knows everything, and when this ends badly—and, believe me, it will—I am the most likely candidate to become the scapegoat. I know that. It is the way the colonel works." Haslanger stood up. "But he can be beaten. We can both be free of him, you and I, providing he does not return. Providing all traces of Joshua Wolfe and his fiendish concoction are wiped from existence."

"He frightens you," Krill said, in words that floated in the darkness like wisps of wind.

"The colonel? Hardly."

"I was speaking of the boy. He frightens you because you know he is smarter than you are. You want me to kill him because he has become more than just a threat to Group Six. The creator, afraid of being destroyed by what he has fashioned."

Haslanger made himself stare across the desk through the darkness until the disfigured face and skull were plain to him. "Yes, I am afraid, and you should be, too. If Fuchs leaves Disney World with the boy's remaining portion of CLAIR, I will have outlived my usefulness to him, and that means so will you. Don't you see? They all must die, everyone in that park. Fuchs will be blamed for it, while we will be spared, as will Group Six. Another Pentagon administrator will take over who lacks the colonel's intimate knowledge of the two of us.

Tell me you see this just as I do. Tell me you share my vision.''

Krill's massive head nodded.

"Very good," Haslanger said, calmer. He stood up and approached the locked cabinet on the side wall that contained a gallery of his creations. "Now let me tell you how it must be done. . . ."

"Found out why you've been having trouble reaching that friend of yours," a grim-faced Sal Belamo told Susan Lyle upon returning to the car that would handle the first leg of their journey to Florida. Belamo had already arranged for a private plane to cover the bulk of it, and if all went according to plan, they'd be getting into Orlando early Sunday morning. "His name is Killebrew."

"Was, Doc. He's dead. Got himself toasted in a blast that took out the CDC's entire containment facility inside Mount Jackson."

Susan felt an emptiness in the pit of her stomach. "My God . . ."

"It gets worse. From what I just heard they're trying to pin the blame for the whole mess on you. Say you went crazy. Calling you a renegade."

"Welcome to the club," McCracken said from next to her in the backseat.

"They can't get away with that."

"Yes, they can," Blaine told her. "You made yourself a convenient target for everyone to cover their tracks. Got yourself linked up with the wrong people inside Group Six. Helped lay waste to that facility and then headed west."

"What are you talking about?"

"Tell her, Sal," Blaine said with his eyes locked on Susan.

"Story is you were just an accomplice. Boss, me and the Indian are getting most of the blame."

"Meaning there's nowhere any of us can turn to for help in Disney World."

Blaine nodded. "Something I've grown used to."

"I haven't. Look, this is still about finding Josh and his remaining sample of CLAIR, and Killebrew was running some crucial experiments on the organism. He would have tried to reach me any way possible.''

"Your voice mail's probably been listened to by anyone who can handle a touchtone by now, Doc,'' cautioned Sal Belamo.

Susan looked toward Blaine. "I set up that private electronic mailbox, just like you suggested, and gave Killebrew the number.''

"I don't recall suggesting giving it to anyone but me.''

"You're not the only one who can think for himself.''

Sal Belamo pulled out his cellular phone. "What the hell? Let's give it a whack.''

Arkansas authorities had no choice but to let the fire that raged through the CDC's Mount Jackson containment facility following the series of explosions burn itself out. It was twelve hours before rescue crews in helicopters could even venture close. Early reconnaissance of the site left little hope there'd be anyone to rescue, but until a closer inspection was made no one could say for sure. The containment facility maintained a number of samples from past investigations in ultrasecure isolation cases which might be salvaged, if nothing else.

The first rescue team arrived in helicopters that could land no closer than a mile from the remnants of the facility due to the still scorching heat. Ten men began the difficult trek through air choked with smoke, following its thickening clouds north toward the rubble.

Susan Lyle held the cellular phone blankly against her ear for several moments after Killebrew's recorded voice had completed its message. She could have replayed it but there was no reason; she had heard his words clearly enough. She just didn't want to believe them.

"You said someone blew up the containment facility,'' she posed to Belamo.

"In a big way.''

"Was there . . . a fire?''

"Still burning, last I heard.''

Susan pressed a number of keys on the cellular and then handed it to McCracken. "You better listen to this.''

                         *   *   *

The rescue team was passing through a blanket of thick
coarse smoke within sight of the containment facility's remnants when those in the lead suddenly clutched their throats.
The men further back could barely even see them through the
daytime darkness and didn't realize anything was wrong until
the first ones in their party dropped and began to roll downward, writhing and twitching.

The men bringing up the rear were the only ones to catch
a glimpse of their friends' bodies shriveling up in front of their
very eyes before they turned and tried desperately to escape.
One managed to yank his walkie-talkie free and was halfway
through the word "Mayday" when he heard a sound like paper being crinkled. He realized with cold terror that it was
coming from inside him. He started to scream but his mouth
locked open in the middle of trying, and he dropped to the
ground in spasm, tumbling to his death with the others.

"If Killebrew's findings were correct, that fire will have
brought CLAIR back to life," Susan said, when the message
he had left on her voice mail finished playing in McCracken's
ear. "Released it to spread unchecked."

"Can it be stopped?"

"If we can find Joshua Wolfe, there's a chance. He's the
only one who understands how CLAIR functions intimately
enough to stop it."

"Then it doesn't matter if the kid mixes CLAIR with whatever he created in Group Six once he gets to Disney World,"
Blaine concluded. "You're saying the Fires of Midnight have
already been released."

"And right now that makes Joshua Wolfe the only one who
can put them out."

CHAPTER 39

"Mister, I really wish somebody would tell me exactly what the hell is going on," Turk Wills snapped. He was in the Magic Kingdom security office located above an old-fashioned ice cream shop on Main Street U.S.A. Six A.M. on the Fourth of July, Wills hadn't been through his coffee yet, and here he was talking to a tense man in a crisply pressed business suit that looked all wrong for the day.

"It's 'Colonel,' if you don't mind."

"I do mind. I mind you army types coming down here and telling me how to do my job without telling me what you're really here for."

Fuchs rolled his neck, searching for comfort in civilian clothes. "You know what you need to know, Mr. Wills. I believe Washington was very clear on that point. Have you circulated the pictures?"

"Sure, of the kid and—"

"Stick with him first, please."

"All my people in the Kingdom got the shots. Be nice if I knew why it was so important that we find him."

"What's important is that your people simply report in if they spot him. They are not to approach on their own. Is that clear?"

"Crystal. Now what about the other picture, the bearded guy?"

"Same rules apply."

"If he represents some sort of danger to the park, I want to know about it."

"What he represents is of no concern to you."

And with that Fuchs turned away and took a long, slow look at the setup in the security center, getting his bearings. A bank of television monitors filled a large portion of the far wall. Manned by a single technician, the touch of a few computer keys could bring up any of nearly one hundred sweeping shots of the Magic Kingdom. The closed-circuit cameras broadcasting them were hidden atop buildings, trees, even rides, providing a complete view of what was happening outside.

"Somebody much higher ranking than colonel got me on the phone yesterday and told me you and the other suits would be coming down," Wills persisted. "Most of them been in the park since last night and it's pretty obvious they were looking for something they must not have found. Now, what I'd like to know is what it is and how it ties into this kid."

Fuchs gave him a long, hard look and spoke in a tone so deliberate it sounded caustic. "Mr. Wills—"

"It's 'Chief,' if you don't mind."

"*Chief* Wills, the Magic Kingdom's scheduled to open in roughly three hours' time. A hundred thousand people expected, I'm told. Your best bet to keep them all safe and sound, so they can leave with their thirty-five-millimeters, their kids and their wallets all fully exhausted, is to do just as I say."

Wills glanced at one of the black and white pictures every on-duty Magic Kingdom staffer throughout the day would be given. "I got a grandson almost as old as this."

"Congratulations," Fuchs said, and then turned back to the action unfolding on the constantly shifting screens. "Just do your job, Chief Wil—" He cut himself off when his eyes reached a screen almost dead center on the bank, widening in disbelief. "Are those . . . *dinosaurs*?"

"Yeah," said Wills, smirking. "We're just full of surprises here at Disney World."

"Looking good, Stace," one of her coworkers complimented Stacy Eagers as she completed yet another test run of the Tyrannosaurus rex's primary programming.

In addition to herself, there were four others working in the room they called Mission Control. Located beneath the Magic Kingdom along one of the sweeping corridors composing the tunnels, they had named the room for its resemblance on a smaller scale to the NASA version. Television monitors enclosed their every move, the dull glow off their screens capable of providing all the light they needed to perform the myriad of commands required to make the creatures come alive.

And that was what Stacy Eagers had come to think of them as: creatures, not robots, actual breathing monsters brought back from the world before man. And why not? So precise was their replication—every movement, gesture and mannerism—that they might as well have been *real*. Stacy Eagers was a thirty-year-old woman who had started out as a computer hacker at age twelve en route to becoming one of the country's most talented programmers. She had never had a boyfriend, couldn't remember if she'd enjoyed her last date, and never even considered exchanging her thick Coke-bottle glasses for contact lenses.

The Disney people had come to her after three others had failed in their assignments to write programs to make dinosaurs come to life robotically. Forget animation. Disney had built dinosaurs to scale. Not puppets made from papier-mâché or plastic, but creatures with skeletons formed of steel beams six inches in diameter. State-of-the-art hydraulics allowed for full articulation of the joints, eyes, teeth, lips—everything. But Disney wanted to go beyond the animatronics that drove comparable beasts at a theme park in Osaka, Japan, and soon would at the rival Universal Studios in California and Orlando. The problem wasn't in the hardware; the problem lay in developing software that could make these magnificent machines come alive.

And that's where Stacy came in. Disney had built creatures capable of a complete range of motion. Stacy's job was to give it to them. The dinosaurs couldn't move, roar, walk or interact until a computer program told them to. But every separate action, every lift of a foot and flap of a reptilian eyelid, required thousands of bits of information and hundreds of commands carried out in a millisecond. Stacy estimated that it would take six programmers four years working twenty-four hours a day to write the necessary programs for a minimum of three multimillion-dollar supercomputers. Not exactly what Disney wanted to hear until she told them the alternative:

Artificial intelligence.

Program the creatures with a series of rudimentary commands from which they would develop their own evolving progressions of activity. *Teach* them to learn to do things on their own within prescribed parameters. Even program them to remember and repeat those sequences which generated the most positive responses from spectators. Disney liked that touch most of all. They would still need one supercomputer to manage the effort but, considering it could handle the entire planned thirty-creature population of Dinoworld alone, the investment was considered worth it.

Stacy wasn't crazy about unveiling the first of the creatures so early, especially in the limited confines of the Magic Kingdom. The park had no open stretch of land big enough for the T. rex and the Steg to really do anything big, just move around a little, do some roaring and make eye contact with the patrons. The site they'd settled on was a barely wide-enough strip of grass on the lagoon bank to the left of Cinderella's Castle. Not a whole lot of room for viewing, but then the creatures were just going to be standing there on display for most of the day. She intended to run a few simple programs at regular intervals; that was it.

The row of television monitors immediately above Stacy allowed her to follow every programmed move the creatures made and to make the called-for adjustments. Another pair of monitors featured the view from the creatures' perspectives, thanks to minicams that had been positioned behind their eyes.

"Okay," she said, zooming in on the T. rex, "let's try one more run-through before we give the world its first peek."

The bearded man pushed the woman's wheelchair closer to the fence as the Tyrannosaurus rex's jaws widened for another gurgly roar.

"Is that what they really looked like?" Blaine McCracken asked Susan Lyle.

"Dinosaurs were never my specialty but, yes, I think this is pretty damn close."

The T. rex sank back to its time-honored hunker and, stretching its neck, scanned its huge head across the gallery viewing it. A few of the kids shrank from their perches. Adults laughed. Fifty feet away, on the opposite bank of the lagoon, the Stegosaurus gazed up from its make-believe munching of grass.

"We'd better have a look around the rest of the park," Blaine suggested, and pulled Susan's chair backwards, their cherished fence-front spots gobbled up instantly.

The Magic Kingdom's official opening time was nine A.M. But guests at Disney resorts could enter an hour before that and so, Blaine learned, could the handicapped. By using the wheelchair he hoped that he and Susan could remain together without attracting undue attention. The remainder of her disguise consisted of sunglasses and a soft, wide-brimmed straw hat that slouched low over her brow. She had also trimmed and colored her hair during a brief stop in a motel room thirty minutes from the park.

Blaine's disguise was equally effective. His goal was simply to mix in amongst the other thousands of park patrons and toward this end he, too, had donned a sun hat. But that was where the obvious ended. McCracken hoped to draw attention to certain features of his disguise, including a belly hanging well over his waist courtesy of a thick motel-room pillow. He had used paste and talcum powder to color his beard gray and then let Susan cut his thick wavy hair short enough to brush straight back. Finally he had added attention-getting sunglasses to the mix, featuring one colored lens and one clear lens, evidence of an eye disorder. Anyone looking at him would take note of his glasses and likely stop there.

"Where to now?" Susan asked Blaine, after they had extricated themselves from the crowd struggling for a glimpse of the first exhibits from Dinoworld.

"A spin around the park. I need to catch my bearings."

McCracken eased her chair along the road that curved left from Cinderella's Castle and banked toward Frontierland. He had never been to the Magic Kingdom before and could only imagine what it would be like jammed with people milling everywhere. Not ready to consider the prospects of that yet, he busied himself with an analytical consideration of the logistics they were facing.

The Magic Kingdom was divided into seven different theme parks he preferred to think of in terms of grids. As such, Sal Belamo had been assigned several in the north and east, in-

cluding Mickey's Starland and Tomorrowland, while Blaine
made himself responsible for the four concentrated to the south
and west. They would continue to make sweeps throughout
the day in search of Joshua Wolfe, maintaining contact with
each other as well as with Johnny Wareagle, who would con-
fine himself to the labyrinth of tunnels that ran beneath Disney
World until his services were required. No disguise, it was
deemed, would be enough to hide Johnny from Fuchs's troops.

From the moment Blaine eased Susan off the Disney monorail and down the ramp for the entrance onto Main Street
U.S.A., the scope of the Magic Kingdom—the countless roads
which weaved and sliced through it—left him awestruck. On
the one hand he took solace in the fact that such a massive
facility would make it all the harder for Fuchs's men to find
him. On the other, it would be equally hard for him to find
Joshua Wolfe. A barbershop quartet had greeted their entry
and now he could hear a marching band approaching.

"Do you think he's here now?" Susan asked as Blaine kept
sweeping and cataloguing with his eyes.

"I wouldn't be. Not enough people to use for cover yet."

"When would you come?"

"Late this afternoon, when the really big crowds arrive.
Maybe even tonight, when darkness makes it all the harder to
find me."

"And yet you wanted to be here as early as possible."

"Because I can't be sure, and because I wanted to get the
lay of the land."

She could feel McCracken's hands suddenly tighten on the
handles as the chair rolled slowly across the litter-free road.
Two men ambled by, looking from side to side, and kept going
even after their eyes had crossed Blaine and his wheelchair-
bound charge.

"Another pair of Colonel Fuchs's men," he said after they
were well past.

"How many does that make?"

"Enough to make the odds of us finding Josh before they
do lousy at best."

"You on today?"

Johnny Wareagle looked quizzically at the man wearing the
cowboy outfit.

"Injun Joe, right?" the cowboy continued. "Tom Sawyer's Island. Live characters today."

"Oh," Johnny said softly. "Yes."

"Should be fun."

Wareagle had crossed paths with the cowboy at a bend in one of the corridors that ran beneath the Magic Kingdom. Located beneath the glitter and crowds, this subterranean maze contained the bulk of the park offices, storage areas and its electronic nerve center as well as access points to virtually all the rides' movable parts. No gears or grease, in fact, were ever glimpsed because they were all contained in "the tunnels," as they were commonly referred to. Problems were accordingly often repaired before anyone noticed anything amiss. Ride stoppages were unheard of at Disney. Nothing slowed the constant flow of people determined to have a good time.

So, too, security guards were a rare sight in the Magic Kingdom. If any needed to get from one spot to another in a hurry, they almost invariably used the park's subterranean world to reach hot points whenever trouble arose. There was no place in the park that could not be reached via these tunnels, which were often used by Disney characters to delight kids by seeming to pop up anywhere without warning.

Johnny Wareagle had been waiting in the darkness for Blaine McCracken to tell him where to go, when a high school band being given a tour forced him to move on. There were plenty of places for him to hide, in the form of storerooms, staff changing and locker rooms, lounges and closets. Each hallway featured clear markings indicating what lay ahead in all directions, both here in the tunnels as well as aboveground in the park itself. Johnny hadn't been paying much attention because it didn't seem to matter. He'd put plenty of distance between himself and the high school band when he had run into the cowboy stuck before him now.

"Well, I got the first stunt show in Frontierland," he said finally. "Good luck."

"Good luck," Johnny returned.

The cowboy started to move on, then changed his mind. "Ran into another big guy not long before you, you know."

Johnny felt his spine quiver, thinking of the monstrous thing Blaine McCracken had encountered in the New York Public

Library and then again inside Group Six.

"Somebody did a great makeup job on him, let me tell you. I figured he was heading for the Haunted Mansion, 'cept I didn't know we were adding live figures there, too." He seemed to think of something. "Come to think of it, he was heading in the wrong direction."

"Which direction?"

The cowboy pointed back, slid easily into his performance drawl. "He went thata way, off to the right. Hey, you know him?"

"Maybe."

The cowboy tipped his cap. "Have a good day, pardner. Don't scare too many kids in that cave of yours."

"No."

"Happy Fourth of July!"

CHAPTER 40

Joshua Wolfe reached the Magic Kingdom at dusk, covering the last stretch of the ride in a shuttle bus boarded in front of the local plaza hotels. The Magic Kingdom was the third stop after Disney-MGM Studios and Epcot, and the four-mile trek took a choking, churning forty minutes. Traffic was backed up for miles, everyone coming and nobody, it seemed, going. The parking lots, especially the Magic Kingdom's, had turned into obstacle courses with buses parked anywhere they could steal a place to squeeze into, only to find themselves unable to maneuver in the mounting clutter. The driver of this shuttle repeated the pickup times but cautioned patrons to be patient. A long night was promised. Anyone who wanted to get home sanely, he advised, should leave before the parade and the fireworks got under way.

The driver opened the doors and people crowded into the aisle impatiently. Josh felt his breathing shorten, suddenly claustrophobic. To settle himself, he focused on the task before him: retrieving the vial of CLAIR and retracing his steps out of the park. The front pocket of his jeans held the small vial of the compound he'd created in Group Six to mix with CLAIR, if he had to—if they made him.

Josh barely remembered leaving the bus, getting the admission ticket he had bought earlier in the week ready, and stepping onto the monorail. His life seemed to start again when the monorail doors opened before the entrance to the Magic Kingdom. They stamped his ticket, gave it back and he was through the turnstile onto Main Street U.S.A. This was Disney's elegant re-creation of a quaint small-town center, complete with horse-drawn carriages, antique car replicas, and old-fashioned trolleys, one of which now featured a barbershop quartet singing in perfect harmony.

Josh moved farther into the world of simulated small-town life. Hair held back by a baseball cap that made him look like every other teenager in the park, Josh ambled dazedly on, lost in the swirl of lights and activity. He smelled fresh popcorn, heard the far-off sounds of a marching band making its way through the park.

And saw the Men. They stood out stiffly, eyes focused nowhere near the attractions. Josh walked toward the grassy, tree-lined park across the square where Disney characters were mugging for photos with speechless children. Nearer to him a group of teenagers in matching navy T-shirts squeezed together for a commemorative picture. Josh approached a boy about his age who was struggling to focus a camera before the group broke apart.

"Hey, want me to take the shot?" he offered. "That way you can be in the picture, too."

"Good idea, man," the kid returned, and looped the camera over his neck. "Just press here," he said, handing it over.

Josh accepted the Minolta and waited for the boy to squeeze in amongst his friends before focusing. They were smiling, laughing, impossible to still. Josh felt the camera tremble in his hand. He didn't want to be taking the picture—he wanted to be in it, too, wanted to be part of something.

"Whenever you're ready," one of them yelled out.

He pushed the button, snapped off a few more and then left them to their clowning. A sea of dark blue shirts, making the kids anonymous amidst the crowd.

"Hey, thanks, man," said the kid, taking the camera back from him and extending his hand. "I'm Andy."

Josh took it in the best grip he could manage. "Josh."

"Hey, you got a camera? How 'bout I take one of you?"

Josh thought of the eyes of Fuchs's drones relentlessly searching for him.

"I've got a better idea," he told Andy.

McCracken greeted the dark like an old friend for the relative cool it brought. The hours had melted away between iced teas and lemonades purchased during sweep after sweep of the park. He pushed Susan Lyle's wheelchair toward the Splash Mountain ride from the Big Thunder Mountain Railroad, watching a constant procession of jammed cars reach the top only to be jettisoned over a fake waterfall on a seemingly straight drop down. Each landed with a thud and skidded across the water, spraying the gleefully screaming occupants who'd waited two hours for the adventure.

"Hey, boss," Sal Belamo called.

"Here, Sal," Blaine returned, pretending to speak toward Susan instead of the jawbone microphone of his wireless communicator. "Where are you?"

"Just went through Alien Encounters in, what the fuck, Tomorrowland. You wouldn't believe the shit they got inside this thing."

"Glad you're enjoying yourself. Our friends still in evidence?"

"Looking a little more nervous now that it's getting dark."

After twelve hours in the park, twelve hours of becoming intimately acquainted with the scope and layout of the Magic Kingdom, Blaine could best describe it as deceiving. On the one hand it seemed as if it must be larger than it really was to accommodate the seven different theme parks located within it. On the other, those theme parks had been fitted economically into a manageable but confusing area. It took Blaine several sweeps before he figured out which road went where. He had his bearings now, could recite all the various eating establishments and souvenir specialty shops, in addition to the rides, from memory.

As the day wore on, it had become increasingly difficult to negotiate the roads through the mounting crowds. Numbers had peaked during the last two hours to the point where moving atop the spotless avenues meant standing still much of the time. McCracken checked his watch. In a little over an hour's time, the Spectromagic Parade would begin, followed immediately by a massive Fourth of July fireworks display in the Disney tradition, the highlight of which was going to be an American flag sewn in the sky by continuous explosions of red, white and blue.

"Fuchs's people are looking for us as well as the boy, aren't they?"

"Could be we've already been spotted."

"Even though they haven't made a move?"

"Insurance. Fuchs isn't sure his people will be able to find Josh, so he's hoping we do it for him. Remember, he doesn't know the kid slipped away from us. Figures we're all still together."

"Like one big, happy family," said Susan.

Everything considered, this last day had been one of the worst in Turk Wills's life. The Magic Kingdom was breaking attendance records every time somebody new came through a turnstile and, in between dispatching his men to hot sites spotted by his plainclothes detail, he had to deal with Mr. Washington. What he would have liked to do was take Colonel Asshole and string him up from the wire running from Cinderella's Castle for Tinkerbell's Flight. See if it would hold his weight.

Mr. Washington had been watching the closed-circuit monitors and nothing else. He was soaked with sweat even though the air-conditioning was cranking as high as it would go. He spoke suddenly now, though his eyes never left the screens.

"I told you he'd be coming in after dusk. I told you to put your people on the alert."

"We got a hundred thousand people in the park right now. My people been on the alert all day."

The man from Washington swung his chair toward him stiffly, neck locked to his shoulders from staring at the screens too long. "I'd like to sympathize with your problem—"

"Thanks."

"—but I need to remind you the matter that brought me here is one of national security."

Fuchs started to come up out of his chair, but Wills spun it around so they were both facing the bank of monitors again. "See that?" he said, gesturing to a quartet of screens picturing different parts of Main Street U.S.A., stretching all the way to Cinderella's Castle. "They're setting up for the parade right now. In an hour I'm gonna have maybe sixty thousand people jammed along that route you see up there. Now, I'm figuring whatever's going to go down here is likely to put plenty of them in danger. So what I can do, I can either pull my men to help you cause it, or I can keep them on watch to protect those sixty thousand from whatever might happen." Wills turned the chair again and looked Fuchs right in the eye. "I choose option two."

"I'll have your job for this," the colonel promised.

"Come midnight tonight, it's all yours, Mr. Washington."

The group in navy T-shirts was part of a teen tour that had originated in the Northeast ten days earlier. They had been working their way south through historical Philadelphia, Washington, Williamsburg, Gettysburg, reaching Disney World as planned on the Fourth of July. The boy whose camera Josh had taken the picture with—Andy—had given him one of the blue shirts and that made him, for all intents and purposes, one of them.

The large group splintered off into several smaller ones, Josh trailing along with a dozen or so who opted to head for the Haunted Mansion. They halted just past Liberty Square when they saw how long the line was.

"Shit," a girl named Wendy muttered.

"What about Splash Mountain?" a boy named David asked.

"Worse," a gum-chewing girl replied.

"Tom Sawyer's Island," Josh suggested a bit nervously, realizing he was running out of time.

"What?" from Wendy.

"No line for the raft over. Entrance is right there and it's closing at dark."

"What the hell?" responded another of the kids. "It's better than nothing."

Josh counted his blessings, concentrating on the matter at hand. He knew the Men would be riding the rafts one after the other. All those potential hiding places in the caves and mines on the island wouldn't have been lost on them. Linking up with these kids was his only hope for safe passage over there.

They packed onto the raft named "Huck Finn" and were squeezed back against the far rail. Josh kept his eyes down, knowing he mustn't invite a chance glance, even in the coming dark. The straw-hatted driver repeated the "Closing in ten minutes" warning and urged all passengers to be quick in their exploring. The raft thumped against the dock on the island and the patrons disembarked into a shack labeled "Aunt Polly's Restaurant."

This really *was* an island, and that was what had attracted Josh to it initially on Wednesday. He had ultimately settled on it as the hiding place for his second vial of CLAIR because of the dark, cool hiding places it offered. After checking out all the possibilities, he had chosen Injun Joe's Cave. When he discovered that finding the perfect spot within it was impossible, he had decided to create one by chipping out a large enough portion of rock with the help of his belt buckle. The resulting gap easily accommodated the vial but, even chipping away further at the shard of rock, could not stop it from protruding slightly once replaced.

That was a blessing now, since it would greatly facilitate his task of locating the spot again in the dark. Sure enough, he found the slight ridge quickly and removed the rock fragment. Then he slid his fingers into the depression and gripped the vial firmly. He eased it into the pocket on the other side of his jeans from the one containing the smaller vial he'd taken out of Group Six. Now that he had what he'd come for he could begin to think about exiting the Magic Kingdom, something that would surely prove more difficult than entering. But if he could stick with this group of teenagers for another hour or so, exit from the park would come infinitely easier in the postfireworks rush.

Moving swiftly, he caught up with the other kids and accompanied them to the landing where the last of the island's patrons for the day waited to be ferried back to the Magic Kingdom mainland. His group squeezed onto the second-to-last raft, "Huck Finn" again. A few minutes later it thumped home against the mainland dock. The surge of the crowd pushed Josh forward onto the landing, then back up to the pedestrian road that sliced through the Magic Kingdom. He followed the others, who stopped when they caught a glimpse of roller-coasterlike cars careening through some nearby foliage.

"What ride was that?" Wendy asked.

"Big Thunder Mountain Railroad," the boy named David answered. "Let's check it out."

And they headed off to the right, the ride just below them, with Joshua Wolfe following along as if caught in the flow.

—

Krill checked his watch, satisfied that it was almost time to move. The fireworks display would be starting in barely an hour's time at the conclusion of the evening's Spectromagic Parade.

Normally, the Magic Kingdom's fireworks were shot off from a custom-made turret pedestal poised in a cement court-yard behind Cinderella's Castle. But tonight's were too elaborate and required too many mortar tubes and Roman candles for the area to accommodate them. So they had been moved to a barge moored in the Seven Seas Lagoon between the Polynesian and Grand Floridian resort hotels.

The change of location, though, would not change the unique way the shells would be shot off. Instead of black-powder charges, Disney fired their charges by air pressure, known as the air launch pyrotechnic system. Similarly, the shells would be set off electronically as opposed to the standard timer launch. The result was a show far less dangerous and far more spectacular, since it allowed technicians to precisely time the release of every single burst of color.

It had taken Krill several hours to disassemble the trio of shells he'd located in the storage closet, properly insert the three canisters containing the nerve gas Dr. Haslanger had provided, and then reassemble the shells. His remaining task now was to load these altered charges into the mortar tubes fastened tight atop the barge. When the fireworks exploded to life, the nerve gas inserted within would disperse over the entire area of the Magic Kingdom. That would give Krill a half hour to escape before it took effect. Fuchs wouldn't be coming out and neither would Joshua Wolfe. With Fuchs dead and taking the blame for the debacle, both Krill and Haslanger would be safe. Group Six would survive in some form, and however reduced it might be, Haslanger would be able to retain his labs and research facilities.

Krill reviewed the remaining logistics of his plan. Take the launch out to the barge and load his three charges into separate mortar tubes. The entire show was controlled by a computer program that would kick in automatically. No technicians

would even be in the area. Krill's plan was to work his way
to the launch once the parade started and go from there.

Krill had just stepped out from the storage room, the three
shells held in a small tote bag, when he saw the huge shadow
approaching an elbow turn in the tunnels ahead. He ducked
back inside but left the door open a crack, just enough to catch
a glimpse of the Indian gliding up the hallway. Krill tensed.
He recognized the Indian from a picture in McCracken's file,
knew he had been party to the debacle at Group Six a few
nights earlier.

He had accordingly expected the Indian to be in the park,
yet not down here stalking him as Krill felt certain was the
case. To confront the Indian now, though, he knew, would be
to threaten the success of his mission. So Krill remained still
and waited until the Indian was out of sight before moving
back into the corridor and heading in the opposite direction,
remembering too late that he'd left the door to the storage
room open.

"Hey! Hey! Up here!"

Josh turned his eyes upward along with the rest of the kids
in the group as they reached the start of Big Thunder Mountain
Railroad.

"Here!"

A boy was straddling the tracks above them, waving. A
camera dangled from around his throat and Josh realized it
was Andy.

"Get the fuck down!" David yelled up at him.

He showed his camera. "I just want to take one—"

The rest of Andy's words were drowned out when a chain
of roller coaster cars swept round the bend. The smile vanished
from his face. He froze briefly as the cars bore down on him.
The *whomp* of a collision followed and Andy was airborne,
tumbling toward the ground.

The girl named Wendy screamed.

"Oh, God," someone else moaned.

Andy hit the bank with a thud and rolled. Above him the
Big Thunder Mountain Railroad cars wavered but somehow
clung to the tracks.

"Help!" a voice yelled. "Someone get help!"

Josh was close to the fallen boy and moved instinctively, pushing forward through some brush to reach his moaning, semiconscious form.

"Help me," Andy muttered fearfully. "Help me, please. . . ."

Josh settled down next to him.

CHAPTER 41

Response to the accident within the Magic Kingdom was swift and immediate. One of the costumed young men working the controls for Big Thunder Mountain Railroad hit the hidden emergency button that triggered a silent alarm, silent everywhere but inside the security office, where a harmonic buzz sounded to the accompaniment of a red light over the bank of monitors.

Turk Wills looked up. "What the hell . . ."

The monitor, crowded a bit by the presence of Mr. Washington, spun away from the screens toward Wills. "Thunder Mountain Railroad, sir." He twisted back and punched his keyboard to bring pictures of the area into view. "Looks like a fall."

"Send medical," Wills ordered. Then, to another worker, "Alert Orlando County MC. Tell them to expect one possible incoming casualty, major trauma possible. Get me a MedVac chopper here in case we've got a critical."

Even as Wills spoke, a fully equipped rescue wagon appeared from a garage hidden in the park. It flashed its lights, hit its sirens occasionally, and headed for Big Thunder Mountain Railroad, slowed by the massive crowds clogging the streets. At the same time, emergency medical response teams rushed on foot to the area via the tunnels, toting black bags. By this time the security monitor had managed to fill six screens with various angles of the accident's aftermath.

"I'm heading down there," Wills announced, halfway to the stairway that would take him down into the tunnels. His eyes fell briefly on Colonel Fuchs. "Sorry for the distraction, Mr. Washington."

But Fuchs was more concerned with the action unfolding on one of the screens, telling the monitor to zoom in closer.

                    *   *   *

Andy wailed in pain when Josh touched his shoulder.

"*My leg!*" Josh discerned through the shrieks. "*My leg!*"

Josh inspected Andy's right leg, which was bent inward at an odd angle. His fingers reached down and felt the steady pulse of blood flowing out of a tear in the femoral artery. Andy could be dead in less than a minute without immediate treatment.

Josh let instinct take over, knowledge from his two years' worth of medical school charging through his brain like information across a computer screen. Knowing seconds were precious, he stripped off the belt from his jeans, worked it around the thick, fleshy part of Andy's thigh, and tied it tight, double-looping the knot.

All the while the boy was moaning, almost wailing.

"This will slow the bleeding," Josh told him.

Andy's shirt was ripped and Josh tore a ragged strip from it and balled it tight. He eased his hand back toward the wound and felt between the knee and thigh for it. He located it blindly and found the point where the blood, not quite stanched but slowed considerably, originated. Probing his fingers through the ragged strip of flesh brought him to the point where the artery had been partially torn. He pressed the balled-up fabric in tight and applied as much pressure as he could.

Josh heard activity behind him and then an unfamiliar voice saying, "Move aside, please. Move aside."

He turned and looked up to see a pair of emergency medical personnel starting to learn toward him, huffing for breath. "Sublateral laceration of the femoral artery," Josh reported, before either could speak. "I have tied the flow off eighteen centimeters above the knee."

"Christ," one of them muttered.

"We'll take over now," the other said firmly.

He squeezed in close and replaced Josh's hand with his own upon Andy's leg. Josh rose and backed away, realizing that blood had splattered onto his shirt and was dripping from his hand.

Standing in front of the monitor board, Colonel Fuchs gasped. Joshua Wolfe's image was clearly visible in the center of one of the screens. His first thought was that the boy had been injured. Then he saw him wipe his hand against his already stained shirt and slip away, eyes darting nervously about. Fuchs locked his stare on his quarry and spoke into the transistorized headset fixed over his ears.

"Target located! Thunder Mountain Railroad, northwest corner of park, bottom of Frontierland. Wearing a dark blue shirt and baseball cap."

The location was perfect, Fuchs realized. The man-made river separating Tom Sawyer's Island from the rest of the park and negotiated hourly by a cruising riverboat would keep the boy from fleeing north or east. The park's steep boundary line lay to the west and was blocked by fencing, leaving Joshua Wolfe only the southern area around Frontierland.

"Form a perimeter along the southwestern stretch of river across to Splash Mountain. I want men on the Frontierland rooftops to get me a spot, but exercise caution." Fuchs took a deep breath. "There's no reason to be rash. We've got him."

"An accident," Susan Lyle said softly, when the rescue wagon came into view near Cinderella's Castle.

McCracken, though, was more concerned with the flood of men in suits surging into the area, holding fast to their ear units, pushing their way through the milling, gathering crowds that wondered what had transpired. He recognized enough of them to know they were Fuchs's men descending on an area somewhere inside Frontierland.

Blaine grasped the handles of Susan's wheelchair and began to push, speaking into his jawbone mike. "Johnny!"

"Here, Blainey," Wareagle responded from the storage closet along the tunnels where he'd been for the last several minutes.

"Sal!"

"Read you, boss."

"Show time, boys. Meet me at the head of Frontierland pronto." He swung the wheelchair to the right.

"Wait a minute," Susan said, swinging her shoulders about. "We're going the wrong way! You're pushing me the wrong way!"

"Depends on your perspective." McCracken brought the

chair to a halt against a railing that overlooked Cinderella's Castle and the beginning of the parade route. "This is where it gets messy. You don't want to be around when we go to work."

"The boy!" she screamed after him, propping herself out of the wheelchair to the amazement of those gathered close by.

"I'll get him," Blaine said to her before he disappeared.

Joshua Wolfe melted away from the scene, into the crowds that thickened along the perimeter of the accident. They thinned slightly as he reached the main avenue of Frontierland where it wound its way past dark wooden buildings lifted from the Old West. Music from a player piano rose out of a brilliantly re-created combination saloon and restaurant called the Mile Long Bar. The flow of human traffic was clearly headed against Josh and bucking it meant standing out. But he had no choice. Losing himself in the mounting crowd headed north for the accident scene meant the risk of trapping himself. So he approached the stretch where passage through Frontierland narrowed in front of the Country Bear Jamboree and Shootin' Arcade.

But the front of Frontierland just beyond that passage was blocked. Josh could see some of the Men making a neat, inconspicuous row across it. And if he could see them . . .

Josh swung round and joined the flow of traffic back past the Shootin' Arcade, skirting the lines winding their way toward the Diamond Horseshoe and Country Bear Jamboree that filled up the larger buildings on his left.

The Men were there as well, more spread out and yet slightly more conspicuous. Watching for him. He realized he must have been spotted on a security monitor while at the site of the accident. There were buildings that he could dodge his way into, a number of restaurants that might offer a back door out to another section of the park. Maybe the Men hadn't had time to cover everything yet, at least not those doors.

Josh slowed his pace, intending to duck into the first likely-looking storefront.

*   *   *

Fuchs flicked his eyes back and forth over three different screens, following the deployment of his men through Frontierland. Suddenly a tall, familiar shape flashed briefly across the center one.

"Go back!" he ordered the man working the keyboard.

"Which screen?"

"This one!" Fuchs blared, pointing. "Slow! Go back slow! . . . There, hold it there!"

He never would have recognized Blaine McCracken beneath the paunch and baggy straw hat, but his giant Indian friend was unmistakable.

"McCracken is entering Frontierland. The Indian is with him," he announced to his troops. "Exercise extreme caution."

Blaine and Johnny Wareagle met up with Sal Belamo just inside Frontierland.

"We got activity up there, boss," Sal Belamo reported, his eyes fixed on the balconies and flat rooftops that adorned the buildings along the main drag.

"Snipers?"

"Spotters, from what I can tell. Boy gets found, it'll be them that does it."

"You handle the ones on the ground?"

Belamo scowled. "You need to ask?"

Blaine and Johnny bolted into a nearby building and charged up the stairs that led to the facade of a second floor. Earlier inspection of the building had shown it had access to the balcony and rooftop for the stunt players who performed regular shows during the afternoon and evening hours. The two men traced the footsteps of the players, Blaine taking a narrow door onto a balcony that ran along much of the street's length while Wareagle continued on to the roof level.

A man standing on the roof and peering downward at the street was speaking into a miniature microphone. Turning, he spotted Johnny and tried to draw his gun. But Wareagle covered the remaining distance in a single lunge and flung the man into the night before his fingers had grazed steel.

The man plummeted to the ground, much to the delight of the nearby crowd, who thought they were watching another installment of the advertised stunt show. The plunge also drew the attention of two more men posted on the roof, each holding binoculars to their eyes. They barely had a chance to drop them to their chests before Johnny was upon them; he trapped a head in either hand and slammed them violently together.

Having shed the cumbersome bulk of his disguise, McCracken dashed across the balcony. As expected, the attention—and guns—of a half-dozen men positioned there turned upward toward the Indian long enough to allow Blaine to begin his surge. By the time they spotted him and steadied their weapons, McCracken had already sighted in and opened fire in a nonstop barrage, empty clip exchanged for a fresh one while barely breaking stride. Bullets flew from the SIG, spent shells flying everywhere to be snatched up by patrons below, eager for a souvenir and avidly watching the spectacle.

By the time a few spectators noted the performers weren't dressed in the expected cowboy garb, Sal Belamo had leveled his .44 Magnum at a grouping of gunmen on the ground ready to open fire on McCracken, exposed on the balcony. Not hitting a bystander was Sal's biggest concern, but the gunmen had helped him here by viciously clearing a path for themselves as they'd advanced. Speedloader held between his front teeth, Sal opened up on the five of them with the Magnum in his right hand, even as he was drawing his backup snub-nosed with his left. He didn't start firing it until the magnum was out, and then only as he ejected the bigger gun's spent shells and drew it to his mouth to pop in a fresh supply.

Sal turned both pistols on the next enemy surge at the same time Johnny Wareagle leaped over the ledge of the roof to join McCracken on the balcony. The Indian had a gun in hand now as well, a Desert Eagle semiautomatic, one of the few he felt comfortable with. He ran in slightly staggered fashion behind Blaine, adding his bullets to the others that traced the retreat of the gunmen.

"The kid, Johnny!" Blaine's voice ordered as he reloaded again. "Find the kid!"

Joshua Wolfe realized the truth of what was happening instantly, the moment the first gunshot sounded and froze him. He turned his gaze to the balcony and glimpsed a bearded man

charging across it. Josh had just recognized the huge Indian
as well when more gunfire split the night almost directly in
front of him. Even from behind, he recognized Sal Belamo
unleashing a series of deafening reports from a huge pistol.

Blaine McCracken and friends had come to his rescue yet
again, but this time Josh had no intention of hanging around
and waiting to be saved. Seizing upon the chaos the gun battle
had caused in the ranks of the Men, he sped toward the gleefully terrified screams coming from Splash Mountain. As he
neared the dwindling line to board the ride, he swung left up
a slight hill and under an overhang proclaiming the entrance
to Adventureland.

Incensed, Fuchs kept his attention pinned to the screen providing the clearest picture of McCracken and the Indian firing
from the balcony. Another screen showed a third man who
must have accompanied them diving behind a concession
stand on the ground to avoid return fire. McCracken and Wareagle instantly turned their pistols on that fire's source.

"No!" Fuchs yelled to himself. "No!"

Another half dozen of his troops had just gone down when
Turk Wills's voice blared over the speaker.

"What the hell is going on, Mr. Washington?"

"It's none of your concern, Chief."

"The fuck it ain't! I'm trying to clear up this damn accident
and all of a sudden I'm getting reports of gunfire in Frontierland and people getting shot for real."

"The matter is under control."

"Stand your men down, mister, before somebody innocent
gets shot."

"That sounds like an order."

"Fucking A right it is."

"Sorry, I have the authority here," Fuchs said, switching
off the speaker and returning his attention to the screens in
search of Joshua Wolfe.

Blaine and Johnny dropped to the street and joined Sal Belamo.

"Kid went this way," Sal said, brushing himself off and
then popping a fresh speed loader into his magnum before

leading them off on Joshua Wolfe's trail.

They charged through a covered arch of small souvenir shops at the entrance to Adventureland and caught a fleeting glimpse of a shape ducking into an attraction two hundred feet away. Guns ready, the trio gave chase, running toward the entrance for a ride labeled "Pirates of the Caribbean." Because the parade was mere minutes from starting, the lines for all attractions, with the exception of Splash Mountain and Space Mountain, were down considerably. In fact, as they sped through the S-like passageway that led to the "Pirates" boarding point, the three of them encountered virtually no people.

A moderately steep decline brought them to the start of the ride, comprised of individual waterborne cars each with seven bench seats. Two were still in sight ahead when Blaine, Johnny and Sal took a car all to themselves, one to each of the middle seats. Blaine could see into the car immediately ahead clearly enough to know Joshua Wolfe wasn't in it. The car in front of that, the one the kid must therefore have taken, had already disappeared into the darkness.

McCracken checked the logistics of the "Pirates of the Caribbean" ride. The cars rode between rails atop a channel of water that looked to be four or five feet deep, enough to allow for currents. On either side the water was considerably shallower, a foot or so of currents sweeping across a hard floor for effect.

Blaine gazed up at the cavelike confines they were passing through. Fake stalactites hung from the dark gray ceiling. Machine-made fog billowed here and there as they came around to the right toward a shipwreck featuring a moving skeleton piloting the remnants of the craft.

"Beware," McCracken thought he heard through an unseen speaker before their car fell into a steep drop. They skidded atop the water briefly before approaching what looked to be a full-scale sea battle between a war galleon and a fort, complete with flashes and bursts of water from near misses. He knew this part of the "Pirates" ride was contained primarily underground amidst the tunnels, which gave him no reason for comfort.

"There he is, Blainey," Wareagle signaled, focusing on the

car two ahead of them now passing through the center of the
battle.

But McCracken's eyes had already been drawn to movement upon the battlements of the fort, brilliantly re-created
beneath a fake night sky awash with gun smoke.

"Fuchs's fucks," Sal elaborated as he glimpsed figures taking cover behind the fort's facade. He shifted position in the
car and steadied his pistol. "How the fuck they beat us in
here?"

"Colonel's got Disney's cooperation. His people got access
to underground doors we don't even know exist."

The fort stretched across the entire length of an imaginary
shoreline, its highest points rising toward the illusion of sky.
While the fort might not have been real, the cover it provided
behind circular gray-brick parapets and atop the raised battlements was just what the gunmen needed. Directly across from
it, the warship *Davy Jones* exchanged imaginary fire through
cannon that recoiled behind a thundering crescendo of fire on
the command of a robotic captain.

Joshua Wolfe's car was passing directly in front of the gunmen poised behind the fort's facade.

"Take 'em!" Blaine ordered.

"*Fire!*" the puppet captain of the *Davy Jones* screamed
from the ship's foredeck at the same time.

The trio's gunfire was all but drowned out by the fierce
sounds of cannon fire reverberating through unseen speakers.

"Take cover, Blainey!" Johnny Wareagle called, lunging
out of the car into the thin stream of water running on the left
side of the track's runner and heading for the *Davy Jones*.

All three had abandoned the car by the time the enemy
gunmen in the fort took aim and fired at it. McCracken and
Belamo ducked behind the galleon's far side, finding it to be
an open, unfinished shell in striking contrast to the elegant
replica on the side the customers viewed. The foredeck and
cannon ports were real enough, though, and Blaine rushed to
the former while Johnny and Sal took up position behind the
latter.

The real fire joined the cacophony of the simulated battle.
The only difference was the chips and shards of wood spewing
on their side and the concrete pieces of the fort sent flying on

the other. The cars passing by after theirs might not have noticed anything was amiss otherwise, or perhaps they thought even that was part of the show.

Belamo made his way to McCracken's side on the foredeck. "Figured it was a good time to break these out, boss," he said, producing a full nine-millimeter magazine wrapped in molded plastic to keep out moisture.

"Splats," Blaine winked.

"Fucking A." Belamo winked.

Sal had the Splat bullets specially made by a friend. Inside each was a capsule loaded with ground glass and picric acid. The glass was there to stabilize any premature reaction. Once fired, the bullet distorted, breaking the capsule and allowing the picric acid to mix with lead. The resulting compound of lead picric gave an ordinary bullet force comparable to a forty-millimeter grenade.

"Give me a minute or so to work my way around behind them 'fore you start firing," Sal proposed.

"Reinforcements will have joined them by then."

Belamo smiled. "More the merrier."

For Joshua Wolfe, the ride passed in terror and second-guessing. He had noticed the gunmen in the fort an instant before the real battle erupted. He ducked low and didn't look back, because he knew it was McCracken returning their fire behind him. It had to be McCracken. He lowered himself to the floor of the car and covered his head, unable to tell the real blasts from the fake ones by sound alone.

As he ducked, his hands went instinctively to the pockets of his baggy jeans, sagging now for want of a belt, and made sure the two vials were still intact inside. He wondered what would happen if he mixed them here, then held the deadly compound out for Fuchs to see from wherever he was watching. Could this be his ticket out? Was there a way to turn the colonel's strategy against himself? Probably not. Fuchs would have him shot and take his chances.

The ride narrowed substantially after the sea battle, the car settling as it snaked its way toward the outskirts of a town besieged by pirates. Any of the mechanical marionettes could be Fuchs's troops made up for cover with guns concealed beneath their costumes:

A man being dunked in a well for torture . . .

Prisoners trying to coax a dog to bring them the keys tucked in its mouth . . .

A man selling garishly made-up women as wives to drunken bidders . . .

Characters spun madly on turntables, swallowing the imaginary contents of rum bottles while pigs wagged their tails, dogs barked and pistols fired. Directly ahead were the orangy hues from a special-effects fire in a multistory building that rose above the rest of the props. The burning building disappeared briefly from view when Josh's car approached a bridge. A drunken "man" was hanging a filthy leg over it and Josh stiffened, certain he was real and would shoot him when he passed under.

Reaching the other side safely, he could barely recover his breath. His car closed on the burning building, its empty windows full of shadows that could belong to those real instead of fashioned. The amber light shone flickeringly over the scene. Josh shut his eyes to wait until the nightmarish ride was over.

"Hey," a voice said. "Hey!"

Josh opened his eyes. Someone was holding the car against a makeshift pier.

"You wanna step out, please."

Josh climbed out of his seat and bolted up the ramp.

McCracken gave Sal Belamo a full minute before firing the Splats from his SIG-Sauer. As a trio of cars passed between the fake and real battle, the Splats blasted into the facade of the fort and carved huge fissures in its frame, decimating it. Shards of rock were blown backwards in avalanche fashion, even as fake cannon fire coughed up plumes of water not nearly as big as the splashes that resulted when the larger fragments of the fort landed.

Blaine used six of the twelve Splats, aiming them toward the areas where the largest concentrations of enemy fire had originated. When he was finished, the central portion of the fort had been obliterated from the trio of parapet watchtowers all the way to the waterline. The remnants of wood framing were revealed beneath the pile of rubble that continued to mount as more of the fort crumbled.

No more fire, real or fake, emanated from within it. Yet in twisted counterpoint the captain of the *Davy Jones* continued to put up a stand that had turned superfluous.

"Boss," Sal Belamo called over the communicator.

"They finished off, Sal?"

"You better get over here."

"Yes or no?"

"You better get over here."

"Good work," Blaine said, standing near the results of Sal Belamo's handiwork.

The entrance to the rear of the fort where it met the Magic Kingdom's tunnels was littered with ten bodies, reinforcements who had not reached their positions because Sal had obviously stopped them.

Sal wasn't smiling. "Love to take the credit, boss, but I found them like this when I got here."

Blaine glanced at Johnny Wareagle, then back at Belamo. "But if you didn't kill them, who did?"

CHAPTER 42

"What do you mean you can't reach them?" Fuchs demanded of one of his field commanders.

"Contact lost, sir."

"Ten more men were on their way over there."

"They must not have made it. I have dispatched another group to find out what happened."

"Is the street outside blocked off?"

"Targets come out of that ride from any exit and we'll have them. Tunnels covered, too."

"Tell your men to stop being selective with their fire. This has gone far enough. Keep me informed."

Fuchs had barely signed off when Turk Wills stormed back into the security center, nearly tearing the door from its hinges.

"What the fuck is going on?" He grabbed Lester Fuchs by the lapels and slammed him against the wall.

"Let me go, Chief."

"The fuck I will!"

"Those are my men who are dying, not yours," Fuchs said, trying to sound like he cared. "And the person responsible is one of those we're after."

"Bearded guy?"

"Yes."

Wills released his hold but stayed just as close. "What's the kid got to do with all this?"

"They're together; that's all you need to know."

"I need to know what the fuck is going on, Mr. Washington!"

"Washington is *exactly* what's going on, Chief, and right now that's me. And I'm telling you that as bad as things are, they're sure to get worse unless you put every man and woman you've got in the park on this while you still have a park to save."

Wills moved to the security center's single window and gazed through the slats keeping anyone on the outside from noticing it was there. Below, Main Street U.S.A. was jammed with people awaiting the momentary start of tonight's Spectromagic Parade. All his years on this beat and he had never once seen the Magic Kingdom more crowded.

"Okay, Mr. Washington, what do you want my people to do?"

"Welcome, ladies and gentlemen, to the Magic Kingdom, and happy Fourth of July!"

The voice of Jiminy Cricket emanating from the park's speakers greeted McCracken, Wareagle and Belamo as they emerged from the building housing the "Pirates of the Caribbean."

"Before tonight's Spectromagic Parade begins, we are proud to have with us a pair of high school marching bands. The first hails from . . ."

The trio joined the flow of pedestrian traffic hurrying to get a view of the parade via a narrow street that cut past a series of Adventureland snack shops.

The enemy gunmen appeared first from within the dwindling line for the Swiss Family Treehouse. Their automatic fire sprayed outward randomly, searching for a bead on the trio in its spill.

"Jesus Christ," Blaine rasped, hitting the ground for safety as bodies collapsed around him. A wave of panic surged through the crowd, which splintered in all directions. Bullets began to pour forth from both major avenues accessing Adventureland as well.

From the ground, McCracken fixed his eyes on a fence surrounding Adventureland's most popular ride, the Jungle Cruise. The thick bushes lining it provided the shelter they needed right now.

"Cover us, Indian," he said to Johnny. "Meet up again on Main Street in time for the parade. Sal?"

"Ready, boss."

Crouching, McCracken and Belamo scrambled off behind

Johnny Wareagle's fierce covering fire. They lurched upright
the last stretch of the way to the fence and catapulted over it,
landing in a thicket of brush that looked like it belonged in
the Amazon.

The Jungle Cruise featured the wildlife, vegetation and local
color of a number of rivers, including the Amazon, the Nile
and the Congo. Blaine could hear a tour guide going through
a humorous litany of some of the attractions as he pulled himself along through the foliage, Belamo just behind him.

They heard a series of thumps to their rear, evidence of
pursuit coming through the dense thickets. For Blaine suddenly the all-too-clean smell of the junglelike greenery was
gone, replaced by the sticky, dank stench of other jungles in
Vietnam. He was back in his element, feeling at home. Those
jungles had made him into what he was. He signaled Sal on.
Belamo resisted briefly, then obeyed, forging ahead of him.
McCracken camouflaged himself in the undergrowth and
waited.

He took down the first man who passed by slamming an
arm in low at his ankles. The man thudded to the ground and
Blaine smashed a rock into the back of his skull.

Regaining his feet, he pressed onward, passing a jungle hut
besieged by a family of robotic gorillas. When he heard the
sound of brush crackling nearby, he took cover behind the hut.
He reached up and grabbed a stringy vine, pulling it toward
him so it draped across the thin path on a diagonal. Then he
sank down amidst the overgrowth.

The second attacker loomed closer, automatic rifle in hand.
The vine Blaine was holding came up level with his chest. He
had started to duck beneath it when McCracken sprang, yanking the vine taut around his throat, twisting and tightening.
The man's face purpled. Blaine kicked his legs out and pushed
him low into the brush as he kept the pressure up until the
man stopped struggling.

He moved on again, past the voices of the cruise leaders in
each of the jam-packed boats, which became the only thing
disturbing the illusion of the real jungle for him. The distraction did not stop Blaine from sensing the approach of two—
no, three—more men. He couldn't risk taking them out with

gunshots. The noise would draw untold reinforcements upon him.

Sliding forward, he came to a clearing where an explorer had been captured by spear-and knife-wielding headhunters going through their programmed gestures and movements. The enemy footsteps shuffled louder behind him as McCracken entered the headhunters' den. This might all have been an elaborately staged set, but the props were real enough, the knives and spears both sharpened at the tips.

Ready for use.

Seconds later, the enemy trio converged on the headhunters' camp and made their way to the river's shoreline to see if their quarry had chosen the water for an escape route. Blaine waited until all had passed his prone position beneath a pair of headhunters wielding spears before he sprang. He rose with a spear in each hand and hurled them outward. One found the throat of a short attacker, while the second lodged in the face of a taller one. The third swung about in a panic before the knife thumped into his chest, and he rolled down a slope toward the shoreline. McCracken dragged his corpse behind cover just before one of the cruise boats slid by.

Hearing the rustling of many footsteps approaching him, Blaine took to the water. He sank into its murky four-foot depth, aware for the first time how much the simulated sounds of birds and insects mirrored the real versions in true jungles. He swam beneath a cascading waterfall and followed the flow of the man-made river toward a family of bathing elephants, taking cover amidst them as another pair of boats cruised by. He could see gunmen perched on every shoreline searching the waters for him as tour boats snailed past. Too many of the opposition covering too many different angles to contend with at this point.

What did that leave?

Another boat sailed by him, its tour nearing an end, and Blaine noted the mooring rope dangling over its side just below the waterline. He took a deep breath and swam out underwater, catching up with its stern. He reached up and took hold of the rope, pulled along for the ride. The boat provided enough cover for him to pop his face above water from time to time for breath.

He hung on until the boat glided up to the dock and was tied down. As passengers began disembarking, McCracken pulled himself on board into the center of the people climbing off. The passengers either assumed that was part of the ride or assumed nothing, because no one said a thing, not even the shocked safari-dressed monitor who eyed him as he passed.

"I guess I got my money's worth," Blaine said and headed off.

Having dispensed with her wheelchair, Susan Lyle pushed herself through the crowd along the parade route searching for Joshua Wolfe. The fact that many of the men from Group Six were posted along the route indicated the boy had not been found yet. If he had managed to recover his remaining vial of CLAIR, this would be the time to escape with it. Right now the second of two high school marching bands was striding down Main Street U.S.A. in the shadow of Cinderella's Castle. The sidewalks along the route were so jammed with people that movement had become extremely difficult.

"Excuse me, excuse me," Susan kept muttering, her voice like a tape playing in her head.

She had reached the sidewalk in front of the Penny Arcade when she saw a familiar shape dodging through the crowds on the other side of Main Street.

Josh!

Dressed in a blue shirt and wearing a baseball cap to hold back his long hair. Baggy jeans sagging toward his hips.

Susan squeezed forward, reaching the front of the curb and ducking under the rope placed there to serve as a barrier. Once in the street, she ignored the protests of blazered Disney personnel and dodged the horn section of the high school marching band to make it across.

She had lost track of Josh, but he was somewhere up ahead, just beyond her, and she continued to push on in his trail.

Once out of the water, McCracken tried unsuccessfully to raise Johnny and Sal on his communicator. Evidently his stay in the man-made river had short-circuited one of its more tender operating chips, leaving him cut off from them.

Hoping the darkness would provide sufficient camouflage

for his soaked clothes and thankful for the warm summer night, Blaine headed toward Main Street and the parade in search of Joshua Wolfe. His wet shoes sloshed as he walked, drawing curious stares he did his best to ignore.

He managed to catch up with the evening's second preliminary band as it crossed between the Penny Arcade and the Plaza Ice Cream Parlor. Twenty feet ahead, just past the Main Street Bake Shop, he saw a woman forging determinedly through the masses of people on the sidewalk. He recognized Susan Lyle just as she reached out to grab the shoulder of a boy dressed in a dark blue shirt and raced toward her.

"Josh . . ."

Susan spun the boy toward her and froze. Her face fell.

It wasn't Joshua Wolfe. She had lost him somehow. She swept her eyes both forward and backward, desperately scanning the huge mass gathered along the whole of Main Street.

He had to be somewhere around here. . . .

She wouldn't give up, wouldn't—

Thirty feet in front of her, another figure making his way through the crowd stopped and swung round. His eyes met hers and Susan's insides turned to jelly. She thought at first he was going to come back for her, but he smiled slightly, then turned back and headed on toward the front of the Magic Kingdom.

Susan's blood turned to ice. She shivered and wavered on her feet, feeling suddenly faint when a pair of hands grasped her shoulders and held her tight.

"Nice spot to watch the parade from," said McCracken.

Krill had recognized the woman and was briefly tempted to approach until he saw McCracken coming up behind her. No sense lay in risking a confrontation with his task this close to completion, so he simply pressed on through the crowd.

Once he reached the shores of the Seven Seas Lagoon, the only thing separating him—and his three fireworks shells—from the unmanned barge would be the security boats enclosing it.

Easily overcome.

The high school band's performance ended abruptly just as

Krill passed under the arch leading out of the Magic Kingdom
and started for the lagoon.

Susan sank against McCracken. "I saw him. I saw Josh."
The last of the marching band was just passing them.
"Where?"
"I don't know. Somewhere close. I followed him, lost
him." She looked down the street. "I thought he must have
been up ahead, hurried after him when I saw . . ." Her
breathing caught up with her words and swallowed them.
"Easy," Blaine tried to soothe. "Take it easy."
"Krill," Susan finished finally. "He's here."
McCracken held her tighter. Neither of them noticed a man
not far away raise a walkie-talkie to his lips.

Turk Wills looked from the communications console to Les-
ter Fuchs. "One of my people just spotted the bearded man."
"Where?"
"In front of the Main Street Cinema. Woman's with him.
Hostage, you figure?"
"She's more likely to be an accomplice," Fuchs responded,
keeping his jubilation down as he prepared to speak into his
headset.
Wills continued before Fuchs could issue his commands. "I
can have my men close in, take him before the parade starts."
"You don't know who you're dealing with."
Wills made sure Fuchs could see the hard stare in his eyes.
"Neither do you, Mr. Washington. I let your people handle
this, things could turn out bloody."
"Not as bloody as they will if your people botch it, Chief."
"You trying to pull rank on me again?"
"I'd hate to see you prosecuted for treason, Chief, but if
your stubbornness ends up aiding and abetting a wanted fu-
gitive, I'm afraid you will leave me no choice."
"The fuck you say?"
"This will all be over soon, Chief. Just leave everything to
me."
A subordinate summoned Wills back to his console and
handed him a microphone. Turk accepted the report, then
looked again at Fuchs.

"Another of your man's apparent accomplices has just been spotted, Mr. Washington. Real big guy. An Indian."

"Prepare to move," Fuchs said into his headset, not about to wait any longer. "On my signal."

Blaine saw Johnny Wareagle only at the last, when the big Indian had drawn abreast of him. His expression was grim.

"They've made us, Blainey."

"I figured as much. How many we talking?"

"Fifty, sixty maybe, along this street alone. More coming."

"Rooftops?"

Johnny's eyes darted briefly upward. "Well hidden."

"Another problem: Krill's here."

Wareagle stiffened, didn't look surprised. "I know. I found a storage room in the tunnels where he'd been."

"He was heading out of the park, Indian. You figure maybe he planted something? You think Haslanger wants to make sure he can walk away from this no matter what?"

Johnny recalled the supply of fireworks loaded in the storeroom: one of the crates had been pried open and several shells were missing from it. "Yes, Blainey, but not planted." He gestured at the sky.

"Oh, shit . . ."

"I must stop him."

"And now, ladies and gentlemen, on this magical Fourth of July night, the Magic Kingdom proudly presents Spectromagic. To fully enjoy the performance . . ."

"I'll cover you as long as I can . . ."

". . . the Kingdom's lighting will be shut off. . . ."

As Johnny started off, all of Main Street went black at the same time a calvacade of multicolored lights approached from Cinderella's Castle, accompanied by music blaring from unseen speakers.

". . . unless I don't have to," McCracken completed to himself, Wareagle having disappeared into the darkness.

"What happened to the lights?" Fuchs demanded. "What happened to the goddamn lights?"

"Let me see what I can do," Wills replied quickly, moving for the communication console.

"There isn't time!"

"Just wait a—"

"I won't risk losing him!"

"Shit, in the dark you—"

"Take McCracken!" Fuchs ordered into his headset. "Take McCracken now!"

Arm clasped to Susan's elbow, McCracken turned from the head of Main Street U.S.A. and squeezed along the sidewalk in search of the first route away from the pedestrian clutter. Gunmen were likely to be closing on them even now and he kept his eyes alert for any sudden movement.

Suddenly the dark he'd been relying on for camouflage was pierced by the lead figures of the parade in the form of neon-costumed, silvery shapes perched within moving balls down the center of Main Street, waving to the crowd as they spun one way and then back the other. Behind them loomed a seemingly endless procession of floats and attractions re-creating favorite Disney characters and films, all ablaze in bright spectral light.

The music reverberated loudly and McCracken found himself even with Mickey Mouse wearing a sequined tuxedo atop a golden harp float by the ice cream parlor, when he spotted a trio of men plowing relentlessly his way. He swung back around only to see another two closing from the rear.

He drew his SIG as stealthily as he could manage. "When I push on your shoulder," he told Susan, "hit the ground."

"But—"

"Just do as I say and keep looking for the kid, no matter what."

The bright light from the Spectromagic Parade was enough to catch flickers of motion on the rooftops behind the facades of the buildings on the other side of Main Street, concentrated atop the magic and bookstores all the way down to the arcade. His Splat bullets had gotten wet back at the Jungle Cruise, rendering them useless. He was facing an army with only a pair of standard nine-millimeter clips to wage a defense.

A float lined with musical notes come-to-life slid past, followed closely by one manned by characters from *The Little Mermaid* as the song "Under the Sea" played. Blaine chose that moment to abruptly push on Susan Lyle's shoulder. He squatted as she went down and turned toward the advancing gunmen, ready for anything except what happened next.

The second-story facades of the buildings lining the other side of Main Street exploded one after the other, taking out large concentrations of the enemy. Hit by what McCracken recognized as *grenade fire*.

Fired by *whom*, though?

Shards of wood sprayed into the air, showering the audience as well as the Spectromagic participants. The parade ground to a halt. The *Little Mermaid* float rocked and then listed heavily to the left, mounting the sidewalk and slamming into the bakeshop. Another series of flashing balls manned by silver-faced figures spun wildly across the road, seeming to chase some of the fleeing crowd. People scattered in all directions as muzzle flashes filled the night with fresh color, aimed expertly and discriminately at Fuchs's troops who'd been closing on Blaine.

What the hell was happening?

McCracken grabbed Susan and shielded her against the ice cream parlor's frame, back to her so he was facing Main Street, watching Fuchs's men swing wildly about in search of the unseen force that was killing them. Panicked throngs of spectators were tripping over the spilled bodies as they screamed and struggled to flee. Blaine glimpsed additional members of the opposition darting for the remaining strategic positions in the buildings across the street. More grenade fire peppered those troops as well and the shower of debris started up anew, intensifying the panic.

McCracken used the opportunity to smash the ice cream parlor's front window with his SIG-Sauer. He shouldered through the remnants of the glass and lifted Susan inside, ignoring the jabs from the remaining shards. He led her around behind the counter, remembering the men Sal Belamo had found inexplicably dead back inside the "Pirates of the Caribbean."

"What's happening?" she managed, ducking low for cover.

"I don't know. Stay here."

Blaine bounced over the counter, ready to join the chaos outside, only to find himself facing an impossibly familiar figure standing sideways to the door.

"What do ya say, Captain?" greeted Harry Lime.

CHAPTER 43

Joshua Wolfe had hoped the Spectromagic Parade would prove enough of a distraction to let him escape from the Magic Kingdom. The darkest moments would come when the section featuring *Fantasia* passed the center of Main Street and, ironically, the eerie chords of the film's soundtrack had just begun to play when the explosions erupted.

Like many others the ensuing chaos caught Josh with the force of a Midwest twister and spun him around at will. He slammed into one person, then another, might have collapsed if there'd been any room on the street to do so. He managed to separate himself from the panicked horde of parents desperately trying to find their children and backed free of the riotous throngs.

The dark *Fantasia* float featuring the Black Demon had tumbled over, and one of the demon's still-extended wings tripped Josh up and spilled him to the ground when he tried to backpedal. Unhurt, he regained his feet, realizing that escape toward the main entrance of the Magic Kingdom was out of the question. He had no choice but to turn and try looping around the worst of the congestion.

Two men extricated themselves from the crowd and started in his direction. Josh glimpsed them long enough to find the recognition on their faces before he rushed off.

"And me thinking you were dead," Blaine said to Harry Lime.

"That's the way it was supposed to be."

"You were in on this with Livingstone Crum's bunch, Thurman and the rest of them."

"Just doing my job, Captain, same as you."

"A lot of people got hurt."

"That's why I'm here."

"How'd you find out?"

"Thurman called me. Said he owed you."

"And the others you brought along for the ride?"

"Key West Irregulars you met that night in the bar, Captain. They always did love a good fight."

A fusillade of bullets shattered what little glass remained of the ice cream parlor's front window. McCracken dropped to a crouch and opened up with his SIG on the enemy troops darting across the street. Harry instantly swept a submachine gun from his shoulder and added his fire to Blaine's. A grenade launcher dangled menacingly behind his back.

"They've certainly got one tonight," said Blaine.

"I'm going down there!" Wills insisted, strapping a gun belt around his waist.

"You'll be killed," Fuchs told him, with a calm that seemed just as unsettling as the chaos that had overcome the park.

Turk wanted to shoot the bastard. "You expected this, you son of a bitch!"

"No, but I should have." He should have known Mc-Cracken would have brought reinforcements with him, lying in wait until they were needed. "An unfortunate distraction, that's all."

"*Distraction?* Are you fucking *crazy*? Look at what's happening out there!"

"The price is well worth the cost, Chief. Rest assured."

"I don't know if I'll ever be able to rest again."

Fuchs completed the instructions to the rear-based team of his men and then started for the stairwell leading into the tunnels.

"Where the fuck do you think you're going, Mr. Washington?"

"Out there as well, Captain. To a different section of the park entirely, where my quarry awaits me."

"Fuck you," Wills said loudly, too late for Fuchs to hear as he disappeared down the stairs.

*   *   *

A single guard had been on duty on the lagoon dock when Krill got there. Krill dispatched him without incident and settled himself into a launch that was identical to the three watching over the barge.

He had almost reached the first when the explosions began inside the Magic Kingdom. Krill paid them little heed, other than to realize what a blessing they were for helping him reach the security launches one after the other virtually unnoticed and dispatch those on board.

Krill tied his launch up to the barge and mounted it quickly. He checked his watch: two more minutes to go before the fireworks commenced. He could see easily enough through the darkness but the sight atop the barge confused him.

Mortar tubes of various diameters were lined up in neat, symmetrical rows interspersed with thinner launchers loaded with Roman candles. Dozens and dozens in all. Disney had also perfected a system for automated reloading, so the number of shells filling the air with color and sound could stretch well into the hundreds. But which would be the tubes to be fired first?

Krill could only guess. Just load his shells into the most accessible tubes as quickly as possible and then take his leave.

He tucked the small bag containing his shells into his right hand and advanced toward the nearest mortar tubes. The barge was heavy and stable, but its wet surface was slippery. He lowered his bag to the deck when he reached the first row of tubes, just behind some of the larger Roman candles. He had centered one of his altered shells over a tube, about to drop it in, when he heard a strange sloshing sound. Krill turned in time to see the Indian he recognized from the picture in McCracken's file lunging for him from the starboard side of the barge. Impact carried him sideways toward the edge, but not before he let the shell drop. It sank down the tube into firing position, ready to be shot into the air.

Josh never stopped running, not even when his breath turned to hot, burning gasps in his chest. But he ran without clear destination, without purpose. He weaved through the rapidly emptying northwest section of the park, hoping to lose himself but quickly seeing the futility in that strategy. By the time he reached Liberty Square near the Hall of Presidents, pursuit by the Men seemed to be closing from all directions.

Boxed in, he dashed onto the boarding platform for the three-tier riverboat that was moored before him. Josh dashed along its length and reached the end just as footsteps thumped across the platform in his wake. Desperate, he jumped into the water and paddled frantically behind the cover of the huge boat. Reaching its aft side, he caught Tom Sawyer's Island in his gaze and began swimming toward it.

The boy was halfway to the island before he was spotted.

"Follow him!" Fuchs ordered his men who had reported from the scene. "Don't let him out of your sight!"

The men obeyed. The first group on the scene plunged off the riverboat into the water and swam after Joshua Wolfe. They had closed the gap considerably by the time the boy reached the shoreline of Tom Sawyer's Island, stumbling, falling and finally regaining his feet. The dual islands, especially this one, offered plenty of places to hide in the form of thick brush and crevices, not to mention the mine and cave. And hiding was exactly what the men expected Joshua Wolfe would do.

But instead he stayed on the move, smashing through the thickets and racing along the paths leading to the footbridge connecting this island with its twin.

"Subject confined to second island, Colonel," reported the first Group Six man to reach the still wobbling footbridge into his walkie-talkie. "We have it surrounded from the shoreline."

Fuchs had abandoned the tunnels beneath the complex to be present when his men captured Josh. Nearing the riverbank, he boarded the ferry and waited for it to transport him across. The colonel thought quickly. There was almost nothing on the second of the two islands, except for more foliage and Fort Samuel Clemens.

"Hold your positions until I arrive," he ordered.

The logistics along Main Street U.S.A. worked to the advantage of Harry Lime's Key West Irregulars, especially since the panicked rush of people prevented the Group Six troops

from using their superior numbers to full advantage. Captain
Jack, Jimmy Beam and Johnny Walker settled into a hit-and-
run, guerrilla-type strategy. Meanwhile, Papa and the Sandman, dressed in his customary bathrobe with extra ammo
weighing down the pockets, had managed to splinter the opposition by luring isolated small groups into the Walt Disney
World Railroad station and Main Street's City Hall. There they
could be picked off in confined spaces that significantly reduced the advantage of superior numbers.

The park was emptying at a remarkable clip, the chaos
transferred to the monorail station where people forced their
way onto train after train, pounding on the doors when they
closed without allowing them to board. Many gave up on the
effort and simply ran to get away.

Inside the ice cream parlor Harry Lime and McCracken reloaded and prepared themselves to rejoin the battle.

"Can I make you a sundae before I leave?" Blaine asked
Susan, who was still perched behind the counter for cover.

"I'd settle for you coming back to get me."

"Count on it."

"Find Josh, Blaine."

McCracken stole a glance at Harry before responding.
"Count on that, too."

Lime led the way back onto Main Street U.S.A., firing the
last shells from his grenade launcher. When it was empty, he
stripped a pair of submachine guns from his shoulders and
glided down the sidewalk with one in each hand. McCracken
snatched a similar weapon from one of the opposition corpses
and pocketed a pair of extra clips for it as well.

Most of the lighting still had not been switched back on,
keeping Main Street in a dull glow. The pall of smoke from
explosions and gunshots hung low in the thick, moist air. Except for the combatants, the immediate area was deserted. People had fled leaving their souvenirs, tote bags and backpacks
behind to mix with the blast-riddled debris and bodies claimed
by the battle. McCracken had seen entire towns leveled by
warring parties, but there was something even eerier about
this.

Fresh gunfire strafed the street from the side opposite them,
originating on the first floors of all three main buildings smol-

dering there. Blaine and Harry ran down the sidewalk letting go with nonstop barrages that shattered what little remained of the windows and turned the contents of the shops into a shambles. For a time they were actually firing back to back, exchanging fresh clips for exhausted ones almost in unison. Then Harry took a hit in the shoulder and discarded the weapon he'd been holding in that hand. He lunged over the sidewalk and joined McCracken beneath the overhang of the old-fashioned cinema.

"Don't look like my boys can hold all of 'em back, Captain."

"Then let's see what we can do about the ones who got by them," Blaine said to Harry as the first of the fireworks burst in the sky, showering them with light.

Wareagle tried to spin away from the edge of the barge back toward the mortar tubes, specifically the one in the center where he'd seen Krill insert his charge. Krill, though, held Johnny off, fighting for time. The two giants grappled across the edge of the barge, jarring some of the mortar tubes forming an obstacle course that threatened to trip either up with a single misstep. Each tried to topple the other off so as to complete his task: Krill, the loading of his two remaining shells; Johnny the disabling of the mortar tube loaded with the first.

Krill's inhumanly long arms and apelike forearms held Wareagle at bay and kept angling for his throat. Johnny realized that just maintaining the stalemate would be a tall order, never mind overcoming this adversary. The elongated face before him looked like a skull with a coating of flesh-colored paint, dominated by bulging eyes and protruding teeth.

Krill's already misshapen features distorted into a snarl. Without warning he snapped his head forward, leading with those awful teeth. Johnny reeled backwards but still felt a burst of piercing agony when Krill's mouth-mounted razors tore a piece of his cheek off. Krill snapped his neck forward again, and this time Wareagle risked freeing a hand to wedge against the monster's chin to hold off the assault.

The move worked at the expense of leaving one of Krill's arms free and he instantly fastened it upon Johnny's throat. His fingers were obscenely long and thick, allowing him to close all the way around Wareagle's expansive neck. A less muscled man would have perished to a crack of cartilage almost instantly. But crushing Johnny's throat took more effort than Krill had anticipated, which surprised him enough for Wareagle to twist to the side and ease the pressure on his windpipe. In the process he withdrew the hand pressed against the monster's chin and rocketed it forward with all the force he could muster.

The Indian's tightened palm flattened Krill's nose and staggered him. Krill backpedaled briefly, a low growl rising from his throat before he swept his other hand outward, fingers curled like a claw.

Johnny felt his shirt tear and flesh rip as if a bear had raked a paw across it. Krill swiped at him a second time in the opposite direction and the fiery pain struck Johnny again, a bloody X now drawn down the center of his chest. Krill used that X as a target for a knee hurled upward. Johnny's breath exploded from him in a rush. He felt the monster's hands curl round his head to snap his neck and he thrust his hands out for a comparable hold.

But the extra length of Krill's arms proved too much to overcome, and Wareagle felt his neck starting to give against the determined resistance of his powerful muscles. A crack followed which sent a burst of tingly static down his spine and turned his legs rubbery. He tried to lurch backwards, but Krill took advantage of his move by thrusting out with both arms against him.

Johnny realized he was airborne only in the instant before he landed hard on the calm lagoon surface. He sank into the black water and instantly splashed back upward. Krill's toss combined with the currents had spilled him ten feet from the barge. Even from that distance Johnny could see the monster approaching the mortar tubes with another of his canisters in hand. A series of powerful strokes got him back to the barge and, as he reached a hand over the edge to help pull himself up, the first fireworks of the evening shot into the sky, fired from far down the row of mortar tubes.

The sudden burst of brilliant light from above sent Krill's hands clinging to his eyes. The second deadly shell he had pulled from his bag went clattering to the deck and rolled away. Krill staggered, eyes lost behind his palms. Johnny pulled himself back atop the barge as another half-dozen mortar tubes spewed their initial shells simultaneously.

McCracken continued to fire barrages of bullets, salvaging a weapon from another downed Group Six man everytime the one he was wielding was exhausted. He and Harry zigzagged their way down Main Street U.S.A. toward the front of the Magic Kingdom where the rest of the Key West Irregulars continued to make their stand.

A mad figure in a bathrobe rose above them atop the train station, holding submachine guns in both hands. Blaine could see the bloody splotches staining Sandman's white robe and knew he was ready to go to sleep for the last time. He dashed ahead of Harry toward a concentration of Group Six men pouring fire Sandman's way.

Before he could get there, the Irregulars he recognized as Jim Beam and Jack Daniels rushed the enemy from behind and cut them down just as Sandman at last fell backwards. Blaine swung to his right at the sound of fresh gunfire in time to see Papa emerging in a sprint from City Hall. Bullets traced him from both levels and dropped him in the middle of the street an instant before the entire building went up in a fiery blast, taking out untold numbers of Fuchs's men.

"Shit," Harry moaned, leaning over Papa's body. "*Shit!*"

He let go with a wild fusillade just as Blaine reached him.

"Come on!" Blaine urged, yanking him upward.

"It ends here, Captain!" Harry screamed between rounds.

"No, it doesn't, Harry. Not even close."

Johnny Wareagle slid silently across the barge beneath a sky bursting with light, skirting between the mortar tubes jettisoning their magic contents into the air without pause. He could see instantly that Krill was still blinded by the resulting bursts of light. The first few rows of tubes that had yet to fire must have contained the more elaborate, climactic American flag display, which would explain why Krill's deadly shell had not been fired off yet.

Just as the monster seemed to finally be adjusting to the wash of light filling the night sky, the bright spray from double rows of Roman candles erupted in a constant stream. He screamed and stumbled, barely holding fast to his third shell, the second teetering dangerously close to the barge's edge.

Krill's attention was so rooted on the mortar tubes that he never noticed Wareagle had reclaimed the barge. Johnny attacked by springing *through* the Roman candle spray. The lunge sent agony down his spine, centered in his neck, which had locked solidly in place.

Krill was lowering his third shell blindly toward another of the mortar tubes when Johnny slammed into him from behind, ignoring the wrenching pain that came on impact. Krill flew over the tubes and crashed to the barge's surface between rows of mortars that began to erupt instantly again. The shell flew out of his hand and rolled into the water. Silhouetted by the dazzling light, Johnny grasped the tube in which Krill had loaded his first shell and tore it from its mounts.

Krill roared and threw himself on Johnny just as the mortar plopped into the water. Their struggle took them back in front of the first rows, a flurry of blows finding Wareagle despite the monster's watery, half-closed eyes. Behind Krill he could see the first rows of mortar rubes finally come to life, and almost instantly the sky showed the forming shape of an American flag. The shells lifted off one after the other without pause, spreading into red, white and blue designs that stitched a pattern in the thick night air.

For Krill they didn't exist, too bright to see. But he didn't have to see Johnny to double him over with a fresh series of savage strikes with fists that felt like cannonballs. A few stung Wareagle in the neck and his legs simply dropped out, the feeling gone in them. Sensing his vulnerability, the blinded monster leaned over and felt for something to grab on to. His hand grasped the Indian's coal-black ponytail. Krill yanked hard and drew Johnny upward, a desperate animal pouncing on its prey.

The sky continued to explode with color, shells rising upward with loud pops from the mortar tubes, joined now by the nearest row of Roman candle spray kicking up white sparks.

As soon as he was upright, Wareagle threw his chest forward and rammed Krill to throw him off balance. Johnny then pushed off with what little his legs would give him, enough to stagger the monster backwards toward the sea of hot, sparkling white. Krill seemed to realize the Indian's strategy and tried to lurch forward. But his feet slipped slightly on the wet surface of the barge and then deserted him altogether. He fell backwards, flailed his arms about desperately for purchase on something to hold on to.

Then the light swallowed him. His eyes exploded in agony in the instant before the heat ate at his flesh. He screamed and lunged away.

Blinded, he lurched straight into the path of a trio of mortar tubes in the first row which fired their shells simultaneously into him, turning the monster into a shroud of blinding, fizzling color. His mouth opened for a scream that never came; his arms stretched impossibly wide to each side, shaking as if electricity was pulsing through his body.

Johnny collapsed to the barge's deck and watched as Krill caught fire. All at once, the flame became an inferno that dropped for the water. The monster's upper body had just flopped over the barge's starboard side when his huge bulk simply locked in place. It spasmed once and then lay still. The stink of burning flesh continued to assault Johnny's nostrils as Krill's legs smoldered, and he watched the shape of the unfinished flag etched against the skies over the Magic Kingdom.

Sal Belamo had emerged from the Jungle Cruise only to be caught in the initial swell of panic, twisted about and carried by the crowd. He managed to extract himself briefly before being stampeded by another rush which separated him from his pistol. The force of the crowd actually carried him along, his feet barely touching the ground. It was all he could do to remain upright. Suddenly one of his legs got tangled in a thicket of limbs and he went down hard, scrambling to avoid being crushed by the advancing hordes.

The feeling of relief Sal felt upon escaping the mobs was short-lived. As soon as he tried to stand upright, an excruciating pain shot through his ankle.

"Fuck," he muttered to himself, exasperated. He was in no shape to join McCracken in the battle raging up the street now and had no weapon, even if both legs had been functional. Further, it didn't seem as if his presence would mean very much anyway. McCracken needed more help than Sal could provide alone under even the best of circumstances.

That didn't mean he was giving up. There *had* to be something he could do.

He leaned back against the fence overlooking the dinosaurs to take the weight off his twisted leg. Turning, Sal found himself just about eye level with the robotic T. rex.

A thrill surged through him.

"Why not?" he asked out loud. "Why the fuck not?"

The lights from the uncompleted flag began dying in the air, returning the sky over Fort Samuel Clemens to relative darkness. Joshua Wolfe sat huddled atop a rampart gazing upward. He had already pulled the vial containing the remainder of CLAIR from his pocket and pinched it between his knees. Taking deep breaths to steady himself, he twisted the vacuum sealer off and carefully extracted the tube of the compound he had created at Group Six. He removed the top from it as well and, after only the shortest of pauses, poured it into the vial already two-thirds-full of CLAIR.

The effort brought the resulting compound dangerously close to the top. Josh knew it would take several minutes for the chemicals to mix and the proper reaction to take place within the unbreakable space-age polymer. He screwed the vacuum seal back in loosely, fidgeting with it until he was confident it would pop off if forced from his hand.

Let Fuchs come after him now. Just let him. . . .

Why wait to release the vial's contents? What was the difference? His life was over anyway. He belonged to Fuchs and the others like him, men who wouldn't be happy until the means of life and death was in their hands. Josh could give them that and the world would be an even more fucked-up place as a result. Might be doing that same world a favor if he ended things right now, save humanity the bother of a miserable future.

"Josh? Can you hear me, Josh?"

The colonel's voice echoed through the stillness of the night, coming from somewhere nearby, as more fireworks exploded overhead.

"Go away!" Josh yelled back.

"I know what you're thinking, son. I know I've gone about this the wrong way. My apologies. Mistakes have been made. The excitement of what you had to offer us got the better of me, I'm afraid. So let's discuss new terms. No more threats, no more ultimatums. Come back to Group Six. Work on any project you want. If you choose to help us in our pursuits, splendid. If not, I will support your decision."

"I've mixed them together, Colonel!"

"Son—"

"I'm not your son! Dr. Haslanger's maybe, but not yours!"

"Josh, calm down, I beg you. I know you hate me. But the action you are considering is worse than any deed *I* could ever perform. So what does that make you?"

"As full of shit as you are," Josh said over the fort's top, letting the wind take his words.

"The world needs me, Josh. It needs Group Six. As unfortunate as that may seem, it's true. I did not make this world and I do not control it. But with your help we can make things better. Come back to Group Six and refine CLAIR. Figure out ways to feed the world and power the vast machines which have multiplied out of control. Accept the challenge!"

"Go to hell."

"You think giving up is the answer? It's not. You have my word, Josh. No more games. Keep the formula with you if you so choose, but come with me. I can take you away from the madness. Group Six can lift the burden that is tearing at you. You belong with us. There is no other alternative."

"You're forgetting one."

"Let me come in. Let us talk face-to-face."

"Don't even think about it."

"I'll give you a few minutes to think about it. Relax a little."

"I'm giving you ten minutes. If you and your men aren't gone, I'm going to release the formula."

"Of course, young man. Of course."

Fuchs turned away from the fort and raised the walkie-talkie to his lips. "Do you have a clear shot or not?"

"Affirmative, sir," replied one of the three snipers in position in the trees overlooking the fort. "But he's still holding the vial. If we shoot him and he drops it . . ."

"Damn."

"He's not going anywhere, sir."

"But we may have to, unless, unless . . ."

"Sir?"

"If I can't talk him down, maybe there's someone else who can," Fuchs said, formulating a new plan as more fireworks burst through the air.

The party in the temporary Dinoworld control room had been going full blast since dusk, when the robotic T. rex and Stegosaurus had been shut down for the night. Even Stacy Eagers herself could not believe how smoothly things had gone. Not a single glitch over the twelve-hour shift, and crowd excitement had exceeded even her expectations.

Totally oblivious to the chaos that was occurring above them, her six-person staff was in the midst of drinking yet another toast to the massive creatures when Stacy noticed a stranger had entered the room, a short, sinewy man with a bent nose and callused ears.

"You ask me, they don't pay you people enough. Great work, let me tell you."

"How'd you get in here?" Stacy wanted to know, trying to steady her thinking.

"Negotiated with the guard," Sal Belamo replied, producing a pistol. "He lent me this."

Stacy suddenly didn't feel drunk anymore. "What's going on?"

"What's your name?"

"Eagers. Stacy Eagers."

"Mine's Sal."

"What are you doing here?" Stacy Eagers asked the little man who looked like a piece of chain mail with eyes.

"Rescue mission," he answered, keeping the gun poised toward the workers holding drink cups for weapons.

"Nobody down here needs saving," she said.

Sal pointed to the ceiling. "Somebody up there does."

CHAPTER 44

The Group Six troops had pulled back somewhat, allowing McCracken and Harry to rendezvous with Captain Jack, Johnny Walker and Jimmy Beam.

"You can make it out now, Captain," Harry told him, gnashing his teeth together. "Lemme go back for the kid."

"Not your style, Harry."

"Never had any style, you know that."

"But you had a plan and that was what you were best at. This is my game."

"Let me go back for the woman, at least."

"Get your men and yourself out."

"No can do, Captain. I helped make this mess. I got to help clean it up."

"Then watch my back and follow me to the ice cream parlor," McCracken said. "We'll split up and go after the kid."

He could hear sirens wailing in the distance now that the ear-splitting roars of fireworks had ceased. Fifteen minutes had passed since the explosions during the Spectromagic Parade. Orlando and Florida State Police authorities must have finally called up sufficient numbers to chance an approach. Blaine let himself wonder briefly about Johnny Wareagle's fate. He took considerable solace in the sight of the large gaps in the American flag's final, lingering design. Obviously not all of the fireworks had been fired and that could only be the result of the Indian's work.

As for the fate of Joshua Wolfe, Blaine could only guess. If the boy had managed to flee, or if he had ended up in Fuchs's hands, the chances of stopping the spread of the reactivated CLAIR in the Ozarks would be virtually nonexistent. Moving swiftly, but taking nothing for granted, McCracken darted down Main Street and ducked into the ice cream parlor to get Susan.

"I'll take a chocolate chip," he said at the counter, leaning over it and expecting to see her still hiding there.

She was gone.

Blaine turned slowly, gun leading.

"McCracken!" a voice called from the street. He dropped low and steadied his weapon for where the windows had been. "We have her, McCracken!"

Blaine peered outward and saw Susan standing between two men, one supporting her, the other holding a gun at her head. Four others stood on both sides of her, widely spaced to preempt any thoughts he might have entertained of shooting them all.

"We will not harm the woman. We will not harm you. Colonel Fuchs wishes to speak with you. Come out into the street unarmed with your hands in the air."

McCracken thought quickly. If all they wanted was to kill him, he reasoned, they could have tried for an ambush as he made his way back here. There must have been some truth in what the man was saying, then. And if he chose to ignore the words, Susan would certainly be killed even if he managed to triumph against however many awaited him in the street. He wasn't alone, after all; Harry would already be moving into position, waiting for Blaine to provide the proper cue for him to spring.

"We're waiting!"

"What does Fuchs want?" Blaine shouted into the street, wanting to give Harry Lime and the other Key West Irregulars more time to move into position.

A pause followed, the question obviously being relayed. Then the man's voice returned.

"There is someone he wishes you to speak with."

"Who?"

"The boy," the man returned, adding, "before it's too late."

McCracken rose and threw his rifle to the floor. "All right. I'm coming out."

*   *   *

The little man limped about the control room. He seemed
honestly impressed with the setup, definitely knew quite a bit
about computers. Maybe it was the booze, but Stacy didn't
feel threatened by him. Behind the two of them the rest of her
staff was clustered in a tight group, having lost interest in their
drinks.

"What exactly is it that you want?" she asked him.

"Already told you: some help. Hey, you got any idea what's
going on up there?"

"What's going on up there?" she repeated.

"Just trust me. Today's your chance to play hero." Sal's
eyes fell on her keyboard and control console. "How much
can you make those monsters do? I mean, I saw 'em walk,
move."

"Anything."

"Huh?"

"They can do anything. They have full joint articulation
and mobility. They behave—I mean, er, perform—exactly as
the creatures they are replicas of."

"Anything," Sal repeated.

"That's what I said."

Sal held on to the gun, even though he was starting to figure
he didn't need it, that this woman was going to like what he
wanted her to do.

"Prove it," he told her.

Seven men surrounded Blaine in a circle while one searched
him. When the search turned up nothing, the man in charge
motioned him to start walking. He caught up with Susan and
extricated her from the grasps of the man on either side. She
embraced him and Blaine could feel her trembling as he
hugged her back tighter.

"I'm sorry," she said softly.

"My fault. I should've anticipated—"

"Keep walking!" the leader ordered, and a pair of M-16s
prodded them on.

Before they could obey, staccato bursts of fresh gunfire
made Blaine take Susan hard to the ground. Around him a
number of Fuchs's men dropped where they stood to the gunfire of Harry Lime and the rest of the Key West Irregulars.

The four surviving members charged down the street in assault fashion, zigzagging, rotating point.

Not yet, Harry, not yet, Blaine thought to himself, watching Harry's floral shirt flapping in the breeze as he slid partway off Susan to reach for a downed man's rifle.

He had just closed his hand upon it when gunfire from the hidden positions he'd feared along the street cut Lime, Captain Jack, Johnny Walker and Jim Beam down in their tracks. He gave up trying for the gun and rushed to Harry instead, leaning over him even as a dozen guns steadied his way.

"I guess I really fucked things up this time, Captain," Lime managed between gasps. "Don't tell the kid I was here. Don't tell him I was . . . part of it."

Blaine nodded and squeezed Harry's hand. Suddenly Harry lurched upward and grabbed him by the lapel, eyes pleading.

"Take care of him, Captain. Whatever happens from here, promise me you'll take care of him."

Blaine nodded deliberately. Two of the gunmen hoisted him away just as Harry's grasp went limp. The others who'd been in concealed positions were emerging onto the streets. If Harry had suspected they'd been there to start with, he could have baited a much better trap, drawn them out before launching a direct assault. But subtlety had never been one of Lime's more noteworthy traits, Blaine reckoned sadly as the men marched him back to where Susan was standing.

Surrounded again, the two of them were led on past Cinderella's Castle and the Dinoworld exhibit on the grassy bank adjacent to it, no one noticing the T. rex was twenty feet closer to the fence.

"Shit," Sal Belamo muttered, peeling his eyes away from the screen that showed a captured Blaine McCracken being led through the center of the Magic Kingdom. The picture came courtesy of dual cameras mounted in the T. rex's eyes. "I want to see where they're going."

"No problem," Stacy Eagers told him, and she worked the controls to move the dinosaur farther forward.

Another camera showed it taking one lumbering step and then another, its head positioned for a clear view of the men advancing forward. Sal returned his attention to that screen and followed the group onto a small keelboat that disappeared into the darkness of the man-made river.

"What's on the other side?" he asked.

"Tom Sawyer's Island," Stacy replied.

Sal was staring at the T. rex again, amazed by its lifelike stature. "Can this boy swim?"

"So nice of you to join us, Mr. McCracken," Fuchs said when McCracken reached the outskirts of Fort Samuel Clemens.

"The kid in there?" he asked, gesturing that way.

"He's being rather stubborn. Doesn't want to leave. Prepared to do a very naughty thing if we act rashly."

"Maybe I should let him."

"Destroy the world? I think not. That's not an option you would favorably entertain."

"What do you want, Colonel?"

"Isn't it obvious? I want the boy."

"As a possession."

"I'd call it a resource. Come now, are we that different, you and I, in what we seek, what we pursue?"

"Considerably."

"I'm talking about safeguarding the interests of our country."

"So am I."

"Joshua Wolfe can help us do that job."

Blaine shook his head. "You're not up to that job."

"Regardless of tonight, you and I fight many of the same battles. Often we are on the same side, though our approaches may be different. But if this boy exposes the contents of his vial to the air it will be a very bad thing for both of us. Talk him down, Mr. McCracken. Bring him out."

"You don't know what's going on out there, do you? I'm talking about the world, Colonel, or what's soon to be left of it."

"I'm afraid I don't," Fuchs said, disinterested.

"Joshua Wolfe never created CLAIR in the first place, at least not the CLAIR you want. You can blame a splinter group of the CIA that's a rival of yours for that, fat man named Livingstone Crum in charge. Ring a bell?"

Fuchs's mouth dropped just a little. McCracken didn't let up.

"Crum's group picked up Operation Offspring when Haslanger dropped it. They monitored the boy all his life and when he came up with something they liked, they took advantage of it. Tinkered with his formula. Killed seventeen hundred people. It's them you should be after."

"But it's the formula I'm after and that's what the boy has with him inside there. I'll send Crum a thank-you note."

"I'm not finished. See, the fat man tried to cover his tracks and ended up reactivating CLAIR in the process. It's loose, Colonel, and it's spreading and Joshua Wolfe is the only person who can stop it."

Fuchs looked interested in the prospects. "And I'll be glad to supervise that process once you deliver the boy into my hands."

"I'm supposed to trust you on that?"

Fuchs glanced around at the force encircling the area and smiled confidently. "I don't think you really have a choice."

"It's Blaine McCracken, Josh," Blaine called from just outside the gate. "I'm coming in."

When the boy made no protest, McCracken swung open the wooden door and entered the fort. He did not think for one moment that Fuchs was going to let him walk out of here, but he also recognized this was the only way he could buy himself time. Sal and Johnny were still out there somewhere, after all, and sooner or later they'd be coming.

"Josh?" he said, moving slowly, making sure his hands were in evidence.

"Up here," the boy returned.

Blaine looked up at the rampart ledge and saw him there cradling something in his fingers. "Bad idea."

"Why, because they can shoot me? Fine, let them. I want them to." He showed the vial. "I've got this just a twist away from opening. If I fall, that'll do it."

"They know that."

"Good."

"Can I come up?"

"Do what you want."

McCracken moved for the ladder.

"He's climbing up," one of the snipers reported. "Got him in my sights. Dead on."

"They've got to be taken out together," Fuchs ordered. "But not until we've got the vial. Understood?"

"Affirmative."

Josh was leaning against the top of the facade, knees curled to his chest, trembling and still soaked from the swim that had brought him to the island.

"You should go," he said when Blaine joined him on the ledge, tone softer and not threatening anymore.

"I'm stuck here, just like you."

"Fuchs sent you."

"Right."

"He's an asshole."

"Right again."

The boy almost smiled, then shook the gesture aside, along with his hair. He moved to bring his hands to his face, then remembered the vial clutched between his fingers.

"You didn't kill anyone, Josh."

The boy looked back up at him.

"It wasn't your original formula for CLAIR you released in Cambridge. Someone added something to it in the lab, the same people behind the Handlers. You came up with a delivery system for a weapon they'd been itching to try. That's all."

"I don't believe you."

"Think, goddamnit! You told me that's what you do best. Well, do it now, kid. You ran all the tests, correlated all the data. Everything checked out and still seventeen hundred people died."

"Because *I* made a mistake!"

"Same one I've been known to make: you tried to help people. You wanted to help them so much you forgot to watch your back."

"I . . . didn't kill anyone?"

"Closest you came was putting Sal and Susan to sleep with that GL-12."

The boy leaned back, feeling suddenly light. "Wow."

"Don't relax yet, kid. You've still got your work cut out for you. . . ."

"What are they doing?" Fuchs demanded.

"Still talking."

"Can you see the vial?"

"Kid's still holding it."

"Don't let it out of your sight. Do you hear me? Don't let that vial out of your sight!"

Blaine could see it in the boy's eyes, his mind racing as he listened to the story of what had happened at the Mount Jackson containment facility.

"Any deaths yet?" Josh asked.

"Undoubtedly. But nobody's about to report them."

"CLAIR will spread on the winds. But up in the Ozarks this time of year, they tend to shift and swirl. That gives us some time."

"Can you stop it?"

"Relatively simple proposition if we get to it before CLAIR spreads outside of those mountains."

"And if it already has?"

"Then I don't think anybody can."

"Stace, I think I'm in love."

Sal Belamo watched in utter amazement as another of the park's cameras picked up the T. rex walking down the middle of the street leading from the grassy bank to Liberty Square and the water. It seemed to be picking up speed, didn't look lumbering or mechanical at all. Though it walked with the hunch typical of a real T. rex, it nonetheless measured over thirty feet from head to ground. Its forepaws flapped as it moved, tail sweeping from side to side.

"You making it do that?" Sal asked Stacy.

"It's doing that on its own in order to maintain balance."

"Just like with the real thing . . ."

"Closest thing to it we're ever gonna see on this earth, in our lifetimes, anyway."

Sal switched his attention to the view as seen from the creature's perspective. The eye-mounted cameras had been installed with built-in stabilizers, so the picture remained still even when the T. rex's head bobbed up and down in rhythm with its pace.

Stacy changed the angle of its head to better display the last bit of land leading to the water.

"Going's gonna get a little slow briefly. Each command's got to be separate since the ground's not flat."

Sal's mind was elsewhere. "Tell me something, Stace, how sharp are its teeth?"

"They're coming down!" the sniper team leader's voice exploded over Fuchs's walkie-talkie.

"Can you see the vial?"

"Negative. But I have direct shots. Repeat, direct shots!"

"Where is the vial?"

"Out of sight right now. Do we have clearance to fire?"

"Negative. We've got to be sure the vial is secure."

"They're on the ground. Shots still clear. I can drop them now. Take them in the head. No chance either of them could open anything."

"No! Not until we're sure," Fuchs ordered.

The door to the gate opened. Fuchs watched McCracken emerge with the boy close beside him cradling the vial in his hands, only its very top exposed.

"I'd back off if I were you, Colonel," Blaine told him.

"Well done, Mr. McCracken. See how far a little trust can go?"

"I said back off."

"Hand me the vial, please."

"Can't. I don't have it." Blaine cocked his head toward trees where Fuchs's snipers were placed. "Wasn't hard fooling them. The vial's still inside the fort."

"What?"

"Hidden and rigged to go off if your men try to find it. Setting it was like working a trip wire. You know, just the right amount of pressure, getting the timing right. Cap's screwed off, gravity all that's holding it in place. Weight shifts and down it goes. Bad idea to send anyone in looking. One of your men steps wrong somewhere and, well, you get the idea.''

Fuchs realized the object in the boy's hand was a watch, the glass of its face having fooled him. His voice turned unsure. "What do you expect to gain from this?"

"I expect you to let the woman and the kid out of here." Blaine's eyes found Susan, who was still being held by a pair of Fuchs's men. "Once they're out of the park and with the Indian, I tell you where the vial is."

"How will they find this . . . Indian?"

"He'll find them. You'll provide a walkie-talkie so he can make the call."

"You're bluffing."

"Try me."

"I'll want to search you, both of you."

"Go ahead."

Fuchs signaled a pair of men forward. One held a gun on McCracken, while the other began the process of a methodical frisk. Blaine raised his hands in the air. The man frisking him checked his hips, then eased up past his waist, his own jacket opening in the process. Blaine noted the presence of a gun the man had neglected to remove before approaching.

"What the fuck is going on here?"

The eyes of Fuchs and everyone else turned to the edge of the clearing, where Turk Wills stood menacingly still, a blue-steel revolver in his hand half raised.

It came up a little more. "You crossed the line, Mr. Washington."

Fuchs stood there, silent. No one else moved except McCracken. He seized the moment of hesitation by snapping his right hand out and grasping the guard's pistol, shooting him first before it had cleared the holster all the way. His second bullet dropped the man holding the gun on him from the front, and then the four men on either side of Susan. Fuchs was his next priority, but the colonel had already dived to the side, scrambling away, his voice blaring into his walkie-talkie.

"Hey!" Turk Wills blared, gun still poised on Fuchs. *"Hey!"*

"Kill them!" the colonel ordered. *"Shoot them!"*

A bullet from the ensuing fire took Wills in the leg and dropped him, in the process giving Blaine the time he needed to find the snipers posted somewhere in the trees above. He spun.

And froze.

In the woods fifty feet away, a Tyrannosaurus rex had captured two adjacent trees in its huge mouth and was shaking them determinedly. McCracken saw the snipers fall out and drop forty feet.

"Get down!" he yelled to Susan as he leaped upon Josh and brought him to the ground behind the cover of a rock just ahead of the barrage of gunfire from Fuchs's ground-based troops. The kid wailed as the bullets bore down on them, forming an eerie crescendo to the rock splintering away as Blaine covered him with his body. McCracken drained the rest of the clip from the pilfered gun, then judged his chances of retrieving the rifle from the other man he had felled nearby.

Not good, Blaine had just deemed, when the T. rex entered the clearing.

"No one's ever going to believe this one," Sal Belamo said to himself, grinning broadly. "No one's ever going to fucking believe it."

Stacy Eagers positioned the T. rex directly in front of McCracken for cover and kept it moving forward. It was snorting and bellowing now, head lopping from side to side as if in search of fresh prey. The cameras in its eyes showed some of the gunmen actually turning to flee from its path. Stacy spun it back around enough to view McCracken.

He had managed to snare a rifle and fired on those troops the T. rex had not chased off before moving to check on Susan Lyle.

Stacy spun the head again.

"Hold it!" Sal Belamo ordered. "Go back!"

The camera eyes showed Colonel Lester Fuchs steadying a discarded rifle he must have salvaged from the ground on McCracken.

"You fuck!" Belamo screamed at him, and watched as Sta-

cy's hands flew across the keyboard. "Get that bastard! Better
yet . . ."

Sal crouched and shoved her fingers off the keyboard, re-
placing them with his own.

"Hey!" she protested, recoiling.

Sal had studied her every move, effectively memorizing the
command sequence and activators, so he knew exactly what
to do. There would have been no time to relay the instructions
to her anyway. The T. rex responded by twisting its upper
body and lurching its head downward with jaws open. Bringing the rifle up had blocked Fuchs's view of it so he saw
nothing until those jaws dropped over him and snapped almost
all the way shut.

"Oops," said Sal, realizing he had pressed the wrong key.

He hit another sequence and the T. rex lifted its vanquished
prey into the air and began shaking its head from side to side.
Only Fuchs's legs were visible between its teeth and they
shook horribly for a brief time before going still altogether.

"I think it's stuck," Belamo said of the T. rex, which kept
shaking its head in spite of Sal's command to stop.

EPILOGUE

Less than a day later, tests supervised by Susan Lyle confirmed that the spread of CLAIR had thus far been confined to the Ozark Mountain range. That gave them all the time they needed to enact Josh's plan.

Following the boy's instructions, the first step was regular airdrops of liquid oxygen over the infected area. Exposure to the much warmer air temperatures created a vapor cloud which shrouded the mountain in a frigid blanket, effectively immobilizing the deadly CLAIR. This gave Josh, working with Susan and other CDC technicians, the time they needed to identify the genetic markers responsible for the mutation and develop an enzyme capable of eradicating them. Five days after the explosion that had destroyed the Mount Jackson containment facility, CLAIR had been effectively neutralized and was left to filter harmlessly through the air.

"Doesn't look like that was enough for you, Indian," McCracken said after delivering the news to Johnny Wareagle.

Johnny turned to face McCracken from the edge of the hillside overlooking the Oklahoma reservation where he had grown up. He had already discarded the surgical collar recommended for his badly wrenched neck and traded it for one of Will Darkfeather's herbal pastes. A thick bandage covered the portion of his cheek where Krill's teeth had made their mark. The scar wouldn't bother him. Down below, somewhere, Joshua Wolfe was getting settled into his new home. Blaine knew the boy needed to disappear, cease to exist. He was too valuable a commodity to allow for any semblance of normalcy in his life. Group Six would not be the only ones after him, vying to reap the benefits of his intelligence.

"I am convinced this is what you must do, Blainey, what

we must do. I am not convinced we will not be sorry for it later.''

''Chief Silver Cloud didn't express any reluctance. I think Will Darkfeather even liked the idea of having an apprentice.''

''Both gave their support because they understood the alternative, as much as anything else.''

''All the same . . .''

''All the same, we know the boy possesses an unstable personality. He has embraced your plan for the time being, but down the road, either long or short, he could change his mind. He could run as he has done before, and next time we may not be the ones who find him.''

''He won't run.''

''You cannot be sure.''

''I have to try.'' McCracken followed Johnny's gaze down the hillside. ''This place is the kid's only chance. I figure he deserves that much.''

An ironic smile crossed Wareagle's lips. ''Strange how we have come to evaluate our lives. No matter how many we save, what decimation we prevent, we continue to define ourselves in terms of the next life that crosses before us.''

''That's what keeps us going, Indian.''

''It also takes its toll, Blainey. Fighting the world's battles is sometimes easier than fighting a single person's.''

''As in this case.''

''If we have to hunt the boy down again, things will not end pleasantly.''

McCracken spotted Josh's figure as he gazed far below at the world Wareagle had grown up in. ''This is his home now, Johnny. He's not going anywhere.''

''Unless someone comes to take him.''

''It's gonna be tough,'' Joshua Wolfe told Blaine before McCracken took his leave, ''giving it all up. The work and all. The science, computers—that sort of stuff. I can't remember a time when it didn't dominate my life.''

''And screw it up royally.''

''You're right, but it's all I've ever known. Not easy turning away. You should know.''

''I've never had to face that, not yet, anyway.''

"Lucky for me."

A mere day in the sun had darkened the color of Josh's face. The taut nervousness had vanished from his expression. He looked like someone ready to learn how to smile, but he wasn't smiling now. True to his word, Blaine had said nothing to him about Harry Lime being in the Magic Kingdom or his complicity in the plan that had nearly destroyed the boy.

"Given a little more time, I really think I could have done it. Wiped out air pollution, I mean, and that's just for starters. I don't know from where, but I get these ideas. They could be great things, wonderful things."

"And what happened in Cambridge, what Group Six wanted you for, shows how close that line is to the one marking disaster. Thing is, kid, somebody's always watching just in case you cross it. They want you to cross it, because then they've got you."

"Did that happen to you?"

"For a while."

"You broke away."

"I got smarter than them."

Josh thought about that. "I could, too."

"You offer too much more. I'm an asset. You're a resource."

"Is there a difference?"

"Assets fight battles. Resources win them."

"And it's all about battles. . . ."

"These people live to fight them. That's how they justify their existence and that's why nothing will stop them from coming after you if you don't lie low. You can't be exactly who you want to be, but it beats being who *they* want you to be."

"Makes sense."

"As much as anything."

Josh shifted uneasily. "I owe you a lot."

"You can repay it all today. Help yourself out in the process."

"Just name it."

"I know I told you you had to give it all up, but there's one more thing you've got to do for me first."

*　　*　　*

"I know this is the best thing for him," Susan Lyle said to Blaine as they drove off the reservation. Her parting with Josh had been difficult, especially since both knew it would not be safe for them to meet again for some time. "But I still can't accept it."

"Because it means he can't be with you helping to find the cure for cancer?"

"I don't know. It just seems like such a waste."

"The alternative is to have Sal, Johnny and me rotate watches for the rest of his life. And even at that we couldn't stop someone from getting to the kid sooner or later."

"And here?"

"You can see people coming from a long distance away."

"A view you must be familiar with."

"Only one I know," Blaine told her. "I got to thinking about that, about Josh. Kid's different. Kid doesn't fit in. All the kid wants is to make the world better and put himself ahead. And all that gets him is being manipulated, exploited. Not for who he is, for what he can do. Sound familiar?"

Susan looked at him, eyes acknowledging.

"Call him dangerous. Call him a rogue. Call him a weapon. I know the terms well. Then all of a sudden I'm on the other side, chasing a mirror. Who was I chasing, Doctor?"

"Psychology's not my field."

"Mine neither. It comes down to chances. How many do you get? How many do you deserve? I've been lucky with chances. I figured the kid deserved the same. I figured the kid deserved something I don't have."

"Home," said Susan, in what had started out as a question.

"Place to go back to when things get finished, call it whatever you want."

"But things never get finished for you, do they? Tomorrow, maybe the day after, you go back to it all over again."

"It's what I am, what I've got."

"Does that bother you?"

"No."

"It bothers me, Blaine. It bothers me because I'm not locked in to any one road. I can walk away from this. Maybe I'll even help find the cure for cancer myself. But you and Josh, your roads are never going to change. You can't get off them, and there isn't any end.''

"If there was, it wouldn't be pleasant.''

"And Josh's road still has a formidable block straight ahead.''

"Haslanger . . .''

"He's the last person left who knows everything.''

"Not quite. There's someone else who needs to be paid a visit.''

"But Haslanger *created* Josh, probably still feels the boy belongs to him.'' Susan tightened her stare. "He'll be coming after him. You know that.''

Blaine's eyes turned to black ice. He smiled, slightly and surely. "There's always tomorrow, maybe the day after.''

Livingstone Crum switched on the tape recorder, so not a single facet of the new recipe he was creating would be lost. He found taking notes much too cumbersome and distracting. With the tape recording his every word and move, he was assured his genius would be preserved.

"Today,'' he began, "I am working on my own version of Braciolette Ripiene, or stuffed veal rolls.'' He catalogued the contents already laid out for him upon the kitchen counter and island just to his rear. "Twelve small slices of veal cut from the leg, twelve small thin slices of lean ham, three tablespoons of pine nuts, one cup chopped parsley, two tablespoons raisins, two tablespoons each of grated Parmesan cheese, olive oil, butter . . .''

Crum stopped suddenly and turned. A small swarthy man with a twisted nose stood behind the center island, holding a helping of the fat man's nuts in one hand, a silenced pistol in the other.

"And two bullets in the brain,'' said Sal Belamo between chews before he pulled the trigger.

On the whole, things could not have worked out any better for Erich Haslanger. The full blame for the disaster at the Magic Kingdom had fallen on the late Colonel Lester Fuchs. Haslanger had been fully exonerated of any wrongdoing. Group Six would continue, because the country needed it, and he would remain at Group Six, because General Starr needed him.

He had already destroyed Fuchs's personal file on him. With all accurate records altered inside the computer banks, the long-ago past had ceased to exist. His life didn't even begin until he joined Group Six and that was all whoever took over as Fuchs's replacement would care about.

There would come a day when Joshua Wolfe would work by his side. There would come a day when the boy realized this was where he belonged. Oh, he might need some coaxing, but Haslanger would give it time. There was no rush. For him there were twenty-four working hours in every day.

Haslanger filled a large glass with water from his office cooler and sat down behind his desk. Project work inside Group Six had been temporarily suspended, pending a full investigation of the events leading up to the disastrous night in the Magic Kingdom. The investigation was window dressing, all coordinated by Starr, the blame already apportioned by the men who made reports, not wrote them. But the corridors of the complex were strangely quiet, the labs abandoned save for experiments where cessation of work would mean deterioration of materials under production.

Haslanger took a hefty chug of water and then another, sighing after the second gulp went down. He did miss Krill, and found it strange admitting that. But Krill's passing meant another link to his past severed. Potentially the last one, potentially—

Haslanger felt his head start to slump and shocked himself alert. Like a man driving a lonely road in the dark night hours. It happened sometimes.

But then it happened again.

Haslanger tore open a desk drawer and rummaged desperately for the stimulants he always kept close for times like this. This was an especially bad one, worst he could remember. He felt it looming over him like an ocean wave he was too far from shore to avoid: exhaustion, irrepressible and relentless, turning every part of him heavy and slow. He popped a pair of pills in his mouth and reached for his water to down them.

His hand stopped halfway to the glass. His eyes fell on the

water cooler and he knew, knew everything. Recognized the effects.

GL-12 . . .

The phone on his desk rang. Haslanger snatched for it dimly, blessing the voice on the other end for being about to save his life.

"Help me!" he blared, steadying the receiver to his ear, trying to dry-swallow the stimulants. *"Help me!"*

"Pleasant dreams, Doctor," said Blaine McCracken.

The phone slipped from Haslanger's hand. He lurched away from his desk and staggered for the door. Halfway there he crumpled. The black wave engulfed him and he couldn't swim out from beneath it to the surface that beckoned above. Then the surface was gone.

Erich Haslanger had fallen asleep.

Here is a preview of
The Walls of Jericho
by Jon Land

AVAILABLE IN HARDCOVER IN APRIL 1997
FROM FORGE BOOKS

CHAPTER 1

"What do you know about the murders, Inspector?"

Ben Kamal shifted stiffly in the chair set before the desk of Ghazi Sumaya, mayor of the ancient city of Jericho. "The same thing everyone else does," he said, still wondering what he was doing here.

"And what is that?" Sumaya asked him.

"Seven in the past year in the West Bank: three prior to the Israeli pullout, four after. The latest occurred here in Jericho ten days ago."

The mayor leaned forward, the massive desk dwarfing his small frame. "You would agree that we're facing a serial killer, then. *Al Diib*, they call him."

"The Wolf . . . because his victims have been savaged, mutilated beyond all recognition."

"The one you caught in America, they had a name for him, too, didn't they?"

"The Sandman," Ben nodded.

"Why? "

Ben lowered his gaze. "He killed entire families while they slept."

"Until you stopped him."

"Yes. "

"That makes you something of an expert."

Ben raised his head again. Shafts of the early morning sun streamed through the open blinds, making him squint. Above him, a ceiling fan spun lazily, catching some of the stubborn light and splashing it across the portrait of Yassir Arafat which hung directly behind Sumaya's chair.

"I have experience, that's all," he said.

The mayor's deep-set eyes sought Ben's out compassionately. "Experience, Inspector, is exactly what we need. I spoke

to President Arafat last night. He has been contacted by the
Israelis. They want to assist us in the investigation.''

Ben's eyes widened. "Assist us?''

"Their offer is genuine, I assure you. I've already conferred
with a representative of their National Police this morning.''

"Did you ask him what they have to gain?''

"Perhaps they have the same thing to lose: peace. And toward that end the Israelis want to send an officer to liaise with
a Palestinian counterpart. Are you interested?''

"No, sir.''

His response took the mayor off guard. "Perhaps you didn't
understand my question. I was asking if you want to officially
take over this investigation.''

"I understood what you meant. I don't. I'm sorry.''

"Perhaps it is I who should be sorry,'' Sumaya said, sounding genuinely hurt. "Sorry for standing behind you when
everyone else was calling for your head.''

"Put me in charge of this investigation and they'll be calling for yours as well.''

"Some already are,'' Sumaya lamented, "more with each
day.''

He rose and moved out from behind his desk. The mayor
wore a suit of an olive shade only slightly lighter than Ben's
green police uniform. He was a small man, but carried himself
in a way that made him seem taller. Sumaya had been part of
the Palestinian delegation that had forged the original Gaza-
Jericho First option. He had gained a masters degree in France
years before and returned to the West Bank to chronicle the
times he instead found himself a part of. His dark graying hair
had begun to recede, adding to the air of authority that hung
over him.

"We have a credibility problem here, Ben,'' he continued.
"These murders have become a symbol for our inefficiency.
They are giving the growing pains we are experiencing a
worldwide forum that the enemies of peace are seizing upon.''

Sumaya walked to the window and drew the blinds shut,
trapping the sun outside where it shone off the chiseled white
stone structure of the Palestinian Authority headquarters on
the outskirts of Jericho. His formal office was located down-
town in Jericho's Municipal Building but, as a member of the

Palestinian Council as well, he preferred using this one.

"The peace talks are scheduled to reconvene next week," the mayor explained. "Six months without dialogue and finally the new Israeli prime minister seems ready to negotiate the final stages of withdrawal from the West Bank." Sumaya tightened his stance, almost to attention. "Almost a year we've gone without an 'aamalivva, an operation, carried out against Israel, and to a great extent your work is the reason. You have helped teach us how to arrest our own, Inspector. Hamas is running scared. We've infiltrated their ranks, preempted their strikes, jailed their militants. So they have seized upon these murders to destroy the credibility with the people we have worked so hard at building!"

Sumaya stopped to settle himself down, but the agitation remained in his voice when he resumed. "You understand what I'm getting at here? There can be *no peace without the support of the people* and these murders have taken that support from us. The talks will collapse, if they ever get started now."

"Which is where this Israeli liaison comes in."

"Let's face facts here. The Israelis don't trust us any more than we trust them. What we have between us is a mutual nonunderstanding. Now, I have spoken to the President and we are of one mind on utilizing your skills and expertise."

"I'm hardly the proper representative for our people, *sidi*," Ben offered.

"I understand your bitterness over the treatment you have received in recent weeks. The behavior of your fellow officers has been inexcusable and I wish I could have done more to change it."

"But I'll need their cooperation, along with that of witnesses, and families of the victims, too. If they read the newspapers, it is safe to assume that such cooperation will not be forthcoming, certainly not in the ten days we have left before the start of the peace talks."

"But we must *try*. Make an effort, a point."

"And if that effort fails, what point have we made? That we are just as inefficient working with the Israelis as we are working alone? Incompetent as well as weak? You're taking a very big risk here."

"The bigger risk lies in doing nothing, Inspector. If Al Diib is still at large one week from Wednesday, there may be no peace talks and everything the Authority has tried to accomplish will collapse. We have nothing to lose. "

"And, of course, at this point neither do I."

"I wouldn't have put it that way." Sumaya cleared his throat uneasily. "You will have my complete cooperation, Ben. "

"And will I have Commander Shaath's, too?"

"I know you have had a problem with him, since . . . the incident."

"The two of us had problems before. That only worsened things."

"He resents foreigners, that's all."

"I'm not a foreigner. I was born here just as he was "

"But Shaath did not emigrate to America as a child."

"That was my parents' choice. I made the decision to return."

"As your father did before you. Did I ever tell you I knew him?"

"You mentioned it once."

"He was a hero," Sumaya reflected softly. "I remember meeting him in 1967, not long after he returned in the wake of the Six-Day War. He said I was too young to help, told me to wait for another time." His voice drifted. "I suppose he knew even then it would come."

"I was seven years old when he left. He never told me."

"I wept the day he was killed. We all did. He was given a hero's funeral."

"My family didn't learn of it until weeks later. They wouldn't ship his body to America."

"And how do you think he'd feel about you returning too, following in his footsteps?"

"I think he'd tell me I made a mistake."

"Why? "

"Because he had something to return to."

"And you . . ."

"I thought I did."

The focus returned to Sumaya's expression, as if his point had been made. "But don't you see? You *have* now. This is your opportunity."

"I'd prefer not to take it."

Sumaya seemed miffed. "You understand I'm under considerable pressure here."

"Because of the murders . . ."

"The murders and your own peculiar status. I went out on a limb for you, Inspector. I kept you from being transferred." His deep-set eyes blazed into Ben's. "Or worse. "

"I appreciate that."

"Then help me now," Sumaya implored. "The Israeli police liaison will be here at three o'clock this afternoon. What should I tell him?"

"That I need more time to think about it."

"There is no more time." The mayor started to shuffle back to his chair. "You see, Inspector, the body of another victim was found in Jericho this morning."

CHAPTER 2

"Danielle!" the voice repeated. "Danielle, can you hear me?"

So as not to attract attention, Danielle Barnea waited until she was far enough from the crowd in Haganah Square to respond quietly to Shin Bet commander Dov Levy's edgy call. "I'm right here. Still in position."

"What happened? Where were you?"

"Trying not to stand out."

"The truck just turned into the market, approaching the warehouse."

Danielle gazed across the street at the man beneath the Ottoman Clock Tower she'd been watching for an hour now.

"Atturi's standing still, checking the time I think," she reported. "Wait a minute, he's moving."

"Which way?"

"East. Yefet Street."

"Yes!" the commander's voice beamed. "We're finally going to nail this bastard!"

Danielle waited until Atturi had walked a safe distance ahead before following. He had done nothing thus far to indicate he suspected any surveillance, but she wasn't taking any chances.

She had been promoted to Shin Bet, the Israeli equivalent of the FBI, after becoming the youngest woman ever to attain the rank of Chief Inspector in Israel's National Police. Quite a bit of fanfare accompanied the promotion, not only because it represented another incredible stroke of career fortune, but also because of the event that had sparked it.

She had actually been off duty when she recognized Ahmed Fatuk, wanted for more than a decade for acts of terrorism, walking into a bakery shop in Jerusalem. Knowing Fatuk would be long gone by the time she could summon backup,

Danielle made her move on him alone when he emerged from the bakery. Pretending to retrieve the contents of a spilled purse from the sidewalk, she had stuck a gun in the back of his head when he passed by. Since Fatuk's arms were loaded down with bags, there was nothing he could do but give up. A week later he was interned in the Ansar 3 detention camp, awaiting a trial the Israeli justice system would take their time in scheduling. That same week found her transferred to Shin Bet.

In the years since Prime Minister Rabin's assassination, the agency had undergone wholesale changes and been forced to endure a purge through its ranks. As a result, high level field positions that almost never opened up were suddenly available, and Shin Bet officials scoured the army and National Police, culling the best from their ranks.

They never bothered to ask Danielle if she wanted the job; no one *ever* turned down such a prestigious position, a career-maker that could provide the ticket to anywhere she wanted to go. Career, though, was the problem. They hadn't asked Danielle if she wanted the job, and they hadn't asked her what had brought her to Jerusalem on the day she had arrested Ahmed Fatuk. Events had conspired to make her a hero, rendering it impossible for her to follow the new path she had finally decided to embark upon. Now that path would have to wait. Again.

The investigation of Ismail Atturi, an Israeli Arab suspected of being involved in smuggling goods into the West Bank and Gaza, was well underway by the time of Danielle's promotion to Shin Bet, though with little to show for it. Neither Shin Bet nor the National Police had been able to directly link Atturi to the operation. Thanks to an informant, though, they had learned of a shipment going out this day from a storehouse located in the famed flea market in the old city of Jaffa.

"The truck has backed up against one of the sidewalk stalls," Commander Levy reported. "I'll keep you advised."

Danielle followed Atturi, easy to spot in his cream-colored baggy linen pants and shirt, down Yefet Street and then left on Oley Tsiyon toward the center of the market. To blend with the many tourists in this part of town, she herself was dressed in casual clothes: a pair of light weight slacks and an oversized blouse baggy enough to conceal the holster clipped to the inside of her pants. The nature of this assignment dictated that she carry her Beretta in that fashion, but the holster's designer must have cared little about the painful bite it made into the hip, to say nothing of the unsightly bulge she hoped her blouse was hiding.

She listened to the shouts of various salesmen pitching their wares from stands on the sidewalk, moving carts, or open-front shops adjacent to the flea market. The peddlers and shopkeepers strained their voices to have their boasts of bargains heard and heeded. Everyone other than tourists knew the quality of the merchandise was generally low, but the spirit of the merchants who battled for street space and customers was keen.

"I'm just entering the market," Danielle reported. "Suspect still in sight," she added, catching a strong whiff of freshly caught fish, the official welcome to Old Jaffa's flea market.

"Agent Tice should be coming into view any moment," Levy told her. "Fall back once he takes up pursuit."

Joshua Tice was a top Shin Bet field agent she had been lucky enough to be paired with in her first months with the organization. A no-nonsense, generally humorless man, he worked as many hours as they would let him and longed for nothing else. Was that what lay ahead for her ten years down the road? Considering that possibility always set Danielle trembling.

Up ahead, Atturi moved past an array of Oriental rugs draped over car roofs and hoods, ignoring the pleas of merchants to come over and admire the fine silk and wool. Following in his wake, Danielle gave the endless row of stalls no more than a fleeting glance, despite the boisterous salesmen hawking flashy, cheap jewelry. One attempted to loop a garish necklace over her neck when she passed, and it was all she could do to fend him off without causing a ruckus.

By then Atturi was crossing the street toward the line of miniature warehouselike buildings that specialized in ancient, rusted appliances. The incredibly high duties levied by the Israeli government on such merchandise when it was new created an extraordinary demand for recycled items such as televisions and refrigerators, often regardless of their condition.

The buildings housing them were no different. Old Jaffa was a city mired in its storied past, the ancient structures virtually untouched by redevelopment or renewal. Torn and tattered awnings flapped in the faint breeze above merchants negotiating every deal down to the last shekel. Windows peeked out from behind shutters more broken than whole. Most of the buildings were constructed of stone, smoked gray or black through the years and laced with a dusty, heated stench Danielle had never forgotten ever since her father had brought her to Old Jaffa for the first time as a child.

Danielle shifted her eyes from Atturi long enough to register a truck backed up through one of the warehouse fronts that looked as old as the merchandise around it. If their informant's information was correct, though, that truck was in the process of being loaded with stolen goods Atturi would be transporting into the West Bank. One of the strange dividends peace had brought. She noted the yellow Israeli license plates, undoubtedly forged, that allowed passage through the West Bank checkpoints without fear of detainment and potential seizure.

When Danielle glanced back at Atturi she saw that Tice had cut in behind him sixty feet in front of her.

"All right, Agent Barnea," Commander Levy instructed her, his voice calmer, "back off and stay alert. Don't move until I give the order for the other teams to do the same."

"Roger," Danielle replied, keeping her eyes on Atturi as he cut a diagonal path across the busy street toward the warehouse in question. Tice lingered well behind him.

Tice had to stop when several cars snarled in the endless grind through the market refused to give ground, leaving him no room to cross the street. Danielle kept her pace steady, eyes sweeping the crowds until she locked on a group of four figures slicing forward, wearing jackets in spite of the sweltering heat. Too fast, too stiff, something clearly on their minds besides buying and bargains.

Joshua Tice never saw them; his attention was riveted on Atturi as the Arab approached the truck. But it was not Tice the men were after. They too headed for the truck, their eyes, Danielle was certain, fixed on Atturi. She felt her pulse quicken and fought to remain calm.

"Go Red," she said into her nearly invisible microphone,

using the signal for imminent danger.

She couldn't see the other agents posted along the street, yet knew they were in motion even now, heading toward her position as relayed by Commander Levy.

Tice had brought a hand to his ear, slowing as he listened, eyes darting about in befuddlement.

Danielle continued to push through the crowd toward him, straining to maintain at least a partial glimpse of the jacketed figures. She caught three in her field of vision again, hands ducked inside their coats now. Still in motion. Taking their time.

Danielle shoved some bystanders aside and drew her Beretta nine-millimeter pistol. She caught sight of Tice holding a twin of her gun low by his hip forty feet from her. The jacketed figures were hidden from his view by the knotted crowd.

A man jostled Danielle from the back. A soccer ball ricocheted off her leg, bounced off a car fender and rolled straight toward Atturi as a sliver of space appeared briefly in the crowd. She saw two of the jacketed men raising their own pistols. A third pulled a sawed-off shotgun from under his coat and leveled it straight at Atturi's back.

Tice turned and took a step sideways to kick the soccer ball aside, placing him directly between the shotgun's barrel and Atturi.

Danielle registered the boy chasing the ball about to cross that path as well. At that instant her instincts took over. She had raised the pistol in her hand and fired before she even knew her finger had moved. The sound reverberated inside her head, as she pulled the trigger again and again.

One of her bullets struck the shoulder of the man wielding the shotgun and spun him just as he fired, causing him to miss the boy who had frozen in place. She was dimly aware of Tice twisting violently and clutching for his face, staggering—his gun useless. The next gunfire she heard belonged to two of the other jacketed men. Their twin fusillades slammed Ismail Atturi into his truck, spraying blood all over the hood and windshield, as Danielle launched herself through the now panicked crowd.

She chanced a fresh series of shots at the jacketed men through an opening, angling herself to cover Tice, who was

writhing on the pavement. She realized the boy in the soccer
uniform was still in the line of fire too and shoved him to the
ground as she squeezed off fresh rounds toward Atturi's slay-
ers.

The fourth man! What happened to the fourth man?

No sooner had Danielle realized she had lost track of him
than the familiar click-clack of submachine gun fire made her
twist to the right, hearing screams erupt on that side of her.
The fourth man was trying to escape, firing wildly on the run,
his bullets felling a pair of pedestrians who had ended up
between Danielle and him. Before she could swing her Beretta
on the assassin, three more of the Shin Bet team charged into
the street firing, one mounting the hood of a car and another
a merchant's cart to improve their aims. The fourth man managed to turn away, then simply keeled over, riddled with bullets. Danielle ejected her spent clip, reached into her pocket
for a fresh one.

The roar of an engine made her whirl back toward the truck
as she jammed the new magazine home. One of the two final
gunmen writhed in pain on the pavement, while the other
stumbled toward her. His left shoulder oozed blood through
his jacket, a pistol trembling in his right hand.

"*Suka!*" he screamed at her, trying his best to steady the
gun and fire.

Danielle dove behind a pair of cars for cover and heard the
windows of the nearer one explode as she chambered a round.
She peered cautiously over the fender of one car in time to
see the big truck screech from its berth in the warehouse. A
violent lurch carried it into the street where it plowed through
stalled traffic and crashed into the final gunman, tossing him
aside.

Danielle noted insanely that its ancient wipers were struggling to wipe the contents of Ismail Atturi's skull from the
windshield, as the truck smashed through another pair of cars
and slammed them into the one she was perched behind, pinning her in place.

The truck bore down on her like a dragon spewing hot,
gasoline-scented breath. Danielle could do nothing but angle
her barrel upward and fire. Glass spiderwebbed around the
three neat holes she drilled on the driver's side of the wind-

shield, blood splattered on the inside now as well as out. At the last instant before it was upon her, the truck turned into a line of parked or abandoned cars, coming to a halt with its ancient horn blaring.

Danielle climbed out from the twisted steel around her and sprinted over to the truck behind four of the team members, led by Commander Levy Another pair had rushed to Joshua Tice, one pressing a handkerchief against Tice's face, while the other fought to hold him still. Guns steadied on the truck's covered rear from all angles. Levy nodded to the man closest who then leaped up on the sill. In one swift motion he drew the burlap flap back and the team braced, ready to shoot.

"Refrigerators," Danielle heard the first one say. "Fucking refrigerators."

"What the fuck?" another blared, climbing into the rear of the truck.

He grabbed hold of one of the refrigerator doors and pulled. The latch resisted at first, then came free when he yanked harder.

A cache of automatic rifles, both American M-16s and Israeli Galils, spilled outward, clacking against each as they tumbled to the pavement.

"*Elloheem!*" one of the Shin Bet agents exclaimed.

"Holy shit!"

The second agent's use of English made Danielle think of what the last gunman had screamed at her, the word *and* the language:

He had called her a bitch. In Russian.

If you would like a longer preview of *The Walls of Jericho*, send your name and address to:

> Jon Land
> c/o Tor Books
> 175 Fifth Ave.
> New York, NY 10010